G000096715

THE RIGHT HAND OF THE SUN

Also by Anita Mason

Bethany
The Illusionist
The War Against Chaos
The Racket
Angel
The Yellow Cathedral

THE RIGHT HAND OF THE SUN

Anita Mason

JOHN MURRAY

First published in Great Britain in 2008 by John Murray (Publishers)
An Hachette Livre UK company

1

© Anita Mason 2008

The right of Anita Mason to be identified as the Author of the
Work has been asserted by her in accordance with the Copyright,
Designs and Patents Act 1988.

All rights reserved. Apart from any use permitted under UK copyright law no part
of this publication may be reproduced, stored in a retrieval system, or transmitted,
in any form or by any means without the prior written permission of the publisher,
nor be otherwise circulated in any form of binding or cover other than that in which
it is published and without a similar condition being imposed on the
subsequent purchaser.

A CIP catalogue record for this title is available from the British Library

Hardback ISBN 978-0-7195-2122-5
Trade paperback ISBN 978-0-7195-2132-4

Typeset in Centaur MT by Palimpsest Book Production Limited,
Grangemouth, Stirlingshire

Printed and bound by Clays Ltd, St Ives plc

John Murray policy is to use papers that are natural, renewable and recyclable products and
made from wood grown in sustainable forests. The logging and manufacturing processes are
expected to conform to the environmental regulations of the country of origin.

John Murray (Publishers)
338 Euston Road
London NW1 3BH

www.johnmurray.co.uk

For Christine

LONDON BOROUGH OF WANDSWORTH	
501425681	
Askews	09-Oct-2008
AF MASO	£16.99
	WWX0003544/0175

Acknowledgements

This book has taken a long time to write and has accrued many creditors. The patience of my friends should perhaps be listed first.

A bursary from Arts Council England financed a sustained period of the writing, and I was given further valuable financial support by the Authors' Foundation. I am grateful to the Hawthornden International Retreat for Writers for a month's tranquillity, in beautiful surroundings, in which to think and write.

A lengthy section of this novel was written, and some of its more intractable difficulties were wrestled with, in a small house by the sea in Ireland. I thank Eva Coleman most sincerely for her generosity.

I
The Crossing

I

The fisherman didn't want to take me to the island.

I had known this as soon as I saw him. Down on the shoreline, looking in the wet sand for a shell. He knew I was there, of course, but ignored me. That could only mean he didn't want what would happen next.

I fingered the beads through the cloth they had come in. New, the cloth, but dimly remembered. The beads, too. They clicked together pleasantly. I did not yet have the word for them, but I had the idea for them. The word would come back.

My stomach was a cave with no bottom. *I* didn't want what would happen next, either. Not now that I was face to face with it.

The fisherman stooped and straightened in one movement, and came walking back to the canoe. The canoe was drawn up high on the beach, and was filled to half its depth with fish. They had been speared. The spear lay on the sand, with the paddle beside it. The fish winked like a hill of mirrors.

I stepped towards the fisherman, the beads in my hand. I greeted him and said I wanted to go to the island.

It lay like a cloud on the water. It looked very close, almost as if you could shoot an arrow there. I knew this was deceptive, that the island always looked thus in the mornings, but that after noon, when the breeze began to blow and the crossing was hazardous, it moved further away.

His face showed fear. I had not expected that, and it disquieted me further. I also thought, if there is something to be afraid of, perhaps I can escape going.

The fisherman said, 'I will not go to Ix Chel.'

'Why not?'

'There is a spirit on the water. In my village they have seen it.'

He made the sign to send away evil. Then he began to throw fish into a woven sack which he took from the bottom of the canoe.

The sun was full on me, but I shivered. Nevertheless I held out the bag of beads and, moving them inside the cloth so that they clicked and rustled, said, 'I can pay you well.'

His eyes went to the bag. He liked the sound. And he was curious.

'What do you have there?' he said.

I untied the bag and looked into the nest of green. I took out two and held them in my palm, letting them take fire from the sun. They were the sea's depths, they were the eyes of the jaguar.

'*Chalchihuites*,' he said in wonder.

If indeed they were *chalchihuites*, they were worth more than all he and his village had. They were worth more than twenty villages. After a moment, he knew they were not the precious greenstone, but something else. Yet there was the colour. The colour could not be denied.

'They are a new thing,' I said. 'They are a sign.'

It was as if someone had put these words into my mouth. I was surprised I had thought of them.

He went on throwing fish into the sack. I put the beads in the bag and helped him. Together we threw all the fish into the sack.

When we had finished, I said, 'What kind of spirit is it?'

'As tall as many houses.'

I felt dizzy, but I carried on. 'I know this spirit,' I said. 'It is my friend.'

He looked at me closely for the first time. He stared at my

4

features until his face cleared. 'You are the slave of the *batab* of Chanek,' he said. 'The one who did not speak our language.'

'I speak it now,' I said.

'There were two of you.'

'Yes. But my brother does not want to go to Ix Chel.'

'I have not said that I will take you to Ix Chel.'

I picked up the beads from the sand. The sun had warmed them so much that when I took them into my hand again they almost burned it.

'Look at these,' I urged him. 'Hold them.'

I tipped them into his palm and he was astonished. It was their heat that convinced him, their supernatural heat, as if they were part of the sun itself.

'All these are yours,' I said, seeing his weakness, 'if you take me today to Ix Chel.'

I had remembered how little time there was. I had been given eight days, and this was the eighth.

He held them a little longer, rolling them in his palm, enjoying the soft clicking of their talk and absorbed by their serpentine fire. Then, saying, 'I will speak to my father,' he picked up the sack of fish and the spear and walked away.

I squatted down in a palm tree's eye of shade. He would come back, but I did not know when.

Heat rose from the sand. There was no wind, and the sea was as flat as copper and intensely bright. My eyes closed and I slept on my heels, only waking when a puff of sand blew against my wrist.

I was wide awake at once. The puff of sand meant the wind was starting. The fisherman had not come back. Now, he would not return today. I stood up and stretched my toes. My feet were glad, the whole of me was glad and thanking the earth and sky that I had been spared from doing what I couldn't do.

I heard a step and there, coming down the path from the village, was the fisherman, walking with an older man who carried a paddle.

☆   ☆   ☆

When the trader found me, I had been weeding the *batab's* flowerbeds. I had soil on my fingers and between my toes. He said he had a message for me. He said my countrymen had come.

I did not believe him.

He put up an arm and took from the back of his plaited hair a roll of paper. He held it out to me with a ceremonious gesture. 'The paper will speak,' he said.

At that, I suspected it might be the truth. I dared not touch that roll of paper. I did not know what would become of me once I touched it. I backed away. I saw his look, the surprise in it. I pretended that I could not touch so sacred a thing with hands that were dirty with earth, and ran into the courtyard where the women were steaming maize and asked for some water from the pitcher so I could wash my hands. All the time I was washing them I was wondering what to do. When I finished, I realized I had to go back to the trader.

I took the paper and unrolled it. The thin black marks jumped at my eyes and for a moment it seemed to me that I understood them, but then they closed themselves to me.

I rolled the paper up again and put it in a fold of my clothing. I thanked him.

'The great canoe will wait eight days,' he said, and told me the place. Then he gave me the bag in which the beads were. 'With these you can buy your freedom from your *batab*,' he said, 'and anything you need on the journey.'

I thanked him again. Inside the bag, the beads made a sound like crickets. I offered him some for his trouble, but he refused. He said he had already been paid by the sender of the message.

He took his leave then, wishing me good fortune. I thought, he thinks I will go. I wished I had looked more closely at him, listened more carefully to his voice, because his look and his voice would surely have told me something about my countrymen. He had stood on the same ground with them, shared the same air with them, looked into their faces. It could not be that he had not been changed by it.

6

I could have asked him questions. My brain had been too slow, it had not been able to recover from the first thing he said. Now he was gone — safely gone — curiosity started to torment me. How had they seemed to him? Had they seemed like gods? What did they have in their hands, or on their feet? How had they been occupied? What were their clothes? None of these questions was any good, whether asked or not: by now I needed to hear and see them myself, nothing else would tell me what I longed to know. Inside this tormenting curiosity, and not recognized until it was too late, lay a different thing: a terrible sadness that they had come, they had come after all this time, and I had not seen them.

The sadness went into my heart like a knife. I found myself weeping. I don't know for how long I wept, before it came to me that I did not have to endure this sadness, that I could take the chance that had been given to me.

That was how it was. That was how I grasped that I could make this journey. As soon as I realized that I could, I knew that I must.

The wind was not too strong. The fisherman and his father paddled steadily. After a time I offered to take one of the paddles, but they refused.

My toes gripped the carved-out wooden floor of the canoe and I did not look at Ix Chel as it came closer. My mind was filled with dread and a shivering excitement. I kept my eyes on the surface of the water, the easy rise and fall of it like a great animal breathing, and the way the sun winked off it.

Because I was looking at the water, I didn't notice the ship until we were in full view of her. Feeling something change in the paddling of the two men, I raised my head. She was sailing before the breeze. She was as stately as a temple, and all rounded fullness and grace. Her sail was like gulls' wings and her mast rose like a prayer. She was as familiar to me as my own hands, and as strange as a dream.

7

The old fisherman asked what they should do. The ship frightened them very much. But she was sailing away from us, so I told them to go round the headland and put me ashore on the beach where the pilgrims landed when they visited the shrine.

When we rounded the headland my heart leapt into my mouth and the fisherman and his father stayed their paddles in midstroke. There rode a host of ships like the one we had just seen, lifting like birds on the water.

The canoe began turning.

'You must take me ashore,' I said, although every part of me wanted to flee.

They started to paddle, and stopped again. The canoe went on turning, slowly, like a leaf that doesn't care where it goes.

I thrust my hand into the bag of beads, and held some out to the old man. He hadn't yet seen them. He laid down his paddle and slowly took one into his hand. It was the colour of the sea in its milky shallows.

After a while he picked up the paddle again, and we went on and came gradually to the shore.

Men stood on the beach watching us. They were hairy and their clothes were outlandish. Their faces were reddened but not with dye: their faces looked raw. Their eyes made me think of glass beads. Large animals ran about among them, with lolling tongues.

Behind the beach, where tufts of grass began, were wooden huts with a thatch covering. Out of one came a man wearing a gold chain around his neck.

With the blade of his paddle in the sand, the fisherman held the canoe steady. I left the bag of beads on the floor of the canoe and stepped into the transparent water. The canoe was already moving away as I walked up the beach.

I knew at once that the man who wore the gold chain was the one who had sent the message. He was standing talking at the centre of a knot of people who leaned their bodies towards him like flowers to the light.

The men on the beach who had watched me get out of the canoe went on gazing at me as if they weren't sure what I was. I felt the weight of their eyes on me. Then something was said in an excited tone, and a man set off running.

The man with the gold chain looked up and raked me with his eyes. My topknot, my loincloth, my wristlet of feathers. Whether I understood the words he uttered or just heard the thought in his mind, I knew that he said, 'I see no Spaniard.'

I was close to him now. One of the dogs, appearing from nowhere, growled at me and bared its teeth, but it was called back. This alarmed me but I went on walking. I came to where he stood, and knelt down in the sand at his feet.

You could hear the silence going up and up into the sky.

I said, then, what I had practised saying, rolling it over and over in my mouth. Although I had practised it, my tongue stumbled. I said, in Spanish, 'Long live our gracious lord King Ferdinand.'

A ripple of astonishment went through the silence.

The man at whose feet I knelt lowered himself to a crouch and looked deeply into my eyes. He was looking for my soul, but as soon as it felt his scrutiny it hid.

He straightened up and spoke a little stream of words. I went on kneeling in the sand. As long as I knelt there, I thought, nothing else could happen. But he bent down, took my hands and raised me to my feet.

'Welcome, brother,' he said, in the tongue I had been born to.

2

Later, a story arose that I had stepped ashore at Ix Chel carrying a Christian prayer book and saying 'It is Thursday,' or something of the sort.

I smiled when I heard it. No book could have survived the shipwreck, the boat, the insects, the rain, the many years I had lived among the *winic*. Those years had folded into one another in my mind. The *winic* did not number years, although they marked their passing: it was days they counted. And not as Christians counted. As I stepped on to the beach at Ix Chel all I knew of the day was that it was Two Dog and a bad day to make a decision.

'What's your name?'

I gazed at him hopefully. A big-faced fellow with hair the colour of wet clay. He had spoken the words in a rush and I hadn't understood him.

'Your name?' He said it more slowly so that I got his meaning.

'Muluc,' I said.

'*Muluc?*'

There was laughter. 'No, no, no,' said someone. 'Your *real* name.'

They were all looking at me. There was a crowd of them, jostling, eager to make my acquaintance, expecting something.

What did they want? Obviously the name I had given them wouldn't do.

'Gerónimo,' I said at last, pushing away the first Spanish name that came into my head, which was Gonzalo.

'Welcome, Gerónimo!' exclaimed the clay-haired man and struck me hard on the back. Then they all began to talk at once, asking me questions, introducing themselves, trying to tell me things, interrupting each other and making such a clamour that I was half-deafened as well as bewildered.

'I am Alonso. At your service.'

'Where do you come from, brother?'

'How did you get here?'

'Were you with Balboa?'

'How long have you lived in this place?'

'If there's anything you want, my friend, just ask me.'

'Ignore this man, Gerónimo. He's from León.'

'What is your *family* name?'

Their breath smelt. It smelt of rotten meat. I tried not to turn my head away or show how much it offended me, but after a while, with the din of their voices and the foul air in my nostrils, I began to feel almost faint. Luckily, at that moment a man pushed his way through the crowd to me, holding an armful of clothes.

'He's good enough as he is,' protested someone.

'The Captain says he has to put these on.'

He made a path through the throng and led me to one of the huts that stood behind the beach, so that I could put the clothes on in privacy.

I felt the fabric of these clothes between my fingers. It felt thick and prickly. It had a faint, rank smell: the smell of meat. I did not want to put on these clothes, in which my body would feel stifled, but it seemed that I did not have a choice.

In the hut I stood still, with the sun coming through a crack and playing on my bare toes. Then quickly I pulled at the loop of cloth so that it fell in a little hill and I was standing naked, my loincloth on one side and the pile of clothes I had been given on the other. I thought, after this moment I shall be different. I began to put on the clothes. It took quite a long time. I had to work out in what order to put them on, and how they fastened, and when I had finished, my limbs felt like trapped animals.

I looked at the shoes. Each was like a boat, and fastened with a narrow strap. I inserted a foot into one of them. The foot told me it was being buried alive. I took it out again.

I left the hut, carrying the shoes and the simple strip of cloth in which my body had moved so easily, and walked into the woods above the shore. I folded up the cloth and left it lying at the foot of a tree, and I left the shoes beside it. I went back to my fellow countrymen.

They congratulated me on my new appearance. Some of them now thought I should change the way I wore my hair as well, but others disagreed. In the middle of all this the man with the gold chain came by.

'Where is your companion?' he asked me.

It was a moment before I understood what he meant. Then, 'He did not want to come,' I said.

'Hernán!' someone else called just then, and he walked away.

It was late in the afternoon by now, and fires were being lit all over the beach. Men began to gather by them. I was beckoned to several of these fires and hesitated, uncertain what to do; in the end someone took me by the arm and guided me to one. I sat on a tree trunk. I would have preferred to squat on my heels, but they were all sitting on the tree trunk and I thought it best to do the same. Just as the sun was dipping down, a sort of soup or stew was passed round in wooden bowls. I looked for a maize cake to eat it with but could not see any. I took a mouthful of the soup. It was very salty, and in it bobbed a greasy morsel of something or other.

I put the bowl down at my feet and hoped nobody would

notice. The man sitting on my right, a broad-chested fellow in a torn shirt, noticed at once. He looked at the bowl, looked at me, and said, 'Don't you want that?' I invited him to take it. He swallowed it in one draught, except for the meat, if that was what it was. This he held up between a thick thumb and forefinger, as if it were a great treat, then popped it into his mouth and chewed with relish. I watched the steady movement of his jaw with fascination. As he put the bowl back on the ground, he said, looking very serious, 'Take my advice, friend. Never give your supper away.'

'Why?' I asked, worried I had done something I shouldn't.

He grinned widely. 'Because there's nothing else.'

A boy sitting on the ground next to him found this so funny that he became quite breathless from laughter.

Soon they began to go to the huts to sleep. I was shown a hut I could sleep in, but I didn't go to it. I knew no sleep would come to me there.

I stayed by the fire until they had all gone, and then I took off the clothes I had been given and lay down by the embers. I stared up at the stars, trying to read them, but they told me nothing of what my new life would be. I slept fitfully. The sound of snoring came from the huts, and once a man called on the name of Lordjesuschrist in terror.

In the morning I woke early and sat for a while on the beach watching light steal over the sea; then I waded into the water and washed myself and swam for a little, just for the pleasure of it and because I did not have to sweep the paths of the *batab*'s garden that day. When I got back to the shore a fresh-faced young man was waiting for me.

He told me, and his words stumbled before they came out, that 'the C-Captain' wanted to see me. Then he added apologetically, 'You must put some c-clothes on.' He indicated his own clothing, in case I didn't understand. He said his name was Sandoval.

He came with me to where I had left my clothes by the embers of the fire, waited while I put them on, and then took me to the man who wore the gold chain.

The Captain was deep in conversation with a Spaniard who had extraordinarily blue eyes. This blue-eyed man was very good-looking; he was tall and shapely, had hair as yellow as maize, and in one ear wore a stone of the same deep blue as his eyes. The Captain saw me and indicated that I should wait. He finished his conversation soon afterwards and the blue-eyed man walked away. As he passed, his glance fell on me, where I sat on my heels in the shade, and there was something in it that unsettled me, as if the wind had begun to blow from an unseasonable direction.

The Captain called me over and looked me up and down.

'Don't you like the shoes you were given?' he said.

They were still under the tree. That is, unless someone had taken a liking to them.

'I cannot wear them,' I explained.

'Perhaps we can find you some sandals,' said the Captain.

I said it didn't matter.

'Indeed it does. You can't wear the clothes of a Christian gentleman and go barefoot.' Then he put his arm round my shoulders and asked how everything was and if I had eaten since my arrival.

I was by now quite hungry. However, I said I had eaten.

'And where did you sleep?'

I pointed to the place on the beach where the fire had been.

There was a pause before he said, 'Let's go for a walk,' and set off walking along the shore. I followed him, and one of the dogs trotted behind us.

He began to talk about how glad he was that I'd been able to join them. He even said that it was a kind of miracle, and must have been the will of *Díos*. He asked me how long I had been living among the *winic*. I said it might have been eight years, it might have been ten: I could not be sure. I started to say

14

something about the shipwreck, which I still lived through in my dreams, but he wasn't interested in that. He wanted to talk about Gonzalo.

I said, as I had said the previous day, that Gonzalo didn't want to come with me. The Captain seemed unable to grasp this. I tried to explain — using my hands because I didn't have the words — the amber in Gonzalo's lip, his tattoos, his honour-scars, his paint and elbow-plumes.

'None of that matters,' the Captain said impatiently.

'He has married a wife, too,' I said.

'He could bring her.'

'He will not.'

I could see that the Captain was very disappointed by this news. 'Perhaps he will change his mind,' he said. 'We shall be on this island for a few days yet. One of the ships has developed a leak and we have to repair it.'

I fixed my eyes on the beach and said nothing.

The Captain then wanted to know how I had been treated all these years.

'They were kind to me,' I said.

He seemed puzzled and looked at me closely. He was waiting for me to say something else. But I didn't, and we walked on.

His next question was whether there was a name for the place where I had lived. Yes, I said, it was called Chanek.

'Is it a town?'

'Yes.'

'How big?'

How big was Chanek? It was just Chanek.

'As big as a Spanish town?'

He was trying to help me, but it was no help. I said, 'Fifty houses,' because the word 'fifty' had just come back to me.

'Are there many towns like that?'

'Yes.'

'And who rules over the towns?'

'The *batab*.'

'Does that mean "chief"?'

'Yes.'

We went on walking.

The Captain glanced up at the sky and said suddenly, 'Do they know what a sun dial is?'

'No,' I said. Neither did I.

The answer seemed to please him. 'Do they know how to smelt iron?' he asked next.

I realized I must be careful. I asked him to repeat the question.

He drew his small blade from the sheath and tapped it with his finger. I remembered Gonzalo's dagger and how he had lent it to me to carve the days on the side of the boat. I was the only person he would allow to touch it, until the *batab* took it from him.

'No,' I said, 'they don't have it.'

I was still thinking about Gonzalo and the dagger when he said, 'Do they use animals for tilling the land?'

As he spoke, there came to me a picture of ridged brown earth, the furrows soft and heavy. This earth was so real that I could smell it, and I knew that if I walked over the furrows it would cling to my feet. It glistened with wetness, this soil, and was speckled with yellow straw. But even as I gazed in wonder at this field, it began to fade and another field showed through it, like something seen through worn cloth. The second field replaced the first. The soil of the second field was dry and chalky, and scrub grew over it. Roots matted it. I walked into this second field. I looked down at myself. My arms and legs were bare, and an axe set with a white tooth of flint hung from my hand.

He had no patience with my dreaming. He had gone on to something else.

'Is there gold?'

That at least I could answer. 'No,' I said firmly.

Too late, I saw it was not the answer he wanted. He frowned

and shook his head. He brought out of his pocket something wrapped in a square of fabric, and spread it on the palm of his hand. It was a small gold ornament, a chain hung with tiny figures of fish. A pretty thing. I had seen them on the wrists of the men who went to the *batab's* house.

I asked how he came by it.

'Trade. One of my men got it on this coast last year.'

He could not have said this. Obviously I had misunderstood him.

He went on, smiling, 'If there is no gold in these parts, where does this come from?'

'There is no gold.' I knew there was none.

The smile vanished and he looked irritated. He said, 'Do these people value gold?'

'Yes,' I said.

'As much as we do?'

'They love *chalchihuites* more,' I told him.

'What is that?'

'Greenstone.'

He folded the little gold thing back into its nest of cloth and returned it to his pocket. Just then we walked past a boy sitting on the ground, who was slowly scooping up handfuls of sand and letting them fall. His eyes were looking at nothing. He was a *winic*, but to my amazement he was dressed from head to foot in Spanish clothes.

'Somewhere,' the Captain was saying, 'there must be gold mines.'

I agreed with him.

'Have you any idea where they might be?'

'No,' I said. After a while I told him, 'They value feathers, too.'

He laughed. 'Why do they value feathers?'

I remembered the glory of the *kukul* in the forest. I shook my head, and let him think that I didn't know this, either.

*   *   *

17

There were several hundred Spaniards on Ix Chel. They were people of all sorts: even on the first day I could tell that some were of high rank, some of low, and that some were servants of the others, and I even suspected that some were not Spaniards, which turned out to be true. There were women, too, because a few of them had brought their wives. From time to time I glimpsed people who lived in the camp and both looked and moved like *winic*, but they were shadowy and disappeared when I approached them and could not be found. So in the end I gave up trying to speak to them.

The great variety of people engaged in doing different things made the camp interesting and just like a town. I enjoyed wandering through it, watching what people were doing, sometimes asking questions if I didn't understand. However, if I was puzzled, I usually tried to work it out myself, because I didn't want to appear too ignorant. A man, bare to the waist like a *winic*, beating out a flat strip of metal over a fire. Another patiently smoothing a shaped piece of wood which he then fitted into a box-like structure, open at the top, the purpose of which I could not guess at. A youth stitching leather with a broad flashing needle of steel (the *winic* used the spine of a fish). Another repairing an object I recognized with shock: thick, padded, as tough as hide but made of cotton, it was *winic* body armour. They boiled it in brine until it was hard enough to stop an arrowhead. The lad repairing it thought I didn't know what it was, and explained.

'It's light, you see,' he said, weighing it in his hand. 'Cooler, too. Better than steel, for here.'

But where, I thought, had they got it from?

Other Spaniards didn't seem to be doing anything at all. They were just sitting in the shade telling stories, or playing some game with dice or counters, or spending all day polishing a spot of rust off a dagger, or sweet-talking a woman, or snoring in a hut. Some of them were clearly bored, and wanted to be off the island and sailing to the next place. But we had to wait for the ship to be repaired.

The sad young *winic* dressed like a Spaniard whom I had seen scooping sand on the beach was still in the same place, still doing the same thing, when I saw him again. The sand ran through his fingers and made a little hill under his hand, which he did not bother to look at. His body sagged, a thing it disturbed me to see in a *winic*. He wore his hair long but did not braid or wash it.

'Bless the day,' I said in the language I call Ahau, and sat beside him.

He sprang up and was about to run away. I grabbed his sleeve.

'What is your name?' I asked.

He stared at me and trembled. I asked him again, and he stammered out the name by which they knew him in his town.

I said, 'Is that what they call you here?'

He tried to tell me the name the Christians called him by, but he garbled it badly and I could only make out the first part, 'Mel.'

I wanted to know where he came from. I thought I might know his town. But I didn't, it was not near Chanek. So then I asked him what he was doing on the island.

Something seemed to have settled on his tongue. Suddenly, a question flew out of him that was clearly the only thing he could think of.

'What are you, lord?'

He must have thought I was a magician. The true answer was complicated and I didn't feel like explaining how I had come to be in the company I was in, dressed the way I was and yet speaking his language. I simply said that I was a friend of 'these lords here'. That did not make him any less afraid. He did in the end, however, tell me his story. Bearded men had come ashore in a boat and captured him. They had also captured his friend, who was now dead. They used him as an interpreter when they wanted to talk to the *winic*.

I wondered how much *cristiano* he had learnt. I thought it couldn't be much, in the time. So I asked how long ago they had captured him.

'Eighteen *winals*,' he said without hesitation.

It was a ridiculous answer. Eighteen *winals* are a year. I was sorry for him, but when he said this I laughed.

He was upset at my laughter, and insisted that he was right. I didn't want to upset him further, so I asked where they had caught him: was it in the town or somewhere else? He said it was on the beach, where he and his friend had gone to get shell-fish.

And where was the beach?

But that he couldn't tell me. I pointed at the part of the coast that lay opposite, which at that time of day showed so bright and clear that you could see a canoe setting off from the other shore to fish, and asked him whether it was to sun's right or sun's left – north or south – of it. He had no idea.

Then he said something that quite astonished me. 'There was a battle,' he said.

This convinced me that being kidnapped by Christians had turned his wits. But since I was curious to hear what he would say, I went on asking him questions. How many of his people had fought in this battle? Warriors from two towns, he said. How many bearded men? He shrugged, as if the number didn't matter. Had any of his people been killed? His eyes went dark. Three twenties had been killed. His uncle had been among them.

I did not like anything he said. It made me uneasy. I stood up, said he must be careful not to tell lies, and left him.

It was an obvious question, but it took a couple of days to occur to me. What were all these people *doing here*? And where exactly had they come from?

I thought I might be able to glean the information from

listening to what people said. I listened carefully. I didn't manage to glean anything. Everyone knew what they were here for, so no one needed to talk about it.

In the end, I asked a man who was sitting on the ground mending his shoe. If he had to mend his own shoe, perhaps he wouldn't laugh at me for not knowing, I thought.

'We've come to trade with the Indians,' he said. That was the word they all used for the *winic*. 'To make ourselves rich.'

'But there are so many of you!'

He did laugh, then. 'A lot of people want to be rich.'

I decided to ask several people, to see if they all said the same thing. I next asked a man who had only one arm and was cooking a bit of fish on a fire. 'Ask *him*,' he said with a look I couldn't interpret, and I saw the Captain walking towards us in conversation with the man whose eyes were so blue.

The third time, I asked Sandoval, the youth who had fetched me from the beach on the first morning.

'I c-came here,' said Sandoval in his halting way, 'because there was n-nothing for me in Spain, and there is n-nothing for me in C-Cuba, either.'

I had gathered by now, from listening to people, that Cuba was the place they had come from. It was an island, apparently not very far away. I hadn't heard of it. It must have been discovered after I was shipwrecked, I thought.

My homecoming, if that was what it was, felt strange. For a long time the strangeness never left me. I found it in my stomach when I woke in the morning and it only slipped away from me when I drifted into sleep. The strangeness of these men, the strangeness of the world they had brought with them. The camp and its activities, the fleet of ships riding in the bay with their white sails furled like sleeves, seemed unreal to me. But perhaps I seemed unreal to them. Perhaps I *was*: that would explain why I felt like a ghost. I felt that when they looked at me they looked through me, as the Captain had when he said, 'I see no Spaniard.'

I told myself it would get easier, and I applied myself to learning again all those things I had forgotten while I lived among the *winic*. The names of the days and months, and how to reckon them. The names of numbers and how to reckon the Christian way, in tens. The names of many simple and ordinary things, which I had forgotten because the *winic* did not have those things, like candles and oranges. With these, I had also forgotten how to walk and sit and eat like a Spaniard and how to button a shirt. And there were things I remembered that were no longer true, for, naturally, while I was living among the *winic* things had happened in the world that I didn't know about. For instance, when I said, 'Long live our gracious lord King Ferdinand,' they had all been astonished because King Ferdinand had been dead for years.

I was dismayed to find how much I had forgotten of my own language. I had assumed, on the day of my arrival, with that torrent of speech beating on my ears, that it would very soon come back; tomorrow, even, I might be able to understand all that was said to me and answer fluently. The days went by and I knew I had deceived myself.

I couldn't conceal how much *cristiano* I had forgotten. However, I could not bring myself to admit to my companions that I had forgotten how to *read* it. I still had the Captain's letter: I kept it in my pocket and from time to time, when I was alone, would take it out and puzzle over it. It was like looking at a wall in which you know there is a gateway, but you cannot see it: all you can see is the wall.

There were moments in those first weeks when I didn't know where I was. It was like looking into the depths of a pool and seeing, in those shadows, a bird fly. In looking down you are looking up, for the sky is reflected in the water, but there is a startled moment when you do not know what you are looking at. Then you understand, and the sky and the water change places in your mind. But until the bird flew across your vision, you thought you were looking down. And you were.

What would happen to me was that I would feel myself to be in an alien place. Everything around me was extraordinary and incomprehensible. In my ears was a babble of unfamiliar speech. I was looking at a roughly-made wooden building, in which I must sleep, behind which the forest grew densely. There was a fire, with food steaming on it. I had just arrived in Chanek. But something was wrong. Was this Chanek? I had just heard a word of Spanish. Everything shifted. The flow of speech in my ears became *cristiano*. It was not maize steaming on that fire, but the evening broth. The wooden building was one of the makeshift huts above the seashore of Ix Chel. The forest was the forest of the island.

There were other times when I would simply, without thinking, feel myself to be back in Chanek. I would be walking among the trees, or perhaps just sitting quietly, with the breeze on my face and hearing the tumble of the sea, and I would be so lost in the sun and the wind's song and the sea's music, and so at home in myself, that I would notice with a shock what clothes my body was wearing and wonder where they had come from.

A man came up and spoke to me one morning as I was sitting on the beach on the eastern side of the island, watching the dawn.

The moving surface of the water, black and lustrous like the stone mirrors the *winic* use for prophesying, had gradually taken on light, turning from ink to steel and then to silver. A few pinpoints of fire began to burn on it, and then a hundred, and then the rising sun was casting a path of gold all the way from the shallows to the horizon. Holding my breath for the glory of it, I was hardly aware of the man coming closer, and then I changed the direction of my look and saw that he had come to take away my dawn.

He was tall and lean. He wore black robes and had a sword belted at his waist. His nose was hooked, and his eyes were bright and sharp under bushy eyebrows.

'Good day, my son,' he said. 'You are welcome among us.'

I said politely that, although he seemed to know me, I did not know him.

'My name is Juan Díaz,' he said. 'Father Díaz. I am a priest.'

He waited for me to say something. I didn't. What next he said I didn't reply to either. 'We have been hoping to see you at Mass.'

Mass. It took a little while to come to me, like something rising unhurriedly to the surface of a pool. I gave it time. Then it was like finding a treasure you lost long ago and have forgotten ever possessing, and now do not know what to do with.

The priest had been watching me. 'Our Lordjesuschrist waits for you,' he said.

My heart leapt when he said that. I looked at him searchingly to see if he knew what he was saying. But all I could see in his eyes was that he did not like being looked at in that manner.

'Return to Our Lord,' he said sternly. Then he thought he had better soften his tone a little. 'He will not turn his face from you.'

'Why won't He?' I said, and he gave me in reply a look that was intended to search out my secrets.

'Whatever happened to you in that place, it was not Our Lord's will,' he said.

This made me angry. Either God had been there in Chanek or He had not. This priest knew nothing. Worse, he was pretending that he did know something.

'Nothing happened to me,' I said, although it was far from the truth.

He placed a hand on my shoulder. 'My son, I know what you have endured. We saw some terrible things when we came to this country a year ago.'

It exasperated me to hear this claim yet again. Where had they been, that they thought they had come here? I wriggled my shoulder out of his bony grip. 'You didn't come a year ago,' I said.

24

He looked surprised. He said, 'We came with four ships, under Juan Grijalva, and I was chaplain.'

'No one came here.'

'But that is how we heard of you and your companion. How do you think we knew?'

That was easy. The trader had told them, the same trader who brought the beads.

'Return to Our Lord, and He will not reject you,' said Father Díaz. 'He loves the lost sheep best.'

'What is a sheep?' I asked.

I knew what a sheep was; at that moment I could see one in my mind quite clearly. I said it to get rid of him.

He glared at me and went away.

In the end I couldn't shut my mind to it any longer. Spaniards had come to that coast before. It even turned out that they had come more than once. There had been an expedition from Cuba the previous year, Grijalva's, and one the year before that. So that this was the third, and there were men here on the island who had been with both the earlier ones — although, surprisingly, the Captain, whose name was Cortés, had not been with either.

At first I could not conceive of it. How *could* they have come, with their ships and their steel and their noise, how could they have fought *battles*, while I was in Chanek? How could they have been so close and not have walked into my dreams?

I went over and over it, each time feeling the shock it had dealt me the first time. I squinted at it from different directions and repeated it in my head, 'They have been here before,' as if it were a riddle. The riddle, I eventually understood, was not that they had come, but that they had come and gone, and what that meant. It meant that the country they had come from and Chanek *existed at the same time.* So that men could stumble upon this place and then go back to Cuba as if all that separated them was a strip of sea.

I huddled over it alone. Then a need to know got the better of me. On these other expeditions, what had happened? I started asking questions of the men who said they had been here before. At what time of year had they come? Where did they land? Did they see towns? What did they offer the *winic* in trade, and what did they get in return? Was it true there had been a battle? But after I had got answers to these questions, I wasn't satisfied, and I realized that they weren't the question I really wanted to ask, and that I couldn't ask the question I really wanted to ask. It was, 'What did you *see*?'

I wanted to borrow their eyes to look at the place I had lived in. I wanted to understand it as they had understood it, because although, of course, I knew far more about it than they ever could, I also believed that they knew something about it that I did not. Wanting to see it with their eyes, I also wanted, when I did this, to see myself in a corner of it. (But I did not want *them* to have seen me.)

So, secretly, I studied the men who had been on these expeditions. When, as they often did, they told stories about their experiences, I listened carefully, weighing the words, the voice, the glances. And at the end of it I came to see that they knew nothing at all.

They spoke of fighting *winic*, of running short of water, and how someone in their company had been stupid enough to mistake copper for gold. They boasted of their own courage and complained that on the last expedition they had been led by a coward, and agreed that Hernán Cortés was a man of different mettle. They talked darkly of what they'd found or fancied they had found in some temple or other. But about the country itself they had nothing to say. They had been in it, but they didn't know what it was. They had eaten its fruit, breathed its air and left their piss in its soil, but all they could talk about was gold.

It was gold they had come for, each time. They had got some by trading – not much, just enough to whet the appetite, they said — but on this visit they hoped to make their fortunes. I couldn't imagine how they were going to do it. Fish, maize and salt were the things I had seen most of in Chanek. Yet there were men in the camp who told me they had sunk all the wealth they had into this voyage, and would be ruined if it didn't succeed.

Before we left Ix Chel, I walked through the forest to a sheltered beach, and far along it.

The water, as the sun rose on it, had a surface like the skin of pearl. I took off my shirt and then my other clothes, and finally I was walking naked, keeping the clothes looped over my arm. Once I turned to look back at the faint tracks I'd made in the wet sand, and saw that the sand and the sea together were already gently smoothing out the little hollows as if I had never walked there.

I came to a place where a narrow bar of sand pushed into the water, like a finger pointing. It was fringed all around with small white shells, through which the water seeped and rustled. A soft, brilliant green weed matted the shallows, and above the weed drifted a cloud of tiny flies that were just winged specks, which vanished as I approached them, so that they were never where I was but always just a step away. Like a thought you can't quite grasp.

I dropped my clothes on the sand and stepped into the shallows. The water was warm and cool at the same instant. The weed wrapped itself round me, it clung to my thighs and tickled my ankles. It was heavy as I pushed through it, now wading up to my waist, but all at once it cleared and the level of the water fell slightly, as if it had changed its mind. I was standing in a shallow pool of the sea, transparent, mysteriously still, as if outside the workings of wind and tide.

The place was full of light. Light danced teasingly on the water, sometimes showing me every grain of sand on the sea bed, sometimes locking my gaze on the silvered surface. Darkness and light wove together: in their fabric, fish might dart, there could be anything.

I stooped over the water. For a moment I saw my own face reflected in it. Then it split and dwindled into two discs of light, and I was looking at twin patches of silver on the back of a fish. A fish as long as my arm to the elbow, and plump. Hanging tranced in the water.

Slowly, slowly, my hands entered the sea. It must be as if my hands were the water, the water was myself. Then the fish would come into my hands, the fish would allow it, seeing no difference between my hands and the water. This could only be done by thinking it done, making it as real as the rest of the world, which was only a thought anyway. So in my mind I made my hands the water and the water myself, and slowly I crept my hands towards the entranced fish, which still hung like a sheet of light in the shallows, motionless except for a tremor of its tail which could also have been a movement of light – and was. For my hands came emptily together in the space where the fish had seemed to be, but had not been, being only a dream of mine and a jest of the water's.

I waded back to the shore. The weed, warmed by the sun, seemed even denser, and small bubbles burst from it, rainbow-coloured. Weed pressed my belly and thighs. Just when I was within a few paces of the shore a handsome red and silver fish, which had become trapped in the weed and was frightened by my approach, leapt right out of the water and into the net of my hands.

When word went round that the repairs to the ship were finished and we would soon be leaving, the Captain called me to him. He said that a group of *winic* was reported to be making its way in our direction, and he asked me if I would interpret.

I said I would be glad to. I had been idle ever since I arrived on the island and a task was welcome. It also seemed to me that I was very well fitted for it, for no one else had picked up more than a couple of words of Ahau and I did not imagine that the kidnapped young *winic* was much use.

I went down to the water, waded into it and, scooping it up, poured it over my head and face so that it ran down and drenched my shirt. For a while I sat and watched the sun make rainbows on the wet sand of a beach I would never see again. Then I went back to present myself.

The Captain's gaze travelled over me, and dwelt on my feet.

'Weren't you given some sandals?'

'Yes, Captain.'

'Then put them on. It looks more suitable.'

I found the sandals and put them on. My toes splayed outward, overlapping the leather soles like fish spilling over the edge of a plate. However, when I laced the thongs the sandals stayed on my feet, and when I walked they came with me. I returned to the Captain.

The *winic* arrived soon afterwards. There were, to judge by their style of dress, five elders and some minor officials of the town. Ten bearers followed them, bringing baskets of fruit and maize cakes.

The Captain smiled at the *winic* and ran a string of glass beads through his fingers. Beside him was Blue Eyes. Behind them, twenty or thirty of our men stood or lounged, all studying the *winic* with interest.

The Captain told me to greet the visitors and thank them for the food.

I was a little nervous: I had never had to speak in front of so many people. However, I was determined to do well and deserve the trouble that the Captain had been to on my account. I employed the ceremonial phrases I had heard while I was employed at the *batab*'s house but had never used myself, because for a slave they are not fitting. I enjoyed the surprise that flickered on the faces of the *winic*, and I was sorry that the Captain couldn't understand Ahau and admire the performance I was giving.

'You speak well,' said the oldest *winic* when I had finished. 'You must be the slave we have heard about.'

I didn't reply to that, but turned back to the Captain.

'You can tell him that we're leaving tomorrow,' said the Captain.

I said, 'This lord and his people will go away tomorrow in their great canoes.'

'We know they will,' said the elder.

I had not expected that. 'How do you know?' I asked him.

'Our gods have told us.'

'What is he saying?' asked the Captain.

'He knows already that we're leaving. He says his gods told him.'

'His gods can tell him nothing,' said the Captain. 'We threw them down the temple steps.'

I was dumbfounded.

Blue Eyes saw me at a loss and thought he should help. 'We threw the idols,' he said, carefully enunciating each word, 'out of the temple.'

It was the shrine of the Moon. It was the holiest place on that coast.

I could not just stand there in silence. In the end, I translated more or less what the Captain had said.

'It is true that this lord believes he has destroyed our gods,' said the elder, 'but he has not destroyed them, because he cannot. It was only because they held us back with their weapons that the temple was violated.'

'He says you were able to throw his gods out of the temple because of your swords,' I told the Captain.

'It was not the strength of our swords but the strength of our faith,' replied the Captain. 'Tell him that if he and his people are wise they will worship *Díos*, and he will protect them. That is why we left the images of our religion there.'

I said, 'It was this lord's god who overcame your god, and you should worship his god, who is now in your temple.'

The *winic* said, 'He has put two things in our temple and we do not like either of them. We do not understand who the woman is, and as for the Yaxché, it is badly made and we do not need him to tell us how to venerate it.'

I was silent. The Captain looked hard at me.

Blue Eyes joked, 'You're not much of an interpreter, are you?'

'Perhaps it was difficult to translate,' said the Captain. His gaze didn't leave me.

'He doesn't seem to know what the new images in the temple are,' I said.

'It was all explained to him carefully through Melchior,' said the Captain. 'The image of the Blessed Mary came from my own cabin.'

'The lord says that his religion has been explained to you,' I told the elder.

'If it had, and even if it did not appear to be nonsense, that is no reason why we should accept it in place of our own.'

'I cannot tell him that, or he will be angry,' I said.

There was a moment's silence.

'What did you just say?' asked the Captain.

'What did *he* just say?' said Blue Eyes.

'Fetch Melchior,' sighed someone.

'Be quiet,' said the Captain. 'I want to know what's going on.'

'He is afraid to abandon his gods,' I said, 'and I have told him that he must.'

'Are you trying to protect him?' asked the Captain.

I said, 'I'm doing my best,' and heard Blue Eyes chuckle.

The Captain said, 'When we leave tomorrow, I want to be sure that the images we have put in the temple will be reverenced, that flowers will be put there, and the floor kept clean, and that there will be no reverting to the foul practices we know they get up to, the spilling of blood and so on. Tell him that.'

I said, 'After we have gone, you must worship the things this lord has given you and not cut your ears to give blood.'

'When you have gone, we shall do what we like. You are foolish to think otherwise,' said the *winic.*

'Did you translate "foul practices"?' asked the Captain.

'Yes.'

'And what did he say?'

'He said he would do as you command.'

'We know they practise sodomy, too. That also has to stop, it's a filthy thing.' He waited. 'What's the matter?'

'They don't have a word for it.'

'Well, we can give them one,' said Blue Eyes grimly.

'This lord also wishes you to cease the way of men lying with men as if they were women,' I said.

The faces of all the *winic* went blank with amazement, and then they laughed. Every Spaniard present, except the Captain, put his hand to his sword.

'Why did they laugh?' demanded the Captain.

'I don't know,' I said. 'I must have made a mistake in the translation.'

The Captain was frowning. All his men were frowning. The *winic* looked uneasy. However, after a pause the Captain seemed to decide that it wasn't worth bothering about, and he handed me the string of beads and told me to give it to the *winic* spokesman.

'Tell him,' said the Captain, 'that it's a gift from a great lord whose servant I am, and who has sent me here.'

I presented the beads to the elder, making a little ceremony out of it. The *winic* thanked me in formal words. Then, looking me straight in the eye, he said, 'You have exchanged one master for another, but who will ransom you from this one?'

He touched his hand to the earth, and the others did the same. The Captain nodded gravely, Blue Eyes yawned and the *winic* withdrew.

The Captain watched them walk lightly away into the forest. He said to me, 'You did well, in the circumstances. Certainly much better than Melchior would have done.'

I murmured something in reply. I was shaken by what had happened and was struggling to find a way of thinking about it that did not set my mind at war with itself.

Blue Eyes lifted a melon from a basket and tossed it into the air. He caught it with one hand and went off to his hut.

We sailed from Ix Chel the next morning.

3

I hadn't been on a ship since the night of the shipwreck, and as soon as I set foot on the deck I became nervous. I began to walk about looking for something to do.

Everyone else was busy. The sailors were setting the canvas: they climbed and clung like monkeys. From the bows came the grunting chant of the boys pulling in the anchor. The deck was all confusion. Men were stowing their baggage below, or taking it out and stowing it somewhere else, or arguing over whose possession a sorry-looking cooking pot was, or searching for something they'd lost.

The Captain went about seeing to things. I heard him say he wanted a tally made of all the food stores on the flagship, and at once offered to do it, but it turned out he had already put a friend of his called Portocarrero in charge. No one else wanted my help, either, and it appeared that unless I had a piece of baggage to lose or quarrel over I would have to be idle. I asked a sailor if I could help him coil a rope, and was laughed at.

In the end I stopped trying to find something to distract me, and got on with being where I was. It wasn't so bad. The ship lifted and fell, lifted and fell, in a regular motion. In a while, my legs began to expect this movement and not fight against it. The wind drummed its fingers in the canvas. I went to the side and watched Ix Chel get smaller. Gradually it melted into the coast-line behind it, until you couldn't tell it was there. Gradually, too, the bustle on deck diminished, and the men settled down to dicing, sleeping or watching the coast as I was. The Captain was sometimes on the upper deck, sometimes inspecting a cask or a sail, and sometimes talking to the pilot, a small, dark man whose name was Alaminos. It seemed to me they did not like each other much.

I watched Alaminos closely. He was the chief pilot. All our lives were in his hands for as long as we were at sea. I didn't think he was to be trusted. He was said to know the coast and the waters, but he seemed to me to know little and to have a great opinion of himself. He seemed unaware, for a start, that the north winds weren't over yet. It was a north wind that had shipwrecked me.

As the first day passed and Ix Chel receded into the distance, I relaxed a little. The sounds of the ship – the slap of the ropes, the dull roar of wind in the sails, the talk of the men and the click of dice on the planking – became a familiar and soothing background. The coastline slipped past, flat and green. Here and there a small temple had been built on the shore, a landmark for canoes and a lookout post. I knew we were being observed from these places now. Eyes followed us for every mile of that seem-ingly empty coast. Occasionally I thought I heard a drum. But it might just have been the wind in the canvas.

At first, as we sailed up the coast, I spent every moment I could at the ship's side, watching the land as we passed it. There was little to be seen, and it was always the same: flat, rising low out of the sea, a green forest fringed by pale sand.

I tried to penetrate the forest with my eyes. I wanted to see places I knew, such as the lagoon to which I had been sent by the *batab* to fetch freshwater fish and the villages I had passed on my way to find Gonzalo. There was no sign of any of them, of course there was not. And with half of myself I did not want there to be, because I did not want these places to be visible from a ship. Yet it would have given me satisfaction to see them, and almost a kind of relief, as if, having seen them from my present place, I could then be quite sure that they existed. And then, of course, I could have pointed them out to my companions.

I was getting used to these men. They had at first been a shock to me. The loudness of their voices, the way they spoke their words right into my face, the hairiness of their cheeks and chins, their smell . . . all this had upset me, I had been repelled by it. Now I was accustomed to the way they shouted, and I raised my voice so that I could shout, too. I stopped noticing their smell. My fingertips told me I was becoming like them: my scalp where it had been shaved was growing a soft mat of hair, and as my chin put forth bristles I let them stay. I didn't bathe because on the ship I couldn't, and if I could not smell my companions I thought it was probably because my own deepening smell was always in my nostrils.

The language was coming back to me, too, but it came back when it felt like it. Sometimes it came back in a rush and I was amazed by what I had just said, and sometimes it came back like the last drops of water in a flask, grudgingly and needing to be shaken.

These things were making me feel more substantial. More – I supposed – like a Spaniard.

The sailors had their own part of the ship, which was separated by a wooden rail from the rest of the main deck. I liked to sit there, among the coils of rope and the barrels, watching the fretting of foam on the wave-caps and the bright pennant that proclaimed this was the Captain's ship streaming in the wind above my head.

I suspected that I wasn't meant to sit there because I wasn't a sailor; however, no one told me to move. I felt more at ease in the company of the sailors than I did in the company of the

Captain's friends. They didn't expect anything of me, and I enjoyed the freedom of their talk, although I didn't understand all of it. It was a relief not to have to listen to gossip about Cuba.

The man who had finished my soup on the day I arrived at Ix Chel had turned out to be a sailor. His name was Salvador and he was on the flagship, as was the boy who had sat next to him that evening. The boy was not quite right in his mind. He laughed, an odd barking laugh, when there was nothing funny, and his eyes jumped around and were strange. Salvador, who seemed fond of him, called him El Loco. A small, wizened sailor whose teeth were jagged and pointed in several different directions, and who had a white scar below his cheek, was often with these two.

All of them bore the Captain a grudge. I asked why.

'He flogged us,' said Salvador.

I wasn't sure I had understood, but the sailor with the jagged teeth raised his arm and brought it down with a sweep that left me in no doubt. 'Why did he flog you?'

'Stealing a side of bacon,' said Salvador.

I felt uncomfortable and didn't know what to say. I thought, here I am trying to make a place for myself among Spaniards again, and the first three people I become friendly with have been flogged for stealing.

'The way I look at it,' said Salvador, 'it was our bacon. Well, it was *my* bacon.'

'News to me,' remarked the sailor with the teeth.

'He owed me a barrel of cheese.'

The boy gave one of his abrupt, worrying laughs.

'I paid a good price for that cheese. There it was, waiting for me on the jetty at Santiago, and the ship was still taking on stores and we were due to sail the next morning, and next minute the anchor was weighed and if I hadn't jumped like a flea I'd have been left on the dock.'

'We sailed in a bit of a hurry, that's a fact,' remarked another sailor sitting near by, and they all laughed at one of those jokes I didn't understand.

'Not a day goes by that I don't wonder who got that barrel of cheese.'

Salvador bit into a slice of fruit and the juice dribbled down his beard and on to his naked chest. It clung in tiny, brilliant beads, each one a little sun, to the curled forest of black hair that ran in a narrowing path from his collarbone to his navel and vanished below the line of his sailor's white pantaloons. Above that line of white, his firm brown belly rose and fell with his breathing. I felt his eyes on me and forced my gaze upward, where it lingered in fascination on those glimmering sticky beads.

'He never had a barrel of cheese,' scoffed the boy.

The pennant whipped. A reek of fish, tar, sweat and piss came up from the warm deck. I went on sitting there, where I shouldn't be, in the drowsy headiness of the afternoon.

As luck would have it, the thin priest was also on our ship. He came by and frowned at me one morning.

'Good day, Father,' I said.

'You have not been to talk to me,' he said. 'Neither to me nor Brother Olmedo.'

'What about?' I said.

'My son, your soul is in danger.'

'My soul is very well,' I told him indignantly.

'Beware, my son. Pride is a great sin.'

'What is a sin?' I asked him. I half-hoped this would send him away, as the question about the sheep had done, but it didn't.

'What is a *sin*?'

'Yes.'

'You surely cannot have forgotten.' As I didn't reply, he went on frowning at me. Then he said, 'You need to talk to me. Hernán allows me to use his cabin for confessions. Come this evening.'

I did not go.

It was natural that being among Spaniards again would reawaken my memories of Spain, but when it began to happen I was at first so astonished at the brightness and beauty of the images that came into my mind that I hardly knew what they were. It was like the sudden rending of a curtain. In the brilliant gap, I would glimpse a ship riding at anchor in a great harbour where warehouses lined the quay; a red-roofed farmhouse among fruit trees; a child looking up from a game on the floor. They did not feel like memories: they were simply dazzling pictures, and they did not identify themselves. Who was this young woman with clear eyes and a pointed chin, standing in a whitewashed room? Whose hands were these that grasped other hands, which might be mine, pressing something into them (a book)? That red-roofed house: was it my home?

As the days passed, the pictures called other pictures to them, and my childhood began returning to me in a procession of people and incidents and fragments of stories. My family had owned a vineyard: I saw it again, marvelled at the springing glossy leaves of the vines, saw how the grapes were blue-black with a ring of redness where the stem entered the flesh. I trod them with the labourers, the wine gushing like blood through the wooden channels. In the drunkenness after the harvest, I saw the villagers dancing naked in a ring. My father found me watching and thrashed me – for my soul, he said.

I had begun to study for the priesthood but I did not finish my studies. It was something to do with the need to sell the vineyard. I walked the corridors of the seminary again. I saw how the light fell from its high windows. Outside were trees, a well, baked earth. A lizard scuttled to a stone. A ripe fig fell.

What had happened after that? Why did I come out to the islands? What did I do, once I arrived? But here the memories stopped. Try as I might, I could recall nothing between Seville, where I embarked on a ship that was presumably the one in the harbour, and the night I was shipwrecked on an entirely different voyage. It was as if time had folded itself along a convenient line and made a pocket in which a year or more of my life was swallowed up. Each time I coaxed my memory to yield up something from that period, it took me, maddeningly, to a scene which appeared quite unconnected, in the *batab*'s palace at Chanek, with the macaw fussing in its cage.

I didn't worry about it. There was enough to get on with.

A little before sundown one day, the wind dropped. The sails sagged like old men's cheeks. I didn't like this, I didn't like the stillness of the sea and the way the air had gone slack and waiting. I looked around to see if anyone else didn't like it, but no one seemed to be worried. Men were settling down to sleep on a coil of rope or a bit of the deck, and the dice players were pleased with the calm because they could light a lantern and go on playing. I lay down in a corner.

In the night, I woke in terror. There was a dreadful shrilling in my ears and the ship was dropping down and down as if it had fallen off the edge of the world. I tried to get up, but the downward dropping of the ship took the power of my limbs away. I lay looking up at the purple clouds rushing across the sky, the moon leering and bloated, and the lantern on the mast dancing like a squirrel in a trap.

Then the ship stopped falling and shivered from stem to stern. We had reached the bottom of the precipice. Now we would be drowned. But no, almost at once we began to be lifted up, the ship groaning and creaking in every timber and starting to roll like an orange from side to side.

I made a great effort and, taking advantage of the ship's rolling motion to pitch myself on to my front, struggled to my knees and then, gripping a rope, to my feet, where I fought to keep my balance against the wind.

Everything was in confusion. Men rushed about the deck, falling into things and colliding with each other, and trying to lash down barrels and crates that had come loose. I saw their mouths open in a shout, but heard nothing because the wind blew their words away. I realized that the ghostly shrilling in my head was the sound of the wind in the rigging. The Captain had

one arm around the mainmast and with the other was gesticulating wildly at Alaminos, who was fighting with the tiller. I made
a run for the ropes, but a sailor appeared in front of me and
yelled at me to get out of the way, so I lurched to the side and
clung to it and stared in horror at the heaving of the sea.

We were perched on the summit of a mountainous wave, but
it was only for a moment. Now, with a shudder, we were sinking
again into the dreadful valley between it and the next. And so it
went on, unceasing, the falling, the being lifted up again, helpless, to the next summit, and the next falling.

We must lower the boat. It was our only hope. Fighting the
wind, I clawed my way to where some sailors were wrestling to
haul in a canvas and shouted in their ears that this was what we
must do. They cursed me and told me to go below if I couldn't
be useful.

I made my way hand over hand along the rail, the deck pitching
and rolling under me every foot of the way, until I found the
boat by bruising my knees on it. My eyes would never have picked
it out, not by the light of the moon and the crazily swinging
lantern, so completely obscured it was by the things that had
been thrown into it, stupid things that had no business being
there, a bundle of rope, a wooden chest, someone's cloak, a set
of padded armour, one boot, a rolled-up hammock . . . In desper-
ation I began pulling these things out and throwing them on to
the deck, and in my haste a few things went into the sea, and
there was Alaminos thrusting his face into mine and bellowing
that if I didn't get below at once he would put me in irons.

I wouldn't have gone, because the thought of being in that
dark place when the ship went down terrified me beyond anything
else. But now a burly figure was making its way towards us. For
a distracted moment I thought it was Gonzalo come to my rescue,
but no, it was the Captain's friend Portocarrero, and he drew his
sword and, gripping a rope to steady himself, held the point a
hand's-breadth from my chest and said that if I didn't get below
he would run me through with it.

As I groped my way down into the hold, a little glow of light rose up to meet me. There were people there and they had a tallow burning. The hold was crammed as tight as a fish barrel with miserable seasick men. Together we began to sit out the storm in the light of a guttering candle.

In the morning the sea was as flat as a tray, and empty. There wasn't so much as a spar of wood floating on it. Not that any of us wanted to see a floating spar, but at least it would have told us something. When a bit of wind got up, we hoisted canvas and sailed along looking for our companions, but the morning went by and we saw no other ship.

In the afternoon the lookouts shouted that there was a sail. We let out more canvas so we could come up with her. By the time the sun went down we had found four more ships; another joined us silently in the night, and two at dawn. The tenth ship, a little single-masted vessel, came into view about the middle of the following morning, and we all cheered, and by now we were certain that the whole fleet was safe. We expected the eleventh ship to appear on the horizon at any moment.

But the eleventh ship did not appear. The sun slipped down to the sea and she still had not appeared.

People began to talk.

'She's gone to the bottom or gone home, if you ask me,' said Portocarrero with a dark look. 'I'd put my money on gone home.'

He was talking to the Captain, who frowned at him.

The five men who played dice on the deck every day were also saying the missing ship had gone home. They were making a lot of jokes about it. Alaminos came by and told them sharply not to be stupid. The ship had run for shelter in the storm and was stuck in some harbour she couldn't get out of, he said, and that was all there was to it. One of the dice players grinned and said wasn't it odd, though, that it was *that ship*?

I needed someone to explain all this to me, so I asked a man who was standing near me at the rail what was special about the missing ship. He told me she was the *Isabel,* and was commanded by an officer called Velásquez de León. When I asked what was important about that, he said that Velásquez de León was the cousin of the Governor of Cuba. I had gathered that there had been a quarrel of some kind between the Captain and the Governor of Cuba, so I asked no more questions.

As it turned out, Alaminos was right. The *Isabel* joined us two days later. She had been trapped in a cove by a combination of winds and currents.

Velásquez de León came on board our ship and he and the Captain embraced like brothers, although for two days nobody had talked of anything but the trouble there was between them.

We sailed on without further mishap, until we came to a place where the sky was full of sea birds. There were so many I thought they would collide in the air. Gulls, egrets, pelicans, all circling and swooping, bringing fish out of the water with a flick. Their beaks streamed, the fish were a wriggle of silver.

I gazed into the water to see what was causing this. The water was turbulent, brownish. A brownish or pale current running inside the sea green, the jade. Inside that brown tunnel turned broken-off twigs and black branches and bunches of leaves, rotting fruit. A dead squirrel looked up at me with its eye of clouded glass.

But that wasn't all. At the edges of the brown water, where it met the jade water, were countless fish. Tiny as an arrowhead. Hanging motionless like a cloud on a day of no wind. Then in an instant all gone, as if they were just a thought of the water.

So that was the reason for the birds.

But why was the water brown?

I saw that, on the shoreline where the strip of sand had always been, there were now banks and shoals of mud. Between these banks a broad river poured into the sea, bringing on its shoulders all the twigs and branches and dead matter I had seen floating. A line of forest blurred into the sky behind the mudbanks.

All of a sudden there was a great bustle on deck. Men were buckling on their swords, coming to the rail and pointing things out to each other. The dogs which were normally kept in one of the holds burst on to the deck and rushed about barking.

'Take her in closer,' said the Captain to Alaminos.

Alaminos said he wouldn't because the water was too shallow.

'Nonsense,' said the Captain.

Alaminos said that if the Captain knew more about this coastline than *he* did, then he should take charge of the navigation.

The Captain asked a little knot of men who were watching the shore whether it was true that the water was too shallow. They said it was and that we would have to anchor where we were, and that this was where they had anchored a year ago.

The Captain didn't like it, but he ordered the anchor to be dropped. He said we would go ashore in the boats.

'You'll come with me,' he told me, 'in the first boat.'

I didn't have any desire to go with him. I didn't like the look of that shore. I said I would rather stay on the ship.

'You'll come with me,' said the Captain. 'We might meet Indians.' Then he took off the cotton *winic* armour he was wearing and that many of them had, and told me to put it on. When I next saw him he was wearing a steel corselet.

I got into the boat. Already in it were fifteen men, three dogs and several crossbows. We set off dangerously low in the water, and rowed towards the shore.

On the islands of mud which the river had carved, perched hundreds of thin-legged white birds like ghosts. Some took flight as we approached but most remained, still and watchful. We glided past them, not talking, listening to the splash of the oars and the unnatural silence. And now the forest itself was coming into view, the forest that lined the banks of that brown river and was the source of the twigs and the squirrel and all the other dead things I had seen floating in the current.

This forest was strange to me. The broad fleshy leaves of the trees were like fat green hands, the twisted trunks seemed to be writing, and the branches arched mightily into a canopy so dense that darkness hung from it like fruit. But strangest of all were the roots.

The roots were a country. They formed a vast, sinewy net of wood, a bony trapwork that straddled and threaded the mud, separating it into blank, glistening, bottomless pockets where a man might sink and die horribly. They crawled right down to the water's edge, and in the other direction crept into the shadows of the forest.

I looked into the shadows and my heart did its best to leap out of my body. In the forest there was an army waiting.

In a single glance, I saw them all and knew what they were. I could tell the warriors who had faced death many times, and the first-time boys with uncut hair. I could see the captains of twenty and of four hundred. I saw their gaping masks and their flint blades, and the spirits they had with them.

'What is it?' said the Captain, who was sitting beside me, and then, because his eyes were sharp for a *cristiano*, he went as still as a post himself.

All this time there had been no sound but the creak and splash of our boats. Then suddenly the *winic* rushed out of the forest and screamed fury at us, and we cowered under the shock of their noise and drumming as if it had been a rain of arrows. The oarsmen faltered, and fifty hands made the sign of the Tree like a flock of birds rising.

'Speak to them,' the Captain urged me hoarsely. 'Tell them we're friends.'

I shouted, but they were making so much clamour they couldn't hear me.

'Try again. Say we only want water.'

'But we didn't bring the casks.'

'Say it.'

I shouted in Ahau that we wanted water. A stone rushed past my head and crashed into the mudbank, splashing muck all over the Captain's face. He wiped it off.

45

'Tell them we mean no harm and would like to land,' he said.

The noise had died down a bit by now, and when the *winic* at last understood that I was trying to speak to them they became quiet. I said we only wanted to land and get water. After a pause, a reply was shouted back.

'They say that if we land they will kill us,' I said.

The Captain said, 'Tell them that if they attack us we will kill them all, and burn their town.'

I did so.

Arrows began to fall around us. Falling neatly around the boat, not touching it.

'Row on,' ordered the Captain. But the rain of arrows grew heavier when we moved forward. One lodged itself in a man's armour, at the waist.

The Captain looked at the river. It was dotted with tiny islands, half sand half mud. Bare of everything except the white birds.

'We'll land there,' said the Captain, and he pointed at a long, thin island a little further from the bank than the others.

We beached the boat where he pointed, and signalled to the other boats to land as well. Soon all of us were on the island.

We lit a fire with some driftwood and spent the night there. The Captain set a watch on the boats and told all of us to sleep in our armour, but no one felt like sleeping. Towards the middle of the night, two boats slipped away from the island and went up towards the river mouth, muffling their oars. They came back many hours later. The Captain moved about, talking to people and looking intently at the opposite bank. Nothing was to be seen there but a dense darkness.

Apart from the occasional beat of a drum, the *winic* left us alone.

In the morning we got ready to go ashore. As soon as we went to the boats, the *winic*, who had gathered again on the opposite bank, set up their war din. This upset the dogs, who started barking loudly and rushing about.

I found the Captain talking to Brother Olmedo. He was our other priest, and I liked the look of him a lot more than I liked Juan Díaz. Olmedo was a fat man who trod lightly and smiled when he saw you. At the moment he was looking very serious. He said to the Captain, 'Hernán, can't you avoid this battle?'

'Not if they are seeking it,' said the Captain.

Brother Olmedo said, 'You are obliged to read them the Requirement.'

'I'm not obliged to read them anything if they are *seeking a battle*.'

'Read it nonetheless.'

We got into the boats and pushed off towards the river bank. It was only a short distance. As we were crossing, the Captain turned to a man sitting in the boat, and said, 'Do you have it?'

The man said he did.

'Then read it.'

The man took a leather pouch from his pocket and out of it brought a folded sheet of paper, closely covered in writing. He began to read from it, in a monotonous voice, and all the boats rested on their oars while he did this. I realized that it was a ritual of some kind, but all the same it seemed such an extraordinary and dangerous thing to be doing in this situation that I paid very little heed to what he was saying, but kept my eyes on the *winic*. Then, belatedly, I remembered that I ought to listen because I might be asked to translate. So I tried to concentrate on a sentence or two, but what I heard made no sense. It was all about the Pope.

A blaring of conches suddenly came from the river bank, and as the sound died away the *winic* shouted and blew their clay whistles. This noise completely drowned the Spaniard's voice, and from that point I paid no attention to the speech whether I could hear it or not.

Drumming had now started. At any moment, I thought, they would fling themselves upon us across that narrow channel, or at least loose a storm of arrows.

The warriors nearest us made a rush for the bank. Then, as abruptly, they stopped, raised their weapons in the air with a wild yell, and stamped their feet four times.

The man in the boat was now saying something about the Catholic kings of Castile.

'Waie-aie-aie!' yelled the *winic*, and more of them rushed forward, thrust their weapons into the air and stamped. A moment later, all the *winic* within sight were performing the same wild dance. Now the entire host was yelling, stamping and blowing whistles and conches with a noise that made my head ring.

The Captain raised his hand. The oars dipped and we moved forward again.

At once, arrows began to fall.

The arrows fell into the mud on either side of the boat and into the planking. The *winic* were not yet trying to kill us. But now our bow glided heavily into a soft cliff of mud and stuck fast, throwing us all backwards, and as we picked ourselves up and put our hands on the sides of the boat, ready to scramble over the net of roots, the drums screamed in rage and the sky rained stones and arrows. A man standing so close that I could feel his breath had his hand pinned to the planking by an arrow. He plucked at it, with a look of horror on his face, and then begged me to snap the shaft. Blood welled up out of the wound and fell into the frondy cracks of the mud, turning the mud blue. As I was staring, transfixed, at this, another man elbowed me aside and broke the arrow shaft, and the wounded man brought his hand up slowly through all the length of the snapped end, his face deathly white, until his hand was free and the blood rushed out in a torrent.

The Captain leapt from the prow of the boat and landed like a monkey on the tree roots. He ran forward, holding his shield up against the arrows. Young Sandoval was right behind him. Then men were pouring out of the boats, stumbling, cursing, but also running forward over the root-net, under the arrows.

I had no shield, nor a weapon of any kind. But I reckoned it would be more dangerous in the boat than on land, so I scrambled out of the boat and ran with the rest.

The roots were slippery and knotted, and we kept falling over them. When we fell we went into the mud, which several men had already plunged feet-first into. They were up to their waists in it and were desperately trying to scramble free, while arrows bounced off their steel helmets. The arrows were coming thickly, filling the air so that you couldn't see the sun. One of our men had caught a spear in the chest; it had gone straight through the leather corselet he was wearing, and he lay spreadeagled across the tree roots.

I stumbled forward, frightened out of my wits and having no idea in my head but that I must keep up with the others if I wanted to survive. In the midst of it all – the stumbling over roots, the noise, the *whoosh* of arrows, the terror – I thought suddenly of Gonzalo and how he would have relished this fight. My next thought was that he might even be here. Thinking this, I fell headlong over a root. As I lay there getting my breath, and trying to pull my left foot, which was stuck fast, free of the mud, I looked up and saw my death rushing towards me. It had taken the form of a jaguar. He sprang with his flint sword raised to deal the blow that would split my head, and I saw his face inside the animal's jaws regarding me seriously. But then there he hung just a little too long, in the mid-air of his leap, as if he'd thought better of it, and I saw the end of the crossbow's bolt sticking from his chest. He pitched feet-first between the roots and fell forward, and the mask skewed sideways on his neck and gaped at me.

I dragged my foot out of the mud, crept to him and pulled off the mask. He was young, for his rank. His town would mourn him. I wondered what they would say about his death, since he had been killed by a thing never seen before. I felt my hands not wanting to let go of the mask, and when I stood up my hands held on to it. Then they put it on my head.

It smelt of copal. It was full of the god. Its darkness fell over me, and then I was looking out through its jaws, and it was sitting on my shoulders as light as a cloud.

We were still in the swamp and were surrounded. My countrymen were fighting furiously, slashing and chopping with their swords, and wherever the steel bit the *winic* fell back. But only for a moment. Then they would surge forward again in another flood. With a cry I had heard other Spaniards giving, I charged to the aid of a Spaniard who was fighting with two *winic*. When they saw me rushing down on them, jaguar-headed, they turned and ran.

I rushed on into the fray. The *winic* fled at my coming, and this caused me no surprise. It seemed to me quite natural that a space should surround me into which no warriors came and no spear flew. Onward I rushed, leaping from tree root to tree root like the animal I had become, shouting the war-cry — on to where the trees of the swamp finally gave way to trees I recognized and the ground was ground that could be stood on. And there I stopped, for in front of me were grass and maize plots, and across them the Captain, Sandoval and twenty others were driving *winic* before them.

Ahead, I saw the town with its temple top and sacred tree, and its houses of wood and stone. The townspeople had put barricades around it, of tree trunks lashed with creepers. I took off the head of the jaguar and hid it in a tree, and then I ran to the barricades to help my companions, and as we were struggling to pull them down a heavy log slipped and crushed a Spaniard's leg.

Once we had got into the streets the *winic* ran to the temple. From it, they loosed a stream of arrows at us, which sent us dodging among the houses. I crouched behind a wall and watched a Spaniard calmly winding his crossbow while arrows flew around him. When it was ready he raised it to his shoulder to fire the bolt. I never saw whether he hit his mark because just then I heard a terrible clamour of shell trumpets, drums and the eerie whistling and screaming with which the *winic* launch an attack. It was coming from the forest.

We are all dead men, I thought, for it was obvious that, having entered the town, we were trapped.

I hid behind the wall, waiting for the attack. My legs were shaking and I couldn't make them stop.

Nothing happened for a long time. The clamour in the forest continued for a while, then abruptly faded. There came new sounds. A number of sharp cracks like the snapping of dry boughs, and then shouts, Spanish shouts. These sounds, mysteriously, were also coming from the forest.

Our men raised a loud cheer and at once rushed at the *winic* who had taken refuge in the temple, and chased them from the town like deer.

Then, marching out of the forest in triumph, came Blue Eyes and about forty men, holding smoking hackbuts above their heads and shouting '*Santiago!*'

The Captain saw me hiding behind my wall and told me to follow him. He walked, with Blue Eyes and Sandoval and several others, to where the sacred tree was growing, close to the temple. He took out his sword and cut it. He made deep gashes in its trunk: one, two, three.

When I saw this I wanted to cry out in protest, but I kept silent because the Captain was saying something. The man who, in the boat, had read the speech to the *winic*, now took an inkhorn, quill and paper from his pocket and wrote busily.

I went up and looked at the tree after they had gone. Sap was welling from the wounds he had made. Held inside the sap, like an eye, was a spot of blood which had come off his sword.

I turned this over and over in my mind in the days that followed. I knew that the Captain had not known what he was doing, but that did not alter the fact that he had done it. The Yaxché grows beside every temple; or if it does not, its sign is planted there. It is the pathway between earth and heaven. The Captain had cut it with his sword.

We slept in the town. We had scavenged through the houses for food, but there wasn't much and in the morning the Captain sent parties out to look for more. He also sent for Melchior, but the boy could not be found. Then it was reported that his clothes had been discovered at the edge of the forest. He had gone back to his people.

I was glad, because among Christians he had become a shadow, but the Captain was furious. He said that Melchior's escape would do us grave harm.

Soon after the foraging parties had ridden out, we heard sounds of fighting. When our men came back, they had prisoners. They said they had run into war-parties of *winic*. The Captain told me to question these prisoners and find out why they had been waiting to attack us.

At first I didn't get very far. The captives were seasoned warriors and they expected the usual death of a captive taken in war. They did not understand why I was asking them questions and took it as an insult. However, I carried on until eventually they broke their silence to put an end to the questions. They said they had not wanted to attack us; they had just wanted to warn us away from their coasts.

'You were mustered in twenties of twenties,' I reminded them. 'You had painted your faces. Your spirits were with you.'

'We wanted you to go away,' they said again, 'and that was all.'

'We only came for water,' I said.

They did not believe me. They said we had come here two *tuns* ago and killed many of their people, and they believed we would do it again. That was why they warned us not to land. That was why they were ready for war.

I was thinking there was a lot of sense in what they said, but also that the Captain wouldn't be pleased if that was all I had to tell him, when the youngest of the captives said, more in anger than boasting, 'We will continue to fight you. We will fight you until you are all dead.'

The others closed their faces. I turned my attention to him. I thought he had said more than they wanted him to.

'How can you kill us all?' I said, and laughed. 'So far you have killed one or two of us and we have killed four hundred of your people.' ('Four hundred' is what the *winic* say for 'very many'.)

'We know there are only a few of you,' said the young warrior. 'The boy you stole has come back and told us.'

I tried to hide my dismay but he saw it. 'We shall kill you all and burn your canoes. We shall eat your flesh and throw down your god,' he said.

One of the others spoke sharply to him, but he didn't care to listen. 'Tomorrow we will fight you with twenty times twenty times twenty. We will bring warriors from all over the land.'

I went to the Captain at once.

He said, 'It may not be true. Perhaps he wanted to frighten us.' He looked at me for my opinion.

'He was telling the truth,' I said.

Several hours after dark, he sent me with three soldiers along a path that led north from the town. He said that, if we managed to reach the ships, I should stay there, since he'd lost one interpreter already and didn't want to lose another. It seemed madness to me, since no one was certain that the path even went to the coast. It was all guesswork and the memories of men who had ventured inland the year before.

The path glimmered palely under half a moon. If it could be seen, we could be seen. I told the other three to put mud on their faces and the backs of their hands, and to wear cotton armour and no helmets, which they didn't like, but they obeyed me. I said the *winic* could hear things that Christians couldn't, and I tried to tell them how to move silently, but they were impatient and said they would move the way they always did. So we set off, making a clatter that could have been heard in Chanek.

North of the town was a flat plain on which grew isolated trees and bushes and a thick-bladed grass. It had been used for crops, and was lying fallow. After a while we came to fields where the old maize stalks stood in dark companies as we passed. Beyond this, jumping like skeletons out of the shadows, were the poles on which beans would twine, and beyond them was the plain again, the grass which rustled too loudly as we walked, the moon which could not be hidden from, the birds that saw us and spread the tale.

We half-walked, half-crept while I watched the journey of the moon and calculated how much was left of the night. And still we had seen no *winic*, although if the path went where we hoped there was no reason for *winic* to be on it, for it went only to the headland where there was no village. But then, if it went to the headland, where was the sea? Should we not already have glimpsed it?

But all the time, the sea was there around us. A moment came when the land drew back its skirts and where it had been the sea rose, gleaming. We stopped then, and I saw, marvelling, that on the broad apron of ground before us were great beasts bending their heads to the grass. They flicked their pointed ears. A sound came from them, a gentle snorting of contentment, and from time to time one of them would move a lazy leg forward to get at a new patch of pasture. I recognized them with a start and then with tears in my eyes, and wondered that they could have endured so long on the ships. How their feet must have longed for earth!

Standing in the shadows, watching our approach, were the three *cristianos* who were guarding them. These three came forward and had a whispered talk with the three I was accompanying, while I kept my eyes open for *winic*. Then we went on again, the grass dwindling into islands lapped by sand, until there was only sand and the suck and splash of the sea.

On the shore lay an upturned boat, bleached by the moon-light. We carried it to the water, tipped it on to its keel and clambered in. The ships looked a long way out, they were just a darkness on the water about the size of a bean-flower, but by rowing hard we came to them quickly.

I went with one other man up the ladder of the flagship, while the remaining two stayed with the boat. On the deck, swathed in

54

canvas like a tall, thin corpse, lay the thing that had to be taken downriver to the Captain. We needed the help of the sailors in raising it. It was as heavy as twenty corpses and as obstinate, and it took six of us, heaving mightily, to get it over the side and lower it, bit by bit, while it crashed against the planking, into the little bobbing boat. Then the clumsy wheeled carriage had to be lowered in after it, which made the boat settle still further in the water, so that altogether I thought it was a good thing I wasn't going back with them or the boat would certainly sink to the bottom.

I stood by the wooden rail, which had taken quite a battering when we manhandled the lombard over it, and watched the boat grow smaller.

'I reckon that thing will be more trouble than it's worth,' said Salvador, coming to stand beside me. 'Don't you?'

He put his hand on the back of my neck.

'No,' I said.

Just after dawn, the sound of distant drumming rolled over the water.

I crawled out of my bed in the canvas and went to the ship's side. All the sailors were clustered there. They were looking in the direction of the shore. I strained my eyes. I could see only the veils of mist the sun was lifting from the forest.

After a long time in which the drumming continued without pause, a flock of birds flew wildly towards us and behind them came the crack-crack of hackbut fire. From the patch of forest to the north of the river, tiny puffs of white smoke were rising. They blossomed like flowers above the tops of the trees and vanished into the pale air.

Then the forest convulsed in whistling and howling, while the beat of the drums quickened. Through the din a brave, small sound rose: the Spanish battle-cry. After that my ears did not need to tell me what was happening: the clash of steel on flint and flint on steel, and the sighing of spears as they rushed through the air to bury themselves in flesh.

Already I could see how it would be at the day's end, as I stood at the edge of the field where the battle had been. Everywhere, Spaniards lay dead, their heads and limbs severed by flint swords, their throats pierced by arrows, their skulls smashed by stones. Blood had made a swamp of the ground, and the flies and the vultures were feasting.

I grieved for the death of my companions in this foreign land, and for the end of all their hopes. But I have to confess that my thoughts were mainly for myself. What would become of me, when the Captain and all his men were dead? Would the sailors take me to Cuba with them, or would they try to avenge their dead companions and be killed as well? Could I still go back and live among the *winic*?

This last idea threw me into a turmoil. I thought, I have left my life among the *winic* behind me: I do not want to go back. Then in a rush Chanek came back into my mind as powerfully as if I'd only that day left it. Its white stone walls, the wild grasses that blew in the margins around the maize plots, the colour of its earth. The hut I had lived in, its three hearth stones and the hole in the thatch above, through which rain came in. Its comforting smell of wood-smoke, food and copal; the murmuring talk of the slaves. And I was filled with longing for it.

These thoughts were interrupted by a loud *boom!* from the forest. The sailors cheered lustily and said it was the lombard we had shipped ashore in the night.

But after the firing of the lombard there was again nothing that told us how the battle might be going, nothing to give us hope. The 'Santiago!', when we heard it, sounded frail and forlorn. I sat on my heels in what shade there was from the masts and rigging, and waited. I sat like that, as the sun grew hot on my skin and misery grew in me, until there came a long, deep blaring of conches and I took it to be a sign that the *winic* had killed or captured every last Spaniard. I put my head in my hands and despaired.

Moments later there was a gigantic shout from many throats and a sound like drumming, low and quick, and then the crackling of many hackbuts fired at almost the same instant. And above these sounds there rose again, this time passionate and like a song, the battle-cry of Spain. From the exultation in those voices, and the great cheer the sailors raised, I understood that we had won the victory, although how it had happened I could not imagine. And I was thankful – that we had been spared, that there would be no more bloodshed, and that now I could go home.

The Captain sent for me to come back and interpret, because he expected the *winic* to sue for peace. However, when they arrived, with gifts of food, he received them politely enough but said he would not talk to them. This went on for four days. I did not understand what he wanted.

'Tell them I will speak only to their highest chiefs,' he told me, and I did so, although I thought it was pointless because he knew nothing about their rulers.

However, on the fourth day a greatly enlarged delegation came, so perhaps his stubbornness had brought in *batabs* from a wider region. The Captain looked pleased when he saw them approaching; nevertheless, as soon as the baskets of maize and fowl had been put down and the phrases of greeting uttered, he launched into a furious speech, telling them that they had attacked us when we came to their shores in peace, and deserved to be put to death.

When I translated this, the oldest among them said, 'We have already apologized twice for attacking you and we do not see why we should have to apologize again. We have suffered greatly in this battle. Moreover, our temple has been violated and the Yaxché harmed. We do not understand why this lord is not satisfied but would like to kill us all.'

The Captain said, 'They have only themselves to blame for their losses. They were warned.' And he began to rail at them again for having made war on us and for their abominable religion, of which he claimed to have found disgusting evidence in the temple we had slept in, although all that had been found were some bones wrapped in cloth in a wooden chest.

The *winic* replied that their religion was their own concern, as our religion was ours, and that as they did not insult our gods we should not insult theirs. This made the Captain even angrier. He got up from the chair in which he was sitting – an ugly carved thing that had been brought from the ship – and began to walk up and down. He told the *winic* that their behaviour had been treacherous and ungrateful. They had made no attempt to listen to the speech we read to them on our arrival, which explained who we were and many other things it would have benefited them to know.

However, said the Captain, still pacing and frowning, he was able to offer them a second chance. If they would now swear to be our friends for ever, and bring gold as a sign of it (and here he took the gold ornament out of his pocket, to make sure they understood), they would be forgiven and we would protect them in future from their enemies. And so that they should understand what would happen if they did not, he would now show them that the god we worshipped had given him power over certain bad spirits which had not yet had as much sport as they wanted.

I'd barely finished translating his words before he brought his hand down in an abrupt gesture. Blue Eyes, who had moved up beside me, put his fingers in his ears.

The earth opened with a roar and flames leapt from it. Something frightful screamed over the treetops and vanished, drawing the branches into a swaying dance behind it. I threw myself to the ground and lay there with my eyes shut. When, after a while, I opened them I saw a little spider climbing up a leaf. It was having difficulty because of something sticky and black that was on the leaf. I then saw that the same powdery, sticky substance had fallen on my skin.

My ears were singing an echoing song like a flute in a cavern. But now another sound came into this, breaking it up. It was a sound like a moth fluttering. This sound deepened, and turned into the sound of laughter.

I got up cautiously. The Captain, with his hands on his hips and head thrown back, was laughing like a boy. Everyone else was laughing, too. Blue Eyes was slapping his thigh with mirth. The members of the *winic* delegation were running into the forest as fast as their legs would carry them.

It was the lombard, Sandoval told me later, and it had been loaded with the biggest charge of powder the chief gunner would allow. He said that Pedro de Alvarado (that was Blue Eyes) had asked the Captain not to warn me, because he wanted to see what I would do.

I was surprised when they came back. I thought he had so frightened and humiliated them that they would retreat into their forests and wait for us to leave. Their priests would find an explanation for these terrible events somewhere in the prophecies.

I was wrong. A subdued delegation visited us the next morning, accompanied by a train of bearers. They brought gold. Necklaces, earrings, bracelets and anklets, small cast figures of animals, masks inlaid with shell. They brought it out and showed him, and it shone as yellow as buttercups.

When he saw the gold, the Captain's face relaxed as if a woman were stroking it. Then the chiefs announced that they would swear to be our friends for ever, and the Captain got up from his chair and embraced them. He made them say it again, putting in a few phrases of his own for them to say, which I translated as well as I could although there was no equivalent for them in Ahau and although I privately considered them to be ridiculous. He had it all written down by the man who had written things down when he cut the bark of the Yaxché. He thanked the *batabs* for the gold and for a further gift they gave us, of twenty women.

He wasn't expecting the women. He passed his hand over his

beard. I could see him thinking that some of them were beautiful and there might be trouble. But his men were smiling as if the rains had come after a year of drought, and he had no choice. He thanked the *winic* and gave orders for the women to be put under guard and watched as closely as the gold.

He still had one of the gold pieces in his hand. It was a figure of a deer.

'Ask them where the gold comes from,' he said to me.

The *batab* who was spokesman laughed when I asked him this. 'It comes from the Meshica, of course,' he said. His face said that he knew nothing good about the Meshica.

'Where do the Meshica live?' the Captain wanted to know. The *batab* pointed to where the sun sets.

4

Two men came up to me on the night before we left Potonchan, when I was guarding the horses in a clearing. They introduced themselves as Don Francisco and Don Sebastián. They had an air of importance but I noticed that all the same they glanced over their shoulders often.

Don Francisco said I was proving to be of great value to the expedition and that they were very lucky to have me as an interpreter. I thanked him. Then he said why didn't we take a walk.

We began to walk around the little circle of the clearing, with the forest a thick darkness on our left and the horses cropping on our right. There was enough moon to whiten the teeth of the horses as they bent their heads to the grass. It was quiet, except for the creaking of Don Francisco's leather boots, the bumping of Don Sebastián's sword against his thigh and the gentle sound of the horses eating.

Don Francisco began to talk. He said he was sure that I was a man of honour, a man whose loyalty to the cause he had undertaken would be beyond doubt. He believed that even though I had lived among Indians for many years, I had not lost the qualities which belonged to a Spanish gentleman.

I said that I had always tried to remember what I was.

He then said, 'So what do you think of the conduct of a man

who disobeys the orders of his chief, takes goods he has been entrusted with and uses them for his own purposes, and falsely claims another man's authority?'

I replied that a man who did those things was a rebel and a thief.

'That is the man who leads us,' said Don Francisco.

For a moment I did not believe that he had said this; then I knew he had and wished I had not heard it. For although I knew there was gossip against the Captain, I sensed that there was more in this than gossip.

I asked Don Francisco what he meant.

He had a pale face and slightly bulging eyes. His mouth was tight. 'You are aware,' he said to me, 'that Hernán sailed from Cuba against the Governor's orders?'

I said no, I had not known. But they seemed to expect something else, so I said, 'I thought the expedition was sent by the Governor.'

'It was.'

'Then why did he want to stop it?'

'He didn't. He didn't want Hernán to command it.'

'But he chose him to command it.' Everyone said this.

'He was badly advised,' said Don Francisco shortly. 'He took back the appointment. Hernán sailed when he'd been ordered not to. Legally, he is a rebel.'

We went on walking. I considered saying something to show that I was not as great a friend of the Captain as they might think, but I didn't, partly because if I did not always like what the Captain said and did, I liked the feeling these two men gave me even less. I also thought that if the Governor of Cuba couldn't make up his mind, he shouldn't be surprised if people disobeyed him. In the end, for something to say, I suggested, 'Perhaps there was a misunderstanding,' at which Don Sebastián laughed so loudly that Don Francisco had to tell him to be quiet.

'There's no misunderstanding,' said Don Francisco. 'He has set aside the Governor's claims in this country.'

'Claims?' I repeated.

Don Francisco jabbed his finger at the ground. 'This land we're walking on. He has claimed it for the King.'

Something rose in my chest and threatened to stifle me. I looked at the moon silvering the grass, and the horses peacefully cropping. Behind them, the living forest, and beyond the forest the ocean.

'How can it belong to the King?' I said angrily.

'Exactly!' crowed Don Sebastián, and clapped a hand on my shoulder.

Just then, a figure came walking towards us from the town. It was Sandoval. Don Francisco and Don Sebastián said that it had been most rewarding talking to me and they would come back at another time. They went off in a hurry.

After leaving Potonchan, we sailed along the coast to a place my companions were calling San Juan de Ulua. We reached it in a few days.

On the last morning of the voyage, as we approached San Juan, the Captain and Portocarrero stood in the bows, talking. They had been there for quite a long time: both of them had been gazing at the shore as if they couldn't get enough of it. I didn't myself think it looked very promising: mainly sand, with a ribbon of trees behind and, rising in the distance, mountains. I went to the other side of the ship to watch a couple of islands we were passing. Two men were at the rail, looking at a temple built above the shore on the larger one.

Pointing at the image of the Yaxché that stood beside it, one of them said, 'There's another of those crosses. See it? Strange that they put those up.'

'I call it blasphemous,' said the other. 'We went into that temple last year. Know what we found?' And they went on to talk about the disgusting rites of the *winic*.

I half-listened, wanting to interrupt but knowing they would not understand my explanations. So I was on the wrong side of the ship, and with my head in a fret, when the most important event that had yet befallen us was about to happen.

There was a sudden shout of 'Canoe!'

I went to join the Captain, preparing words of greeting. Approaching us was a big trading canoe paddled by ten strong, good-looking *winic* with unbraided hair. They came alongside. They had baskets of fish, and other baskets filled with woven goods and copper. Perhaps there would be gold. I felt the Captain's eyes searching for it, down there in the baskets among the bare Indian feet.

The man at the front of the canoe shouted up to us. I couldn't make out what he said, but I called out a greeting. He shouted again. I still couldn't catch the words.

'What's he saying?' asked the Captain.

'He wants to come aboard,' I said, since that much was obvious.

A sailor threw down the rope ladder. The *winic* who had shouted to us started to climb up, quickly followed by another one. As they climbed, the men still in the canoe talked to them: I didn't understand what *they* were saying, either. Even the sound of it, the rise and fall, was unfamiliar.

Now the first *winic* was stepping on to the deck, making the hand-to-the-earth greeting. The second followed him. Everyone smiled. The first *winic* made a little speech. Pattering, incomprehensible. Everyone turned to me.

There was nothing in my head. It was quite empty.

'Aren't you going to translate it?' asked the Captain.

'I don't understand what he's saying,' I confessed.

'What d'you mean, you don't understand?'

'It's a different language, Captain.'

A long pause. 'And you don't speak it?'

'No,' I said.

Another pause, this time a short one. Then he turned away impatiently, turning his back on me, to give all his attention to his guest.

* * *

I had been having more and more doubts about the nature of this expedition, and the more doubts I had the less keen I was to be its interpreter. So I should have been relieved when my role was taken away from me. However, I wasn't: I felt humiliated. And I realized that, although I had been in two minds about being the Captain's interpreter, it had simplified things for me. It had told everyone who I was, and it had told me who to *be*.

Now, I thought, I shall have to start again. I wasn't sure what I meant by that. I wandered over to the starboard rail and stared into the water.

After a time I found that the Captain's page, a pretty boy we called Flea, was at my elbow. 'The Captain wants to see you,' he said.

I didn't care what the Captain wanted. The Captain had just turned his back on me. 'What about?' I said.

'One of the women.'

'What?'

'One of the Indian women. You know.' He pointed backwards with his thumb.

The women who had been given to us at Potonchan. Clearly frightened out of their wits, they had huddled in a corner of the temple before we sailed. At the last minute the Captain had divided them up among the three largest ships and put them in the personal charge of the commander of each. There were eight of them on the flagship, and they had not left their quarters while we were at sea. As a result, we'd forgotten they were there. At least, I had.

I went to where the Captain was. A crowd had gathered but I pushed my way through. The Captain, with his thumbs in his belt and looking like a man in a fog, was watching as one of the Potonchan women chattered away to the two *winic* from the canoe.

'Where have you been?' he demanded when I arrived. Then, without waiting for an answer, '*She* can understand them, so why can't you?'

The woman was laughing and chatting with the *winic*, who

were all smiles. Behind us, the other women clustered in the doorway of their tiny cabin, looking on with wide eyes. I was suddenly very angry – with everyone: with the Captain, who wouldn't leave me alone even when I was no use to him; with the *winic*, who didn't speak the language I knew; and with the woman, who was at the centre of this scene and was clearly enjoying it – and I said to her in Ahau, without stopping to think whether she would understand me, 'What do you think you're doing? You should be with the other women.'

She turned to me boldly and said in perfect Ahau, 'If you want to understand what these men are saying, you had better let me stay.'

The men from the canoe looked curiously at the two of us, not understanding this exchange. The Captain's stare went from me to the woman and back again.

'Will you explain all this?' he said.

'She speaks two languages,' I said.

'What? Are you sure?'

'Yes, Captain.'

At the same moment the woman said to me, 'Do you want to know what these men say, or not?'

'What do they say?'

'They bring you greetings from their *batab*. They have brought fish and maize as presents and tomorrow they will bring other things.'

'Well, that's very welcome,' said the Captain when I translated it. 'Tell them that we've come a long way and would be glad of any hospitality they can offer.'

I put this into Ahau. The woman translated it into the other language. The *winic* from the canoe bowed.

'Meanwhile,' said the Captain, beaming, 'perhaps we can offer *them* something. A drop of wine?'

Winic drink strong liquor only at festivals, but then they drink until they fall down. When the wine was brought, the men from the canoe first sipped it cautiously and then drank it in great gulps. In a short time they were very drunk. The Captain and Portocarrero watched them with amusement, refilling their cups and drinking a little themselves to encourage them. The two *winic* staggered around the deck, fell down, had to be helped to their feet again, laughed as if it was the funniest thing that had ever happened to them, stopped laughing and began to fight with the rigging, then fell on their knees and spewed up everything in their stomachs.

The sailors got them half-way down the ship's ladder, and from there their friends hauled them into the canoe.

After they had gone, with much shouting of farewells, the Captain stood stroking his beard and looking hard at the woman. She didn't flinch under his stare, but kept her eyes lowered.

'What a strange thing,' he murmured. 'The hand of Fate is in this.'

We went ashore the next day. The Captain said he liked the place and we would stay for a time. He would have had to say so, whether he liked the place or not, because the men who had come here before had been talking about this place since we left Ix Chel. They had done well here and could have done better, they said, if Grijalva had not been such a fool and stuck to the letter of his instructions. There was gold, they had seen it. The Indians dived into the rivers for it and came up with the grains held in their mouths, and between daybreak and sundown an Indian could fill a hollow tube the width of his finger and the length of his forearm with gold.

I thought they were dreaming. The air was thick with mosquitoes and all I could see was sand.

It stretched, this sand, to either side of the shallow bay where we were anchored. A pale yellow sand, rather coarse, rather unpleasant when it got inside your shirt, as it quickly did, or into your eyes or the roots of your hair. It also got up your nostrils and into the cavities of your ears, and under your fingernails, and naturally into your mouth even when you didn't open it, and into your bed if you were lucky enough to have one. I had to admit that the sand was beautiful. The wind had formed it into shapes like the waves of the sea, and every day the shapes were a little different. The trouble was that you couldn't walk on this sand, only *in* it, because it clutched at your feet. The horses hated it. So did the soldier in charge of the heavy guns, who had been told to position two of the falconets on it to protect the camp, and had to think of a way of preventing them sinking in deeper every day until the sand was trickling in through their mouths.

But no one except the gunmaster, the horses and me minded the sand much to start with, because things had begun so promisingly. The *winic* not only welcomed us, but helped us as soon as we came off the boats and began to look for a way to make ourselves shelters, for the sun was cruel on those sand dunes. They were suddenly there bringing wood and matting, working alongside us as we fixed stakes in the soft ground, making a thatch out of an armful of leaves with astonishing speed. And it was all done with such smiling willingness that even the surliest *cristiano* was touched by it. Or so I thought until my feet took me past Blue Eyes, cursing the stupidity of a *winic* who was building his shelter in the wrong place.

This work went on all day until sunset, by which time we were all very tired. Just as we were giving up our labours because there was no longer enough light to work by, and wondering what we were going to eat, a large crowd of *winic* arrived with baskets of food, which we fell on hungrily. They were very friendly and eager to talk to us. When we asked what this region was called, they said it was known as Anahuac, and when we asked who its lord was they replied that it was subject to the Meshica, who were ruled by a powerful monarch who lived beyond the mountains.

The Captain was keenly interested in this ruler, of whom, it seemed, our men had heard talk when they came to this country the previous year, and he wanted to find out more, but the *winic* could not tell him more. They only said that the chief man of the district would come to visit us soon. So the Captain had to be content with that, and I thought he probably was content, for they had told us that we were close to the Meshica, from whose land gold came.

We lit fires and sat round them, and ate the food. The pale dunes filled with a flicker of firelight. The Captain went from one fire to another, talking to the men. What he said to them I didn't hear, but I saw their faces turned towards him, and their faces were rapt.

The first thing we did after we had set up camp was celebrate Mass, because it was Easter. The Captain ordered everyone to attend.

I went to the place and found they had stood some barrels on end and laid planks over the top to make a table, and this had been covered with a white cloth. On the cloth, right in the middle, blazing so bright in the sun that you couldn't look at it, was the Tree.

The thin priest I didn't like, Father Díaz, and the other priest, Brother Olmedo, came to stand behind the table in white and gold robes, and Brother Olmedo picked up a little bell that was there and rang it.

Then walking over the sand dunes in tens and twenties came all our men, with their eyes meekly lowered, their swords set aside and their heads bare. As they reached the place, they fell on their knees. Brother Olmedo, whose voice was melodious and pleasing, began to chant.

All these things, as they happened, I remembered. As I knelt in the sand and listened to the singing of Brother Olmedo, a deep happiness filled me. Brother Olmedo sang beautifully, and the Tree dazzled my eyes.

Brother Olmedo and Juan Díaz began to move among the kneeling rows of us, each carrying a silver cup. Each kneeling man raised his head as the dish reached him, and a white morsel was put on his tongue.

The priest Juan Díaz moved along our row, full of calm and authority. He placed the white morsel on each tongue. He came to where I knelt. He paused, went by me and placed a white morsel on the tongue of the man at my side.

I couldn't understand what had happened. I gazed at the pale wrist of Juan Díaz, bending first in one direction and then the other, as he took little pieces of the god's flesh out of the cup and placed them on waiting tongues. I stared at his retreating robe, and as he came to the end of the row and turned to work his way along the next one, I looked into his face.

It was stone. It told me I was nothing, an offence on the earth.

I knelt for as long as the others stayed kneeling. When they stood up, I stood up, and when they walked away, I walked away. I did not know whether to hide myself in the depths of the earth or seize Juan Díaz by the throat.

Next day we got our first inkling of the sort of place we had come to.

The *winic* dignitary who arrived, in a canopied litter accompanied by flute-players, fan-bearers, numerous attendants and a cloud of incense, was clearly not just an important man in his own right but the representative of a very powerful ruler. Everything about him said this, from the pride of his bearing and the gravity with which his eyes rested on the Captain to the ceremony with which he presented his gifts. He tried to take the Captain's measure in that first calm, searching look, which the Captain returned frankly and smiling. He did not want his words translated by a woman, I saw, but the two of us were standing at the Captain's side ready to interpret, and the woman from Potonchan had already put the Captain's words of greeting into the Meshica tongue, and he realized that he had no choice.

So he welcomed us to the country on behalf of his lord, the great Muctezumohatzin, who had instructed him to make sure we had everything we needed. It was to our visitor, we discovered, that we owed our palm-leaf shelters and the food the *winic* had brought us. His name was Teutlil and he was the Meshica governor of the district. He was at our service. Very politely, he asked us who we were and where we had come from.

I was taken aback by the Captain's reply. He launched into a speech that bore, it seemed to me, very little relation to the truth. He said he was the servant of a great lord who ruled many lands on the other side of the ocean and who, hearing of Muctezumohatzin's fame (he could not pronounce the name, but left it to us), had ordered him, the Captain, to visit him. For this reason, said the Captain, he would like to meet Muctezumohatzin as soon as possible, and he hoped it could be arranged.

I felt a respect for this *winic* governor that did not go well with telling lies to him, and it was in my mind to ask the Captain why we could not simply tell our visitor the truth, but I reflected that it is the duty of an interpreter to translate what is said, so I put the Captain's speech into Ahau so that it could be translated into Meshica.

It did not have the intended effect.

'You have only just arrived here,' Teutlil rebuked the Captain. 'How dare you ask for an audience with the *tlatoani*?'

This was not a good start, I thought. However, the Captain was not much chastened by it. He apologized, but there was an obstinate look in his eye and he did not withdraw his request. Fortunately we now moved on to safer ground. There were all manner of gifts to be presented.

Muctezumohatzin had sent us a mountain of cotton cloaks. The cotton was of the finest, white and soft. The Captain liked the cloaks but they weren't what he was waiting for, nor were the cane shields covered in featherwork that were the next gift, although some of the feathers were tinier than a fingernail and in each piece the colours rippled like water.

Then the gold was laid before him.

'Ah,' he said.

Our men at once were all round it, peering into the basket, stroking the gold with their eyes. They hung back from touching

71

it until the Captain reached down and took out the pieces one by one, and then they took them and held them reverently, and at the same time hungrily, as if there could never be enough of this metal. They fingered the little chains, the tiny bells and the modelled animals with delight. They told each other they had not seen better workmanship anywhere.

'Does your lord have a lot of this gold?' the Captain asked, as casually as if he'd been asking if Muctezumohatzin had an abundance of flints.

'His palaces are full of it,' replied the governor, and after I had put this into Spanish there was a heaviness in the air that made me wish I had not translated it so scrupulously.

The Captain made a speech of thanks and presented our own gifts in return. I supposed he had not expected to be put in this situation and had not brought suitable presents for a ruler in his baggage. At any rate, our gifts were not generous. They were the carved chair which he had sat in when talking to the *batabs* at Potonchan, a velvet hat and, lastly, 'a thing,' he said, 'that we hold in high esteem'.

The Meshica did not have glass, of course. Perhaps they had seen some that had been traded on earlier expeditions. However, that would have been in the form of beads, whereas what lay in the basket the pages now brought to the governor was engraved glass: a large goblet for drinking wine and various smaller pieces. It was very pretty, winking in the sun, but I knew that if they did not know how to carry it, it would be broken in a day.

The steward thanked us for our gift of the beautiful substance, to them unknown, which we esteemed so highly, for the interesting seat of carved wood and for the hat. Then he asked for something.

One of the Captain's men was wearing an unusual helmet: it came to a point like a cone. The governor asked if he might take it to show to his master. The Spaniard yielded it up, rather unwillingly, and the Captain, handing it to Teutlil, wanted to know why it had caught his fancy.

'It resembles the headwear of the sun, whom we call Hummingbird,' said the steward. 'Muctezumohatzin takes an interest in all things to do with the *teotl* and will wish to see it.' He held it in his hands with devotion. 'I will return it when I next visit you.'

'You can put some gold in it when you bring it back,' suggested the soldier it belonged to, without any shame. I wasn't going to translate this, but the governor asked what the man had said.

'He asked,' said the Captain, who could think faster than any man I have ever met, 'that you return it filled with gold in grains, or in whatever natural form this metal occurs here, because, just as your lord will be interested to see the helmet, our king will be interested to see the form in which gold is found in this country.'

By this time, we had all noticed that Teutlil had brought painters with him and they were making pictures of us. The Captain asked to look at them.

He smiled with pleasure when he saw the paintings. They must have seemed strange to him – the four colours that were never mixed, the odd way the ships were depicted, looking like temples on the water, and the little seated figure that seemed to float in mid-air, with its knees drawn up to its chin in a way that no Christian ever sat. But he saw at once that nothing had escaped the painters. They had captured the colour and roundness of our eyes and every detail of our clothing: belts, boots, swords, kerchiefs. The helmet that the governor had asked for. A white bandage around one man's arm. The Captain's gold neck chain.

'Clever,' he said. 'Very clever.'

The governor said the paintings were for Muctezumohatzin, who wished to know what 'these *teotl*' looked like.

I had heard the word *teotl* several times and deduced that it meant 'god'. But it sounded as if the Meshica were using the same word for us. I asked the woman from Potonchan about it.

'It is what they call you because you are not like them,' she said.

Teutlil and his retinue stayed with us for several hours. Before they left, the Captain offered them refreshment, of which they took only a little, and, lastly, an entertainment.

He led his visitors to the edge of the dunes. Down on the wet strip of sand that ran beside the water the horses waited, lifting their feet, the little bells on their harness jingling, their coloured cloths gay in the clear light, their riders clothed in steel that the sun turned to fire.

Teutlil turned pale and he went as still as a rock. Not a *winic* moved or spoke. They have never seen horses, I thought; they do not know what they are seeing. And by now I knew it was the horses that had saved us at Potonchan. But then the attendants began to murmur, and the painters remembered what they were for and their hands began to fly over the bark paper.

A signal must have been given, but I did not see it. I saw the horses move forward as if they had been a single beast. They trotted prettily to the music of the harness-bells, then they stretched out their legs and, as I held my breath, began to gallop as if the spirit of the wind was in them. When they had become small in the distance they wheeled like a flock of birds and came back towards us. The beach trembled with the shock of their hooves. They swept past us in thunder.

I glanced at Teutlil's face and saw both awe and terror on it, and I knew that this, as well as the request for a meeting, was the message the Captain wished to send to Muctezumohatzin.

'I hope all their names aren't like that,' said the Captain. He had got no further than 'Muckety' each time he tried to say it.

'His name is Muctezuma,' explained the woman from Potonchan. '"Tzin" means "lord". Many people are "tzin". Do you want to know what this name says?'

The Captain did. He wanted to know as much about Muctezuma as possible.

'It says' — she put it into Ahau for me — '"Lord-Who-Is-Severe".'

The Captain was pleased. He was pleased with everything she did. His eyes followed where she went.

On our first night at San Juan de Ulua, the three of us had sat in the Captain's cabin, talking by the light of a candle. The candle attracted mosquitoes, of which there were enough already, and it would have been pleasanter to sit outside, where the moon and stars were plenty to see by and burned like a lace of fire above our heads, but the Captain did not want to be overheard. Which meant that twenty versions of that conversation were circulating in the camp the next morning.

She told us her story and it was a remarkable one. She had been born in a place not many days' journey from here, she said, but had left it as a child, having been sold into slavery by her parents. That was how she had ended up in Potonchan, and how she came to speak two languages. She told us a great deal more than this, stories of having been born to great riches and disinherited in favour of a brother, and how her parents had plotted to steal the body of a child of one of their servants and pretend it was hers, and other things of the same kind, and I passed it all on faithfully to the Captain although I did not believe a word of it.

I knew it wasn't uncommon for the *winic* to sell their children into slavery, but they only did it if there was a shortage of food. They would sell themselves into slavery for the same reason: it was a way of keeping alive. Later, if these slaves managed to accumulate some wealth, they would buy their freedom. But it was not the nobility who did this: of course not. It was the nobility who *bought* the slaves because *they* had enough to eat.

I was sure the woman had become a slave in this way and not in the way she described, because the *winic* are very fond of their children. And in that case, it was equally obvious that she was not of the class she claimed to be. I thought the whole story was an invention for the Captain's benefit.

He didn't question it. 'It's a sign,' he said. 'Her coming to us. As yours was.'

75

I made no comment.

'Ask her what her name is,' he said.

She told us, and nobody could pronounce it, so he said we would call her Marina (which, of course, *she* could not say, since the *winic* cannot manage 'r'). However, within a short time nobody except the Captain was calling her that. She had become known as 'the Tongue'.

And, by that time, he had given her to Portocarrero when he distributed the twenty women. That was unexpected, because he had already slept with her and I assumed he would keep her for himself.

The camp was suddenly full of *winic*. They came every day to look at us or trade, or both. As often as not, they brought their families. After a wave of children rushed up to the falconets and peered into their mouths, the man in charge of the guns roped them off and put a guard on them. So friendly were these *winic* that some of them even put up their own palm-leaf shelters on the edge of the camp and lived next door to us. The camp became quite crowded.

One day, walking through the camp, I found Salvador, the mad boy and the sailor with crooked teeth engaged in trading. They were trying to persuade a *winic* to part with a roast fowl and a basket of maize bread in exchange for a broken horseshoe. The *winic* was turning the horseshoe over and over in his hands. He was uncertain whether it was a piece of rubbish or a thing or great value. The shoe had a jagged edge at the last nail-hole where the iron had snapped. The other surfaces were pitted and rusting, but the break itself was clean and grainy. This inner surface, where the secrets of the metal lay exposed, fascinated him.

Salvador grinned up at me. 'Where've you been? Haven't seen you for weeks.' That was true. I had kept myself to myself since Potonchan. When I didn't reply, he said, 'Talk to this character, will you? He can't make up his mind, and Vasco and me and the boy have got an appetite.'

'I don't speak the language,' I said apologetically. It was proving difficult to explain this to people: quite often, when I couldn't translate for them, they thought I was just being lazy.

Salvador appeared to believe me and wasted no more time on it. He took the broken horseshoe out of the *winic*'s hands and pretended almost to drop it because of the weight. 'Iron, that is,' he told the *winic*. 'It's a horseshoe.'

'A broken horseshoe,' the boy pointed out.

'Doesn't matter to him, does it? He hasn't got a horse.'

The *winic* took the horseshoe and began turning it over in his hands again.

'He likes it,' said Vasco, flashing his terrible teeth.

The *winic* looked at me as if I could help him.

'These men are scoundrels and the thing you are holding is worthless,' I said to him in Ahau.

Although he could not have understood a word, he put the horseshoe down and picked up his baskets.

'Hey! What did you say to him?' protested Salvador.

Vasco put out his hand to detain the *winic*. He smiled his ugly smile into the man's face and held out the horseshoe.

'I'll tell you what,' said Salvador. He dug in his pocket and brought out a brass fish hook. 'I'll throw that in as well.'

The *winic* took it and held it up in his fingers.

'You can catch fish with it,' Vasco explained.

'He can catch fish already,' I said.

'But not with a *brass fish hook*,' said Salvador.

'Tell him he can catch fish with it.'

The boy was doubling up with laughter. 'That's enough,' Salvador told him. 'He'll think there's something wrong with it.'

The *winic* put the fish hook between his teeth. He replaced his baskets on the sand, picked up the broken horseshoe and walked away.

The Captain's demand for a meeting with Muctezuma had taken me by surprise, and I wasn't the only one. There were quite a few who said we hadn't come here to go on wild-goose chases after native rulers.

The Captain was very interested in Muctezuma. He plied the Tongue with questions.

'How tall is he?'

'Of normal height,' she said.

'How old is he?'

'Not young, not old.'

'What is his character like?'

'They say he is cruel,' she said. 'But the Meshica are cruel in any case.'

I had noted her dislike of the Meshica. So had the Captain: he gave her a curious glance.

'Do his people fear him?'

'Of course. He is a *teotl*.'

'How large is his realm?'

'It stretches from the sea on this side of the land to the sea on the other side of the land.'

'Where is the sea on the other side of the land?' the Captain asked quickly.

She said it was a long way away, and could not be more precise, although he pressed her hard on the subject. In the end, as if to prove how large Muctezuma's realm was, she said, 'Four hundred cities give him tribute.'

'What do they give as tribute?'

'Cotton, feathers, turquoise. All sorts of things. Maize. Seashells.'

'Gold?'

'Gold, yes.'

'How big is his army?'

'He has many warriors,' she said. 'The Meshica are born to fight. They always win their battles.'

A look that was half-amused and half-thoughtful passed between the Captain and Blue Eyes.

'Where does he live?'

'In his city, Tenochtitlan.' She put it into Ahau so I could

78

translate it for him. 'This says "Cactus-on-the-Stone". It is the greatest city in the world.'

The Captain laughed. 'It can hardly be greater than Seville.'

'It is as large as a mountain and as light as a cloud. It floats on the water. In his gardens there is every kind of plant and tree. In his palaces he keeps the jaguar and the *kukul*-bird.'

Neither the Captain nor Blue Eyes was smiling now.

'I only tell you what people say,' she said.

A little stream, in places so narrow you could jump over it, flowed through the dunes to the sea. It gave us water for drinking and for washing our clothes and pots and pans. One day, walking over the sand, I saw a young man, bare-chested and wearing white pantaloons, bent over this stream with a cooking pot, which he was rubbing in a vague manner with a twig as if his mind was on something else.

He had the proud cheekbones and copper skin of a high-born *winic* in Chanek, although he did not have the hooked nose they admired. His was straight, above a wide mouth. His eyes brooded. I recognized him as one of the elusive *winic* I had seen and never managed to speak to on Ix Chel, and had not thought about since.

When he saw me he looked alarmed. I greeted him in Ahau, hoping it was a language he understood. He frowned. He looked away from me, at the cooking pot, and cleaned it again with the twig.

I repeated the greeting. When he still did not reply, I spoke to him in Meshica, of which I had learnt a little.

He did not respond to that, either. He went on studying the cooking pot as if it was the only thing in the world that interested him.

I stepped forward. I was determined to talk to this man.

But it appeared he would do anything rather than talk to me. As I moved forward, he rose from his crouching position by the stream and began to walk away. Back towards the camp.

I followed him. There was no point in quickening my pace,

because he would quicken his, and we would end up both running towards the camp, which was undignified and might give the impression that he had done something wrong. So I began to talk to him, again in Ahau and gently, because although I could not understand the reason for it, it was clear that he was afraid. I asked him who he was, where he came from, and whose servant he was, and I told him my name.

The camp came in sight, with its cooking fires and prowling dogs. He stopped walking as he saw the dogs, and stiffened. He spoke, then.

'What you want with me?' he said.

He had spoken in Spanish.

How stupid I had been! Elated that he had broken his silence, I said, 'I only want to talk to you.'

'Why?'

But a dog was coming towards him with its fangs bared, and he stood rooted to the spot in fear. Then, slowly, he turned his head towards me and his eyes entreated.

I picked up a piece of driftwood and drove the dog off with it. It gave a growl or two and trotted back to the camp.

He waited until it was almost out of sight, and then he murmured something that might have been thanks.

'What is your name?' I asked.

Again, he was silent.

'I drove the dog away,' I said. I was getting impatient with this *winic*. 'You could at least tell me who you are.'

'Taino,' he said.

He walked away, and I let him go.

The Captain sometimes went back to the ships to sleep because he said it wasn't a good idea always to spend the night in the same place. We were on the ships when the ambassador from Muctezuma's court came. As soon as he set foot on the deck I knew they had resorted to magic, because he bore – as much as a *winic* could – an uncanny likeness to the Captain.

There were a lot of formalities, bowing and incense burning and speeches of welcome on both sides, and it emerged from the speeches that this visit had nothing to do with Teutlil's but its purpose was solely to deliver a personal gift from Muctezuma to the Captain. The gift was carried in four heavy wicker baskets and it was quite a task to hoist them on to the deck.

As, one by one, the things that were in the first basket were taken out and held so that the sun touched them, before being laid on a mat, my head started to swim. They were items of clothing and personal ornament: they were part of a costume. In fact, there were two costumes. The Captain never understood that. When he talked about it to his friends afterwards, joking, puzzled, admitting that at least the workmanship was excellent, he spoke as if the precious things they gave him were just an extravagant jumble of objects. But there were two distinct costumes.

A mask inlaid with many tiny pieces of turquoise, the work so fine, the pieces of stone so highly polished it was like looking at a shaft of light falling into the depths of the sea. A head-dress of magnificent *kukul* plumes, the headband woven with threads of gold. A collar of *chalchihuites*...

Treasures. Even he could see they were treasures. But then, when they were all laid out on the mat, the ambassador indicated that he was to be dressed in them.

He wasn't prepared for that. When he saw that they wanted him to take off his cotton armour and his sword and be dressed, he drew back. He said later that he was afraid they would stab him under cover of it, but there was no reason for him to fear that and I thought he was afraid of being mocked. But we were all standing there, wanting to see what would happen next, so he had to submit to it.

They began by covering his face with the turquoise mask. On his head they put the crown of *kukul* feathers. After this, a cloak of very fine cotton was fastened on his shoulder and the collar of *chalchihuites* was hung over it. They encircled his hips with a belt made from hundreds of little polished discs of the black stone that winks like mirrors, and they sheathed his legs in silver. A shield was put into his hand; it was gloriously fringed with blue feathers and at its centre shone a moon of pearl inside a sun of gold.

The slaves took from the basket the last piece of the costume, the sandals, and laid them before him. The sole of each one was carved from a single piece of mirror-stone.

They invited him to step into the sandals, but he wouldn't. He had stirred uncomfortably as they put the belt of tiny discs around his hips. His eyes inside the mask shifted from side to side.

'Is that all?' he said.

With reverence they took the lovely things from his body and replaced them in the baskets. Then the second set of baskets was uncovered. For, so far, only half the gift had been presented.

The slaves took from the second pair of baskets a mask of polished mirror-stone, and covered his face with it. On his head they put a diadem from which hung an eagle's feathers clasped in gold. Next they put a cloak of fine cotton on his shoulders and hung over it a collar of seashells and corals. The belt they fastened on his hips was made of tiny pieces of winking silver, and the greaves on his calves were of pure crystal. The shield they put in his hand was stitched with featherwork held by a golden thread, and in the centre of the shield was a turkey's claw fashioned in gold.

The sandals were covered in pearls.

The wonder with which I saw the first treasures unwrapped had long since turned to dread. I said to the Tongue, 'What does this mean?'

'It means nothing,' she said. 'It is a gift.'

The ambassador then spoke. He said that with these gifts Muctezuma welcomed the Captain to 'his own realms, his own house'.

'What does *that* mean?' I asked the Tongue.

'It is just what they say,' she said. 'It is politeness.'

'What have you not said?' I asked her.

'I speak everything I hear.' I thought she looked afraid.

'Why have they put these things on him?'

'For his honour.'

'Why are there *two* costumes?'

'I do not know.'

'What are you two talking about?' asked Blue Eyes.

Everyone was waiting for the Captain to say, or do, something. But the Captain stood motionless as if he'd been struck dumb, just breathing rather loudly inside his mask of black stone.

Then he took off the mask with an abrupt movement. His face was red and there was a deep mark on his nose where the mask had rested. He started to pull off the other things they had put on him, and the slaves hastened to help him so that the precious objects should not be harmed.

When all the parts of the costume had been replaced in the baskets and the Captain had put his armour back on, he seemed to relax. He thanked the ambassador and ordered a pair of embroidered shirts to be brought from his cabin and presented to him. He tried to find out from him whether Muctezuma had received his request for a meeting, but the ambassador said that the message he brought was the gift itself and he could say nothing more.

I had not seen Juan Díaz since the Mass at Easter. Then one day there he was right in front of me. Since I could not avoid him, I decided to confront him.

'Why did you refuse me the flesh of Lordjesuschrist?' I demanded.

He said, 'I was surprised that you expected it.'

'Why?'

'Because I had not heard your confession. Neither I nor Brother Olmedo. Without confession, you cannot receive the body of Our Lord.'

I was confused. Was this an excuse he was inventing? I knew he did not like me. The *winic* only confess when they are going to die. But confession among Christians is different. He had said something about confession when we were on the flagship.

'What should I confess?' I asked cautiously. For, indeed, I did want that morsel of the Lord's flesh that Juan Díaz had denied me. I wondered if it might be better to go to Brother Olmedo. However, it was Juan Díaz and not Brother Olmedo who had first spoken to me, there on the beach at Ix Chel, and I thought this was significant. I took it to mean that it was Juan Díaz I had to deal with.

'You must confess,' he said, 'everything you have done to offend our Lordjesuschrist since you made your last communion. Everything you can remember, and ask pardon for those things you cannot. God is merciful: he does not expect you to remember everything.'

I considered what I might have done to offend Lordjesuschrist. It was by no means the first time I had asked myself this. I had asked that question frequently in Chanek. It was no easier to answer now than it had been then. For a while, I had thought His absence was a punishment and had punished myself doubly for deserving it, but I no longer thought so and in any case had He not returned to me in a different guise? None of this could be said to Juan Díaz.

'What offends God?' I asked.

'Do you really not know?'

'I am asking you.'

'Then, did you never eat meat on a Friday?'

I laughed at him, and he thinned his lips. 'A slave does not eat meat,' I said.

'Very well. Have you committed fornication?'

'What is that?'

'Acts with women, for instance.'

'No,' I said. He did not believe me.

'You lived among the heathen. Did you never, even once, burn incense to idols?'

Copal. Its sweet scent filled my nostrils again. It was as much as I could do not to let my eyelids close with pleasure, not to try to draw it into my lungs.

'What are idols?' I muttered, for something to say.

'False gods.'

'Why should I burn incense to *false* gods?'

His face darkened. 'You have done more than burn incense,' he said. 'I have seen the scars on your ears. It is an evil thing, my son. It is the Devil you have sacrificed to.'

He made the sign of the Tree in the air. Then he stalked away like one of those long-billed shore birds that peck the living flesh out of shellfish.

Teutlil came back after eight days, accompanied by a train of porters carrying baskets.

The emperor had again been generous. He had sent more towering armloads of cotton, more *chalchihuites*, more *kukul*-feather headdresses and exquisite featherwork inlay. He had sent gold.

A whole basketful of gold, each piece carefully wrapped in cloth. Necklaces, pendants, ornaments, the little cast figures of animals and gods they did so pleasingly. He had sent them by the score. He had also, as the Captain requested, filled the soldier's helmet to its brim with grains of gold.

But these were not the principal gift. The principal gift needed eight slaves to carry it. When it was laid on the ground, on woven mats that had been put down to receive it, such a hush fell on the assembled officers that you could hear the crack of a pebble flung against another by the sea below.

Again, it was not one thing but two. Two great wheels, like a sun and a moon, one beaten out of gold and the other out of silver. Each was as wide across as a sword's-length. They were worked all over with figures and designs. Teutlil began to explain some of the things that were shown, but the Captain wasn't interested in what the designs meant. He was staring at the gold wheel as if it was a lake he would like to jump into.

When he was able to take his eyes from it, he thanked Teutlil for this magnificent gift and presented his own gifts in return. These were as paltry as his earlier gifts. Then he asked how Muctezuma had received the news that we wished to meet him.

It seemed he had not received it well.

'You will not meet the *tlatoani*,' said Teutlil gravely. 'He will not come here, and you will not visit him. His city is too far away, it is too great a journey and too dangerous.'

'Danger is nothing to us,' replied the Captain with some impatience. 'Nor is distance. We have come from the other side of the ocean.'

Teutlil said that all the same it was not to be thought of.

'I don't think it's as far as you say,' persisted the Captain. 'It has only taken you a week to travel there and back, and your porters were heavily laden.'

'It is fruitless to pursue the matter,' said the governor. He was embarrassed, I could see, by our rudeness and wanted to end the conversation as quickly as possible.

The Captain's face took on a look I had seen before.

He said, 'My king has ordered me to meet lord Muckety, and nothing short of death will stop me. Take that message back to your ruler, and ask him to send me a proper invitation.'

By nightfall, the rumour of the gold and silver wheels had spread all through the camp. Sitting on the sand dunes as the day cooled, I heard it go on its way. I saw men's heads lift by their cooking fires, and knew it had reached them.

In the morning they came to see. They were polite about it, respectful, but firm. They formed a line all across the dunes. They didn't talk much. They stood in the sun patiently, swatting at the mosquitoes that settled on them. When their turn came, they would duck under the curtain that covered the entrance to the Captain's shelter, where the treasure was laid out on mats and guarded by Portocarrero and the quartermaster Olid, and they would stare with the eyes of beggars. Some went down on their knees. Then they would have to leave, to make way for the ones behind them. When they emerged, they rubbed their eyes as if they had been blinded — not by the light they were walking into, but by the light they had just seen. They walked away as quiet as they had come.

The next day, the talk began. It was feverish. It was a wild mixture of hope and fear. The hope was wilder-eyed than the fear. But the two could not live together, because they pulled in opposite directions. Fear said we had stumbled on greater power than we had ever dreamed of, and we should make haste to go back to Cuba while we still could. Hope said we had stumbled on greater wealth than we had ever dreamed of, and we should stay here and make it ours.

I lay under my palm thatch. I did not want to hear the arguments that were going on all over the sand dunes. The unending talk of gold, which at the beginning had aroused my pity because it seemed to come out of some dream or delusion, had begun to fall like rain on my mind. The sound of that rain went on behind every conversation I heard in the camp, behind every talk we had with the *winic*. I saw that it would always be like this, as long as we were here. There would be nothing else, because the rain fell on everything, and whatever it fell on it dissolved.

5

Many times I had taken the Captain's letter out of the leather pouch I kept it in, which I had got from a saddle-maker in exchange for a fish, and tried to read it. The writing was now blurred and faded. The letters, individually graceful in their sweeping strokes and curves, were a thicket I couldn't penetrate. Every time my fingers touched the pouch in my pocket I was reminded of my failure. I decided to burn the letter when no one was looking.

The day I was going to do this, I took it out for the last time and unfolded it. It had come to me from my new life to my old life, but it had turned out to be a sign I couldn't interpret. I held it regretfully in my fingers.

One of the marks separated itself from the others and seemed to rise off the paper. It hung before me, a clean shape, strong and arching, that, with a shock of delight, I knew. It was the letter 'n'.

I walked through the gateway of 'n' and, one by one, over the following days, each of the letters revealed itself to me.

Making my way through the words required a lot of effort. But in the end I deciphered the message the Captain had sent me.

Brothers,

Having arrived on these shores in company with a number of Spanish gentlemen, I have been given to understand by the native

people that two Christians are living in these parts in captivity to
a chief. I have reason to believe that he will be willing to release
you in return for a gift. I am therefore sending with this message
a quantity of glass beads, which the Indians prize, so that with
them you will be able to buy your freedom and make your way
to us. A ship under one of my captains will wait for you, for
ten days from the date of this letter, at the island that is a league
off the eastern coast. I urge you to make all haste, and join

    Your brother in Christ, and fellow servant of their Catholic
Majesties of Spain,

Hernán Cortés

16ᵗʰ day of February, 1519

It told me nothing I didn't know already. In fact, it told me
nothing at all.

Daily, a file of *winic* came into the camp carrying baskets of
food. But now there were fewer baskets and they went only to
the Captain's palm-thatch shelter. The food was divided among
the officers. Everyone else had to fend for himself.

The stores we had brought with us were now quite rotten. The
cassava loaves were green and stank. The salt pork had blackened. Both were thrown into the sea. We waited for the tide to
take them away, but the sea didn't want them. The cassava loaves
bobbed about in the shallow water, every day greener, slimier and
surrounded by rings of bubbles which winked strange colours in
the sunlight. They began to trail soft streamers like hair. They
were so like human heads that I was afraid to look at them.

Meanwhile about eighteen of our men had died. A story went
round that they had died from eating the bad food, in spite of
the fact that everybody knew they had really died of the wounds
they got at Potonchan, or from the vapours that drifted across
from the marshes when the wind was blowing that way. Some

people were saying that this was an unhealthy country and we shouldn't stay here any longer than we had to. They said it was all very well to talk about the friendliness of the Indians, but one day the Indians were likely to turn on us, as had happened in other places. They said the mosquitoes were more than anyone could bear.

And it was true that the mosquitoes were very bad. It was true, too, that the sun turned the sand dunes into an oven and most of our men spent the day lying prostrate under their palm thatch. But we had to stay on the dunes because we were waiting for Teutlil to bring back Muctezuma's reply to the Captain.

One evening, Don Francisco and Don Sebastián came and sat beside me on the dunes. I was sitting with my back to the camp, watching the sea. It was a quietly breathing mass of darkness, off which came gleams of light. The vast bowl of the sky, pierced with fire, rose above us.

'A beautiful night,' said Don Sebastián, and I agreed with him.

Don Francisco asked how well I was eating.

I said I was eating well enough.

'I'd be surprised if that were true,' said Don Francisco. 'No one else is.'

A little funnel appeared in the sand near my left foot. Sand trickled from the sides into the centre, which continued to sink as if something were sucking it away. The funnel widened until it was about half a finger's length across, the sand all the time slipping down it and disappearing at the bottom. Suddenly two small scaly legs appeared, and then a pair of indignant eyes on stalks.

They lived under the sand and came out in the cool of the evening. I liked to see them. This one came out of its burrow as cautiously as a maiden, then darted on its toes with surprising speed and vanished sideways over the dune.

Don Sebastián's eyes followed it. 'Can you eat those?'

I told him they were poisonous, which was a lie.

Don Francisco said, 'In a few days' time that Indian will come back with another message from Muckety, and Hernán will have to make up his mind whether to go on with his harebrained scheme to march inland or whether to go home.'

'And we all know what he *wants* to do,' said Don Sebastián.

I went on looking at the sea.

'Do you think it doesn't concern you?' asked Don Sebastián.

'I am just the interpreter,' I said.

'But you're *here*, along with the rest of us. Baking in the sun, bitten by insects, short of food . . .' said Don Sebastián.

'Sitting on the edge of Muckety's empire, hoping he won't decide to wipe us out,' said Don Francisco.

I said, 'Why are you talking to me?'

'When things come to a head,' said Don Sebastián, 'it may be too late to ask who's with us and who is not.'

I didn't ask, With you in what? because the answer seemed fairly obvious. So instead I said, 'I owe him something. He ransomed me with beads.'

'An honourable answer, but not a wise one,' said Don Francisco. 'Give it more thought.'

'But don't take too long,' said Don Sebastián.

Because of the shortage of food, some Spaniards who knew how to fish had started catching fish to sell to other Spaniards — for gold, if they could. There was anger about this; it went against the spirit of the expedition, people said, the men who could fish should share what they caught and not expect payment. However, the only person who could stop it was the Captain, and he refused to. The fish was needed, he said, and if he stopped the selling of it, the catching of it would cease, too.

Salvador, Vasco and the mad boy had been doing their share of fishing. Salvador had a slender gold chain in his hand one day.

'How many fish did you give for that?' I asked.

'Ten,' said Salvador. He smiled at the chain, and let it fall from his thumb and forefinger into his palm.

'He's a liar, he's a liar!' shouted El Loco in excitement. 'It was only six.'

'You be quiet,' said Salvador good-humouredly.

The boy had a freshly-caught squid in his hands. He had just taken it out of a net. Holding it by the tentacles, he swung it against a stone. A jet of purplish ink spurted out of it and landed on Vasco's arm. Vasco scowled at his arm, and then at the boy. The boy giggled.

'Easy,' cautioned Salvador.

I sat down beside them. I was glad of the companionship, on a day when I had nothing to do because nothing needed to be interpreted and there was a feeling of unease and ill-temper in the camp. However, the prevailing mood seemed to have infected them as well. Vasco had a look like a gathering storm on his face.

He pointed a black-nailed finger at the gold chain in Salvador's palm.

'We all caught those fish, don't forget.'

'I ain't forgotten,' said Salvador.

'Don't.'

The boy had been deftly cleaning and cutting up the squid. He now put it in a foul-looking iron pan to cook on the fire. Before long, it was hissing and singing. A drop of liquid flew out of the pan and landed on Vasco's ankle. Vasco yelped. He glared, enraged, at the boy.

'He's just a kid,' said Salvador.

'His bloody squid!'

'So? He caught it, and you're going to eat it.'

Vasco stood up in a swift movement, pulled the boy's head back by the hair and hit him with his fist. The boy sprawled on his back in the sand with his arms and legs out like a starfish. Then he picked himself up and there was murder in his face.

Salvador stood up and hit the boy before the boy could hit

Vasco. Then he hit Vasco. Both the boy and Vasco sprawled on their backs in the sand with their arms and legs out like starfish.

Salvador wiped his knuckles on his thigh. He opened his other hand and saw that he was still holding the gold chain. He slipped it into his pocket.

He saw me watching him, and winked.

I did think about what Don Francisco and Don Sebastián had said to me. The truth, of course, was that I had no more desire to go inland and meet Muctezuma than they had. This was not why I'd joined the Captain at Ix Chel.

However, not long after that conversation, as I was standing outside my palm thatch shaking the sand out of my shirt, the Captain walked past. He asked me, with a kind look, how I was.

I said I was well.

He said some people were unhappy because there was a shortage of food, and asked me how I was managing.

I thanked him and said I could catch my own fish.

He then said, 'You're a very important member of this expedition. We couldn't do without you. I'm sure you realize that.'

I made some reply or other.

'Remember this,' he said. 'To *me* you are indispensable, but to *them* you are nothing. They would as soon throw you overboard on the way back to Cuba.'

When Teutlil came again it was a cloudy afternoon, threatening rain.

Gifts were exchanged. Muckety had sent more towering armloads of cotton, more beautiful featherwork. He had sent *chalchihuites*. The Captain gave them a glance; he was waiting to see if there would be more gold. There was. Not a great deal, I could feel the men behind me thinking, but still it was something, and there would be more where it came from.

Our gifts in return were a few more bits of engraved glass and a shirt. Teutlil's manner became haughtier. Either he was offended by our meanness or he was preparing to deliver Muctezuma's second reply to the Captain. Or both.

The second reply was the same as the first. The *tlatoani* was honoured that we had visited his realm but he would not meet us in person. It was useless to think of making a journey to Tenochtitlan. It was equally useless to send any more messages.

'Be damned to that,' said Blue Eyes.

The Captain took it badly. He tried to smile, but managed no more than a grimace. And no doubt he didn't like to be rebuffed in front of his men.

Brother Olmedo was standing by, as he often did in these meetings with the *winic*, and he had in his hands an image of the Tree. The Captain snatched it from him.

He strode up to the governor, holding the Tree, and thrust it in his face.

'This is what we worship,' he said, 'not devils made out of wood and stone who demand the blood of children.'

He swung round and said to the Tongue and me, 'Translate it.'

The governor's face was as stiff as a carving.

'This is the sign of *Díos*, in whose name we have come here,' said the Captain. 'He is mightier than your emperor, and it is He who commands me to visit lord Muckety and tell him that his wicked deeds must stop.'

He continued like this. The Tongue and I translated as best we could. The Captain kept thinking of more things to say. Olmedo tried to interrupt but Blue Eyes stood on his foot. The governor looked both baffled and affronted. The sky was becoming heavily overcast with purple clouds that had rolled in from the sea.

Finally the Captain stopped. His outburst seemed to have taken him as much by surprise as it had everyone else. Behind me, a Spaniard gave a bit of a cheer.

Teutlil waited a while before he answered. Then he said coldly that he would report this meeting to the emperor. He advised us not to attempt to see Muctezuma, since we would not succeed. He left without any further ceremony.

A nasty wind whipped up as we stood watching his procession walk over the sand dunes, and a moment later we were all drenched by a squall of rain.

The next day there wasn't a *winic* to be seen.

We stood on the dunes shading our eyes for a sight of them. Their shelters next to our camp had suddenly a sad and flimsy look. All that day, not a *winic* appeared on the beach.

Nor did they come the next day. Nor the next.

The Captain's curiosity about Muctezuma had not diminished, and he continued to ask questions of the Tongue. What useful information he thought he could get from her I didn't know, considering that, if she was telling the truth, she had not lived in this country since she was a child. But he went on plying her with questions, and he appeared to believe her answers.

'He eats a hundred dishes at every meal,' she said. 'He has kings to serve him, and they have to walk barefoot.'

'He must be as great as the Khan of Cathay,' murmured the Captain. 'Did he inherit the throne from his father?'

At first she said yes. But then she thought about it and said the *tlatoani* was chosen.

'Chosen?'

'Yes. They meet and choose. But always from the same family.'

'What does *tlatoani* mean?'

She shrugged. 'It is what he is.'

'Does it mean "emperor"?'

I translated this as 'lord of lords'.

She hesitated for a moment or two before putting it into Ahau. 'It says "He-Who-Speaks".'

'Who does he speak to?' asked Blue Eyes.

'His people, presumably,' said the Captain.

She said, 'He speaks to the Lord of the Near.'

*   *   *

Walking back from the beach with a large fish I had caught, I saw Taino again.

He had been collecting driftwood for the fire, and had a bundle under one arm. His face went watchful when he recognized me, but I thought there was a hint of a smile in it. He had a cut above one eyebrow, and the flesh around it was purple.

I greeted him in Spanish. He returned my greeting shyly, and then his eyes fell on the fish. They lit up, and he exclaimed in surprise. He told me the name of this fish in his language, and that they did not usually grow so big.

I gave it to him.

His gratitude was touching. He said he would cook it for his master. I did not want him to cook it for his master, that was not why I had given it to him, but I thought he probably had no choice in the matter and that at least his master would be pleased with him. I asked him who his master was.

He said his master was the priest. The thin one.

I could hardly take the fish out of his hands. I managed not to say anything, either. I changed the subject.

'Where do you come from?' I asked.

'Cuba,' he said.

It was not the question I should have asked. The expedition had sailed from Cuba, and therefore so had everyone in it.

'But is Cuba your country?'

'Bohío my country,' he said.

'Where is that?'

He pointed over the sea. It could have meant anything.

'They call it Hispaniola,' he said.

Something stirred in me at the name. It was an uneasy stirring.

'If Bohío is your country, why did you leave it?' I asked.

He gave me a strange look, as if he could not quite believe I had asked the question. His face started to crumple.

'I go with my king,' he said.

I did not understand this. He had definitely said 'king'. I wanted to ask him who his king was, why his king had gone to Cuba, and how he himself had come to be in the service of Juan Díaz, but my questions seemed to have upset him so much that I thought it better not to ask him any more.

After the *winic* went away, the Captain had doubled the watch. He expected an attack. However, nothing happened to worry us. For a while, nothing seemed to happen at all. Just the heat and the mosquitoes.

Then one morning Flea, the Captain's page, came to me in a hurry when I was sitting under my palm thatch watching how the breeze would raise a fine drift of sand from the dunes, blow it a little way like a curtain and then drop it. The boy told me in excitement that some new Indians had come.

There were five of them. They were not like the ones we had been dealing with. These had a looser look about them and their faces were broader. Their cotton was heavily embroidered and they wore flamboyant plumes. They had a taste for big jewels: their earlobes, lips and noses were opened to allow for the insertion of large, glossy stones, and the ones they wore in their ears were so large that the ears hung not far above the collarbone. Little gold chains decorated with tiny bells were on their wrists.

The Tongue was talking to one of them. The others were staring around them at the camp, the armour piled up here and there, a dog that wandered past.

She turned to me. 'They come from a town called Cempoala. They want us to visit them.'

'Tell them we are very pleased to make their acquaintance,' said the Captain, 'and that we shall visit them as soon as we can.'

Several of the *winic* now broke into the conversation, speaking what I realized, after careful listening, to be yet another language. I asked the Tongue to confirm this.

She said it was a language she did not speak either, and that it was as different from Meshica as Meshica was from Ahau. She said it appeared that quite a lot of the Cempoalans could understand the Meshica language but refused to speak it, because these people hated the Meshica, who had conquered them and took too much tribute.

The Captain was getting impatient, hearing us talking to each other, so I explained to him that we had come across yet another new language and that we were lucky to be able to talk to these people. I told him what the Tongue had said, that many of those who could speak the Meshica language refused to because they hated the Meshica for demanding too much tribute.

I thought this business of languages would interest him because it must mean that it was indeed a large country. However, the Captain had apparently heard only one word of my explanation.

He said, 'Did you say "*hate*"?'

While we were waiting on the dunes for the *winic* to come back, the trouble that had been brewing in the camp for a long time finally came out into the open.

Velásquez de León, the Governor of Cuba's cousin, was at the centre of it, and all the men who wanted to go back to Cuba supported him. They did not want our return to Cuba to be delayed any longer, and they saw no point in paying a visit to the Cempoalans. They demanded that the Captain read out, in front of everyone, the commission he had received from the Governor of Cuba, which would make our situation clear. They had a list of complaints against him, as well, such as that he had not ordered a record to be kept of the gold we obtained from the *winic*, and had not set aside the King's share of it.

It was a complicated and angry affair that went on for days, and I stayed out of it. I was surprised to see, one day, Salvador, Vasco and the mad boy among a huddle of Velásquez' men on the dunes, but when I asked Salvador about it he denied that they had been there.

The Captain dealt with the trouble very cleverly, and even managed to work it to his advantage, but that did not mean it was the end of the trouble. Nevertheless, after a week or so things were quiet enough for him to give the order to march to Cempoala. By that time, a ship he had sent up the coast under Don Francisco had come back with news of a more sheltered harbour, so he sent the fleet on ahead to wait for us there.

The Cempoalans welcomed us rapturously. They came out in their hundreds as we trudged the last mile over the grassy plain which eventually succeeded the sand dunes. They escorted us into the town with music and dances, and threw flowers over us as if we were coming to a wedding.

It was a larger town than I had expected, and its broad streets, gardens and brightly painted houses gave it a very pleasant look. It was clearly prosperous: we had passed abundant maize fields, and the streets were busy with the vendors of fish, fruit and other goods. At the centre of everything, pulsing above the rooftops like another sun, rose the crimson slope-sided walls of the temple with the god-house at its summit like a box of jewels. The Captain squinted at it.

'How the Devil do they get up there?'

'There's a stairway,' I pointed out.

'Damned steep.' He turned his attention to the Tongue, who was walking near by, and said something tender to her, and, whether or not she understood, her face glowed.

We were given quarters in one of the priest-schools, where the *batab* visited us in the evening. This *batab* was a fleshy, talkative old man. He overflowed the litter in which his slaves carried him. He wanted to tell us the history of his people, but his minister suggested that we might want to rest after our long journey and that the *batab* should confine himself to what was most important. At this the *batab* began to complain bitterly about the Meshica.

They were wringing the country dry, he said. Every year the tribute rolls were longer. Every year the arrogance of the tax collectors grew greater. Every year the punishments for not complying with this, and not delivering a sufficient quantity of that, increased.

'What sort of punishments?' the Captain enquired.

'They take our young people to their city,' the *batab* said.

'For what? To be slaves?'

'They give them to Hummingbird.'

'What does that mean?'

'They sacrifice them,' explained the Tongue.

Blue Eyes leaned forward. The Captain looked shocked. 'How many are sacrificed?'

I put this into Ahau, the Tongue put it into Meshica and the *batab* said something.

'Twice twenty,' the Tongue said. Then she changed it to, 'Four times twenty.'

'Are you sure?' I said.

'What did he say?' demanded the Captain.

'It is twenty times twenty,' said the Tongue, and I lost my patience.

'Tell the truth, woman,' I said angrily in Ahau. 'Tell us what he says.'

Her eyes flared. 'He says twenty times twenty. Who are you, a just-now slave like me, to tell me I am lying?'

'Will you two stop arguing with each other and tell me what he *says*?' demanded the Captain.

'He says forty, or eighty, or four hundred,' I said. 'Four hundred just means many . . .'

'I don't want your explanations,' the Captain said. 'I want to know what he says.'

After that I kept my thoughts to myself as I translated the Captain's speech about how he grieved to hear the troubles of the Cempoalans and how this news would anger the great monarch who had sent him here. He had been sent, he said, to explain our religion to the Cempoalans and to bring them justice.

'You may have heard,' he threw in casually, 'that our god gives us such strength in battle that we cannot be defeated. You may have heard what we did at Potonchan.'

There was a pause. The *batab* said thoughtfully that yes, he had heard what we did at Potonchan.

When I translated that into Spanish, I heard a sound like a sigh, and the air seemed to change. It was a roomful of Spaniards standing a bit more at their ease.

We had not been in Cempoala long when a party of Meshica tax collectors arrived.

It was clear the *batab* hadn't known they were coming and that our presence in the town was the greatest disaster that could be imagined. All the *batab* could think of was to rush us back to our quarters and tell us to stay there, while whisking the tax collectors off to another part of the town and entertaining them with food and drink.

The Captain watched the feverish activity – Cempoalans running hither and thither with dishes, maize cakes, incense-burners, flowers, embroidered mats – through a hole in the curtain that hung over the entrance to our building. The hole had been there in the first place but he had enlarged it with his sword.

'What the deuce is all the fuss about?' he wondered. 'They can't be so afraid of five tax collectors.'

But they were, and when evening came we found out why. These were tax collectors with an unusual mission. Muctezuma had heard that the *batab* was entertaining us without his permission and had imposed a punishment. Forty young Cempoalans were to be taken to his city as slaves.

The *batab* came in person to explain to us, carried through the back streets in an undecorated litter because he could not afford to be seen visiting our quarters. He was trembling, and kept glancing at the curtain over the doorway as if he thought there was a Meshica listening on the other side. He covered his face and apologized for causing us such trouble. He said he would never recover from the shame. But we must prepare to leave the town.

'Do you have a jail?' the Captain asked him, quite calmly.

Chanek had possessed no such thing. As far as I knew, there was no word for it in Ahau. The *winic* seemed not to use imprisoning as a punishment. I racked my brains and eventually asked if the *batab* had a granary that could be sealed from the outside. He could not imagine why we were asking such a question, but said that of course he did.

'Put the tax collectors in it,' said the Captain.

The *batab* stared at him without speaking. I explained that, among us, this sort of place was used for keeping dangerous people out of the way.

It took a little while for the *batab* to grasp what the Captain meant. When he did he was still silent, but out of fear. However, the Captain didn't budge, didn't look as if he was out of his mind, didn't laugh as if to say it was a joke, just stood there relaxed and perfectly serious. In the end, faintly, the *batab* said that the Captain did not know what he was saying.

'We will stand beside you,' the Captain told him. 'We will defend you from Muckety's anger.'

The *batab* said that Muctezuma ruled the world, and no one could defend a man from his anger.

'*Díos* is more powerful than any emperor,' said the Captain. He went on to say that the King had ordered him to find Muctezuma and force that ruler to mend his ways, and he would do it whether or not the *batab* helped him. 'But if you do as I say now, I shall know that you are on my side,' he said, 'and if you don't, I shall know that you are not.'

This, too, the *batab* took a few moments to digest, but then he swayed on his feet and I saw what the Captain, no doubt, had been seeing all along: the frightened old man, with his four unnerved servants, standing like a collapsed sack of flour in the midst of us, and us in a hard ring around him, fingering our steel, and the dogs with their heads lifted sniffing the smell of Indian.

Tears began to trickle down the *batab*'s face. Through the tears he said that, though he was afraid it would cost him dearly, he would do it.

'To make it easier for you, my men will guard them,' the Captain said. 'But you must arrest them yourself.'

I didn't know what he was doing, and I had a sense that he himself only half-knew, and was feeling his way.

About an hour after sunset, a messenger came to tell us the tax collectors had been arrested. We were all sitting around on the woven mats they'd given us to take the damp off the floor. There was talk and the rattle of dice. Someone was playing a lute, uncertainly, as if the song had escaped him.

The Captain chose six tough-looking men and sent them to guard the prisoners. After they had gone, he came to me and said quietly that he would send for me later on.

At about the middle of the night there was some coming and going, and I heard him in low-voiced talk. Then an interval of quiet. As I started to doze, there was a touch on my arm.

The Captain was in a curtained inner room lit by candles. With him were Blue Eyes, Portocarrero, a few others he trusted and the Tongue. And, with their hands tied in front of them in the native fashion, two trembling and bewildered Meshica.

'Ask them,' the Captain said to me, 'why the *batab* locked them up.'

While I put this question into Ahau and the Tongue put it into Meshica, he drew his dagger and severed the cords that bound them.

They said they had no idea why he had done it, but that when they found themselves in that place, with our men guarding them, they expected to be killed.

103

From the way they looked around them, at our faces pale and bearded in the flickering light, and the weapons we carried, and the tiny-flamed candles the Captain had stuck in the wall that dripped hot pools of wax on the floor — all of these being things they had never seen before — I could tell that they still expected it.

The Captain told them, 'I knew nothing about this until it had been done. If I had known what he meant to do, I would have tried to stop him.'

It was so quiet in the small room that I could hear the candles burning.

'It was a rash and foolish act and it will bring down the wrath of lord Muckety on this city,' said the Captain, 'but I could not prevent it. Go back and tell your lord that.'

Slowly their eyes came up from the wax that glistened on the floor and met his eyes. So open and frank his eyes were at that moment.

'I am sending you home,' he said. 'My men will escort you to a safe place outside the town.'

When this was said to them they fell on their knees.

'Tell the emperor, when you report these events to him, that I am his respectful and loyal friend, and that I will come soon to visit him,' said the Captain.

At dawn he sent an urgent message to the *batab* that two of the Meshica prisoners had somehow escaped. He said that, to prevent the escape of the remaining three, he had had them taken immediately to one of the ships.

The *batab* came to see us at once. He was terrified. The two who had escaped would go straight back to Muctezuma and report what had happened to them, he said. The Captain agreed that they would. But then, he said, Muckety would soon have known in any case. The *batab* said he did not know what to do. The Captain suggested that he summon the commanders of his army and tell them to prepare for war.

The *batab* trembled. He begged the Captain to have pity on his age, his flesh, his wives and children, and his little realm. Cempoala had been a beautiful and prosperous land before the Meshica came, he said. Now it was robbed of its produce and the pride of its young men had been broken. Did the Captain want to bring down still more disasters on its head? Muctezuma was harsh, but at least if they paid the tribute his people were left in peace. Now the country would be invaded by a Meshica army thirsty for revenge. The warriors would be taken for Hummingbird. Nothing would be left.

The Captain cut through all this with a wave of his hand. What was done was done, he said. The *batab* must have courage.

Muctezuma was not slow in sending his answer.

It came in the form of an embassy, not to the *batab* but to the Captain. It consisted of two high-ranking Meshica, attended by the usual fan-bearers, incense-carriers and so on, and followed by twenty porters bringing gifts of cotton cloaks and feather-work.

The Captain greeted them with every appearance of pleasure and invited them into our quarters. He closed the curtain behind them and posted a Spaniard at the entrance to discourage any Cempoalans who might want to listen.

It was clear that Muctezuma did not know what to think. First his officials had been insulted, presumably with our encouragement. Then two of them had been rescued and returned to him by us, with a friendly message. He wasn't sure whether we were playing a trick on the Cempoalans, or the Cempoalans were playing a trick on us, or both of us were playing a trick on him. In these circumstances, he seemed to have decided to treat the Captain as a friend until he had evidence to the contrary, since that was the safest thing to do. Or perhaps that was not his thought at all, but what he wanted us to believe he thought.

The Captain was as sweet as honey.

'Tell your emperor,' he said to the ambassadors, 'that I receive his gifts with great pleasure and that I hope to visit him soon to make my thanks in person.'

The *batab* came to us shortly after the ambassadors had left. He was in a state of terrible nervousness, and desperate to learn what they had said.

'They brought us greetings and gifts from lord Muckety,' said the Captain. He ordered the gifts to be shown to the *batab*. The *batab* looked at the baskets as if they might be hiding a snake.

'Why did lord Muctezuma not send envoys to me?' he asked.

The Captain said he really didn't have any idea, but he thought the *batab* would not have wanted them.

'Why is he not angry with you?' protested the *batab*.

'Because he is afraid of us,' said the Captain. 'He has heard what we did at Potonchan.'

The *batab*'s eyes returned unwillingly to the gifts.

'The best thing for you to do now,' said the Captain, 'is make an alliance with us.' Turning to me, he said, 'Make sure he understands what an alliance is.'

I had been very slow. Only now, when the Captain said this, did I see what he had been driving at in the past days. In a flash I saw both that the *batab* had no choice and that the Captain was thinking far ahead. And now I could not mistake what his aim was.

'This alliance,' said the Captain, 'will require you to swear allegiance to the King of Spain, who is our sovereign lord. In this way, you can be sure that we will protect you. We will help you against your enemies, and you shall help us against ours. Do you understand?'

The *batab* was very unhappy. He protested that Muctezuma would not allow it. The Captain replied that things had gone much too far already for the *batab* to be worrying about what Muctezuma thought, and that the *batab* would be wise to take the friendship that was offered him.

Then with a feeling of dread I saw the scribe who had written things down at Potonchan take a quill and inkpot from a box he carried, and the old *winic*, as if understanding what these instruments meant, began to weep.

6

It was clear now. I could have grasped it earlier, but I had not wanted to grasp it. I had told myself that the Captain's cutting of the Yaxché at Potonchan and the little speech he'd made when he did it had been an empty flourish, a piece of rhetoric. Now I saw it as part of a plan. At Potonchan, when he made the chieftains of the region swear allegiance to Spain, I had said to myself that it was nonsense because how could such allegiance be enforced? But now I saw that one day he would build on it, because he never wasted anything. The proof of his intentions was his dealings with the *batab*, whom he had tricked and frightened into a military alliance. He would use the alliance to threaten the Meshica. Such was his madness that he would try to make *them* swear allegiance to Spain, as well.

The moment I had begun to allow this knowledge into my mind, there flooded into it a black tide of memories dammed up throughout my years in Chanek. *Winic* shuffling in chains, *winic* killing themselves by hanging or drowning rather than endure slavery to Christian masters. *Winic* forced to forsake their customs and villages and call their children by Spanish names. *Winic* who walked with their heads bowed. *Winic* so different from the *winic* I had lived among that they seemed members of a different creation. But they were not. They were simply *winic* who had been forced to submit to Spain, and who had reached the condition that these *winic*, those of Cempoala and Potonchan and Chanek, would reach if they, too, were forced to accept Spain as master.

I had seen the havoc wrought upon the *winic* in the islands. The ship on which I embarked at Seville had taken me straight out to Hispaniola.

I sought out Taino in the priest-school we were camped in. He did not want to be found, so I lay in wait for him. When, as I knew he must, he appeared to cook his master's supper, I stepped out from my hiding-place.

'I want to talk to you,' I said.

'No. I not talk.'

There was the weal of a belt across his back.

'Who has hurt you?' I asked him.

'No one.'

'Was it Juan Díaz ?'

'No one.'

'Taino,' I said, '*I* am not going to hurt you. But I want to talk to you. I want you to tell me what happened when you went to Cuba.'

'Nothing,' he said.

'What happened to your king?'

'Why you asking these questions? You mocking me.'

'I am not mocking you.'

'I not answer.'

I could not make him answer me. But then a thought occurred to me. 'Does Cuba have another name?'

No doubt he thought this question was harmless.

'Before, they call it Fernandina,' he said.

That was a name I knew. On the voyage that ended in shipwreck, there had been excited talk of an expedition to put down Indian rebels on Fernandina. A very successful expedition, apparently.

✳   ✳   ✳

After the *batab* had sworn the oath of allegiance to Spain, I kept my own company for several days. To anyone who asked what was wrong with me, I said I had eaten shellfish that were bad. And it was true that I had eaten shellfish.

Eventually the Captain sent for me. I didn't go. He came to see me.

'What ails you, my friend?'

I told him I had poisoned myself with shellfish.

'Well, *you* should know about shellfish,' he said. 'You don't look too sick to me, in any case. Would you like me to send you my physician?'

'No, thank you.'

'We're moving out tomorrow,' he said. 'Going further up the coast. I hope you'll be well enough to walk.'

We marched to the new harbour. It was not a bad place, flat and grassy with a broad river flowing into the sea. There were game and fish. 'This is where we shall build our town,' the Captain announced.

Founding a town had been one of the things agreed on (agreed, that is, by some and not others) while we were still on the sand dunes. At the time, I hadn't thought it would really happen; I had thought it was another of his manoeuvres. But no, the town was real, and in no time we were marking out ditches for foundations and digging them, and sawing timber.

The Cempoalans (we had started to call them Droopy-ears) helped us build it. It was named Villa Rica and it was laid out like a Spanish town with a fort at its centre. In a few weeks it had a church, a jail, a courthouse and about a dozen wooden houses. It even had a gibbet for hangings. As Salvador remarked, all it lacked was a brothel.

I had gone in search of Salvador and his friends that day because they gave my mind a rest from the Captain. However, it was the Captain they were talking about, and with an unusual degree of bitterness. He had asked every member of the expedition to give up the gold they had come by in trading, so that he could send it to the King. As a proof of the expedition's loyalty.

Salvador, Vasco and the mad boy had done well both out of trading with the *winic* and selling fish to other Spaniards. They had amassed quite a little hoard of gold trinkets. They were angry at having to give it up. As I listened to them I realized that in fact they hadn't given it up: they had only parted with a few small items. However, they had forgotten this in their indignation at having to give up any of it.

I supposed that if the Captain was sending gold to Spain to prove his loyalty, this only made it more certain that he would pursue his plan of going inland to seek a confrontation with Muctezuma.

I did not know what to do. If the Captain's purpose was to make the *winic* on this coast accept the rule of Spain, I did not want to help him achieve it now that I could see what he was doing. However, if that was also his intention with Muctezuma, it was an aim so ambitious, so extravagant, that I did not see how he could possibly achieve it. Faced with a powerful and civilized empire, and obliged to deal with a monarch considerably sharper-witted than the *batab* of Cempoala, I thought he would find a graceful way of extricating himself and come back to the coast. Indeed he might not be able to go inland at all: the Velásquez party was still a power to be reckoned with and they might yet force him to return to Cuba.

There was also the question of where, if I left the expedition, I would go. It was surely much too late to go back to Chanek.

I decided to wait and see what would happen.

All the time we were building the town, the Captain was sometimes there, supervising the work, and sometimes in Cempoala. When he went to Cempoala he would take the Tongue and me with him, and about fifty of his men. No doubt he wanted to keep an eye on the *batab*, in case the *batab* changed his mind about us.

However, if anything was likely to change the *batab*'s mind, I thought it was what the Captain did in Cempoala.

We were looking around the town, accompanied by the *batab* in his litter and the *batab*'s usual retinue. We came to the temple.

The Captain cast his eyes up the stairway. It was not that high, compared with others we later saw, but the steps, as always, were very narrow, barely enough for the full length of the foot, not a human foot. Steps that were not quite steps, on which you couldn't rest but must always press further upward. They were steep; they were the pathway of the god. And they were splashed and spotted with blood.

The Captain reined his horse. Behind him came the rustle of Christian anger.

'These foul practices must cease,' he said.

The *batab* was hidden behind the drapes of his litter, as was normal when he was taken through the streets, and when the Tongue and I translated this he made no reply.

'The time has come,' the Captain said, fixing his gaze on the stairway, 'to tell you about the truths of our religion.'

Brother Olmedo, who was standing close to me and pouring sweat in the heat, said loudly that it was a stupid time to talk about the truths of religion and we should cut short our walk and find some shade, but the Captain ignored him. The Captain began, there and then, sitting on his horse in the blinding sun, to preach a sermon. From time to time he would stop to allow us to translate.

It was impossible to put more than a small part of it into Ahau because there were no words for the things he was saying, so I concentrated on the parts that the *winic* would understand. The creation of the world in six days, the disobedience of First Man and First Woman, the drowning of mankind as a punishment, the saving of two of each creature so the world could begin again. All this time, there was no response from behind the *batab*'s curtain.

'But the wickedness of men did not stop,' said the Captain, checking his horse, which was restless, smelling the blood. 'At last, *Díos* sent His own son to teach men how to live properly. This son was born of a virgin . . .'

'What did you say?' the Tongue asked me.

'Born of a woman who has not jigged.'

'How can anyone be born of a woman who has not jigged?'

'Just translate it, please.'

'They will laugh at me.'

'What is the matter?' asked the Captain.

She said something in Meshica. The Droopy-ears grinned.

The Captain was becoming increasingly irritable as we struggled to translate what he was saying. 'When he grew to manhood, Lordjesuschrist performed many miracles. He fed five thousand people on two loaves of bread and five small fishes.'

'Five loaves of bread and two small fishes,' said Olmedo.

'He made water into wine. He walked on the sea. Finally, He brought a dead man back to life.'

I was starting to feel faint from standing in the sun and from the smell of blood that wafted down from the shrine, and from trying to concentrate for so long.

'Satan, who is the enemy of men, tempted a follower of our Lord to betray Him to the priests. He died on a Cross. He was sacrificed for us.'

'I do not understand this,' said the Tongue.

'Just translate it,' I said.

'Who is this Satan? What is this about priests and the Tree?'

'Just say something, please.' The steps were wavering in front of my eyes.

'What is the problem now?' demanded the Captain.

'Who was he sacrificed *to*? *Díos* or this Satan?' When I didn't reply, she turned to the Captain and tried to ask him in Spanish, but he didn't understand her.

'I think I'll do it next time,' said Olmedo.

The Captain said with determination, 'Because of this we worship the son of *Díos*, and we urge you to do the same and abandon the worship of demons.'

There was a pause after the Tongue translated into Meshica, and then from behind the *batab*'s curtain came a mighty snore.

'Enough,' said the Captain. He swung himself down from his horse and gave the reins to Flea. He drew his sword.

'Captain, what are you doing?' I protested.

All our men were drawing their swords.

'Are you mad?' cried Olmedo.

'If it is mad to fight for Christ, then I am mad,' said the Captain, and leapt up the staircase. Blue Eyes, his brother Jorge, Sandoval and a man called Ávila were right on his heels. Then up the steps were running twenty, forty men in a tide. The *batab* had woken up and was clutching the edge of his litter like a drowning man clutching a raft. The Tongue was talking to him in a torrent of Meshica.

The *batab* tried to get out of his litter but was too agitated to manage it and fell back, clutching his chest. From all sides of the temple square, Droopy-ears were running out of their houses. The ones in the *batab*'s retinue were trying to push their way through to the temple steps, but Spaniards stood shoulder to shoulder and blocked them and ten men with naked swords now stood a weapon's-length apart along the base of the stairway.

The Captain had reached the top. I saw him rest for a moment, getting his balance, and then he disappeared from sight into the shrine. Almost at once there came a loud cry and the sound of something toppling.

Two priests came fleeing down the stairway with panic-stricken faces. More sounds of heavy objects falling came from the sanctuary. Most of the Spaniards who had set off up the stairway had now reached the top or were near it, but I saw them suddenly move apart to the sides of the staircase as if a hand had divided them. There was a confused movement and then, dragging with it a rumble that seemed to come from the depths of the earth, a motion that you couldn't mistake.

'Out of the way, quick,' said Olmedo.

The gods were rolling down towards us.

Their huge wooden faces ground pits in the stairway and left gouts of paint on the lime. The sharp stone edges cut them, mangling noses, chipping eyebrows and scarring their necklaces of skulls and shells. As they fell lower they bounced on the ungiving stone, and at every bounce something broke off from them, another piece of wooden flesh, and another wail went up from the priests who tore their robes at the top of the stairway and the stricken crowd of Droopy-ears who were witnessing all this on the ground.

When all of them had come to rest, all four lying askew with their colours half-stripped from them and their eyes blank, there was a long stillness in which not a blade of grass moved or a bird called. Then the Captain stood again at the top of the steps and began to walk down them with a measured tread. I heard the little grating of his soles on the chips of stone and the way the leather creaked with the flexing of his ankle.

He had put his sword away and there was a smudge of black on his cheek. His right knuckle was bloody. His eyes shone.

At the bottom he stopped and looked at us. He took in the stunned and speechless Droopy-ears, the tense cordon of Spaniards that stood between them and the temple steps, the *batab* anguished in his litter, the hatred in the eyes of the priests.

'I have done the will of *Díos*,' he told the Droopy-ears. 'Now let's see what your gods can do.'

Their eyes stared back at him.

Recollecting where he was, he turned to me.

'Translate it.'

Four days later we were back in our little wooden town. With us were many Droopy-ears whom the *batab* had sent with food and gifts. The *batab* was subdued. His gods had allowed themselves to be burnt in the street.

The Captain was in high spirits but there was a nerviness in his manner, as if he was expecting something to happen. I kept my ears open but heard only talk about the journey we were going to make inland to meet Muctezuma and the route we were going to take. The *batab* had advised us to head for a country in the mountains called Tlascala ('the land of grain,' translated the Tongue), whose people had been at war with the Meshica for years. They would no doubt welcome us if we made clear that we, too, were enemies of the Meshica.

Late one night there was movement in the space between the wooden houses. By the dull gleam of a shrouded lantern I saw six men walking quickly, sword in hand, towards one of the houses. I heard a knock, voices, a scuffle and then Blue Eyes cursing steadily.

They came back the same way soon afterward. They had uncovered the lantern and I could see them quite distinctly. The thin priest, Juan Díaz, was in the midst of them, pale and with a cut on his forehead. Blue Eyes's arm was bleeding.

In the morning there was a prickling in the air and Sandoval and Blue Eyes's brother, Jorge, were making a serious show of standing outside the door of the lock-up, which still didn't have all its roof.

'Who's in there?' I asked.

'Friends of yours,' said Jorge, who took his lead in all things from his brother and liked to make life difficult for me.

'Juan Díaz isn't a friend of mine,' I said.

'Juan Díaz isn't in there,' said Sandoval.

The voice of Salvador came from inside the jail, imploring me to get him out.

'You'd better be moving on,' said Jorge, and put his hand on his sword hilt.

I passed the Captain's house and five or six of his friends were standing outside it. Angry voices – the Captain's, Blue Eyes's – came from inside the house. Also a voice that I recognized as the priest's, raised in denunciation of someone. I walked on in the direction of the shore.

When I returned, having caught two fish, the sun was well up, fires for breakfast had been lit and the Captain was strolling about with a smile on his face talking to people. He came up to me as I knelt by my fire. I offered him a fish.

'No, thank you,' he said. 'We've had a spot of trouble. I expect you've heard about it.'

'No,' I said.

'There was a plot to steal a ship and sail it to Cuba. Luckily it was discovered in time.'

'Who was in the plot?' I asked, turning the larger of the fish over and slitting its belly with a shell. There were eggs inside.

'Most of them are the ones you would expect. They've been making trouble for a long time.'

I inserted my fingers into the cavity where the roe was and began to scoop it out.

'A few of them are known to you, I think. Some sailors.'

I laid the roe on a leaf and began to scale the fish with the blunter edge of the shell.

'But I'm sure you knew nothing about it.'

'I didn't,' I said.

'That's what I thought.'

I went on preparing the fish. The scales were in a glimmering heap. I put the fish in a cool part of the fire to cook. With the shell I dug a small hollow, scooped the scales into it and covered them with sand. The Captain watched.

He said, 'I could give you a dagger made in Toledo if you wanted one.'

'I have a knife,' I said. I had been given one on Ix Chel.

'Then why don't you use it?'

'It rusts. For this, a shell is better.'

'You're an odd fellow.'

I rolled the roe in a leaf and put it in the ashes at the edge of the fire. I said, 'There is something you could give me instead.'

'What is it?'

'I would like the Indian who is the servant of Juan Díaz for my own servant.'

He was silent for a moment. He seemed very surprised. He thought about it. Then he nodded and stood up.

I ate the roe when the leaf in which it was wrapped was beginning to char. It was delicate and pink. It tasted like sea mist.

That day there was a trial in the Captain's house and two men were condemned to be hanged. Juan Díaz was not condemned to anything because he was a priest. Salvador, Vasco and the mad boy were condemned to a flogging.

'You should choose your f-f-friends with more care,' Sandoval told me reproachfully.

I went to see them flogged, because not to go felt like desertion.

The whip was a long snake of rope, one end of which was wrapped round the huge hand of Mejia the artillery captain. In turn, Salvador and the other two, bare to the waist, were bound by the wrists to a wooden pole fixed between posts.

Salvador was flogged first. The rope bit his shoulder, drawing a line of blood to the skin. It bit a second time, the other shoulder. Then remorselessly as the sun rose higher in the sky the rope swished and tore, swished and tore. Salvador's back became raw meat, then something that looked like jelly. There was the salty smell of blood and the sweet smell of Mejia's sweat in the air.

'Enough,' said the Captain.

Salvador was half-led, half-carried away.

Vasco did not have Salvador's strength, and when he had received only half the number of lashes he collapsed and hung from the bar.

The boy screamed like a wild thing from the first stroke to the last. The Captain stopped it before very long.

When the day was cooling, I went to look for them. I could not find either Vasco or the boy; they had disappeared, leaving Salvador lying face down in the shelter of a palm thatch outside the walls of the town. His back was a livid pulp.

I went to the forest and gathered *membé* leaves. When the sun had gone down on them, I pounded them to a paste in a hollow stone in the stream, put the paste in a gourd and mixed it with a little seawater. I said to my god, Heal thou the man on whose flesh I shall put this. I went back to where Salvador was, and laid the paste of leaves on his back.

I sat by him until it was light. I sat by him for most of the second day. That afternoon, I gathered more *membé* leaves.

On the third day he grumbled and said, 'What's this muck you've put on me?'

The next day I made him some soup with mussels, and he ate it all. The crust of blood had blackened and hardened, and covered his back like a shield.

In a week the new skin had begun to grow on Salvador's back. I saw it where a corner of the crust had flaked off. It was pink like the tail of a mouse.

In the time it took for Salvador's back to heal, we were preparing to go inland. The *batab* came several times to visit us. He was advising us on the route we should take to Tlascala and talking about how many fighting men and porters he should give us. For the Droopy-ears would march with us, being our allies.

The Captain was keen to discuss all these things, but most interested of all in the *batab*'s son. He wanted the boy to come with us.

The *batab* at first refused. He had six daughters but only one son. He had sworn the oath the Captain demanded and it had been written on paper. Was this not enough? He would not give us his son.

'It will be an education for him,' pointed out the Captain.

The *batab* offered us his nephew instead.

The Captain said he would be glad to take the nephew as well.

The *batab* said in that case he would never see either of them again.

'I shall care for your son and nephew as if they were my own flesh and blood,' said the Captain. 'In that way, I shall know that you will care for my brothers, whom I shall leave in the town we are building, as if they were *your* flesh and blood.'

The *batab* assured us that we had no need to worry about the men we were leaving behind. The Captain said that nevertheless he would insist. He reminded the *batab* that he had by now put himself in a position where he could not do without our help. The *batab* wept again.

'This Indian is starting to annoy me,' said Blue Eyes.

'Am I not going to face lord Muckety on your behalf?' asked the Captain. 'I am sure you would rather I faced him in his lands than in yours.'

The *batab* replied that he was not such a fool as to believe that we had come to his country in order to right the wrongs of the Cempoalans.

Many such conversations were held. Finally, one morning, a sad-faced procession made its way over the plain to us. In it sat the twelve-year-old son and the fourteen-year-old nephew of the *batab*. The Captain made light of it, but he was relieved.

He was impatient to start the journey. The sooner we left the coast the better for him, I thought. In the past two days he had just faced down an open revolt. Even now, with bags being filled, weapons polished and the horses' hooves getting a last inspection, half his men were ready to cut his throat.

I would go with him. None of us was leaving, he had made sure of that, but he had bound me to him in another way as well. I had been with him too long, I had helped him do too much, to think now of going back to the *winic*. But I had also realized that in staying with him I had a chance to do some good. As his interpreter, I was better placed to protect the *winic* from the worst that might happen to them than was anyone else. And no one else would try.

On our last morning I watched the Cempoalan porters tie ropes around the cannon and hoist them on poles, from which they hung like huge black fish. For everything – the barrels of gunpowder and of wine, the Captain's travelling chests, the anvils for beating out horseshoes, the inkpots of the scribes, Brother Olmedo's chalice and a hundred iron cooking pots – must all be taken over the mountains. This fantasy of his cannot succeed, I told myself, but now this thought, which earlier had comforted me, brought a regret with it. For, as it became more certain that we would embark on this journey, a desire had grown in me to see the magnificent city of Muctezuma and to meet the emperor who had sent the costumes of the gods to the Captain.

II
These Gentlemen

Alonso de Ávila

Á vila had seen it coming. He had seen it coming as far back as the Grijalva expedition, that hamstrung venture that could have achieved so much but managed no more than a few trinkets of gold, a man dead and a tooth knocked out of the commander's mouth by an arrow. From the moment that expedition touched land, there had been war between its two ruling spirits: daring and caution. Caution won. Grijalva was the nephew of the Governor of Cuba and a mutiny was not a good idea. It had nearly happened, all the same.

And now it looked certain to happen. This time the shoe was on the other foot. It was the commander who possessed the daring, the cautious who wanted to mutiny. But the cautious were still the same men. They were the kin, the household, the friends of the Governor of Cuba.

Ávila was not the closest of the Captain's circle. To be an intimate of Hernán's, you had to come from Hernán's native soil, the soil of Medellín. Nevertheless, Ávila was the Captain's man. He had made his mind up long ago: he had made it up in Cuba, when the first rumblings of Diego Velásquez's discontent with the commander he had only just appointed began to be heard.

Hernán was too enthusiastic, that was the problem. Entrusted with the expedition, he had set about finding ships, men, provisions and equipment with astonishing alacrity and expenditure. Within a few weeks, he had a fleet. Diego Velásquez became alarmed. This was not what he had expected. It smacked of ambition. *Independent* ambition. Doubts were fed into his ear by relatives and hangers-on. Diego Velásquez asked the Captain what he thought he was doing, and the Captain gave him a soothing answer and sailed for the port of Trinidad, a hundred miles along the coast. It was there that Ávila, just returned on the first of Grijalva's ships, joined him, and it was there that orders arrived from the Governor cancelling Hernán's appointment and requiring him to be sent back to Santiago de Cuba as a prisoner.

But there was a fever in the air. Grijalva's men had brought back dazzling stories. Those who had been to that shore were impatient to go back, and those who hadn't were impatient to go and see for themselves, and all of them wanted to sail under a commander whose dreams were the same as their own. It didn't matter that Hernán had served in neither of the two earlier expeditions. What mattered was what he was doing now. You don't amass — do you? — nearly a dozen ships, sixteen horses, assorted blacksmiths, carpenters and other useful tradesmen, as many hackbutteers and crossbowmen as you can lay hands on, several casks of gunpowder and ten artillery pieces, if all you want to do is trade with the Indians. And in addition he was making promises.

The two officials in Trinidad to whom the Governor's orders were delivered did nothing about them. One was Diego de Ordaz, the Governor's own steward, whom (it was an open secret) he had placed in the expedition to keep an eye on Hernán. Hernán by this time was in a strong position, with nearly five hundred men under his command and half the length of the island between him and Diego Velásquez. He wrote a polite letter to the Governor and, after stocking his ships, moved on to Havana, where he planned to take the horses on board.

While the expedition waited for the horses, Diego Velásquez's messengers caught up with it again. The Governor was by now very angry. He instructed his kinsman Velásquez de León, who had joined the expedition, Ordaz, who had failed him in Trinidad, and the chief magistrate of Havana to seize Hernán and return him to Santiago.

Again, no one did anything. The magistrate said he thought Hernán was in the right. Ordaz never received the order because Hernán had sent him off to collect a supply of salt pork. As for Velásquez de León, he had a grievance against his cousin which he made no secret of, and after Hernán had had a talk with him he simply ignored his instructions. The horses were boarded, the salt pork was stowed, the Captain wrote another letter to Diego Velásquez, and the fleet sailed.

You could draw several conclusions from all this. The first was that Hernán had made a powerful enemy and there would be a reckoning. The second was that the first conclusion should always be borne in mind, for he who followed the Captain would share the Captain's fate unless he made provisions for the contrary. (Some gentlemen were therefore making them.) The third was that, sooner or later, the underlying rift between the men who owed loyalty to Diego Velásquez, and now had as many excuses for being on the expedition as a bramble bush has berries, and those who had thrown in their lot with Hernán, would come to the surface. The fourth was that, when it did, the fundamental ambiguity in the expedition's purpose, which had been seeded by Diego Velásquez himself, would be laid bare. And *that* would be what the fighting was about.

Were they here to trade for gold, to explore the coast further and to rescue Spaniards who were languishing in captivity to a native chieftain? They had done all this. They could, and should, go home now, said the partisans of Diego Velásquez. On the contrary, said Hernán's men. They had come here to settle the country. The Captain had been quite explicit about it. They claimed that Diego Velásquez had also ordered them to found a settlement.

Had he? Well, yes and no.

'How can the Governor delegate an authority he doesn't have himself?' Velásquez de León had scornfully demanded at an angry meeting outside the Captain's palm thatch. Velásquez de León had been stirring up trouble since before Potonchan. But he had, Ávila thought, put his finger on the nub of the matter. Diego Velásquez did not have a licence to found a settlement, and since he didn't have it, naturally he couldn't confer it on the Captain. But he *wanted* the expedition to found a settlement – in his name, of course – so that later, when he could legally do so, he could claim the land that had been settled. Before anyone else did.

He had come as near to saying this as he dared. So much became evident when Hernán publicly read out the commission the Governor had given him. Until that moment nobody had been quite sure what was in that commission.

It turned out to contain only the list of instructions everyone had by heart. The bit about the desirability of settling was in the *preamble*, hedged about with a great deal of *whereas* and *hereunto*.

After the Captain had finished reading from this double-faced bit of paper, there was a thoughtful silence. The Captain folded the commission and put it away.

'I'm grateful to these gentlemen for asking me to read out this document,' he said, 'because it clarifies matters about which there has been some confusion. It is now apparent that we have carried out what we were supposed to do and it is our duty to return to Cuba. Preparations to embark will begin straight away.'

The camp was in an uproar within half an hour. He was a clever devil, Hernán.

Velásquez de León

Velásquez de León had been three months in the Captain's company and still did not have his measure. When Hernán announced that they would prepare to embark for Cuba, he went back to his palm thatch and started to gather his belongings together.

A rising tumult came to his ears while he was doing this. A tramp of feet that disturbed the sand. Voices raised.

He sent his servant to find out what was happening. Then, realizing this was stupid, he went himself.

They were all outside the Captain's hut, all those who had pinned their hopes on him and now were desperate that he would not give them what they wanted. They were clamouring for him to revoke his order to embark. They were arguing passionately that they must stay, they must found a settlement, that if they went away now the Indians would never let them land again. Some of them even pulled from their pockets their little bits of gold – the gold they should not have had! – and held it out as if they wanted the gold to talk for them.

And Hernán was listening and nodding and looking like a man full of scruples and regret and good intentions.

'Our instructions don't permit it,' he said at one point. But then, a little later, 'No one wants to go back to Cuba the poorer, and certainly *I* don't. I shan't recover my outlay.'

Velásquez de León returned to his palm thatch. He would not intervene again. He would wait and see what came of this.

The Governor of Cuba had a name for open-handedness, but he had closed his hand to his cousin. He had not given Velásquez de León enough Indians. As a result, receipts from the estate were not enough to cover his expenses. A rash venture or two at the gaming table, which might have improved matters, had made them worse. That was what Velásquez de León was doing on an expedition whose leader he distrusted and the aims of which became murkier by the day.

In the third week of their miserable sojourn on the sand dunes, his patience had snapped. He had demanded that the trading for gold which even the rank and file were doing should stop at once. He reminded Hernán that the licence to trade for gold was restricted to the leader of the expedition, who was supposed to be setting aside one-fifth for the King's tax and keeping the rest secure so that on return to Cuba it could be handed over to the Governor.

'Let Hernán produce his commission, *if* he has bothered to keep it,' challenged Velásquez. 'Let him read it out. Then we shall see.'

Hernán was standing outside his palm thatch, with Pedro de Alvarado beside him, listening to this. Velásquez's demand, made in front of a crowd evenly divided between Hernán's supporters and his own, nearly started a riot. When Hernán could at last be heard, he turned out to be saying, to everyone's amazement, that Velásquez de León was quite right.

'A man should be nominated to take charge of the gold and the King's fifth,' said Hernán. 'You must choose someone straight away.'

The ground cut from under his feet, Velásquez de León was still groping for his next move when the Captain slipped into his shelter and reappeared a few moments later holding a stained and creased document. He unfolded it.

'Contrary to this gentleman's belief,' he said, 'I have not lost my letter of commission, nor torn it up, nor used it to wipe my boots with.'

There wasn't a murmur while he was reading it out.

Three things came of the vehement protests against the Captain's order to sail. The first was that the Captain cancelled the order. The second was that he sent a ship commanded by Francisco de Montejo up the coast to look for a more sheltered harbour. The third was that he ordered Velásquez de León to take fifty men into the neighbouring countryside to reconnoitre it.

Velásquez was extremely angry at what had happened, but all the same he was glad to get away from the camp. The mosquitoes, the gossip and the perpetual idleness all dispirited him. Even a little way inland the air seemed sweeter; it caressed his face as he rode in the generous shade of the forest, and brought to his nostrils a delightful scent of well-watered earth.

This was a rich country, and large. It was not another island, he was sure of that; the size of the rivers, the looming mountains, the number of languages that had been encountered, all pointed in the same direction. This was the mainland. But which mainland?

The sense that he was on the edge of a vast unknown thrilled him. Here, away from the camp, away from the constant grumbling about hunger and the incessant talk about whether to settle or to go home and how much gold Muctezuma had, he felt free, he felt like a boy again, and he welcomed into his soul the spirit that had prompted him to join Hernán at Trinidad and that many considerations had since conspired to make him forget: adventure.

For, truly, what a magnificent adventure it was! New lands, new peoples. Exotic treasures, tales of a great empire. Who knew where it might end? At moments like this, he could even see the thing from Hernán's point of view – stay here, seize the chance, follow the adventure.

But no, he could not do it. He was not a pirate. He was a Velásquez. And there would be another time.

Hernán had not been precise about what Velásquez was to do on this foray into the interior. He should, naturally, investigate any towns he came to, and he should note what crops were under cultivation. He must not disturb the local Indians more than was necessary. He must return in three days. Hernán always liked to know what was over the next hill and it made good military sense, but Velásquez was puzzled by the timing of this mission. He knew Hernán was thinking of moving his camp; that was why Montejo had been sent off to look for another harbour. And if Hernán was concerned about a threat from Indians in the vicinity, he had taken a long time to do anything about it.

He liked to have more cards in his hand than he would need, Velásquez supposed, as he rode through cultivated but empty fields. It was even possible he was doing, belatedly, what his commission required him to do: explore. None of this explained the suddenness with which Velásquez had been despatched: the Captain had summoned him and told him to pick his men and leave that afternoon. However, that was typical of Hernán: he would keep everyone waiting for days while he deliberated over something, but once he had made a decision it had to be acted on immediately.

Velásquez de León did not disturb any local Indians because he did not find any. They had all fled, leaving behind their huts, their orchards and their maize and chickens. In a small lagoon, he found some ingenious fish-traps; perhaps they had just been emptied, because they contained no fish.

On the afternoon of the third day, Velásquez de León turned his horse's head towards the camp. Away from the marshes, the region would not be a bad place to settle, but for the exposed anchorage – and the need to return to Cuba.

However, that was not what Hernán wanted. He supposed he would find out what Hernán wanted when he got back to camp.

He did.

Pedro de Alvarado

The ground had been prepared. Only Hernán's supporters would be there. Guards posted at the edge of the meeting would ensure there were no unwelcome visitors. As a final precaution, it would be the middle of the night.

Pedro de Alvarado sat with his brothers. He liked being with them, he liked the ease of it and the warmth of their bodies. Their presence relaxed him. It steadied him, too, and that was not a bad thing because something in him was apt to fly off like a hawk from a wrist. He would feel the lightness as it left, and wonder what it would do this time.

The meeting spilled out of the area covered by the Captain's palm thatch and on to the bare sand. Roughly a hundred men were present. Dependable fellows, all of them. They were keyed up and quiet, waiting for Hernán to speak.

Alvarado knew what he would say. Hernán would say that a final decision had to be made that night about whether they would stay and pursue their fortunes in the country or return to Cuba, and that he had called them here so that the arguments could be properly thrashed out without interference from the friends of Diego Velásquez. Hernán would listen to their arguments and appear to think about them, and then, pretending to yield to great pressure, he would agree to stay. After that, the meeting would go on to talk about the town that was going to be founded, and elect its officials.

As he spoke, the Captain placed an hour-glass beside him on the wine cask on which he was sitting. They must finish their business by dawn, he said.

Only about a dozen men knew that the decision had already been reached. For the rest, Hernán's invitation unlocked, all over again, their wildest hopes and their fears that whatever they'd gained would be taken away from them by Diego Velásquez. Alvarado played his part, but said no more than he believed. 'We have a foothold here. We fought hard to get it. This is the third time some of us have been to these shores. If we go home now, all that work is wasted. And what a chance we have of glory!'

Each speaker that night spoke with the same urgency, as if no one else had said the same things. Hernán kept his head slightly tilted towards each man who spoke, resting his palms on the sloping sides of the wine cask. He looked pale.

In the expectant hush after the last man had spoken, he seemed to consider. Alvarado waited confidently for him to say that the arguments he had just heard were overwhelming.

'I never regretted studying law at Salamanca,' Hernán said, 'until now.'

With consternation Alvarado listened as Hernán enumerated, remorselessly, the various reasons why they must go back to Cuba. All of them hinged on law. He had attended carefully to every argument that was put to him, he said, and they were good arguments, but he had not heard the one thing he needed to hear, an argument that offered him legal justification. Without it, they had no choice but to go home. That is to say – and here a current that had run behind the speech flowed out into the open – *he* had no choice. It was all very well for them to count their gains and want to keep them and never mind the risk, but he was the one who would *take* the risk. *He* was the one who would be hanged as a rebel if things did not turn out well. He was in trouble already, as all of them knew, because of the expedition's abrupt departure from Cuba – in which, he added as a seeming afterthought, some of those present had encouraged him.

There was a silence when he finished speaking. It was the silence of despair. No one stirred. Hernán was sitting stiffly, leaning forward a little to gaze at the ground, an expression of sadness, of resignation, on his face. Even *he* cannot do it, thought Alvarado. Then indignation took him.

He stood up. 'To Hell with the law and to Hell with Diego Velásquez!' he said, and put his hand to his sword. 'Hernán, defy the Governor and we are with you!'

A rumble of assent arose that caused the Captain to raise his hands swiftly, warning them to be quiet. He got up and, disconcertingly, walked out of the shelter towards the shore. After a few moments Alvarado followed him. Hernán was standing motionless on the sand dunes, looking at the sea. Understanding that he wished to be alone, Alvarado remained at a distance, in performance of his unofficial role as Hernán's protector and also as a reminder to Hernán that he could not escape his duties.

When Hernán turned and began to retrace his steps, Alvarado followed him. Hernán took his seat again on the wine barrel.

'I will agree to your demands,' he said.

There was uproar. Useless now to tell them to be quiet: it was a fiesta. All that was missing was the fiddle.

Hernán was trying to say something. They wouldn't let him. They wanted to rejoice. Hadn't he already said the only thing that mattered?

'On one condition.'

Gradually the hubbub lessened. He had an addendum to make. They prepared, tolerantly, to hear it.

'I will take one-fifth of the gold, after the King's fifth has been subtracted.'

There wasn't a sound. It was as if all the air had been sucked out of the place.

Then, 'I'm damned if you will,' growled Cristóbal de Olid.

'The risks I'm running are much greater than yours,' the Captain pointed out. 'My investment has also been greater. I have bankrupted myself to outfit the fleet. I am therefore entitled to a greater share of the proceeds.'

A murmur started slowly, as if no one could believe he had heard what he'd heard until certain that someone else had heard the same thing. The murmur grew. It became dangerous.

Hernán didn't budge. He sat facing them, hands resting again on the curved sides of that damned barrel, quite calm. His gaze passed over them, his followers, who surely were about to mutiny. Those closest to him were angriest. For they had believed they were in his confidence and all the time he had planned this stroke.

They will kill him, thought Alvarado, and he deserves it. A fifth of the gold: what impudence! He would not lift a hand in Hernán's defence. He was amazed at the coldness of his own rage. He waited to see who would first draw sword.

But no one moved. They cursed him, yes. They cursed him darkly and profoundly. But they did not rise to lay hands on him. And Alvarado, whose own hand lay clenched and motionless on his knee, understood why.

For, in what lay ahead, who else would lead them?

A man as bold, as resourceful, as quick . . . A man who could carry all these men's dreams . . .

He looked into himself and knew he could not do it. He glanced to left and right and saw the rest of them – Portocarrero, Ávila, Olid, young Sandoval – looking into themselves and finding they could not do it.

To mutiny, you have to know what comes next.

The sand in the hour-glass had run through for the second time. With a deft movement of his finger Hernán reversed the glass.

'We are half-way through the night,' he said, 'and there is a great deal still to do. Do you accept my condition?'

They accepted it.

Gonzalo de Sandoval

Trouble was to be expected, and trouble there was, when Velásquez de León returned from his foray into the countryside and heard what had happened in his absence. The expedition had dissolved itself and its former members had become the council and citizenry of a town; the Captain, elected Chief Justice and Commander-in-Chief of the army by his friends, had repudiated the authority of Diego Velásquez and now based his legitimacy on 'the vote of the town council', and the next thing they were all going to do was build the town that had made this conjuring trick possible.

The Captain bought off most of the trouble, or talked his way through it, but Velásquez de León couldn't be bought or persuaded. He was a stubborn man. And courageous, Sandoval conceded. Even when all his allies had deserted him, he stood there with his black-as-jet beard jutting like a spade and his brows knit like thornbushes, demanding – ridiculously – that the Captain hold to the letter of instructions that had lost any relevance they might ever have had. In the end, Hernán had tired of it and put him in irons.

It was Sandoval who escorted the prisoner out to the flagship. Velásquez didn't say a word all the way, just watched the rising and falling of the oars. Sandoval found his gaze irresistibly drawn to the iron on Velásquez's wrists. It was dull and rust-pitted, the colour of a thundercloud, the colour of defeat. It looked immensely heavy.

And now, four weeks after the nocturnal meeting under the Captain's palm thatch and three weeks after Francisco de Montejo's return with news of a harbour (how niftily Hernán had got *him* out of the way!), their town was a reality. Trenches were being dug, foundations put in, a church was going up and so were houses and a fort in case the Indians turned hostile. And a gallows, stark as a bone. And now, too, Velásquez de León was back from his spell on the ships, looking a bit paler and thinner but not a whit subdued, and he walked past that gallows twenty times a day without even glancing at it.

Building the town was hard work. The Droopy-ears helped: they felled the timber and brought it. But it was Christian backs and sinews that dug the pits, laid the stone, hoisted the roof-beams and mixed the mortar. Not everyone was happy. Ávila and a few others reminded the Captain that they were gentlemen and that gentlemen did not do work of this kind. The Captain, whose own hands were caked with soil, said if they were too good to share in the building of a town he hoped they would remember it when the town was rich (as its name said it would be).

Sandoval fixed the roof timbers. Day after day he balanced at the top of a makeshift ladder or crouched precariously on a spur of wall. It wasn't this that made him giddy but a feeling that often came to him that he was back in Spain. As a small boy he had loved to climb trees, scaffolding, ivy, anything that offered a foothold. So powerfully did his childhood visit him during these days that one afternoon, in a dazzle of sunlight, he distinctly saw his mother's hand setting down on the flagged floor a dish of milk for the cat. Later, he interpreted this vision as meaning he would never see his native land again.

The ship appeared when they had been building the town for about a week. She stood out to sea and a boat made for the shore.

The Captain straightened up – he was supervising the digging of foundations for the fort – and smoothed his hands down over his thighs. In the hush that had fallen he watched the boat as intently as if it were a fish he was bringing in.

They seemed to be Spaniards. Indeed, what else could they be? But it was a fearful shock to see them, off that shore where no other Christians should be. The Captain did not relax until the boat was well into the shallows and he could see who sat in it. Then at last his face lightened.

'It's Saucedo,' he said.

It turned out that the Captain had bought a caravel in Santiago de Cuba right at the start of his preparations and left her there to be refitted, with orders that she join the fleet when ready. Now, here she was – with, it was to be hoped, more recruits. In the boat were Saucedo, an old friend of the Captain's, and four other gentlemen.

A cask of wine was broached. Work, for a time, ceased. The safe arrival of the ship was celebrated.

Finally: 'What news from Cuba?' asked the Captain.

'Diego Velásquez has got a licence from the Crown to explore and settle undiscovered lands.'

Every eye fastened on the speaker.

'The licence,' Saucedo went on, 'makes particular mention of this coast, which is believed to be part of the mainland, and of the island of Yucatan.'

'It is not the mainland,' said Alaminos irritably. 'There is a strait to the south that has been missed.'

No one bothered to answer him.

'I suppose,' said the Captain, 'the licence also makes mention of what proceeds Diego Velásquez may take from these so-called undiscovered lands.'

'He is entitled to everything,' said Saucedo, 'except the King's fifth, which is reduced, in view of the expense to which he will be put, to one-tenth.'

Sandoval thought Hernán would break the goblet he nursed

in his hand. But the Captain merely drew in his breath very hard and held it.

They all went back to building their town after a while. It had been a mistake to drink the wine. The afternoon sun was tigerish, the light like a sword, and in a very short time the fumes from the drink had set Sandoval's head throbbing.

That night, two officials of the new town, Diego de Ordaz and Francisco de Montejo (neither, you might think, a friend of the Captain's, but these days a lot of people were changing sides), went round the camp taking men aside and talking to them on Hernán's behalf. They were asking them if they would be willing to give up the gold they'd acquired on this trip, if they'd be willing to give it up for the King.

It was all going to be sent to the King, that was the Captain's idea, and all the officers had already agreed because, like it or not, it was the best way out of the position they were in. The intention was that they would keep nothing for themselves, and that with the gold they would send a letter signed by every man of the expedition, declaring that they were the loyal servants of His Majesty and here was the token of it, and the Captain would write a letter to the King – he was writing it already – explaining why Diego Velásquez must not be allowed to found settlements in this land. Portocarrero and Montejo would take the gold and the letters to Spain in the flagship, and Alaminos would go with them as pilot.

There was no compulsion to give up your gold, said the men who were making the circuit of the camp and talking so confidentially into reluctant ears, but it was for the general good and, so far, no one had refused.

By the time the camp settled down for the night, there was still no word of anyone refusing, and the next day the gold began to be handed in.

Sandoval went to see it, having a curiosity about what an amount of wealth that would forever be beyond him might look like. It was piled up in a corner of the Captain's house, which hadn't yet been roofed. Two of the Alvarado brothers were guarding it. The sunlight fell vertically between the walls and kindled the heap of gold that lay there as if at the bottom of a light-filled well. Gold chains, gold shells, necklaces of gold beads, little figures of deer and frogs and turtles cast in gold, gold rings coiled like serpents, bracelets of embossed gold, gold earrings studded with turquoise and hung with feathers, gold masks of gods, a bow and a quiver of golden arrows the length of his finger.

He was astonished at how intricate the work was. He had never properly looked at the jewellery the Indians wore or thought about how it was made. Now he wondered what tools they used. They had no steel. They did not seem to use wheels of any kind. How did they engrave their gold, polish their gems, cast those little figures? With what strange bellows did they blow the fire?

'It's beautiful,' he said eventually, and in surprise, because he had not thought that Indians would be able to create beauty because they carried out human sacrifice.

'Beautiful or not, it's going to Spain,' said Jorge de Alvarado, who could only hold one idea in his head at a time.

Sandoval thought the Captain was wise in choosing this means of countering the machinations of Diego Velásquez, who had powerful friends at Court. However, he also realized how dangerous it was to ask people to give up their gold. To most men in the camp, it was what they'd come for and it was all they had. They had fought, gone hungry, seen their friends die, put up with wounds, sickness and mosquitoes for it. He thought a lot of them would not give up all their gold but would never forget having been asked for it. (He had given up all of his. It was simpler that way. He wanted to be able to look Hernán in the eye. And he knew there would be more.)

He stood watch with Olid a few nights later. The camp was quiet. In the distance, the sea gleamed like silver. Something was brewing. He could feel it.

Cristóbal de Olid

It was being said in the camp that Hernán had given a thousand gold pesos to Francisco de Montejo. If it was true, it was going to make Olid very angry. Plotting paid better than loyalty, it seemed.

Olid was a fighter. Some people said he was a brawler, but they said it in a tone of respect. He had grown up in the mountains of Andalucia. He knew about physical hardship, he was acquainted with hunger and he had been aware from childhood of how the lack of material things can corrode a man's pride. He had joined the expedition to make sure that a lack of them would not corrode his. He understood tenacity: for two generations, and for scant reward, his family had faced the last Moorish kingdom in Spain and his father had died in the conquest of it. Olid had learnt that there was no justice in the world and that you had to take what you wanted and pay the price, but he also believed that the laws of loyalty were intractable and must be observed, because otherwise a gentleman-at-arms was no better than a bandit.

He had no patience with the dilemmas of Velásquez de León, who had enlisted under Hernán's banner to better his prospects but was nevertheless bound to the Governor of Cuba by kinship and duty; or for Ordaz, who had been placed in the expedition to report on it and could neither do so, since there was no means of communicating with Cuba, nor do anything else either since everyone knew he was the Governor's stool-pigeon; or with Francisco de Montejo, who apparently would go wherever his advantage lay but did not seem to know where it lay. People shouldn't get themselves into such tangles.

There was a conspiracy in the camp. Hernán, who always had his ear to the ground, had lately given everyone work to do, hard, heavy work, not the kind of work that could easily be combined with hatching a plot. However, with the arrival of Francisco Saucedo and the preparations to send a ship to the King, work on building the town had slackened – which, since it was still just as urgent, could only be explained by saying that the focus of their thoughts had shifted. From this hot coastal plain, backed by mountains, to the streets of Seville and the scented labyrinths of the Court. And also, once more, to what lay beyond those mountains. For the Captain was talking about Muctezuma again.

A delegation of men went to see him in his house on the square. Olid heard from Hernán's own lips what had happened. There were about twenty of them and they said they represented the wishes of forty more. Among them were Velásquez de León, a man called Escudero, formerly a town constable in Cuba, whom the Captain had not forgiven for putting him in irons five years previously, and Ordaz, who nowadays was swinging like a weathercock between the Captain and the Governor. Velásquez de León said the town they were building was illegal, that the Captain's sleight of hand over resigning the position to which the Governor had appointed him and getting himself elected as Commander-in-Chief instead would avail him nothing, and he demanded that the Captain allow those men who wanted to go back to Cuba to do so. It was, he said, the only way the Captain had of avoiding the retribution that otherwise would surely catch up with him.

Olid had observed that it was never a good idea to threaten Hernán.

However, Hernán had agreed with Velásquez's request as if it were perfectly reasonable. He said he would put a ship at the disposal of the men who wanted to go back, and he gave them permission to make whatever arrangements they needed for their departure.

For a week after that the camp was full of bustle. Nobody who was going now felt shy of saying so, and there was much selling of equipment that would no longer be needed and composing of messages to be taken back to Cuba.

Then the Captain said they couldn't go.

He was sorry, he said; it wasn't his fault. It was the town council of Villa Rica that had made the decision. The reason was that, on the journey they were about to make to find Muctezuma, every man would be needed.

Olid was present at this announcement: most of the camp was. He saw Alvarado bite his lip to hold back a grin, but didn't bother to bite his own. His sword-arm felt a pleasant anticipatory tingling.

The Velásquez men weren't ready for a fight, though. Quite a lot of them were cowards, and that was why they wanted to go home. Trek inland to meet an emperor? No thank you. There might be battles.

They slunk off, or stormed off; at any rate, they didn't force a showdown. Possibly the worst of it from their point of view was that they had revealed themselves. Hernán knew who they were now, every last man of them, and so did anyone else who had taken an interest. Now all the grins were open.

That was when the conspiracy started, Olid thought. Not earlier. It was born out of the bitterness of being shamed.

Sandoval came to Olid's quarters late one night, and put his finger to his lips. Olid grasped his sword and followed him. Outside, standing by the still-unfinished wall of the fort they were building, waited a phalanx of Hernán's people, and Hernán in the middle of them with his mouth set hard.

They set off between the half-built houses and stopped at one that had a bit of sacking nailed over the doorway. Half a dozen men went inside with weapons drawn. Olid heard a strangled shout, some blundering-about and a furious oath. When Hernán's men came out again they had with them, disarmed and with their hands bound, Ordaz the Governor's spy, the ex-constable Escudero and a man called Cermeño who was a pilot. With these three in their midst, glaring about them like cornered rats, they went on to another house where the Captain sent in to ask whether Velásquez de León would be kind enough to accompany them.

Three other calls were made (by this time half the town was awake), the last of which netted, to Olid's satisfaction, the priest Juan Díaz. Olid had no time for priests. They had taken an unwelcome interest in his family ever since his grandfather's conversion.

It turned out that the plan had been to steal a ship. (They were going to get their ship by one means or another.) They would sail it, of course, to Cuba. They had already started to provision it, surreptitiously, using Cermeño's perfectly legitimate excursions out to the fleet. Some common sailors were also in the plot. All of this came out in shabby detail at the court martial that was held the next day. What most angered Hernán was what these traitors proposed to do when they reached Cuba. They were going to tell Diego Velásquez that a ship loaded with treasure for the King was about to set sail from this shore, and suggest that he intercept it.

'You may rest assured,' Hernán told them, 'that His Majesty will hear of this.'

They could not have damned themselves more completely. It had been very stupid, Olid thought. Sailors were loose-mouthed, and the preparations on the ship would soon have aroused suspicion. No wonder the man who betrayed them had taken fright. There were those who remarked, after the trial was over, that the accused had not been allowed a defence, to which Olid replied that there would have been nothing they could say if they had been.

He went to see Escudero and Cermeño hanged. They had been the ringleaders. Everyone wondered about Velásquez de León, but the Captain said there had been no evidence against him. He decided not to proceed against Ordaz, either, beyond putting him in fetters 'to give him a chance to reflect'.

The hanging was done without ceremony. A second gibbet had been erected beside the one that was already there, in spite of the shortage of timber. The sailors were flogged. Olid thought Hernán had dealt too lightly. He himself would have hanged both Ordaz and Velásquez de León, of whose guilt he had no doubt. He would have dealt justice to Juan Díaz, too, who could not be punished because he was a priest: there were ways of doing these things.

A day after the hangings he went to look at Escudero and Cermeño. They revolved slowly in their chains, nudged by the breeze from the sea. The unseasoned wood creaked with their weight. The iron hung mute except when a more vigorous turn than usual of the corpse caused one link to strike against another, when it resounded with the flat, purposeful note of a hammer in a forge.

Fools, thought Olid, and a fierce joy came over him at being in the flush of his life, and at the starkness of the world's choices and that he had made the right ones.

Alonso Hernández Portocarrero

He loves the lifting of the ship and the *crack* the sails make when they are full to bursting with wind. He's going home.

He did not ask Hernán for this commission to the King: Hernán, very politely, asked *him*. It would, Hernán said, be the greatest service Portocarrero could render to the expedition and to His Majesty — thus, necessarily, also to him, the Captain. It occurs now to Portocarrero that Hernán might have been subtly referring to his performance at Potonchan, where, it was true, he lost his way in the forest during the first battle, which prevented him from taking much part in it, and then was too sick to fight in the subsequent ones. He dismisses the idea, however, since Hernán has always shown a warm affection for him, and since it is beyond dispute that Portocarrero is particularly well qualified for the task that lies ahead.

He knows the Court. He has spent much time at it, in the company of his cousin, the Count of Medellín. He knows its deep places and its shallows, its deceits and manoeuvres, its ancestral memory for slights and its mole-like blindness to the world beyond it. He knows the desert that waits there for hope and the precipice that waits for ambition. He knows his way through them as Alaminos (or so it's to be hoped) knows his way through the shoals of the Bahamas. He — with the help of Francisco de Montejo — will steer Hernán's venture through.

Montejo strolls up behind him.

'They will start their journey to Tenochtitlan today, God willing.'

'So they will.' It is the second Sunday in August, the date fixed on by Hernán. 'May God protect them.' Portocarrero isn't given to uttering pieties, but feels in this case it is called for.

'Do you have — frankly, now — any idea what Hernán intends to do?'

Portocarrero closes his lips on the reply that comes to them, which is 'No.' If he is going to Court, he must get out of the habit he has acquired among Hernán's buccaneers of saying what he thinks.

'He intends to meet Muctezuma,' says Portocarrero.

'And then what?'

There is no answer that can be given. Portocarrero knows the overweening boast he carries in his baggage. *I will make him a vassal of Your Majesty's or put him in chains.* Hernán showed him the letter. It is to be presumed he also showed it to Montejo. Montejo, once a formidable enemy, has come over to the Captain's side. Hernán now trusts him, and Hernán doesn't usually make mistakes. All this having been said, Portocarrero is still reluctant to utter, in Montejo's hearing, that boast. In case it excites ridicule.

'It appears,' says Montejo, 'that Hernán intends to put him in chains.'

'I have no doubt,' says Portocarrero, 'that if anyone can do it, Hernán can.'

'Oh, no doubt.'

They stand together and look at the indigo sea. Cuba is four days' sailing away, but they are not going to Cuba. They have strict orders to proceed direct to Spain.

'Tricky business that, just before we left,' observes Montejo. 'I think he only just got away with it.'

'The hangings?'
'No. The ships.'

'I want you,' Hernán had said to the grizzle-haired ship's master sitting across the rough table from him, 'to carry out a thorough inspection of your vessel tomorrow and then to come to me and say that she is worm-eaten.'

The man took his time. 'But Captain, she is not. She is a sound ship.'

'Nevertheless,' said the Captain patiently, 'I want you to find worm in the timbers.'

The old sailor looked him in the eye. The Captain returned his gaze calmly.

'Why?'

'I will then order her to be beached, and the tackle taken off.'

'With your permission, Captain, that is not an answer to my question.'

'We have too many ships,' said Hernán. 'I have just had to hang two men and flog three others for conspiring to steal one of them.' He paused. 'They were planning to kill the ship's master, too, which you may not have heard.'

'One ship the less is not going to put an end to conspiracies.'

'That is a matter for me to worry about,' said Hernán, 'not you.'

The master said nothing for a while. Outside, the fort was being built. There was the sound of stones rolling heavily out from the barrow that had been put together from a gun carriage, and the loud squeaking of the pulley that needed to be greased. The wooden bucket knocked against the stonework. Someone cursed.

'I won't do it,' said the seaman. 'I won't destroy a good ship.'

'That is what I expected you to say,' said Hernán, 'and I understand it. Now I would like you to try to understand *me*. We are about to go inland, over the mountains, in search of the source of *this*.' He took from his pocket, and unwrapped from its cloth, a hollow gold bracelet in the form of a serpent, with two tiny rubies for eyes. He let it rest on the table in front of the master. 'We have no idea what we will meet, and the only thing we can be sure of is that it will be dangerous. There are men here who will fight like lions if they have no choice, but whose heart will not be in it if they are looking over their shoulders for a way of going home. I have to make sure that they cannot go home.'

There came a terrible clatter outside, followed by an awed obscenity and then silence. After an interval, voices were raised in mutual accusation.

'You are going to destroy *all* the ships?' asked the master.

'As I have said, that is a matter for me.'

'It's a fearful thing to do, Captain. Most men would quail at it.'

'It is a great enterprise we're embarked on.'

The master ran his fingertips over the surface of the table, which consisted of two planks laid across a pair of barrels. His fingers loved timber, Portocarrero saw. They caressed the grain without knowing it.

'Suppose I say that I will beach the ship,' said the master. 'I will run her into the shallows for you. But I will do it because you order me to do it. I won't say a ship's rotten when she isn't.'

'Yes, you will.'

They held each other's gaze.

'Otherwise it can't be done,' said the Captain simply.

As the master stood up to leave, the Captain pushed the bracelet towards him. 'I wouldn't offer you a bribe,' he said. 'But take this, if you like it.'

He spoke to all the ships' masters individually. He was capable of taking great trouble. He made each of them feel that the fate of the expedition rested on him. The story about the rot in the timbers was essential, of course, not only to deflect the fury that would undoubtedly break over his head when the ships were run aground but also because some of those ships belonged to Diego Velásquez.

The thing was done in two stages. First, four of the ships were grounded. This was done at night, and by the time anyone saw them, the four ships were in the shallows, lying at a rakish angle as if drunk.

The Captain went into the little square and called for everyone's attention. He had unfortunate news, he said. It had been reported to him by four of the ships' masters that their ships were infested by wood-beetle and he had therefore given orders for them to be beached. The tackle and guns would be taken off them for future use, and their sailors would be assigned fighting and sentry duties like everyone else.

There was dismay and a lot of anger. What right did he have to run these ships aground without a general consultation, the Captain was asked. Now, if one ship was going to Spain, that left barely more than half the original fleet to take them all back to Cuba. When they eventually went.

'We can build more ships,' the Captain promised them. He pointed out that there was a town now, so some men would be staying. He added that in any case there had been no help for it because the rot had spread into the keels.

That evening, a group of soldiers went to his house to ask him if he was quite sure the ships were unseaworthy. Of course he was sure, he said: what kind of fool did they think he was, to be throwing away his own investment? But if they doubted him, they could go and inspect the ships themselves.

They didn't, because by then it was dark, and in the morning the hulls had been opened, the sea had flooded in and there was nothing to be done about it.

He scuttled the rest a few days later. It turned out, he said, that the rot had spread into *all* the keels.

This time there was not a man in the camp who believed him. He had thrown down a gauntlet to all of them. Portocarrero had no doubt that he had done the right thing. In the game of high stakes Hernán was playing, the boldest move was the safest one. He might end with a length of steel in his stomach, all the same.

As Portocarrero and Montejo were rowed out to the flagship, now the sole remnant of Hernán's fleet, they passed the sunken relics of her companions, buffeted in the swell. They looked, these sunken ships, like another little town, one that had been built too near the water and had not been able to escape an unusually high tide.

Two mornings later, Montejo comes to stand beside him on the deck.

'I have a proposal to make to you. We call in at Cuba. There is a harbour only half a league from my estate. We can stay a few days and take on fresh provisions: wine, fruit, some cheese. It's very pleasant there. What d'you say?'

'We are under strict instructions not to call at Cuba.'

'I know that, my dear fellow. But it's the other end of the island from Santiago. And what the eye doesn't see . . .'

'Alaminos won't agree.'

'I have already spoken to Alaminos.'

III

The Land of Grain

I don't remember how my mother looked. I cannot hear her voice. But I know she hated me.

I had a brother. He was younger than me. Everything he did was right. Everything I did was wrong. My mother would say, 'Why can't you be like him?' and punish me by making me breathe the chilli smoke. All I had done was something like break a pot, an accident. My small brother would dance around me, laughing, while I choked and cried.

I stopped crying. I never cry now.

I thought, why is he better than me? He is not better. He is a boy, that's all. He has nothing to do with pots, he plays with arrows and sticks. If he had to carry pots, he would break them, too.

I thought it would be better to be a boy, because you would be more important. And I thought, if I were a boy, my mother would love me.

As for my father, all I remember is the size of his hands when he lit the New Year's fire in the hearth.

All the time, I knew there was something very bad about me but I didn't know what it was. It didn't seem to be something I had done, like breaking the pots. It felt like something so big and terrible that I could not possibly have done it, because I wouldn't have been able to think of it. And when would I have had time to do it?

It hung around me like a cloak, this thing that was my fault but that I hadn't done. People saw it and looked away. It didn't occur to me to ask them what it was they saw: it was part of my badness that everybody knew about it except me.

One day I decided that since I couldn't help being bad, whatever I did, I might as well do what I wanted. I caught my little brother while he was playing beside the stream, and pushed him into it.

He didn't die. Somebody heard him screaming and pulled him out.

That was probably the day they decided to get rid of me. I heard a conversation between my parents when they thought I was asleep.

'What are we going to do with her?' asked my mother.

I don't know what my father's answer was. They went on talking late into the night.

Nobody spoke to me after that, except to say things like 'Fetch wood' and 'Bring the bowl here.' Even my brother didn't speak to me, but just glared at me like an angry dog. He would have hurt me if he could, but they kept him away from me.

Then one night my mother called me to her and told me what the terrible thing was that I had never known. I understood that while it wasn't my fault in the way that breaking the pot had been my fault, it was, beyond any doubt, my fault and no one else's. She gave me twenty maize cakes wrapped in a leaf and put my hand into the hand of a man who stood at the entrance.

I became a slave as I stepped out of my parents' house. I only understood this later. At the time, all I knew was that a great change had taken place and that I was the one who had caused it.

The greatest change was that I no longer lived in a house. At first, this seemed to me a terrible punishment. I had never heard of anybody who didn't live in a house. Only animals didn't have houses. The shame of this affected me more strongly than anything else, more than the walking all day until I thought I couldn't go a step further, more than the way my clothes got dirty and tattered, more than the meagreness of the food and the way the countryside altered so that in the end it wasn't like anywhere I knew, but flat like a plate whichever way you looked and even the birds different.

The shame of not living in a house was worse than the fact of it, which was just that at night we slept under the sky. In the end, I liked that. I liked looking up at the stars. Not at first, though; I was afraid to look at them at first. Somewhere in them, hidden only from me, my guilt was set out.

I assumed that I didn't live in a house because I was too bad for one. Of course, the merchants didn't live in a house, either, and they hadn't done anything wrong, but I didn't think of that. All my life, I thought, had been moving towards this point, this tramping of the roads by day and sleeping under the stars at night; it was the final judgement on me, and nothing worse could happen.

The merchants weren't unkind. They never made me breathe the smoke of chilli. But they had somewhere to get to and they made me walk. We walked for months, through mountain villages, along the shores of lakes, through ravines and forests where we could hear the roaring of wild beasts. We passed through towns, and although the merchants stopped there to trade goods they had bought in other places, we never stayed in them. We walked until the rains came.

When the rains came we were in a swampy, green place full of trees and with a great river going out to the sea.

The merchants sold me to the first person who enquired about me. He was the steward of the *batab* of Potonchan.

*   *   *

159

I don't like to think of the time when I was a slave in the *batab's* house. If I think about it, I might find that I'm back there, grinding the maize. Whenever those days come back to my mind I think instead of how they ended.

At first it only seemed to me that things had got worse. I was very frightened the day the *batab* gave me with the other nineteen women to the strangers. We thought they were going to kill us and eat us. We couldn't think what else they could want with us. Instead, they put us on enormous canoes, like houses on the sea. No one had ever seen anything like them. Why didn't they topple over, why didn't they sink? On the canoes were large squares of cloth, which were unfolded so that the wind came into them with a noise of thunder, and we began to rush over the water. All the women screamed except me, and I put my knuckles in my mouth so I wouldn't.

After that, they shut us in a small room and we had to endure the sickness. I didn't wail with the others because I am stronger, but it was horrible in the dark place they shut us in, and it went on for days and nights.

I have always been glad that, on the day when my new life began, I had saved some water in a gourd I had concealed and had been able to wash my face. After we were let out of our room, the skin of my face felt good out there in the wind and sunshine. I greeted the sky and the land joyfully. The land looked strange to me, hills of sand and no forest, but I was filled with thankfulness to see it at all. We hadn't had any idea where we were going: we weren't even sure that we were going anywhere in this world. We didn't know whether this voyage was just a journey after all, although a fearful and mysterious one, or a new form of death.

So then there we were, standing on the wood with the wind in our faces and it was as if we hadn't died but instead had been reborn, and I heard a man talking in the language of my child-hood. For a moment I did wonder if I had died.

Then my tongue spoke when my mind was still fumbling.

He heard me. Not the fellow I spoke to: he, of course, heard me. I mean the one in whose gaze I live.

He heard me, and he understood. Oh, not the words. What did the words matter? They were nothing. He understood what I could be to him.

Muluc (I call him by his slave name because I cannot say the other one) is an odd creature. I saw straight away that he was not like the others: I saw it even before he uttered a word, by the way his body moved as he walked towards us and a number of small things like the way he tied his hair. I was curious about him, but I could see he did not like me although at the same time he was obliged to be glad of my presence. I did not find out until much later what disgrace I had rescued him from by speaking when I did.

He had been a slave, like me, and that was how he had learned the language of Potonchan. My lord had gone to a lot of trouble to obtain his freedom. I thought he should be grateful. *I* was so grateful that I would have done anything my lord asked, and he hadn't gone to any trouble for *me*, only fought a battle which he was going to fight anyway. But Muluc wasn't grateful. He didn't seem to care whether he pleased my lord or not. In fact he once told me that he wished he hadn't joined my lord and his people when they came to the place where he was living. I couldn't understand him.

Once it was realized that I could speak the language of the country we had come to as well as the language that was understood by Muluc, so that between us we could allow my lord and the ambassadors of the Meshica to talk to each other, I was no longer treated like the other women. My lord kept me close to him, and when we were not talking to the ambassadors of Lord-Who-Is-Severe or to the Cempoalans he would ask me questions about the country we were in. Sometimes the questions were easy, but sometimes I didn't know the answer and would have to guess in order not to disappoint him.

I worked hard to please him. It seemed to me that if I pleased him a great deal might come of it, and I might never have to go back to being a slave. I knew he liked me, because he showed it in all sorts of ways, like seeing that I got better food than the other women and did not have to grind maize or wash clothes. Sometimes he gave me a present from the things the Meshica had given him. He had taken me to his mat almost straight away, and for a time he continued to want me, but then one day he gave me to one of his friends. I was unhappy and wondered what I had done to offend him. I did not like the friend much. But in time I came to realize that they had an agreement, because sometimes I would be with one of them at night and sometimes the other. The friend did not take such care of me as my lord, and I was glad when he was sent away to his own country. After that, I was able to be with my lord all the time.

The work I had to do was very important, and no one else could have done it, because no one else spoke those two languages. I was aware of what a responsibility rested on me, particularly when we were negotiating with the *batab* of Cempoala and persuading him to make a treaty with us against Lord-Who-Is-Severe. This was a complicated business and took many days.

It was clear that Lord-Who-Is-Severe was worried about us. He didn't know what we were doing on his coast and he wanted us to go away. He tried all sorts of tricks to get rid of us, including witchcraft. Once he sent a man from his court who looked like my lord, as much as a Meshica could. Many people noticed this. But they thought it was a joke of some kind, and I knew it wasn't. There were sorcerers and astrologers in every embassy the Meshica sent to us, and this alarmed me because I know how powerful these people are.

Fortunately nothing came of it. My lord's power was greater than theirs. I didn't say anything about it, at the time. I had grasped, from certain things that had been said, that my lord had a hatred of our religion, so I thought it best to pretend that I knew nothing about such matters. So, whenever any questions were asked that had to do with gods or rituals or magic, I said

I didn't know or said that it was foolishness. Therefore I could hardly say that Lord-Who-Is-Severe was sending magicians to bewitch my lord and he must be careful. However, later I regretted my cowardice and resolved that if ever I thought there might be a threat to my lord, even if I wasn't sure, I would say something.

My chance came when we reached Tlascala.

I had never been more than a day or two's journey from the sea in my life. I couldn't imagine what the country would be like beyond the mountains. When I knew that we really were going to go inland, that it wasn't just a game of my lord's, I used to study that line of mountains and wonder what it would be like to set foot on them and whether it was possible that people lived on them. There was one that was white. Pure white. In the dawn it turned to coral. I thought, if there can be a white mountain, a coral mountain, who knows what else there might be? As a child I had heard the wonderful stories about Cactus-on-the-Stone. I thought perhaps the land behind the mountain was full of magicians and the white mountain was a sign of this. I was very ignorant at the time.

Then there was the business of walking. I hadn't expected it. I don't know why, I don't know how I'd thought we were going to get to where we going unless we walked. Perhaps it was the fact that my lord and his friends went everywhere on the backs of their animals: perhaps I'd thought that I would have an animal, too. I hadn't thought about it. Suddenly, there I was walking again, and very often not even at my lord's side. Day after day. Not living in a house. It was like going back to the time when my mother gave me to the merchants. I was miserable, although I didn't show it. After all, everyone else was in the same situation. Even the men who had animals often didn't sit on them, but walked beside them because the way was so steep and covered in loose stones.

And it was cold. It was so cold in the mountains that I thought I would die of it. The worst was when it rained, because the rain was colder than anything you could imagine and how can you light a fire to dry yourself when everything is wet? The Cempoalans were miserable, too; they shivered all the time. My lord was concerned about them; he was afraid they would die. And in fact some of them did, but not from the cold. They died because they fell over the precipices.

When we had climbed right up into the mountains, we came down one day into a valley where there was a town that belonged to Lord-Who-Is-Severe. Its governor was a proud, unfriendly man who did not want us there but was obliged to give us shelter. He tried to persuade us to turn back. To frighten us, he told us that not only was Cactus-on-the-Stone the most magnificent city in the world, but it was also so cleverly built for defence that it could not be overcome in war. 'You must reach it by a narrow bridge of stone,' he said, 'and in the bridge the Meshica have put sections made of wood that can be taken up as an enemy approaches. Therefore, no one enters the city whom the Meshica do not want to enter it, and no one leaves whom the Meshica do not want to leave.'

My lord and his men were not deterred by this. While we were in the town we discovered a very large display of skulls of captives who had been offered to the Lord of the Near, and this enraged them. I thought it might make them think again about going further, but it seemed to make them more determined.

Before we left, we sent a message ahead with some Cempoalans, asking the rulers of Tlascala for permission to travel peacefully through their country and saying that we would like to help them in their struggle against the Meshica. The Cempoalans didn't want to take the message. We had started to hear worrying things about the Tlascalteca by this time — that, although they hated the Meshica, they hated everybody else as well, and that being shut in for so long behind their mountains had made them mad.

The Cempoalans at first refused to go alone into Tlascala, but my lord talked to them, explaining what a service they would render to their city and how everyone would always remember it, and in the end they went.

*　　*　　*

It was true that the Tlascalteca hated everybody. They had built a wall right across the valley, joining two mountains, to keep people out. It had a hidden gateway, a sort of tunnel inside the wall, cunningly made so that only a few people could go through it at a time. It took half the day for all of us to go through, what with all our animals and weapons and the baggage, and the large army of Cempoalans. The *batab's* son refused for a long time to get out of his litter, which could not be got through the tunnel, and my lord himself had to persuade him. Then, no sooner were we all on the other side and getting ready to move on than we were attacked.

The first I knew of it was when an arrow stuck in the grass by my feet. I couldn't understand where it had come from. Then, looking around, I saw a band of warriors standing on a low hill ahead of us, raising their bows to shoot again.

My lord and his friends rode furiously at them and tried to capture some, but they all got away. It seemed to me not a good beginning.

It was late by this time, so we made camp. As we were doing this a group of villagers came up and apologized for the fact that we had been attacked, saying that it was nothing to do with them. They said the people who had shot arrows at us were ignorant savages employed to guard the frontier.

I did not believe them, and when, in the following days, we were attacked again, I knew I had been right. But the new attacks were much more serious.

Day after day, the Tlascalteca came in hordes to fight us. They got more than they bargained for, because my lord and his men would each fight twenty of them at a time, and would split their heads open and cut off their arms. I saw this because sometimes I went, afterwards, to the place where the battle had been. It was horrible; I had never seen a battle before, and I did not know it was like this. But I told myself that the Tlascalteca did not have to come and attack us, so really it was their own fault.

165

After a few days, the Cempoalans we had sent ahead with the message came back to us. They rushed out of a temple as we went past it looking for food, because the maize in all the fields had been harvested and we had nothing to eat. They were terrified. They had taken the message to the four rulers of Tlascala and it had been scoffed at. The rulers had told them that everyone who ever came to Tlascala was an enemy and that if they didn't leave at once they would be killed. They had been hiding in some wicker chests in the temple.

I lost count of the battles. I watched them all, from my place among the baggage with the other women. The other women were very frightened, and expected to die at any moment. I reassured them; I told them my lord could not be killed, and would make sure none of us was killed, either. They believed the first of these things because they had often seen how arrows and spears could not harm him, but they didn't believe the second.

When we weren't fighting we went out in twenties to burn villages. My lord and a few of his friends would ride their animals and the rest of us would walk. He always took me and Muluc in case he found villagers to talk to, but usually they had all fled. He wanted to send a message to Shiko Tenka, the commander of the Tlascaltec army. We knew his name from prisoners we had captured. My lord wanted Shiko Tenka to know that all we desired was peace, but that if they attacked us we would go on killing them and burning their villages.

Not finding any villagers, we had to give this message to our prisoners and send them back to him. We sent a prisoner back every day. We had sent five or six messages in this way before Shiko Tenka deigned to reply. Then he said he would drink our blood.

Just when it seemed things couldn't get any worse, the ambassadors of Lord-Who-Is-Severe came to visit us and wouldn't go away.

Lord-Who-Is-Severe didn't like it at all that we were in Tlascala and wanted to know what our intentions were. He had probably heard about the message we had sent ahead to the Tlascalteca, so it must have pleased him that we were fighting each other, although his ambassadors pretended to be very concerned about it. We should leave this wretched, poverty-stricken, backward country at once, they said. We could go to a beautiful city called Cholula, where Lord-Who-Is-Severe would see that we were properly welcomed. They added, no doubt wanting to be rid of us, that we would find it easier to get back to the coast that way.

My lord said that he never left a place until he was ready to, and he wasn't ready to, but otherwise he was very polite to them.

By this time we had begun to find out what was happening in Tlascala, because the Cempoalans had been talking to the local people and they came back and told us what had been said. It seemed that the ruling council of Tlascala was quarrelling over what to do about us. The four elders wanted to make peace, but Shiko Tenka — who, it turned out, was the son of one of these elders — was opposed to it. He said we were dangerous and the only thing to do with us was drive us out of the country. We also heard from the Cempoalans that there had been quarrelling inside the army itself, and that because of it one of the commanders had taken his troops home in the middle of a battle.

Naturally we were very interested to hear about these disputes, but we wondered, of course, what would happen to us if they made up their differences and decided that Shiko Tenka was right. It was a miserable time for us and a lot of my lord's men seemed afraid, no doubt because the attacks on us never stopped and the Tlascalan armies were so large, and however many we killed there seemed to be as many of them the next time. Many of our soldiers were very badly wounded. All of the animals were wounded, too, and the Tlascalteca had even managed to kill two of them. That frightened *me*, because I had not been sure what they were, but I could see how in the battles they fought like *teotl* and often saved us, and now I knew they were just animals and could die like anything else. And every day we were hungry and every night we were cold, because when the sun set behind those mountains all the warmth of the day vanished. I could see how dejected even my lord had become at this time. I also saw how groups of his men would come to him, usually at night, with sullen looks, and there would be talking that would soon turn angry and in the end he would send them away; and I learnt later that they had come to him demanding to be allowed to go back to the coast.

Then one day something new happened.

A long line of porters came to our camp (we were living in a temple on the top of a hill) with baskets of food. We were all so hungry we would have fallen on it without question, since the only thing we had eaten for days were some roasted squirrels, but of course my lord wanted to know who had sent it and why.

It turned out that Shiko Tenka had sent it. The four elders had ordered him to.

'Did he send a message with it?' my lord asked.

No, he had just said that it was food for human beings.

'What did he mean by that?' my lord demanded.

Apparently the elders had ordered copal to be burnt before us, in case we were not people but *teotl*, but Shiko Tenka had refused to send any.

The food — maize and eggs, and a few roasted fowls — was eaten very quickly. In a short time there wasn't a scrap left, and the dogs growled over the crumbs. We felt contented and began to hope that after this there might be peace. The Tlascalteca who had brought the food wandered about the camp looking at things and peering at us with curiosity, but they were friendly and we let them stay, partly because it gave us a good opportunity to look at *them*. They weren't armed, naturally, being only porters. They were so interested in us that they were still there the next morning.

That was when the Cempoalan leaders came to me. I had noticed them watching the porters closely the day before, but had thought it was jealousy. Now they came to me and said it wasn't right that the porters should be allowed to come and go as they wanted in our camp, peering at everything and poking it with their fingers, and they were afraid the porters had been sent to spy on us.

I could see at once how likely this was. After all, Shiko Tenka had not done what the elders wanted before, so why should he obey them now? I also thought it strange that the only message he had sent had been about the food. Perhaps, I thought, the food had been bewitched.

I went to Muluc and told him what the Cempoalans had said. He tried to dismiss it. Muluc was never interested in saving us from danger, and if it had been left to him we would all have been dead. I pointed out that the porters were still loitering about the camp when they had no reason to be, and he said it meant nothing and that when we were on the coast the local people had been so curious about us that they came to live in our camp. I lost my patience with him and said that I was going to see my lord about it whether he wanted to help or not, which meant that he had to come with me or he would have got into trouble.

My lord was on the temple platform, looking across the valley. He listened carefully, as I had known he would, and then he called two of his officers and set off walking through the camp, telling me to follow. We came to where a young porter was watching a soldier cleaning his weapons. My lord put an arm round his neck and dragged him to a room of the temple, where he began to question him.

At first the Tlascaltec denied everything. He said he had been given no orders except to bring the food. When he was asked whether it was poisoned (because this was what I had said to my lord, not wanting to mention witchcraft), he replied proudly that if Tlascalteca wanted to kill their enemies they fought them on the battlefield. Fortunately this did not satisfy my lord, who went to look for another porter to question, and the second one, when a sword was put to his throat, admitted that he had been told to watch to see whether we ate the food or not.

My lord, after this, believed what I and the Cempoalans had told

him, but Muluc became agitated and said that it was a misunderstanding and he was sure that the food had not been poisoned. He
told me to ask the second porter if it had been, and I refused
because the question had already been asked several times, and we
were arguing when my lord intervened and said he had heard enough.

I have to admit I was not prepared for what happened next.
He had all the porters gathered together in an open space, and
our men standing round them in a circle with their weapons
ready, and then he made a speech. He told the porters that Shiko
Tenka had sent them to spy on us and had sent us poisoned
food because he was not able to overcome us in battle. In order
to show Shiko Tenka that he would not overcome us by these
means either, my lord said he was going to send the porters back
to Shiko Tenka with a message Shiko Tenka could not mistake.
And this was the message.

One by one, each of them was brought forward, held by several
of our men, and his hand was cut off. They screamed terribly
as this was done to them, and wept for their hands, which were
on the ground in a heap. When all of them had had a hand cut
off, and were weeping and comforting each other, he turned them
out of the camp and chased them away.

Not all of them went back to Shiko Tenka. They were ashamed.
They stayed near by, hiding in the ruins of the villages we had
burned. I saw them when I went out with my lord on an expedition to find food. They were yellow and looked like ghosts. I
don't suppose they lived long.

There was no fighting for a while after that. The Meshica ambassadors, who had made their own camp on the next hilltop so
that they could watch us, came to see us every day. They praised
what we had done, and seemed to think we were ready to leave
Tlascala now.

My lord said he was not ready, and that when he did leave
Tlascala he would go to Cactus-on-the-Stone.

Many times the ambassadors tried to persuade him to go to

Cholula instead. It was not possible, they said, for us to go to Cactus-on-the-Stone. One day they tired of this conversation, which was always the same, and brought a number of small objects in a basket which they laid out carefully on a cloth in front of him. First, they set out a collection of feathers. There were an owl's feather, a turkey's feather, a macaw's feather, an eagle's feather and a duck's feather. They asked him which he liked best. He chose the duck's feather, although it was not as pretty as the macaw's feather. They were alarmed by this, although they pretended not to be. Then they laid out other things: seashells, coloured stones, fruits, the polished bones of animals. Each time they asked him which he liked best. All the time they were doing this they were laughing and smiling as if it was an entertainment. Finally they placed two cloaks before him. One was woven from good cotton and was decorated with a spiral pattern like the whorl of a seashell; the other was woven from a fibre which I didn't recognize, and it was dyed blue and had a thread of dark green running through it. He chose the second one. It seemed they had been expecting him to choose the first, because for a moment, when he pointed to the one he meant, they seemed bewildered. However, they laughed again, and packed all the things up in a beautiful cloth and presented them to him. He didn't want them, but he thanked the ambassadors graciously.

They were trying to find out who he was. They thought the things he chose would tell them. Then they would use witchcraft against him. But they were not able to do that, because the things he chose did not make sense to them.

I was glad, and thought that it served the Meshica right. Not that I believed he had deliberately avoided their trap. I thought he was unaware of it. He was like a soaring eagle which silly boys are trying to bring down by throwing stones.

They did not do this again, but they continued to stay close to us.

*　　*　　*

It was soon after this that Shiko Tenka made his most cowardly attempt to get rid of us. He sent his warriors by night.

I was fast asleep at my lord's side in a small room of the temple. I heard a shout in the depths of my dream, and suddenly my lord leapt up from the mat and rushed out.

I sat up, not knowing whether I was asleep or not, and heard running feet and shouts. The dogs were barking like mad creatures. I put on my clothes and went to find out what was happening.

The moon was full and you could see quite clearly. The field of maize stalks at the bottom of the hill was thrashing about like a net full of fish. Tlascalteca had obviously been hiding there, waiting to attack us; our sentries had seen them and we were fighting them hand to hand.

I knew we would win this battle because the enemy had foolishly counted on surprising us and there were not many of them. Indeed, they seemed to have lost heart already and some were running away over the plain. But I was worried by this attack: I thought, if Shiko Tenka tries to kill us by sorcery or poison and then, when we discover it, he sends his warriors to kill us by night, what will he do next?

In this I was wrong. He did not do anything else. He sent his messengers to ask for peace.

The city of Tlascala seemed very grand to me, but that was because the largest city I had ever seen at that time was Cempoala. The Tlascalteca were proud of their city but at the same time they kept apologizing for it. They were poor, they said, and they lacked all sorts of things because the Meshica prevented them from trading. Also the Meshica sent their armies every year and took Tlascala's young men to give to Hummingbird. All this was because they would not pay tribute to the Meshica. If they did, they would have a quiet life and salt to put in their stew, but they would not do it.

We went to the palace to meet the four elders. My lord had a fever, he had tossed and turned in his bed all night, but when

I tried to persuade him not to go he would not listen to me. The four elders were waiting for us in the garden. Shiko Tenka was also there. He was a heavy man with a scarred face. He was wearing warrior dress and holding a beaked helmet under one arm. I didn't like the look of him.

Only one of the elders spoke. His name was Maxicatzin. He said we were the bravest enemies the Tlascalteca had ever fought against and they were proud to make peace with us. He said they were not in the habit of making peace with their enemies, but rather fought them to the death, and that was why Tlascala had no salt, but in our case they were making an exception since we were clearly not like other human beings. He was not sure, in fact, whether we were human beings or *teotl*, but in either case he offered us friendship.

My lord was pleased, but he was glancing at Shiko Tenka, who hadn't said anything yet.

When Shiko Tenka did speak, it was like waiting for pebbles to drop into a well. He measured out each word as if it was costing him blood. He said that Tlascala had got used to being invaded by enemies who pretended to be friends. They gave all sorts of excuses for being on Tlascalan soil but it always turned out that they were in league with the Meshica. Naturally, he had thought the same of us. He pointed out that the Meshica ambassadors visited us every day, which also made it look as if we were friendly with the Meshica, and this of course was true.

My lord wasn't happy. He shifted around on his cushion. But then Shiko Tenka said that he now accepted that he had made a mistake. He would like to hear why we *had* come, however, since that was still not clear to him.

My lord smiled deeply at this, and I saw that it was a question he wanted to answer. He made a wonderful speech in reply. He praised Tlascala and its brave people, and said that he had been sent here by a great lord to put right injustices, and that the injustice done to Tlascala by the Meshica was the worst he had ever heard of. Then he talked about Cempoala, and how we had helped the Cempoalans drive out the Meshica tax collectors.

'This is how we help our friends,' he said, 'and this is how we would like to help you.'

The four elders were sitting up with their eyes wide open by this time, although it seemed to me that Shiko Tenka's eyes had, if anything, got narrower.

My lord now told them that their years of struggle against the Meshica were over. 'You have never been able to defeat them by yourselves,' he said, 'brave though you are, because Lord-Who-Is-Severe has too many armies. But now everything has changed. With our help, with our miraculous weapons, you can throw down the pride of Cactus-on-the-Stone. Here is your chance of revenge and glory.'

The elders were very excited, although, because of their dignity, they could only applaud by tapping their *pulque* cups. My lord's face was white from the effort he had made. Shiko Tenka looked like a cloud getting ready to rain.

The elders gave the only reply you could expect them to make at that moment. They said they needed to think about it.

I knew they would accept, because it would be stupid to refuse, but it took a lot of talking and bargaining for us to get there. Shiko Tenka took part in the talking, but I could tell he didn't like what had happened. When my lord, who also seemed aware of this, asked him directly what he thought of the alliance we were making, he didn't answer. All he said was that the will of the four elders was his will.

We were more than twenty days making all the arrangements. When finally we left the city of Tlascala, a whole host of Tlascaltec warriors, porters and guides came with us. My lord gave permission for the Cempoalans who wanted to go home to do so, and most of them did, looking very pleased about it. First to leave were the *batab*'s son and nephew, and nobody was sorry to see them go since they had been nothing but trouble.

The Meshica ambassadors, who had come to the city with us, went home as well. We suddenly realized they weren't there. They must have packed up and slunk off by night. They would have known about the alliance, of course, and I suppose they hurried back to tell Lord-Who-Is-Severe about it.

We were going to Cholula first. This was in spite of the fact that everyone said we shouldn't. The four elders said it was dangerous: Cholula was a large city, the shrine of a great *teotl*, it was full of priests and spies and was in the hand of Lord-Who-Is-Severe. When they learned that we were going there because the Meshica ambassadors had suggested it, they were even more alarmed. They thought it was a trap.

'That is a good reason for going there,' replied my lord. He explained that, if we didn't take up the invitation, the Meshica would think it was because we were afraid. He wanted to show them that we were not afraid of anything.

For once, I thought my lord was wrong. His reason for going to Cholula seemed to me a very bad reason, and I agreed with the four elders. However, no one asked me what my opinion was. As it turned out, in Cholula I was given another chance to serve my lord, and if I hadn't been there it might have been the end of everything.

All the time we were in Tlascala I had been thinking that we should get out of it as soon as possible. I didn't like the ring of mountains, which made me feel shut in. When we eventually did leave, I was glad to be going but unhappy about the large Tlascaltec army we were taking with us. It seemed to me it would be easy for them to kill us all as we slept, or lead us into an ambush or put us on a path through a ravine where they could roll rocks down on us from above.

I didn't mention any of these fears to my lord, because he had worked very hard and fought a lot of battles to win the friendship of the Tlascalteca, and I knew he wouldn't be pleased. In addition to which, although I had learnt some of his language, it wasn't enough and I still had to talk to him through Muluc, who, I suspected, very often misrepresented what I said. So I kept quiet about what I was afraid would happen. But in the end

I was right. I was only wrong about where the danger would come from.

Cholula was certainly a great city, and grander than Tlascala. The streets were all paved, and the buildings were tall and beautifully painted. The temple of the great *teotl* towered over everything and his likeness was on many walls and plinths. My lord was impressed by the place and pleased with all sorts of things, in particular the robes of the priests, which were decorated with small crosses. This interested him very much. But what I noticed were the stones. Piled up on the roofs in little heaps.

After we had been taken to the place where we were to stay, I spoke to Muluc about these stones on the rooftops. He hadn't noticed them but said he thought it was not unusual to have stones on a roof and why was I making a fuss about it. When I insisted that he tell my lord, my lord replied that he saw nothing to worry about, either. At least, Muluc said that was what he said.

I didn't let it go at that. I'd learnt that if it was an important matter, I might have to try many times in order to get through the obstructions that Muluc put in my way. I drew my lord's attention to the narrowness of the streets, the height of the buildings and the way many streets were blocked off by the wall of a temple, because there were as many temples in that city as houses. I said it would be very easy for the Cholula to trap us in the streets, where we would not be able to find our way out, and kill us with the stones they had collected for the purpose.

My lord laughed. He said something (or Muluc said he did) about it being a woman's nature to be fearful, and that his men could deal with a few stones dropped from rooftops. But he thanked me for warning him, and told me to continue to keep my eyes open.

At my lord's request, the Tlascalteca had made their camp outside the town. They were old enemies of the Cholula and he thought there would be trouble if they came in with us. The Tlascalteca resented this. Nevertheless, a few of them had come to visit us in our quarters, carrying their weapons upside-down as a sign of peace to the townspeople. I talked to them. I still didn't completely trust them, but I trusted them more than I trusted the Cholula, and one thing was quite clear: the Tlascalteca and the Cholula weren't going to join forces against us.

The Tlascalteca I spoke to had seen the stones as well. They had also seen barricades of cane and other things that puzzled them in the streets. They said they did not know why they were there, but that we should leave the town straight away in case some mischief was being planned.

I repeated this, through Muluc, to my lord, who said, as he'd said in Tlascala when the Meshica ambassadors urged him to leave, that he never left a place until he was ready to.

Everything seemed peaceful in Cholula for the first two days, and the people brought us plenty of food. Then on the third day they didn't bring any, and when my lord sent for the chief men to come to him to explain why there was no food they could not be found. This made my lord understand that the danger was real, and he asked the Tlascaltec commanders to come to him again and told them to send some of their people into the streets to find out what was happening. Muluc, naturally, maintained that there was nothing wrong and that the city was probably preparing for a festival, which would explain the barricades and why the leaders were busy. I asked him what, in that case, the stones were for, and he couldn't answer.

We waited and waited for the Tlascalteca to come back with their report, but they didn't. In the end, realizing that if anything was going to be found out I would have to find it out myself, I slipped out and went into the town.

Although there were numerous priests in the streets and precincts there weren't many ordinary people about, which in itself made me suspicious. I spoke to several women who were coming from the market, and who did not want to talk to me because I was a stranger, but I went on walking beside them until they had to speak. They all said the same thing: a lot of people had left the city because they had heard there was a large army of Tlascalteca, accompanied by devils, on the way. When I asked about the priests, they said that the priests could not leave because they had to serve the *teotl*.

I went on walking around the town. Everybody looked at me sideways, and some people went indoors when they saw me coming along the street. I passed the precinct of the great temple, which I recognized by the two enormous carvings of feathered serpents that flanked the central stairway. I went inside to have a look around, and there indeed I saw several long pieces of wood that had been fashioned together to make a screen or barrier. I was going to investigate further, but a priest appeared and drove me away, telling me to mind my own business.

In the market I pretended to be looking at things to buy, so that I could listen to what people were saying. However, they stopped talking when I was close to them, or quickly changed the subject, which suggested to me that they had been talking about something they didn't want me to hear.

I left the market and walked down a narrow, crooked street that had a little stream running down the middle of it, in a paved channel. Never having seen anything like this before, I was interested in it and decided to follow the stream to see where it came from, because my lord had said to me that if ever I came across a source of water I must tell him about it. I followed the stream almost to the edge of the town, on the opposite side to where we had come in. As I was walking along, an old woman in a house I had passed called out to me and asked what I was doing.

The street had become just a dusty track, and the houses also were not much to look at. They were made of mud, not even plastered, and with just a thin layer of thatch. There were a few fowls pecking at the ground. Apart from that, the street had seemed quite empty until the old woman called out.

I stopped, and greeted her politely. She seemed poor, but she was dignified and her clothes were mended and clean.

She asked me again what I was doing. I said that I had been

to the market and I was now on my way back to the place where I lived.

She said, 'You are going the wrong way. You must go that way,' and pointed down the street, the way I'd come.

I said, 'How do you know where I live, mother?' to which she replied that she knew who I was, that I had come with the Tlascalteca and the devils to speak for them, the whole town had been full of it, and that I was a fool to think I could make anyone believe I was a native of Cholula, speaking the way I did and dressed the way I was dressed.

After that she laughed in a kindly way, because I suppose I looked downcast, and invited me into her house.

It was, as I'd thought it would be, very plain. There were a few pots on the walls, a shrine in the corner, and a stick was smouldering in the hearth. A number of empty baskets were stacked up against one wall.

She offered me refreshment, and I accepted because I had become thirsty from walking around. She started to talk to me. I listened at first out of respect for her age.

She told me that her husband had died twelve years ago when a rock fell on his head as he was going through a gorge. The night before his death she had dreamed it, she said, but she had been unable to persuade him not to travel through the gorge that day. He had said that if it was his fate to die, he would die. Now she lived with her son, her daughter and her daughter's husband, and they all made baskets and sold them in the market. That was where they were now, at the market, and I had probably seen them if I had come from there.

I thought I had, I said, to be polite.

She said, 'You shouldn't wander about the town on your own.'

I said, 'Is it dangerous, mother?'

'No,' she said, 'but you may be taken for a prostitute.'

I was annoyed, but didn't say anything. She laughed again, and said I must excuse her because of her age. Then she said, calmly, 'I have the seeing power, you know. My husband's death was not the first thing I had foreseen. People come to me when they want to know what their fate holds, and often I can help them.'

I wanted to leave at this point, because talk about fate always makes me angry. People are so stupid about it, they tie themselves in knots and end up afraid to do anything. But it would have been impolite to leave just then, and a moment later she said, to my relief, 'So I did know who you were as soon as I saw you, and although it's true that everybody was talking about it yesterday, I would still have known who you were.'

I smiled and said something or other, and wished she would stop looking at me in the way she was, very intently. A moment later I heard her say, in a tone of horror, 'It will be terrible!'

I must have stared at her. 'What will be terrible?' I managed to ask.

'I see what will happen.' She put her hands over her eyes as if to protect them.

'What do you see, mother?' I asked her gently.

'Killing. So much killing. I see the bodies piled in heaps like maize cobs. I see the stones falling from their places.'

That I should have wandered through the whole city, to hear the truth in this unlikely place!

'When?' I demanded.

'I cannot tell.'

I got up from the floor, pulling my shawl around me. I knew I must get back as quickly as possible.

'Daughter, don't leave yet!' she cried, and put out a hand to stop me.

'I must leave right away,' I said.

'The evil may still be averted.' She began to talk very rapidly, in her anxiety to persuade me. 'Don't be like my husband, who believed that nothing can be done and brought his death on himself. Great danger surrounds you, but you do not have to go back to them. You can stay here. You will be safe. No one will find you.'

'*Here?*' I said. 'What would I do?'

She looked helpless. Then she flung out her hands and said, 'My son needs a wife. You could marry him.'

I thanked her and rushed out of the doorway. There was still no one in the street. I ran all the way through the town until I reached our quarters, and I just had breath to gasp out to my lord the crime that was planned against us.

He only did what was necessary. If we hadn't killed them, they would have killed us. He wasn't to blame for what happened afterwards, which was that the Tlascalteca came in and looted the bodies. They were supposed to be cleaning up, because the place where it had been done was awash with blood. Before we left, he ordered the temples to be burnt. It was impossible to burn all of them because there were so many, but I saw the great temple, the shrine of the city's *teotl*, in flames and the roof crashing down into the sanctuary.

After that, we set out again for Cactus-on-the-Stone.

Lord-Who-Is-Severe sent us his ambassadors on the second day. They were very angry that we had killed so many of the leading men of Cholula. My lord explained that we had discovered a plot to murder us, and when they said that was impossible because Cholula was in the hand of Lord-Who-Is-Severe, who knew everything that happened in it, my lord replied that in that case Lord-Who-Is-Severe must have been behind the plot. They seemed shocked by this, and went away.

On the following days, Lord-Who-Is-Severe sent more messengers, but they did not talk about Cholula. They put all their efforts into trying to persuade us to turn back from Cactus-on-the-Stone. They said that the roads were too difficult because of the unusually cold weather, that the journey was dangerous, and so on. At other times they said that Lord-Who-Is-Severe was too poor to entertain us, that his storehouses did not have enough maize or his ponds enough fish. However, he was still sending us presents of cotton cloaks, *kukul* plumes and gold. It was obvious that he would do anything to keep us from getting to Cactus-on-the-Stone but could not hit on the right way to do it, and once he even sent a message offering us whatever we wanted if only we would stay away. I could have told the ambassadors myself how silly this was, but I faithfully translated everything that was said, and my lord's patient replies.

They had told us the truth about one thing: the roads *were* difficult. We had to find our way between two very high mountains. Both were white, as the mountain had been at the start of our journey many months earlier, and to my amazement there was thick smoke coming from the top of one of the peaks. It looked as if the mountain itself was on fire. I was walking beside my lord in case he needed me, and I saw how struck he was by it, too. He ordered some of his men to climb the mountain and find out what caused the smoke. I thought we would have to wait for them to return, but we went on. It was getting very cold again. The paths were steep and slippery, and once or twice we couldn't take the path we wanted to because it had been blocked with branches. Our Tlascaltec guides said the Meshica had done it, and that they wanted to ambush us.

As we came over the pass between the two mountains I saw Cactus-on-the-Stone lying below us in the valley, and it was more astonishing than any story I had heard about it. The bridges linking the city to the land were so long and slender that I couldn't imagine how they had been made. All around it, the water was the colour of *kukul* feathers. I could see dark specks moving on the lake, leaving a wisp of white behind them, and supposed they were canoes, and it seemed to me that there were also larger objects like islands that were moving, too, but I told myself that that couldn't be.

We all stood there for quite a long time looking down at Cactus-on-the-Stone. At last my lord gave a sort of sigh and kicked his animal with his heels, and we began to go down from the mountain.

The last ambassador sent to us by Lord-Who-Is-Severe was his own nephew.

We were travelling around the shore of the lake by this time, and there were many cities there, with fields and orchards. The name of Lord-Who-Is-Severe's nephew was Cacamatzin and he was the lord of the most important of these cities, Texcoco. He invited us to visit him in Texcoco later, after we had made ourselves comfortable in Cactus-on-the-Stone. It was the first time anyone speaking on behalf of Lord-Who-Is-Severe had accepted the fact that we really were going to Cactus-on-the-Stone, and my lord was so pleased that he gave him a pearl.

We walked all that day. The lake was full of bays and inlets, islands and channels, and we hadn't been able to see the whole of it since we came down from the mountain. In fact the closer we got to it, the more confused I was about where we were, and it didn't help that for a lot of the time we couldn't see Cactus-on-the-Stone at all.

In the evening we crossed two wide channels to a town that was built on the water. The houses stood on wooden poles that went down into the lake. Canoes were moving among them, under the houses, bringing fish or coming back empty, I supposed, from the city. My lord said we would stop there for the night, and we were able to use a lot of the houses to sleep in because the townspeople had left. They were frightened by us, perhaps. As darkness fell, the lake lit up with what looked like fireflies. They were lights in the canoes that were still moving across the water.

No one wanted to sleep, knowing we were going to enter Cactus-on-the-Stone the next day. My lord did not come to bed until very late. I could see a red glow on the lake, which disturbed me because it looked like blood, but I realized later that it was caused by the fire of the temple braziers which the Meshica kept burning all night. When dawn came, the first canoes were already gliding through the mist.

We stepped out proudly along the stone bridge. It was wide enough for six of us to walk abreast. As we went along I noticed the wooden sections the unfriendly governor had told us about, which the Meshica could take up if they didn't want enemies in the city to get out, or enemies outside to get in.

The lake was crowded with canoes, because the Meshica had come out to see us. We took no notice of them, but went on marching with our banners floating in the breeze and our weapons held high and flashing in the sun.

At a place where a second bridge joined it, the bridge we were on became quite wide, and here many Meshica nobles had gathered to welcome us. I was pleased to see they were honouring my lord in this way until I realized that every one of them was going to make a speech, and that all the speeches had to be translated. Then of course my lord had to reply. All of this took so long that when we set off again it was late in the afternoon and my head was going round from all the words and from standing in the sun with the dazzle off the water.

Soon we were in sight of the wharves and houses of the city. And then my heart almost stopped, and a murmur went all down our line, for, at the place where the stone bridge launched itself out on the water, a great plumed chair like a throne, with a host of attendants, was setting out. Lord-Who-Is-Severe was coming to meet us.

I was suddenly filled with dread. I could see, without looking at them, the flute-players with their white-ringed eyes and owl-feather bracelets, and I heard their music more clearly with every step we took. Already I could smell the copal. Moment by moment it came nearer, the moment when my lord would speak, and then Muluc would speak, and then I must speak. The moment when I must raise my eyes to the face of Lord-Who-Is-Severe.

The music grew louder, the scent of copal grew stronger. My eyes were down and I was looking at the shapes of the paving stones, the glint of the water and the strange feet of my lord's animal. Then I felt a slowing in the pace of everyone I was walking with, and I knew the moment had come. Ahead of me was the feathered throne. I could see, without looking at it, how it glittered. I felt the flute-players and the incense-bearers stand aside to let it pass. I saw flowers fall on the ground in a rain. In the corner of my eye I glimpsed my lord swing himself down from his animal: but he was shadowy, it was all shadowy, except for the *tlatoani*, who was surrounded by light and could not be looked at.

I knew I must raise my eyes.

IV
Behold, the City

I

Afterwards the thing he remembered most vividly was the sandals. The emperor had golden sandals.

Perhaps that was why his feet weren't allowed to touch the ground. The attendants strewed flowers ankle-deep over the stones, then lifted him out of the chair he rode in as if he were a doll.

A slender, well-framed man of middle height, perhaps forty years of age. An intelligent face. Dignity in the face, dignity in every fibre of him. Something else, too. Something just beyond the grasp.

The Captain dismounts.

His feet touch the ground and the emperor's feet touch the flowers that cover the ground at exactly the same moment. On the emperor's feet are golden sandals.

Hand to his breast, steel helmet doffed, the Captain bows. It is his first bow since he landed in the country. He has been saving it up: he does not intend to bow often. His officers are all bowing behind him, or at least had better be (Alvarado is not to be relied on in these matters). He can't see whether the emperor is bowing, but he presumes not.

Muctezuma speaks. His voice is pitched a little high. The two interpreters who are always with the Captain, and appear to hate each other, translate. The emperor has said, 'It gives us great joy to welcome such noble visitors to our realm. You must be tired from your long journey. We hope we can recompense you for the great trouble you have taken.'

The Captain appreciates irony and has a good command of it himself. He replies that no trouble would be too great for the pleasure of meeting this mighty sovereign and his people, and hunts – fruitlessly – for a flicker in the eyes of his host.

Then, on an impulse (impulses have always served him well), he steps forward to embrace the emperor in Spanish fashion.

There is a swift movement, he is knocked off balance, there is a stink of resin and feathers in his nostrils. His men growl.

Gerónimo, the castaway Spaniard who interprets for him, says nervously that he thinks the ruler's body is sacred and must not be touched.

'You should have warned me,' the Captain rebukes him. The man has a sort of soft reticence that is not Spanish. He has a whiff of the savage still about him, too. Soon he will not be needed because Marina, who is very intelligent, is learning *cristiano*.

The emperor is lifted back into his chair (*someone* is allowed to touch him!), the Captain gets on to his horse again and, after some fussing over the order of the procession, they cross the last wooden drawbridge and enter the city's outskirts. The breeze drops, now that they are off the lake, and the Captain's orange banner droops lifelessly.

We are walking into a perfectly devised trap.

The cannon thunder that night.

And why not? Never mind that gunpowder is precious (though an idea is already tickling the Captain's mind about how it might, possibly, be replenished). There are times when a show is what counts. And hasn't he something to celebrate? Even Hannibal didn't have to *fight* his way across the Alps.

Six weighty tubes of iron are laboured into position around the sprawling palace that is the Spanish quarters, under the curious eyes of Meshica who are pretending not to watch. Each one points down a road along which an attack could, if things go wrong, be launched.

As the smoke lifts after the firing of the first falconet, Indians are seen fleeing in panic for their homes and the priests come out on to the temple platforms carrying incense. After the second gun is fired, the priests begin to chant. After the sixth, there is not a sound to be heard in the whole city. Then a dog being fattened for the table whimpers, and a horse calmly lifts its tail and drops a soft, sweet-smelling mound of dung, plop, on to the emperor's paving.

Later, priests come out and collect the dung, very carefully, in a copper pan and take it away to one of the temples.

The Captain makes a note of the date. It is the eighth of November, 1519.

'The king I serve is a very great monarch, and has ordered me to visit you,' the Captain informs his host at their first interview.

'He has heard of us?'

'Certainly. Many years ago he received reports of Your Majesty and this beautiful realm.'

'What is the name of your lord?' enquires the emperor.

'He is called King Charles.'

He sees his host searching for meaning in the strange word 'Charles' and finding none.

'It is puzzling that we have not heard of him.'

'That is easily explained, since his realm is on the other side of the ocean.'

'Nevertheless, news travels as readily in one direction as the other, we suppose.'

'I imagine the reason Your Majesty has not heard of him is that the canoes of your people are not designed to travel such great distances as our ships.'

'That may be so.'

Muctezuma is wearing a short cotton cloak richly embroidered with featherwork and gold filigree. His brown arms are encased in bracelets of embossed gold. A heavy jade pectoral, fringed with tiny golden bells, hangs on his breast. On his head is a diadem of iridescent green feathers each as long as a man's forearm. Pearls are stitched into the thick, throne-like cushion on which he sits. The cushion rests on a woven grass mat that covers a third of the large, shadowy, tapestry-hung room, around whose edges hover slaves, courtiers and attendant dwarves. All have bare feet. The dwarves make it seem eerily like a European court, but it is not, for the Captain's haunches are resting on the mat unsupported by a cushion and he is obliged to cross his legs, which is uncomfortable and makes him feel like a woman.

'Tell me more about your king,' commands Muckety.

In well-rehearsed words, the Captain begins to draw a portrait of his sovereign that is calculated to inspire awe: his might, his mildness, his overarching wisdom, his passion for justice, his love of his subjects, even the lowliest, his goodness and magnanimity . . . but the emperor interrupts him.

'What colours does he like?'

'*Colours?*'

Is he being laughed at? No, the emperor is perfectly serious. Is even looking at him quite intently.

'Red and blue.' (Some reply has to be made.)

The emperor considers this, then, after an interval, asks, 'What food does he like to eat?'

The Captain bites back an angry reply. 'Venison and other game,' he says as pleasantly as he is able. 'I believe he is fond of roast suckling pig. On Fridays, of course, he eats only fish.'

The interpreters have trouble with this. It's the Fridays, he realizes. They don't have Friday here. The brutal thought that shortly they will, which he finds in his head, has perhaps been put there by Pedro de Alvarado, sitting beside him.

'We, too, enjoy venison and meat that is hunted,' says the emperor. 'We invite you to accompany us when we go hunting.'

The Captain is glad to accept. Hunting presents an opportunity to show off Spanish skill with weapons. Also, anything that will reveal the emperor's nature to him is welcome. Then, before his host can ask another ridiculous question, he returns to his subject. He says that kings and princes count themselves fortunate to be the vassals of the monarch he serves.

He is not sure, when he says this, whether the Indians understand the concept of vassalage. However, from Muckety's next remark it seems they have a good enough grasp of it.

'In the time of our grandfather's grandfather, our people paid tribute to a city of this valley and were in the hand of its ruler. Tenochtitlan was then a humble village. Later, we fought a war against that city and our *teotl* Lord Hummingbird gave us the victory. We made war against other neighbouring cities, and we continued to make war until we had conquered all the valley and beyond it. Now we take tribute from all Anahuac, and Anahuac is in our hand.'

'You don't take tribute from Tlascala,' notes the Captain.

'Tlascala!' The emperor laughs. 'We could conquer Tlascala in a day. But if we did, where could we send our warriors for training?'

For the second time that morning, the Captain bites his lip. An insult to his allies is an insult to him. He lets it go.

'Do you play *patolli*?' The emperor tactfully changes the subject. He flicks his fingers and an object is brought to him by a dwarf. It's a board of tawny polished wood, somewhat smaller than a chessboard, and inlaid in it with a perfection of craftsmanship that gives the Captain pause are squares of a darker wood that make the form of a cross. He pauses at that, too.

'I do not know the game, Your Majesty.'

'It is a favourite pastime of ours. We will teach you.'

The cross beckons him. He cannot refuse it. 'Among us, Your Majesty, this shape has great significance. It is a symbol of our religion. I hope to have opportunities to speak to you on the subject.'

'We shall be pleased to hold such conversations.'

'I think Your Majesty will find what I have to say very interesting.' He ignores Olmedo's look. 'We worship a God who, out of love for us, made Himself flesh.'

'We also have a *teotl*-made-flesh,' remarks the emperor. 'We call him the Lord of the Near. He is made flesh every year at Toxcatl. You may hear his music outside the palace now, if you listen. He is playing the fourth of his flutes. It is beautiful, is it not?'

'Your Majesty –'

'I think we have talked long enough, today.'

The audience is over. The Captain gets to his feet with as good a grace as he can manage. The light strikes his eyes harshly as he comes out of the royal palace.

He has no idea what to do, now that he's got here.

The Spaniards are shown the city.

It is breathtaking. How can such weighty masses of stone, the labyrinthine palaces, the mighty temple-pyramids, the broad paved terraces and plazas, the dizzy cliffs of stairway – how can they seem so light, how can they seem to float on the water?

There is water everywhere, observes the Captain. Canals. The city is built on the lake (how? who taught them to do that?) and the lake lives on inside it, furnishes its pathways, veins and arteries, its digestive system. (The canoes, ceaselessly ferrying goods to and fro. Including fresh water, because, as has been explained to him, the water of the lake is salt. He will remember that. Also removing waste. Human manure in one of the canoes. Being taken to the vegetable plots. A valuable resource. He held his nose but admired the principle: everything used.)

Markets! He has never seen such a market as they have to the north of the priests' quarter. Every conceivable thing to be had there, including blocks of greyish stone the size of your fist, used in cooking they said but he can't believe it, and slaves, and sixty different kinds of the peppers they can't live without, and feathers, likewise – piled up in pyramids, again very neatly (not the slaves, of course, the slaves were bound in an orderly row), and each commodity in a street or lane of its own in that bewildering market, and right at the end, next to the sellers of gold dust which made his palms sweat (sold in hollow quills of various length, he wanted to know for how much but how can the value of gold be measured?), sat magistrates specially appointed to hear disputes arising out of the market's business. The Captain cannot but admire.

He has a lawyer's mind, although to see him in a crisis you wouldn't think it. The drawing up of legal documents in one dusty office after another occupied many of his formative years. If, now, he can't imagine how he stuck at it, all that pen-pushing instilled in him a deep respect for due process. He sees it here. There is much he respects here.

These are cultured people. There's no doubt about it. It has even occurred to him that in some ways they may be more cultured than Spaniards. Courtesy, for example, is carried to a degree that is a form of art. He is beginning to realize what a mistake he made in attempting to embrace the emperor. Ceremony, too. That the emperor's feet may not touch the ground is only one brick in a wall that separates the ruler from the rest of humanity. He must not be seen to eat. A screen is placed in front of him when the first of countless dishes is brought from the royal kitchens. He never wears the same suit of clothes twice – not because it is unbecoming, but because it is *defiling*. He *must not be looked in the face*. On this matter he has made an exception for Spaniards, as he had to, since otherwise he would have had to kill them all.

He yet may.

The Captain raises his eyes, shading them against the glare, to the temple which overlooks the palace in which they lodge. Yesterday he went up the staircase, with a dozen good men behind him, to the twin shrines at the top. Each was a slaughterhouse. Fresh blood lay on the tiled floor, so that when he turned away quickly he almost slipped on it. A vivid pile of flesh, still warm, in a stone bowl held by an idol. Jellied gouts of blood on the face, if it could be called such, of the malformed thing they worshipped. They do this to other human beings – not even

195

their enemies, but to their own people. He knows the details, they have been made clear to him. The victim is thrown backwards over a stone, a priest holds each limb and a fifth priest cuts the heart out. That was what was in the stone bowl. The heart.

Nor was this the end of it. The flesh was eaten. He has covertly looked for it in the market, but was not able to distinguish any among the unfamiliar meats and unfamiliar ways of cutting them. It was possible – he supposed it was even inevitable – that the emperor himself ate human flesh.

This last thought was too much, for the emperor was standing beside him. The Captain's body convulsed in a shudder and he made for the fresh air, and that was when his foot went from under him and he was saved by the quick arm of Sandoval.

He looks at the temple now and a rage rises in him that Spaniards have to eat their innocent bread in the shadow of this vileness, that God's sun doesn't touch their skins until it has climbed above the hellish stairway. Then the rage ebbs and leaves behind it a sense of desolation. Yesterday from the summit of the pyramid he looked down on the whole bright, threaded city, saw how the cobalt lake lapped its edges and the causeways held it like a jewel suspended by three slender chains to the land, and the beauty of it entered his heart like a sword.

'Your Majesty, I must tell you that the rituals your people observe – the tearing out of hearts, the eating of flesh – I must tell you that I find them shocking,' says the Captain. 'I cannot understand how a people so cultivated and intelligent can perform such terrible deeds.'

'Do you not offer sacrifice to your *teotl*?' the emperor asks.

'No. At least, not of that kind.'

'Then of what kind?'

'For instance, some of us mortify our flesh.'

'What does that mean?'

The practices of certain ascetics are described to him, not without problems of translation.

'I do not see the difference between this and cutting the ears,' says the emperor eventually.

'It is quite different, Your Majesty.'

'Why?'

'. . . because . . .'

'Because the point is not the blood but the pain,' elucidates Olmedo.

'Your *teotl* does not require blood, but wishes you to feel pain? How strange.'

There are solaces. There's the woman.

The Captain left a wife in Cuba and is glad he did. A campaign is not the place for a Spanish gentlewoman, although a few of his officers thought otherwise and are now rueing it. In any case, a man needs to keep more than his sword-arm free. The Captain has always striven to do so, but every life has its salting of defeats. He counts his marriage as one. A youthful indiscretion, turned into a millstone by the girl's family. The difficulties compounded by the interference of Diego Velásquez, to whom the family appealed. The Captain's relations with the Governor of Cuba have a long history, and include episodes that are not talked about even among his friends.

But now there is the woman, Marina. He noticed her right away. It wasn't her beauty, although she is pleasing to his eye and well-bosomed. Nor that she walks like a queen, a thing to be wondered at when she has been a slave for more than half her life. No, it was something that happened on the first day, in the little stone plaza at Potonchan surrounded by gaudily painted houses, plumed chiefs, wreaths of incense. Twenty native women with their heads bowed and their hands nicely clasped before their waists, and, among them, *her*, whose head, yes, was bowed, but not as low as the others and not for as long, either, because she raised it for an instant and looked straight at him. At him, the Captain. It was only a moment, she didn't meet his eye, but he knew it for a moment of insubordination and sensed that she had never accepted her lowly place. That was why he believed the story she told, which was far-fetched enough. Yes, there was something remarkable about her. So when it turned out that she spoke two languages and could get them out of the impasse they had come to, he wasn't completely surprised.

Now she is his woman. She is also his interpreter, his guide to the customs of the country, and at times his adviser. Is this not something to marvel at? What would he do without her? (What *did* he do without her, when he gave her to Portocarrero? But that was politic, and not of long duration.)

He requires a lot of her, he has the sense to realize. Actually, he requires everything. For that reason he has given her a servant of her own, a Tlascalan girl. And he gives her presents. Earrings, bracelets. She loves these trinkets. Presumably she has never had any. She has never had anything. The happiness with which she gazes at his latest gift touches him. (He contrasts it with his wife's insatiability in the matter of presents.) He enjoys giving her things; he feels an expansiveness of his soul as he does it. A tenderness. He knows, at the same time, that he is ensuring she will never leave him.

'Come and sit here,' he says, patting the straw mattress, for she is squatting Indian-fashion in the corner of the room, watching him without appearing to watch him, waiting for his command.

It is the middle of the afternoon, and nothing much to be done with it until the heat has gone out of the day. A man deserves a rest. And Adam must be served. Marina rises to her feet in that fluid way they have, that no Spanish woman could manage, all in one movement as if by an impulse of the earth, and crosses the stone floor to him. He notices again that she is tall for a woman, almost as tall as he is, but that it does not inhibit her movements. Her body sways slightly, crossing the floor. She's wearing a gold bracelet he gave her. Her hair, black as a raven, is tightly braided. She smiles at him, a smile at once docile and expectant.

He indicates the space at his side and she sits, placing a slender, long-fingered hand on his knee, pressing it (they are strong, those brown fingers), divining his needs, not that they need much divining he supposes. Adam is just about bursting out of his confines already. His hand goes to her breast, high and firm under the embroidered blouse, and lingers there, while the heat of her body communicates itself to his palm, before withdrawing to thrust itself under the fabric and taste flesh, warm yet slightly cool, oddly muscular, moist, living. His mouth falls on her mouth and it's like diving into a deep, fronded pool – he surfaces breathless and flings off his sword-belt and pushes her back to lie on the straw. The cotton skirt has risen to her knees; he pulls it up further and runs his thumb along the crack between her thighs, gently, to the top. She sighs and turns her head on the mattress. She's all his. She's all his and, unbuttoning himself with suddenly clumsy fingers, he takes her.

For a while, he dozes in a little pool of sunlight that comes from an aperture high in the wall.

Music comes to his ears. Outside in the street, the boy is playing his flute again. It sets his teeth on edge. In Seville, you could give him a coin to go away.

Marina stirs under him. The movement, the renewed intimate contact with her body and its orifices, the animal warmth of the day, combine to inflame him and he's hungry once more, definitely hungry.

Five days pass. Muctezuma has made his guests welcome. He has given them, for their accommodation, the palace of Axayacatl, built by his father, adjacent to the great temple and facing his own palace across the plaza. He provides food in plenty, bedding and firewood, and servants to wait on them. There is no hint in his manner of the lengths to which he went to dissuade them from coming.

'My heart is glad to see you,' he says each morning when the Captain visits him, and at each visit he showers the Captain and his officers with gifts. The Spaniards have never seen such munificence and are confused. They admire and suspect it. They find themselves despising the giver for not knowing the worth of what he gives. The emperor's generosity makes them feel small, for which they resent him. They speculate over how much more gold he has tucked away.

While the Captain and his officers inspect the city, the common soldiers are confined to their quarters. They are bored. One morning, a scuffle breaks out. An artilleryman careers backwards into a section of wall that appears to have been freshly plastered. It receives his weight with a hollow sound.

The man who fell against the wall picks himself up, sees that his opponent is more interested in the wall than in him, and turns to inspect it. He taps it with the handle of his knife. Together the two men tap out the area of what, clearly, used to be a doorway.

They don't need to talk. They know exactly what they are going to do. Stored with the baggage they find an axe, crowbar and hammer and set to work. Their friends join them. In no time at all the door has a jagged hole in the middle of it.

A man squeezes through the gap and they all hear his intake of breath. There is a metallic clatter as something falls, and a curse. Then through the gap comes a hand, holding something. It is a slightly dented gold drinking vessel.

At this moment Pedro de Alvarado walks past. He takes in at once the broken door, the cup, the men whose hands are starting to reach towards it. He grabs the nearest soldier by his hair.

'Fetch Hernán,' he orders.

Under the Captain's eye, since it is now too late to do anything else, the remainder of the panel is removed and laid tidily on the floor. The soldier who had gone through the gap is ordered to come out again, and the Captain steps across the threshold into Muctezuma's treasure room.

It is roughly six paces in length and four in width, and from every surface winks gold. Golden masks, golden plates and bowls, golden ear-pendants and breast-ornaments, golden bracelets, anklets and collars, golden figures of animals and gods. Here is gold in every conceivable shape, and also in its natural form, the little pellets that are found in streams, here heaped into bags and piled up against a wall. There is something terrifying in being given so completely what you want.

'Come and look,' he says to one or two. As he must, for this is a co-operative venture and they must share everything with him, the guilt, the knowledge.

So they come and they look, and then, using any timber that can be found, the doorway is blocked up again and some matting is fixed against it to conceal what has been done. It will fool nobody, of course. In a few hours, every Spaniard has heard about the treasure and it has grown more dazzling with each repetition of the story.

The Captain knows he does not have much longer. And it is at just this point that he receives unwelcome news from the coast.

He called me to translate as soon as the messengers entered the palace. I could see they were Cempoalans and had been travelling hard. I looked at the dust on their clothes and their anxious faces, and I knew what they were going to say.

'There has been a battle, Malinche. Some of your people were killed.'

'How many?' I asked quickly, before putting it into Spanish for the Captain.

'Ten,' said the Droopy-ear. I was sure that was what he said because he showed the number with his fingers.

'Twenty,' said the Tongue.

I felt a familiar rush of anger at her, stupid woman who did not care what she said in her desire (which I never understood) to cause trouble between us and her people.

'There has been a battle in which ten *cristianos* were killed,' I told the Captain.

He sucked in his breath. 'Who?'

I thought the Cempoalans mightn't know. But the first name they produced was a name that caused the Captain to pale and a pulse to beat in his cheek.

'Esca-lante.'

The commander of the garrison at Villa Rica.

Blue Eyes cursed.

The Captain said, 'Pedro, you will tell no one of this.' To me he said, 'Ask them what happened. Where. Who did it.'

The battle had been near a place called Nautla.

'Where is that?'

'We stopped there with Grijalva,' said Blue Eyes.

Nautla, the messengers said, was in the hand of lord Muctezuma. It had a Meshica governor.

'It was the governor who was responsible?' demanded the Captain.

'He asked for tribute and they would not give it,' said the first Droopy-ear.

'There was an ambush,' said the second.

'I don't understand,' said the Captain. '*Whom* did he ask for tribute? I thought we'd settled that matter.'

But it was not the Cempoalans the governor had asked for tribute: it was the towns in the neighbourhood of Nautla. We had not had any dealings with them. The Captain was frowning.

'The people in these towns saw that those of Cempoala were not paying tribute to Muctezumohatzin, so they said they would not pay tribute,' explained the Tongue.

'So the governor sent his army to attack Villa Rica?' asked the Captain.

'Yes,' said the Tongue happily, as soon as I translated the question into Ahau, but I stared at her until she put the question to the Cempoalans.

No. Apparently, what had happened was this: the governor had threatened the towns that refused tribute with the usual penalties, they had appealed to the Spaniards at Villa Rica, and Escalante had ridden to their aid with a combined force of Spaniards and Cempoalans and had been ambushed.

Or had he? The messengers seemed to be uncertain as to whether there really had been an ambush, although there had certainly been a battle. They also agreed that the Spaniards had burned a town, Escalante had died of his wounds, and these events had had a disturbing effect in Cempoala.

Blue Eyes raised a knuckle to his lips and chewed it thoughtfully. After a while he looked at the Captain and said, 'That is what *you* would have done.'

'That doesn't mean *he* should have done it,' said the Captain.

There was another silence. The Captain took a couple of paces around the room. The Tongue watched him.

'It doesn't make any difference, does it?' said Blue Eyes.

'That he should have stayed in Villa Rica? No, it doesn't.'

Another pause. Then, 'Do you think,' mused the Captain, 'that Muckety had anything to do with this?'

Blue Eyes didn't answer. The Tongue did. She had understood the question, or perhaps just recognized the name.

'Of course,' she said in Spanish.

When they have been his guests for about a week, Muctezuma invites the Captain and his officers to a ball game.

The Spaniards have never seen this game played, although they know of its existence. There was a ballcourt in Cempoala, admirably laid out the Captain thought. Rectangular with high sloping sides and, at the top, stone benches for the spectators. The usual evil carvings along the walls.

He accepts the invitation. He takes with him, among others, Velásquez de León, who has become, finally, a good friend after judicious flattery and generous presents of gold. A hot-tempered *hidalgo* but reliable, the Captain judges, and better on one's side than not. He wonders, as he wonders every day, what the Governor of Cuba is doing to destroy him.

The ballcourt is enormous. You could fit a Moorish palace inside it. The Meshica nobility sit chattering on tapestried cushions. At the far end of the court, priests congregate. They wear black. Their hair, long and uncombed, is stiff with blood. Alvarado looks at them and spits.

The Spaniards, out of long strategic habit, decline the invitation to sit in a row and settle themselves on the benches in a compact group. The emperor, seated beneath a feathered awning, talks to a courtier and from time to time dips his hand into a silver bowl. The Captain watches him out of the corner of his eye. His host is an enigma to him.

The emperor notices that he is being watched, and, misunderstanding (or perhaps not?) the nature of the Captain's interest, directs a servant to offer the silver bowl to him.

'We have a weakness for these,' says Muctezuma, 'but we think you will not be able to eat them.'

The bowl contains small red pointed fruits in a thin liquid. The Captain knows what they are and that he must eat one. He puts a smile on his face and a fruit into his mouth. Having no alternative, he bites.

His mouth explodes. A bitter fire floods his throat. He cannot stop the water that streams from his eyes, but he chews on, swallows, rides down the cough that threatens to convulse him, and all the while he keeps the rigid smile on his face as if it were nailed there.

The emperor's remote eyes gleam faintly. It is impossible to know whether with satisfaction, amusement or respect.

Now the players are walking on to the court. There is some ceremony involving incense and the cutting of earlobes. Obsessed with blood, thinks the Captain. A haze shimmers above the stones. It's going to be another very hot day. The air is thin in these regions, there's nothing much between the fiery sun and a man's skin. If the air is thinner, does that mean the blood of the people is thinner? Or perhaps thicker? He looks at the earlobes to see if it runs more or less readily than Spanish blood, but it seems to do neither and he doesn't recall that there was any difference at Cholula.

There are two teams, four players in each. The players, young men, bare to the waist, well muscled, wear knee-pads of leather and an extraordinary belt-like contraption around their hips. The ball is about the size of a small cannonball and that in fact is what it looks like, which caused him to shiver when his eye fell on it, as he did when he saw painted on one of their shrines a Christian cross with, of all blasphemies, a dog-faced creature carrying it under one arm.

He presumes the ball to be an inflated pig's bladder but, as the game begins, he sees that it is both too heavy and too springy. Its springiness astonishes him.

He speaks to the Spanish interpreter at his side. 'Ask what the ball is made from.'

'Soul' is apparently the emperor's answer.

'What? Ask him again.'

The interpreters confer in their common language. 'This word also means "blood",' the Captain is told at the end of the discussion.

'It can't be made of *blood*.' (Can it?)

He will pursue it later. Everything must be investigated because anything might be useful. The mysterious ball is now fiercely in play. It is propelled back and forth by the players' bodies, not their hands: once the ball touches a player's hand the game at once stops. The players strive to strike the ball with the parts of their bodies that are protected – the hips and knees. Back and forth the ball flies, propelled with a skill that begins to entrance the Captain although he cannot make out what is the purpose of the game. There are two large rings of stone that project vertically from the sides of the ballcourt, seeming to ask for a ball to be put through them, but it would be exceptionally diffi-cult to do that, particularly without using the hand to aim, because the hole is barely wider than the ball. In any case, the players don't seem to be trying to do it. He can't see what they *are* trying to do, unless it's simply to keep the ball in play.

He turns to Velásquez. 'What is the point in all this?'

Velásquez has no more idea than he does.

The game is like a dance. At times the players seem to fly. Twisting and turning, leaping to meet the ball and deflect it by a thrust of the hips, diving *upwards*. He cannot perceive any contest here. Yet when he turns to Muckety for explanation of this baffling game, the emperor forestalls him with a question of his own.

'Which team do you think will win?'

The Captain admits he is at a loss.

'We are wagering our cloak,' Muckety says, touching it with a ringed finger, 'on yellow.'

The only visible difference between the teams is that one wears a yellow wristband and the other a red.

'Then I will wager my cloak,' says the Captain, 'on red.'

Fortunately he has a spare cloak in his travelling chest. It is interesting that the emperor is a gambling man. The Captain is by any reckoning a gambling man, but normally he likes to choose his gambles.

At present he is neck-deep in the biggest gamble of his life, and now that he is committed to it he can't see how it can be pulled off. Was it stupidity to come here? What, so far, has he gained? The emperor appears friendly but may turn against them at any moment. If he does, they will be hard put to it to fight their way out, four hundred men against a hundred thousand and the only exit from the city a narrow causeway. In any case, they didn't come here to fight their way out.

So what did they come for? To conquer the empire? You might as well seek to pull down Rome in its pride. Yet something has to be done, and soon, or they are all dead. They cannot just leave gracefully. They have promised the Tlascalans too much, and the Cempoalans, and anyone else who would believe them. They have killed too many people. And they have uttered too many boasts to Muckety.

What is to be done?

He looks at the emperor, contentedly eating peppers amidst a handful of his court, and an idea that has nothing to recommend it except its fantastic audacity pops into his brain.

On the sun-filled court the players leap and weave. Yes, it is like a dance, this game of which he has no understanding and on which he has wagered his best cloak. It occurs to him that if he is wagering his cloak on the outcome of this game, he might as well raise the stake. If red wins, he will carry out the plan that has just come to him. If yellow wins, he will do something else.

He sits back, relaxed now that a decision has been made. Sitting above the game, he watches both the wheeling movements of the players and the quite different motions of the ball, which rebounds from their agile bodies as if alive. He has watched too intently. There comes a moment when, dazzled by the light that blazes off the burnished white walls, he sees on a background of darkness, like a net, the luminous trace these movements have left in the air. A moment later, it is as if this net is being pulled. It is being pulled into a spiral. He sees the spiral, sees it tighten, and in the next moment the turning motion into which the ballcourt, the benches and the players have been sucked has sharpened to a point like the tip of a feather, and the ball, flying before it, is shot unerringly at the gap in the stone ring and passes clean through it.

The emperor chuckles with pleasure. His fingers stroke and take up a necklace of shell and turquoise that lies on a cushion beside him. He tosses it to a player, who catches it with an outflung arm and carries it to his forehead.

The emperor rises from his cushion. The Spaniards rise.

Smiling, the emperor hands his cloak to an attendant and the attendant presents it to the Captain. It seems that the Captain has won the bet.

'This is what I suggest we do,' says the Captain to his officers. He tells them of the plan that has formed in his mind.

After an amazed silence, such a savage shout of joy goes up that he fears Muckety, in his palace on the other side of the temple compound, will hear it and guess what is being plotted.

These dignified gentlemen cavort like schoolboys, they clap and stamp. Alvarado, look, is dancing with a vase of flowers.

The Captain, smiling broadly himself, recalls them to order. 'We need to discuss it,' he points out.

They don't want to discuss it. They want to *do* it. *Now.* A week of idleness in an overwhelming city has stretched all their nerves, diminished them. They are afraid of becoming afraid.

The Captain needs them to discuss it because there may be something he hasn't thought of. No, that's not it. He needs them to discuss it so that, when it turns out there is nothing he hasn't thought of, the idea shall not be wholly his.

Because if it fails . . .

The day that will decide all their fates starts unpropitiously. Just before dawn, when the Christians are stirring and warming themselves at the emperor's braziers, for the early morning is cold at this altitude, a dog somehow gets loose. It slips between the guards, evades the lunge of the chief gunner who is checking his cannon, ignores anxious yelling and sets off at a lope down the street. It is hungry.

It terrifies two girls who are carrying maize cakes wrapped in a cloth to the priest house. They drop the maize cakes and run home, screaming. The dog eats the maize cakes, which are freshly made and still warm from the fire, and then goes in search of something to accompany them. It finds a turkey which has escaped its owner's vigilance and is fussing through the narrow streets north of the temple enclosure. It closes on its prey with silent speed and carries it off, fluttering, to enjoy in some private place. It chooses, for this purpose, a deserted yard which happens to be separated by a low wall from the rear of a temple precinct. As it is the month of the god to whom this temple is dedicated, sacrifice has been offered in the past hour. The steps are still wet with blood, the heart is still burning in the altar dish. The body still lies at the foot of the stone staircase, where, according to custom, it was flung by the assisting priests.

The dog, with the turkey in its mouth, leaps the wall and stops in amazement.

It is a trained dog and, in this happy moment, training is in accord with instinct. It has been trained to tear apart Indians. Here is an Indian on whom the tearing-apart has already commenced. The dog drops the turkey and turns its attention to the remains of the sacrifice, resisting all attempts by the horrified priests to drive it off.

By the time the Captain, a handful of officers and the dog's owner have been found and mustered, the sky has paled and there is no hiding the disgraceful truth from the eyes of the city's inhabitants. The Captain is angry: it is a complication they could do without. He hangs his troops when they steal from the natives in peacetime (Pedro de Alvarado cuts them down before they die, obviating what would otherwise be a rash waste of resources). But what is the point of hanging a dog?

He has given the animal's owner the sharp edge of his tongue. But there is a smirk on Alvarado's face, he can feel it. Alvarado thinks it's not such a bad thing if the Meshica are scared out of their wits by the dogs.

The priests have sung the chant of the sun. The drums have been put away until the following sunrise. The emperor will have finished his morning beverage.

'Time to be getting on,' orders the Captain.

By the middle of the morning there are ten of them conversing, he hopes convincingly, with the urbane ruler of Anahuac. More Spaniards are in the rooms beyond. They have dropped by to pay their compliments to Muckety: the first time they have done such a thing, but what of that?

The Captain has decided – terrifying acts have to be anchored to something mundane or the mind cannot approach them – to set the thing in motion as soon as his page informs him that Sandoval has arrived at the palace gate. As the boy comes, bowing, into the room, the Captain feels a sweat spring out like dew on his brow and wishes blindly that he could undo everything.

Something in his mind never loses its purpose. He thinks of it as like one of the little cross-legged gods the Indians put in their paintings, sitting above the fray. Curious that a man can be made of so many parts. The Captain turns his head to the page's whisper. Across the room, his eyes meet those of Alvarado. What would he do without Alvarado? Alvarado preserves his madness for him, like an egg in vinegar.

'Your Majesty,' says the Captain, for the moment has come, 'there is a matter I wish to raise with you. It concerns the killing of some Spaniards.'

Two hours or so later, they are no further on.

Muckety was at first bewildered and the Captain had to explain what he was talking about. The emperor promptly denied that he had had anything to do with the ambush and reminded the Captain of the hospitality with which he and his men had been received. It was appropriate. Shortly before this exchange, he had offered the Captain one of his daughters as a wife. The Captain refused. It would have been too awkward.

Having grasped the situation, the *tlatoani* effortlessly outplayed them. He summoned officials and sent them to arrest the governor who was responsible for the attack on the Spaniards, and did this so swiftly that they were out of the room with their seal of authority while the Captain's two interpreters were still stumbling through their explanation of what had happened. It was all he could ask for, wasn't it?

Thrown off balance by the speed of his host's response, the Captain resorted to bluster. Such a thing might happen again. It had nearly happened at Cholula. He needed assurances that it could not happen. His king needed assurances. Some token, some symbol of amity, was required. What better assurance could there be than . . .

Alvarado had to say it for him. The words unaccountably

stuck in his mouth. What girlish reticence was this? Could it be shame?

'You must move in with us!' chortled Alvarado.

The words produced no response.

'We do not grasp your meaning,' said the emperor.

'You must come and live with us. In the palace of Axa-what-ever-it-is. Your Majesty.'

'We live here,' said the emperor, frowning.

'It is not good that you live here any longer,' said the Captain.

So there it was, lying open between them, the unheard-of demand, the most brazen piece of impudence that could be imagined, the only slender bridge to safety. Muctezuma must allow himself to be kidnapped. He must come with them, voluntarily, if such a word makes sense, into captivity.

Of course, this was denied.

'Everything will be as before. You will have your people to attend you.'

'Your visitors, your meals, your musicians, all as before.'

'You will rule as before.'

'You will just be in a different place. Your Majesty.'

'Do you take us for a fool?' asked the emperor at last.

Naturally, he refused to come. What on earth can one expect? This is a prince whose feet are not supposed to touch the ground. So far beyond his experience lay what was being said to him that it was quite a long time before he could do more than stare at them like an outraged bird.

Then, in vain the Captain's eloquence that never failed before. In vain the explanations of why the removal is necessary, of the many benefits that will result. You cannot put a gloss on this. It reeks of violence.

This is the point they have reached and seemingly cannot get beyond. The talk goes in circles. The *tlatoani* is adamant, the room is full of rage and fear. It will only take a shout to alert Meshica in the corridors of the palace to what is happening.

It's Velásquez who cuts the knot. He loses his temper. He spins on his heel and turns on the Captain, roaring, 'How long will you let this continue? By God, I will kill him myself if I have to!' He draws his sword.

All of them are armed, needless to say. There are thirty swords in that room (Spaniards have been dropping in to pay their respects, and not leaving after paying them, for quite some time), but all sleep in their scabbards. Now, Velásquez's blade leaps from its rest and blazes like the Cross, and in a moment its twenty-nine fellows have sprung to join it and burn in the golden light.

Does Muckety flinch? Not flinch, exactly, but there is a drawing back of the will, an unsteadiness. Then the emperor says, and no words could be less open to doubt, 'If you lay a finger on our person, your blood will make another lake.'

To which the Captain, with a sudden insight, retorts, 'Then the blood that will be shed today will drown this city.'

He sees, without understanding why, that he has struck his target.

It is as a direct result, apparently, of that statement, that a few minutes later Muctezuma's four bearers, followed by a frightened retinue of courtiers who do not know whether they are supposed to attend on this appalling humiliation or not, set out from the palace to carry the emperor into exile among strangers. *In the heart of his realm.*

In front of the feathered litter, which has taken on the aspect of a bier, walks a court factotum holding a wand, intoning that the emperor is going at his own wish to reside with friends. There can be nobody who believes it.

In fact there is nobody about. Deserted the streets, deserted the plaza. No priests on the temple stairway. But the eyes the Captain cannot see, the eyes that see all this and will never forget it, these eyes are in the stones underfoot and the mosaics on the walls; the whole city is an eye and they are caught in the beam of it.

The Captain's heart is so high in his throat it is nearly suffocating him, but still nothing has happened, no one has shouted
'They are taking away our lord!' Still there is no furious drumbeat or wailing of trumpets. Still there is the painted smile on
the emperor's face.

And now they have reached the gateway of the palace of
Axayacatl. They are passing under its lintel, which does not fall
and crush them. And at last they are among their own and
breathing Spanish air.

The Captain turns to give orders to the guard. Out of the
corner of his eye he watches the tail-end of the woebegone
procession as it enters the building, just in case something extraordinary happens, in case it rushes out backwards through the
gateway to a shrieking of flutes, pulling all the palaces, temples
and Indians in this city out of the trance into which they have
sunk. But nothing happens.

Lord Hummingbird.
Speak to your servant.
Your servant, your flesh, is in darkness.

2

In the palace built by his father, Muctezuma is allotted four rooms. In the largest of them he receives his visitors. The Spaniards refer to this room, not all of them with irony, as the throne room.

The emperor's advisers wait on him after he has finished his morning repast, which he eats an hour before noon. Prepared in the royal kitchens, it now has to travel across the plaza, covered in cloths and kept warm with braziers. A screen, as always, is placed around him while he is eating so that no one may see him during this act, although now there is no one who could see him except two shamed attendants and the Spanish soldier who is always stationed inside the room and who, in any case, politely turns away when the emperor seems to require privacy. There is something about the prisoner that compels politeness.

When the emperor has eaten, the dishes are taken away again. After a short while, the first courtiers arrive. They walk with frozen faces through the rooms and corridors. Their eyes convey disbelief of everything they light on. The Spaniards mock them in mime as soon as they have passed.

Shortly another delegation will arrive, and the first will leave. Then perhaps the priests will come. The priests are not mocked behind their backs, they are spat after. Or the air is crossed behind them, to cleanse it. For half the day, a stream of plumed dignitaries goes to and fro from He-Who-Speaks.

Then it is time for the emperor's afternoon meal. More dishes arrive, an uncountable number of them, or so it seems to the Spaniards, but they are eating tolerably well themselves these days and so do not resent it. They have fish, meat or fowl every day, as well as other things less recognizable. It is presumably a great drain on resources, but who cares? The emperor can afford it.

After his second meal, Muckety is entertained. This is when the Captain and a few chosen companions visit him. The emperor does not reproach them for his captivity. With a forbearance (a nobility?) that would be remarkable in a Christian prince, he does not even allude to it.

The Spaniards enjoy visiting Muckety. He has some of the tastes of a Spanish monarch. They like the jugglers, the acrobats, the hunchbacks and dwarves who amuse him, although they are less keen on the tuneless, unnerving music. They always enjoy the games the emperor invites them to play for a wager. He loves gambling as much as they do. This goes a long way to redeem him, in their eyes. From those things from which he needs to be redeemed.

'I may have misled you when we were talking about sacrifice, Your Majesty.' The Captain returns persistently to his attempts at conversion.

'Indeed?'

'We believe that the only sacrifice God has required is the sacrifice of his Son, who died for us.'

'That is interesting. How did he die?'

'He was crucified.' The interpreters flounder. 'He was nailed to two pieces of wood.'

Nails have to be explained.

'We do not have this form of sacrifice. The sacrifice of the heart, the fire, the arrows, the combat with the unbladed sword, yes. Beheading, too, we have. But not nailing to two pieces of wood.'

'The means of death is not important . . .' protests the Captain.

'Surely it is essential. One does not fish with a digging-stick, or catch birds with a loom. One uses the instrument that is right for the purpose. However, we are mystified as to what purpose would be served by nailing to two pieces of wood. Let us talk of this further.'

A week after the emperor sent men to arrest the governor who was responsible for the deaths of Escalante and the other Spaniards, the envoys return. They have arrested not only the governor but anyone else of rank connected with the incident, including his sons. It is a substantial procession that advances along the causeway from Ixtapalapa and makes its way to the emperor's palace, where with deep shame it is informed that the emperor is no longer there. The envoys redirect their steps to the palace of Axayacatl.

The Captain knows they are coming. The Tlascalans told him so as soon as the procession was sighted in the valley. He makes sure he is with Muctezuma when it arrives. They are playing *patolli*.

He moves a counter and here is Ávila at his side, murmuring that the procession is entering the plaza. Minutes later there is a slapping of sandals in the stone passageway and then a pause. Then the room, which is all at once too small, fills with feathers, the smell of incense and the simultaneous bowing to the ground of thirty or forty Indians.

He notices that they still do not look Muckety in the face. He wonders what it would take to make them do this.

The *tlatoani* casts his eye over his people. He adjusts the hang of his cloak in an uncharacteristic gesture, and the Captain sees with interest that for an instant he is uncertain what to do.

Then, with a weary disdain, he turns the business over to his jailer. 'They are your prisoners,' he tells the Captain. 'Interrogate them as you wish.'

*　　*　　*

217

The governor is questioned first. He is interrogated with time-honoured techniques brought from Spain. This takes place in a tiny room a long way from Muckety's quarters. The room has been chosen because in the centre of it stands, at roughly knee-height, a stone bench convenient for securing a prisoner.

The governor makes only the smallest sound, a bitter sigh, as he is burned with a stirrup-iron heated in a brazier. He does not reply to the questioning. Two thick tears run from the corners of his eyes into his braided hair.

The Captain has expected this. He knows he will have to persevere for a long time to get the truth. The Meshica are a stiffnecked lot.

'Carry on,' he says, and the iron is thrust back into the fire.

He is considering a harsh punishment. With a stiffnecked people (who eat human flesh) he presumes only the strongest measures will inspire fear. And fear there must be or the whole game will fly into the air like a *patolli* board knocked by a careless hand. From that point of view, it makes no difference whether the weeping Indian on the bench tells him what he wants to know or not.

Later the same day, Sandoval inspects the armoury.

It is in a round tower on the edge of the temple complex. The Indians don't usually build round structures. Even their statues are straight-lined and squarish, but then at the last moment something is softened on the edges. It makes him queasy.

But here is this building, presumably made out of the same dark red, pitted stone as the others (you can see it in the few places the builders have left unplastered), and entered by the same tapering, doorless opening, and it looks, more than anything, like the turret of a Moorish castle in Spain.

The task he has been given is half-inventory, half-raid. To carry out either properly he needs to see what's in front of him, and this tower has no windows, only the daylight that streams past the pulled-back curtain and gradually loses itself in the gloom. He should have brought a light. There might be anything in here.

The swords, first. They aren't real swords, being made of wood into which are glued sharp flakes of flint. He would be scornful, if he hadn't seen what they can do. He has seen one cut the head off a horse.

He takes a sword from the stone bench it lies on, slides it out from its wooden scabbard and tests the edge. He feels the warm, welling blood before he feels the cut. Then the pain bites, deep, near the bone.

He takes the weapon to the light. He is alarmed to see that the teeth set regularly and firmly into the edges are not chipped from flint, but are flakes of an unknown material that is black, shiny and glasslike. It's as sharp as steel. It might even be sharper, if the way his thumb is bleeding is anything to judge by. But surely God will not allow there to be something sharper than steel.

He puts back the sword where he found it, picks up another. The weapons are not lying in the sort of order he would expect, all the swords followed by all the spears, for instance, but have apparently been put down at random. He peers at each sword as he picks it up and finds many of them bladed with the same black, murderous flakes. He takes them to the entrance and throws them down on the floor.

He returns to the benches. He picks up a spear. The head of the spear is as long as his hand from the wrist to the tip of his middle finger, and it is made from the same black glasslike stuff. The arrowheads are made of it, too. And the length of those arrows! Almost as long as a man is tall.

He has been walking slowly away from the entrance. The further he goes, the dimmer the light. He does not like this, he does not like the deepening obscurity into which he treads, in this place where devils are worshipped, and he is in the act of raising his hand to his forehead to make the sign of his Redeemer when pure evil leaps at him, a basilisk sneer carved on a mask, and, hanging below it, unspeakable, a bag of skin, a man's face.

He retches. Then he crosses himself with resolution and treads on. He has a task to do. He is beginning to sense that the way the weapons are clustered on the benches is not as haphazard as it looks. They are arranged in accordance with some *idea*. No sooner has he realized this than he seems to feel its perverse vibration, this idea, in the closed air of the tower. He is in terror lest it enter his mind.

It is not their fault. How many times has he told himself this? God in His wisdom has withheld from them the knowledge of Christ. Therefore they have fallen into the clutches of Satan. As a Christian, he must pity their ignorance and strive to deliver them.

He feels no pity. He has tried, and he cannot. He has stood in the shrine of the temple and seen a human heart in a stone dish. It turned his own heart to stone.

He finishes his inspection of the armoury and heaps up most of the weapons near the entrance. What is left he sweeps into disorder, anything being better than the order that glimmered at him from those benches. They will be burnt, all of them.

It begins with a drumbeat.

Most spectacles in this city begin with a drumbeat, but this time it is a Spanish drum and no one is dancing.

The weapons have been piled up in the great paved space between the temples. In the end several armouries were discovered, and all have been pillaged. There are a lot of weapons. Among the arrows, javelins and spear-throwers, the leather slings, the cane-and-feather shields, the heavy clubs and swords set with a multitude of wicked blades, are mingled harmless things, wooden carvings, wickerwork and woven hangings from the palace of Axayacatl. Olmedo reproached the Captain for this, but the Captain replied that, in what they were embarked on, a few pieces of furniture were neither here nor there, and that in any case the hotter the fire the more merciful the death.

Twenty stakes stand in the ground amid this sea of kindling.

The area has been ringed by Spaniards for the past day and night, while the weapons and other things were brought and the stakes hammered in. The priests have watched with stony eyes from their temple platforms. They do not ask what is being prepared or why their domain has been invaded. Forced to detour through obscure courtyards and alleys to avoid the open space that has been occupied by the Spaniards, they behave as if this is the route they have always taken and it is not in the slightest degree inconvenient.

Their calmness angers Pedro de Alvarado, strolling past the woodpile. He would like to wipe the disdain off their thin faces.

The drumming has been shivering the air for a quarter of an hour before there is any discernible happening. But then, winding its way slowly from the rear of the palace of Axayacatl, comes a procession. At its head ride the Captain, Sandoval and other officers. Behind them march a dozen Spaniards with swords drawn. Behind *them* shuffle, in single file, a line of Indians chained together at the ankle. The Indians wear their feathers and insignia of rank, but these are dirtied and bloodied and their bearing is cowed. They look like bedraggled birds. Spaniards march on either side of them. The drums are continuing to beat.

The procession halts at the woodpile and, one by one, the prisoners are released from the shackle and bound to a stake. The Captain dismounts and gives his horse to a page.

He goes to the soldier who is collecting up the discarded leg-irons and takes a set from him. He walks back to the palace of Axayacatl.

Muctezuma is sitting on his ceremonial mat like something carved. Not even his eyes move as the Captain comes in. The soldier who is on guard duty in the room changes his stance, then stares.

The Captain kneels in front of Muckety.

'Forgive me,' he says.

He doesn't have the interpreters with him, so it is unlikely that the emperor understands these words.

He takes one of the royal ankles in his hand. Muctezuma reacts slowly. Astonishment has paralysed him. Then, belatedly, he tries to pull his limb out of the Captain's grasp. But the Captain is strong and the soldier has put his sword at the emperor's throat.

The fetter is placed around Muctezuma's left ankle and locked with an iron key. He does not resist when the second fetter is placed on his right ankle and locked. Between them stretches a chain the length of which would just allow him to walk, if he wished to. The Captain slips the key into his pocket.

He stands up. He moves backwards from the fettered emperor, as if the better to see what he has done. Then he lowers his head in an ambiguous gesture. It is not a bow. But it is not nothing, either. He leaves the chamber.

The soldier coughs awkwardly and retreats to the doorway. It's not his turn to be on duty; he took this watch to oblige a friend. He wishes he hadn't.

In silence, the *tlatoani* weeps.

The prisoners have been bound to the long row of stakes, the piles of weapons have been augmented by a load of firewood that has turned up from somewhere, and the people of the city, who have been collecting outside the ring of Spaniards since early morning, have been allowed into the enclosure. They observe in silence. There are several hundred of them. They have not been allowed to bring weapons. It is impossible to know what they would do if they could, because their faces are without expression.

The Captain, on horseback, raises his hand.

A soldier steps forward with a brand lit from a brazier in the palace.

He plunges the flame into the bank of tinder at its central point, where the governor stares straight ahead. Fire roars through the pile and reaches the bound man almost instantly. Only then does the first smoke rise.

The soldier who is starting the fires works his way along the line of Indians, although it is hardly necessary because, left to itself, the fire would soon spread to engulf them all. A worry niggles at the Captain. He doesn't want to burn down the city.

The Indians burn quickly. They melt like candles. Perhaps there's a lot of oil in their bodies. He wonders about the soul: do they have souls? Presumably not in the same way as Christians. He is glad they burn quickly because he is taking no pleasure in this and in any case a long-drawn-out spectacle is dangerous. The smell is overpowering. It will take days to disperse.

He has watched the watchers carefully. Their utter silence surprised him but he finds nothing threatening in it.

When the last flame of the last Indian is guttering, and a clotted smoke bunches over the pyres, he returns to the emperor and releases the royal feet from the shackles. The emperor does not move.

I went out of the city that day. Like a coward, I wanted nothing to do with it. I walked to the place where the market was held – the great square was deserted, only a few scraps of cloth flapped above the wooden stands – and then to the shore of the lake. I took my servant Taino, who was not my servant, as a companion.

By the lake, we sat on our heels and tossed small pebbles into the water to hear the sound they made. I noticed how quiet it was. Wherever there are *winic* houses there is always the noise of children, of women's voices, the soft thud of maize being ground, the chink of clay pots. But that morning I could hear only the lapping of shallow waves on the shore, the effortful wing-beats of a duck as it raised itself from the water, and the plop of our pebbles into the lake. The ripples spread, into stillness.

Then I heard another sound, which mystified me. It was rhythmic. A thump, followed after an interval by the sound of cascading water and a loud splash. After a brief pause, another thump, and the same sequence. Accompanying it, a faint swishing of water. It sounded like something heavy, a laden boat or canoe, being poled over the lake. But the Meshica did not use poles for their canoes.

Then a long ripple, not a circular ripple caused by a pebble but a straight ripple like the wake of a boat, ran to the shore and died at my feet.

I looked up. The sky was drenched in light. Shading my eyes against the radiance I saw, moving slowly through it like an enchantment, an island of flowers and grasses and, in the centre of it, a tree hung with yellow fruit.

Rabbits ran through the grass and stood on their hind legs on the tree roots. In the boughs of the tree, a bird sang. Sun glanced off the intense red of peppers twining up a wicker frame. At the further end of this vision, on a platform of rushes, the *winic* tirelessly raised and lowered his wooden pole.

In Tenochtitlan, six weeks pass.

In those weeks, the impossible is done. Daily.

The emperor holds court. He administers his realm. He hears disputes, he awards honours, he speaks with the priests about ceremonial matters. He scans tribute rolls and gives instruction to stewards. From the roof he observes the sky at midnight, as he has done every night since his accession. He visits the great temple, under Christian escort, and returns. He does all this as if his heart is not broken, and as if there is not always a Spaniard within a few feet of him.

The conversations about theology continue.

'I think I have failed to make myself clear, so, with Your Majesty's permission, I will start at the beginning.'

'If you wish.'

'There is only one God. No other gods exist. This God is the Creator of everything. He made the world and all that is in it in six days.'

The emperor listens carefully.

'This God is both One and Three.' (At the Captain's side,

Olmedo sighs.) 'He is Father, Son and Holy Spirit. However, these are not three different gods. It is important to understand this. They are one.'

'There are interesting likenesses between your religion and ours,' remarks the emperor.

'Yes?'

'For instance, while you say that your *teotl* is one-and-three, we say that our *teotl* is one-and-four. So we understand quite easily what you tell us. We even think that perhaps it is the same thing. One-and-three and one-and-four: why should they not be the same thing?' The emperor picks up a blue feather from the mat and plays with it.

'Your Majesty, they are not the same thing at all.'

'We think they may be. What you say about the creation of the world also interests us. But we wish to ask you, how many times has it been created?'

A pause.

'Once.'

'Our people say that it has been created five times. This is the fifth world.' The emperor opens his fingers. The feather drifts to the floor. 'Every day we are afraid that it will end.'

One would almost think he genuinely was a guest. The Captain is grateful. Nevertheless, the fiction is a fragile one and has to be publicly preserved. For this reason, excursions are organized, under heavy guard, that will serve the double purpose of keeping the emperor amused and showing him to the people. A hunt is arranged in a lakeside park where the *tlatoani* keeps game for the purpose. Muckety turns out to be an excellent shot with the bow. Alvarado spears one of the wild pigs of the country.

The emperor accompanies his captors when they go sailing on the lake.

Sailing? The Meshica, to whom it has never occurred to ask Lord Wind to propel them over Lord Water, are at first astonished, then admire. Four little ships have been built at the Captain's wish in a tremendous hurry, using timber from the forested hills and the tackle, brought up from Villa Rica, that was taken off the scuttled fleet. They have been built by a man called Martín López, who can turn his hand to most things but had never built a boat until the Captain told him to.

There has been much coming and going. To Villa Rica and other places.

'Where does the gold come from?' asks the Captain of his captive host.

The emperor smiles sadly. 'Always gold.'

'It is of great interest to my king.'

The emperor summons a servant who brings a map painted on cloth. The Captain and his officers pore over it. The gold is found in rivers. The main source is about a week's march to the south-west. There is another important deposit on the coast, which they must have passed on the voyage.

The Captain despatches reliable men, with Meshica guides and the emperor's blessing, to both places. After a short interval, taking advantage of Muckety's continued co-operation (is the *tlatoani* frightened? broken?), he sends men to look for silver, for land suitable for vineyards, for a second harbour and for a route to the other ocean, which he knows is there somewhere on the edge of this country. (His imagination is boundless. The empire is already at his feet, it is already dwindling in significance against the next enormous prize, Cathay, at which Columbus aimed and missed.)

He knows that sooner or later the Governor of Cuba will move against him. That is why he must get as much as possible done now, while the emperor is soft to his will and the city's population still bewildered. He has a growing confidence that, in the long term, the game will succeed. Settlers will come from the islands to hold what has been won. From Spain, too. The King has surely received the treasure by this time, and, with it, the letter that explains everything. His Majesty will favour the enterprise. He will see what great services are being rendered here.

*   *   *

'The objects made of gold which you found in the hidden room of this palace,' Muctezuma tells the Captain, 'belonged to our ancestors.'

The Captain inclines his head in acknowledgement. He would have been astonished to find the emperor did not know about the hole they made in the wall and blocked up again.

'We give them to you.'

As the Captain holds, arrested in its progress, the counter he has picked up from the *patolli* board, the emperor continues, 'You say your lord loves gold. Take these things as a gift for him.'

The Captain does not know what to say. To conceal his confusion, he takes off the velvet hat he wears, on principle, in Muckety's presence, and sweeps it in a bow.

'Your Majesty's generosity passes all bounds.' This sounds cold; yet how can he say the truth, that it will make him the richest man in the Indies, bind his men to him with a chain stronger than steel, and settle his problems with Diego Velásquez once and for all by providing him with a gift his sovereign cannot ignore? He could kiss the hem of Muckety's cloak.

He tries again, hunting for words that are heartfelt but not demeaning.

'This will never be forgotten. I thank Your Majesty most humbly. I am in your debt for ever.'

Muckety is smiling.

'I will send workmen to open the treasure room,' he says. 'They will come today. It is Nine Deer, a good day for giving.'

The stone corridors of the palace are full of light as the Captain walks, humming a tune, back to his quarters. He sends his page to summon Alvarado, Sandoval and Velásquez de León. He looks forward to seeing the expression on their faces, and, after that, the expressions on the faces of certain other gentlemen. There will be no more talk of going back to Cuba after this.

While he waits, he takes a quill and a piece of paper on which he is drafting a letter (to the governing council of the islands in

Hispaniola: powerless, in practical terms, but not necessarily useless), and makes a few calculations on the back of it.

The nib squeaks and splutters. He remembers that, if the emperor had not given him the treasure, he had been intending to take it.

The news spreads faster than you would think possible, and arithmetic begins.

A fifth of the gold is the King's. After that is taken out, a fifth of what remains is the Captain's.

This was agreed to. They agreed to it on the coast. No point in complaining about it now.

After the Captain's fifth is taken out, he has to be reimbursed for his outlay in buying and outfitting several of the ships, and provisioning the expedition. Well, of course: did anyone think he had done it for nothing?

Then a sum has to be set aside for the garrison at Villa Rica. Surely nobody will quarrel with that.

The rest is to be divided equally among the army. In a sense. It is right that the horsemen should get more than the infantrymen because not only are horses expensive but without them they would all be dead. By the same reasoning, the crossbowmen and hackbutteers must get more, though less than the horsemen. Anyone who does not see the justice of these arrangements does not understand the world he lives in.

Violent arguments over the gold have broken out in the camp long before anyone has received his share. By now it has been calculated that the footsoldiers will get no more than a hundred pesos. It will be a week at least before the division is made. As is perfectly obvious, these golden trinkets cannot be fairly distributed in the form they are in: they must be melted down and made into ingots.

Muckety's own goldsmiths will do the melting down. The Tlascalans can have the feathers and jade. The camp is scoured for a pair of scales.

*   *   *

'Do you ever wonder about your family?' the Captain asks his mistress. Sometimes she understands what he says, sometimes she doesn't. 'Do you want to go back and see them?'

She is combing her hair. Long and glossy with some scented water she puts on it, it reaches below her shoulders. She watches him with her tactful gaze, deferential but not obsequious. He is her entire world: he knows it. She will be whatever he wants her to be. Yet she is a mystery to him.

'Your family,' he says again, for she has not understood. 'Your mother.'

An expression of distress crosses her face and he wishes he hadn't spoken. Yet it is an idea so foreign to him, to be without family, that he can scarcely imagine it. How must it be to lack that comforting company – of course there's always a black sheep, a lunatic third cousin, a jailbird, something of the kind, but they're a comfort, too, in their way – jostling in your head? With what could you possibly fill that vacant space?

Her look has become angry. 'Mother?' she repeats in a harsh voice. 'I don't have mother.'

The Captain wants to protest, but tells himself it is not his business. Perhaps motherhood doesn't matter very much here. It is not a Christian country. When it has become one, the example of the Mother of Our Lord will be given to them and they will change their ways. However, he started the conversation because it had occurred to him that he might do a meritorious deed.

'I could help you find your family,' he says. He has thought of sending a small detachment of soldiers to escort her to wherever the village is. He might even, if he has a few days' leisure, go himself. It's always useful to see a different part of the country.

'Find?' She looks horrified.

'Never mind.' It was a mistake. Best to forget about it. He looks at her as she stands by the tapestried wall, starting to plait her hair into the braids that she will then pile up in a coil on top of her head. The Tlascalan girl was asked to do it a few times but didn't do it properly, and is now in disfavour. It made him smile. She knows how to command, this ex-slave woman who shares his bed.

He suddenly has a tremendous thirst for her. Thirst is what it is: his throat is literally dry, he wants to gulp her down. He gets up from the straw mattress on which he's lying and goes towards her. There's a tiger in his step. Her hands drop to her sides: is that apprehension in her face? He won't hurt her. He pushes her back against the wall, more forcefully than he meant to because she gives a little gasp, slips his hand inside the stitched blouse and fondles the proud and swelling breast that offers itself. Her smell fills his nostrils: earth, pine, pepper, a citrus hint of sweat. He tries to bury his face in the breast, but the blouse gets in the way and he pulls it off and plunges his head into the welcoming softness of flesh, tonguing the nipple. His right hand gropes between her thighs, seeking and finding, probing beneath the cloth, then impatiently pulls up the skirt and goes to its goal unhampered. His hand explores and luxuriates. The warmth of a woman. The pull inward, like quicksand, impossible to resist.

She wriggles as if the stones of the wall are digging into her back, he moves to recapture his position and between them they have dislodged the tapestry, which falls down on both of them. Laughing, he flings it off – it knocks over a bowl of grasses – and cannot wait any longer. Quickly, he frees Adam from his encumbering clothing. And it is at this moment, as he is poised on the brink of delight, that his ears pick up a distant and un-welcome sound. The footsteps of Flea, approaching in rather a hurry.

Empires are won or lost like this. It's a matter of fine judge-ment, required just at the moment when judgement is least to be found. There's nothing, thinks the Captain, that can't wait a little longer. He goes to it, somewhat trammelled by his sword, which he has forgotten to take off (too late now), and conscious of Flea's breathing on the other side of the partition, but these impediments to pleasure mysteriously serve to increase it instead. He romps and plunders like a delirious boy in the moist, elastic body pinned between him and the wall of Muckety's palace. Such joy God has given to man. Oh, the sovereignty of the flesh.

The Indian is nervous. He comes from one of the lakeside cities. The Captain will have to ask him to repeat its name. For the moment, however, the only name that matters is that of the rebel.

Cacama, ruler of Texcoco.

It is explained to him that he has met this prince. The Spaniards were welcomed at the lake, were they not, by a lord who greeted them in the name of the emperor, his uncle?

To the Captain these high-ranking Indians all look the same – pride, plumes and a reek of incense – but, yes, he remembers the haughty young nobleman who claimed to be Muckety's nephew, and to whom he gave a pearl.

'Cacama and who else?' he asks. For no one plotting a rebellion ever failed to look for friends.

The Indian gives him three names. They are the names of the rulers of three other cities in the lake region.

'Does the *tlatoani* know of this?'

The Indian's eyes slide away from his. He knows he will not get an answer.

'When will it happen?'

'When they have gathered their armies. Also the priests say that the festival of Woman-Snake has to be held first.'

'What are they planning to do?'

'Make war.' The Indian smiles apologetically. 'They will kill you all.'

'And what else?'

'They will set lord Muctezuma free.' The messenger is still looking apologetic. Perhaps it is in bad taste to imply that the emperor is not free at present. 'Afterwards, Cacama will be *tlatoani*.'

This last piece of information takes a moment to sink in.

The Captain goes to see his prisoner. He takes Alvarado and six others.

'Your Majesty,' he says without further preliminary, 'it has come to my ears that your nephew prince Cacama is plotting to make war on us.'

It is not the emperor's time to receive the Spaniards. It is not his time for his councillors and petitioners, either. It is the time when he sees his wives.

There is a flurry as the Spaniards enter, and two women rise and slip into a side room. The emperor regards his visitors coldly.

'He is plotting to make war, you say?'

'I am informed so.'

'By whom?'

'An official of high rank. I have been asked not to divulge his name.'

'Your informant is lying.' The emperor stares into the Spaniard's eyes, then drops his own to the *patolli* board and moves a counter. He seems to be waiting for the Captain to leave.

The Captain seats himself on a cushion.

'He has no reason to lie,' he remarks amiably.

'We have men in our service at Cacama's court and we know everything that happens there.'

'That is why I am sure Your Majesty is aware of the plot. And as one of its purposes is to remove Your Majesty from our custody, I imagine that you are in fact the instigator of it.'

There is a flash of anger in Muckety's eyes.

'We agreed to come here and live with you,' the emperor says. 'We could have commanded our guards to fall on you and kill you. We did not. Why should we plot war now when we did not want it then, and when, to please you, we have even handed our steward and his family over to be burnt?'

All this is perfectly true. The Captain does not understand why Muckety acquiesced in his kidnapping. Every time he tells himself that it was quite simple, just cowardice, or a superstitious fear of bloodshed in the streets of the royal city, his mind shrugs off the explanation with impatience. At the moment, however, he does not need to think about it. He does not need to know, either, whether Muckety is behind this planned rebellion; he suspects not, since, if he were, why should he be willing for Cacama to supplant him?

'In that case,' he says, 'you won't object if I take some of my men to Texcoco to deal with the matter.'

Muckety does not reply for a time. He moves a few counters on the *patolli* board. He is playing a game against himself, it appears.

'You do not need to go to Texcoco, Malinche,' he says at last. 'Malinche' is a name the Indians have given to the Captain. The Captain is puzzled by it but accepts it. 'Cacama will be delivered into your hands.'

The Captain studies him. He wonders what is going on that he doesn't know about.

'I shall want those who conspired with him, as well.'

'They will be delivered to you, also.'

'The lordship of Texcoco will be vacant.'

'It is easily filled. There are many candidates.'

The Captain's suspicions deepen.

'With a man who will be loyal to us,' he insists.

'Such a man will be found.'

There is nothing more that can be asked. The Captain leaves it at that. If Muckety doesn't keep his word, Spaniards *will* go to Texcoco and blood will be spilt. That is the thing Muckety seems anxious, at all costs, to avoid. This squeamish reluctance for war squares with nothing the Captain has heard about the Meshica or sensed in his first meetings with Muckety. There is something here that is beyond him.

The emperor's slender hand moves a counter on the *patolli* board. If he isn't scheming, wonders the Captain, how can he endure his captivity?

On the morning of Christ's birth, Sandoval puts his foot in the stirrup and rides for the coast. He has a handful of men with him: it's enough, the country is safe for Christians after the burning.

The morning is white with mist and the sun lances through it. He shades his eyes as he trots along the causeway. On either side of him lies liquid pearl. Barely aware that he is doing it, he counts the wooden drawbridges as he goes over them: one, two, three . . .

Can it hold, this fantastic piece of bluff?

It needs to hold only until reinforcements come. More men, more guns. More wine, too: they have finished the wine and without wine they cannot have Mass, and since the whole enterprise depends entirely on God . . .

Sandoval is going to command the garrison at Villa Rica. He is going to replace the officer the Captain sent in place of Escalante. The Captain, who seldom misjudges a man, made a mistake with Alonso de Grado. This lazy, greedy knight has spent his time at Villa Rica gambling, bullying the local Indians (whom it is vital to keep sweet) and – apparently – trying to intrigue with the Governor of Cuba. Sandoval has been ordered to send him to Tenochtitlan in irons.

He will do it with relish. Sandoval hates disloyalty more than anything else in the world. It is a fault he can't understand. Surely it is the easiest thing on earth to stay true to a cause, or a friendship? What kind of man values advancement, or a bit of gold that can be won or lost in a card game, above the steady warmth of fidelity? He despises men like Alonso de Grado, who come and go with the sway of the tide. They are without depth, and at the mercy of every squall of chance and politics.

Sandoval thanks God for his anchorage in Christ and for the leader God has given him. He has fitted little silver bells to his mare's bridle, and they jingle a celebration as he trots her up the grassy slope at the end of the causeway.

On the feast of the Three Kings (modestly celebrated, because there is no wine), the Captain surveys the kings who are in his keeping. Not three, but five. Muckety, Cacama and the three princes who plotted rebellion with him. One of them is Muckety's brother, Kweetl-awac (he is getting the hang of these names). Alongside them are half a dozen other sorry nobles who lent themselves to the plot. All except Muckety are in chains. There is quite a call for chains at the moment. Sandoval will have to send some more from Villa Rica.

The rebellion has been nipped in the bud, for which he has God to thank and also, he imagines, the pusillanimity of the emperor, who would not avail himself of freedom when it offered. The throne of Texcoco has been bestowed on a brother of Cacama's – not, to the Captain's surprise, the brother who brought him bound to the Captain on a dark night. Palace intrigues: they don't interest him. But it cannot be allowed to happen again.

Or, if it does happen again, because the Captain is not so foolish as to imagine that an alien rule can be imposed on a nation without risk of rebellion, it must be made quite clear whom the rebellion is against. So that it is quite clear who will extinguish it.

The kings are unchained for the ceremony. The proceedings must be clothed in as much dignity as possible and no one can pretend that an iron chain is dignified. It is also desirable – the Captain gnaws at his lower lip, torn between a black laugh that wants to force itself out of his lungs and a feeling of vertigo that occasionally visits him as if he were looking into the Pit – it is also desirable to pretend that these lords of the Meshica are doing what they are doing of their own free will.

He has assembled a sober-looking clutch of his men. They include the notary Hernández, who will write it all down in his careful hand, pursing his lips as he does so, and would write down the Last Judgement with the same stolidness. The notary is the most important Spaniard here, apart from himself, because the writing down of it is what it is all about. The clutch does not include Alvarado. For this occasion, Alvarado is too . . . *showy*. He also has an effect on the Indians which the Captain has often noticed. He seems both to fascinate and frighten them. Not

Alvarado, then. But he could do with Sandoval, whom he has sent to the coast. Sandoval is one of those rare men of whom you need two.

The Captain's heart is skipping along like a boy on a beach, and there's a light sweat on his forehead. Too much heat in this room from that damned brazier Muckety keeps burning all the time – or has he caught another fever?

The kings sit on the cushions they have been given, waiting. Muckety has told them what to expect. They sit like statues; he can barely see the rise and fall of their breathing. They don't seem to be inside their bodies, a curious thought. Their bodies are half-naked and filthy, he notices with a start. He hasn't really looked at them since he chained them up.

Do they understand what is about to happen?

He begins to speak. He has sketched out a speech in his mind, thinking the occasion was too important to leave to the inspiration of the moment; but now, leaning forward to address to these five Meshica nobles the most outrageous demand they have ever heard in their lives, he finds that the speech has put a taste of ashes on his tongue.

He lets it die, that speech. Following an impulse, he begins to talk about something quite different which has just, in the past few minutes, swum to the surface of his mind like a great golden fish.

'Your Majesty,' he says, addressing himself to the emperor, for whom at this moment he feels a surely Christian compassion, 'although our coming here was a cause of great amazement to you, you already knew of us, in that you knew of our God. I have seen the crosses in your temples and on the robes of your priests, and from this I know that many centuries ago the apostles of Our Lord visited you and stayed among you, teaching you all manner of things that were to your good. And when they departed, they told you, for missionaries always do, that other followers of the same Lord would come after them and you would not be left alone. It has taken many centuries, because the knowledge of this land was lost; but now we have come, as was promised. We have come to dispel the darkness into which you have again fallen, to restore you to the love of God, and to restore this land and its people to their rightful Lord.'

As his words are laboriously translated, he watches the emperor. He is thrilled to see a tremor run through him, like the shivering of a grass blade as an ant climbs up it.

He leans forward with urgency. 'Lord Muctezumohatzin' (he has got it right by some miracle: the interpreters look amazed), 'this is the meaning of our coming here.' He wills the emperor to believe this because it will make what is about to happen easier for him. (And it will make it easier for *him*, the Captain.) 'I know that you have often pondered our arrival here, why we have come from the other side of the ocean and are unlike any other people you have seen before, and have weapons unlike anything you have seen. I believe that in your heart you already understand the truth. The long wait of your people is at an end.'

The silence, when he finishes, has a perfection to it. Surely nothing else can be said. The clock of the world has stopped. No one is breathing, the rise and fall of the Indians' bodies has ceased. But no, there are Muckety's eyelids opening and closing at regular intervals, the only sign that he is alive.

Then a dog barks, somewhere in the labyrinth of the palace, and the Spaniards shrug their shoulders as if to get rid of a burden. The notary's pen scrapes across the paper with some afterthought.

The emperor speaks. Not to the Captain. He ignores his jailer and, turning to the Meshica lords who sit in a row to his left, he talks to them in the pattering language that sounds to the Captain like the shifting of pebbles.

'What is he saying?' the Captain demands.

His interpreters cannot help. 'He is talking about things concerning his *teotl*,' is all they can say.

Muckety finishes speaking and still does not reply to the Captain. Disappointed, the Captain addresses him again. 'Your

Majesty, we have come to return you to the knowledge of God, and, as a means to that, to enrol you and your subjects as vassals of our most Christian king. That is why we are here now.'

The interpreters flounder over something or other. As they stumble to a halt, the emperor's gaze, wholly aloof, considers them for a moment and then is withdrawn.

He *must* submit. Look, an hour ago his chiefs were in shackles and he himself is a prisoner. Not only that but, for some reason, he is afraid of war. All the same, the Captain prays he will be gracious, will say something that lifts the burden of brutality from these dealings and will sit prettily in the records.

Muctezuma says nothing.

The Captain sees what he must do. It is no good waiting for an answer from this slippery barbarian: moreover, it's not fitting. Who is in charge here?

He steps forward. The Indians tense. He places his hand on his sword, draws it a palm's-breadth out of its resting-place. He says, 'Lord Muctezuma, I call on you in the presence of these witnesses to swear obedience by all you hold sacred to His Majesty, King Charles of Spain.' He beckons the notary and takes a scroll of paper from him. 'Are you ready to do so?'

If he does it, the others will do it. At a stroke, everything will be simplified. In place of this muddle, there will be order. Majestic. Legal.

The emperor utters something between a breath and a sigh.

'Malinche, you are in your own house,' he says.

The Captain hears the thundering of his heart. He unrolls the paper he has been given and finds that the dampness of his hands, or someone's, has made the ink run. No matter. The words are still clear enough. It is the oath of submission.

He reads it, phrase by phrase. The interpreters render it into the Indian tongue.

One by one, beginning with the *tlatoani*, the lords of the Meshica pledge with stony faces to obey the King of Spain.

Lord Hummingbird, turquoise one.
Smoke-of-the-Mirror, mighty and subtle one.
Speak to your servant.
Your servant sickens, lord.

3

The city is celebrating one of its eighteen festivals. This one involves a gladiatorial combat in which the captive who will die has to fight, in succession, four Meshica warriors using a sword that is bladed with feathers. The warriors wound the victim with care. With tenderness.

The usual offerings continue. Hummingbird is hymned and fed. In the streets, a youth in the livery of the Lord of the Near plays the flute and accepts homage. He has been given seven flutes. He is playing the fifth.

From the doorways of their palace, and from the roof to which the emperor goes nightly to observe the stars, the Spaniards watch the processions up the temple stairway with loathing. The sacrifices taking place less than a bowshot away from them poison their air and their food.

How long have they been in this city? Months, now. What have they achieved? Everything and nothing. The emperor is their prisoner and the whole country is at their feet. Gold is even coming in from the regions to which Muctezuma has helpfully directed them on his bit of painted cloth. They have regularized their position, which frankly was dubious, by forcing him to accept the authority of Spain. They are conquerors now, not chancers. And all the time, under their noses, Satan is being served with blood sacrifice, hacked-off limbs and the eating of human flesh.

'We should not allow this insult to God,' murmurs the Captain.

Yesterday a group of his men got into the House of Birds and came back with armfuls of loot. It appears that Muckety keeps gold there, or did. They need to be given occupation.

Alvarado takes a bite from a pheasant's leg. He says, 'We could pick off the priests as they run up and down that damned stairway.'

He would do it himself, except that he is not a particularly good marksman. A terror, yes, with the sword and lance. And born to the saddle. But the crossbow does not obey him, and with a firearm he is a danger to his friends. He despises weapons that give him no contact with the enemy's flesh, the Captain thinks.

'What I had in mind,' says the Captain, 'was driving the Devil out of that shrine and installing Christ.'

'We have to bring them to the Faith first.' This, naturally, is Brother Olmedo. 'A Christian chapel in the midst of these rites invites sacrilege.'

'How are you progressing with the conversion of the emperor?'

'I am progressing.'

'I was getting along quite fast, myself.' The friar has removed Muckety from his instruction.

'He didn't understand what you told him, Hernán.'

The Captain throws his bone to a skulking dog. They don't get enough meat.

Velásquez, who visited the House of Animals, has told him that Muckety's tigers are fed on human flesh.

In the end, he left it to God and God did not fail him.

He was walking across the plaza in front of the main temple. Andrés de Tapia, a young officer but reliable, was with him, together with several others. The priests had been drumming again, which probably meant that another poor wretch would have his heart ripped out before the day was done. The sun was

241

at the zenith, and not a morsel of shade anywhere. He drew level with the great stairway and felt his steps slow. The weight of the air changed: it was like walking through water.

Now, said God.

The Captain's eyes flew up the stairway. Empty, but two priests stood at the top. He could smell them from where he stood.

Now.

'Go up there, Andrés, and say we intend to pay them a visit.'

Tapia blinked once, set his hand on his sword, either for courage or so that it should not knock against the stairs, and began to climb.

'Bring a dozen men,' said the Captain over his shoulder, 'and seal off the emperor's quarters.'

Andrés was a third of the way up. The Captain could feel those steps under his own feet: perversely narrow, unnaturally steep. The two priests were coming down.

There came a moment when the priests stood flanking Tapia and then, turning, began to mount the stairs with him between them. The Captain did not like this formation.

He set his foot on the bottom step and began to ascend. The steps were newly splashed with blood and sprinkled with bits of glistening bone. *This I shall do for the honour of God.* Passing the point at which Tapia had been met by the priests, he noticed with a small shock how perfectly this stairway commanded the rooftop of the palace of Axayacatl. He trod on upward. The smell of blood grew stronger. The steps here were treacherous with it. It would be fatal to slip. God would not let him slip. The priests never slipped. They went barefoot. Such devotion in the service of evil.

The platform descended into his view. A flat expanse of stone, four clay braziers blackened with smoke, between them the unspeakable slab on which the priests performed their sacrifices. Behind these a tiny – in proportion to the mass of the pyramid – walled shrine, the Devil's house, set so far back from the stairway that even when you were almost at the top of the steps it could not be seen.

The doorway was curtained.

Where was Tapia?

He thrust through into the slaughterhouse. It was dark and suffocating. Tapia materialized at his elbow and steered him to a corner. He glimpsed the priests in the shadow, staring.

'There,' said Tapia.

It seemed to him that the image was the source of all the darkness in the room. Yet he could see with frightful clarity every feature of its inhuman face. What most appalled him were the eyes, which were perfectly round and started from their thick-rimmed sockets like the eyes of fish. There was a small, beaked nose which he found quite horrible, and below that a mouth filled with triangular fangs like the teeth of a saw. The lips were slack and voluptuous. The face was painted in garish colours, but the colour daubed on the lips was blood. Around the neck of this abomination hung a garland of flowers.

He turned to look at what else was in the place. He had been breathing in the stench of blood for some while now: his lungs were full of it and his stomach was queasy. Above the sickly-sweet smell of men newly killed hung the heavy sweetness of the incense they burnt constantly. The two mingled with disgusting readiness, as if some secret sympathy existed between them, becoming one smell, one reek, so that he could never breathe the smell of their incense, however far from a temple, without thinking he was breathing the smell of blood.

The forms of Hell were pressing in on him. He whirled round on a movement: it was the flickering of the coals in the censer reflected on the polished surface of a mask. Copper? Gold.

The curtain was pulled aside and the dozen men he had sent for now came crowding into the place. There wasn't room for everyone. They stumbled over things, there was stifled laughter, riding nervously on top of horror. The priests were pushed back against the wall to the left of the principal idol, where an inex-plicable collection of objects hung from hooks — straw masks, baskets filled with shells, things made out of paper, bunches of dried maize cobs, a single feather, many coloured ribbons, a mummified rabbit, a baby's skull, and — a countless number of these, in all sizes from the length of a finger to the length of an arm — *cloth bundles*, tightly bound with hemp string, each one enigmatic and so *filled with something* that it strained against its cord.

His gorge rose, finally. Only aware as if from a distance of what he was doing, he drew his sword and slashed above a priest's head at the largest bundle. As the blade entered the softness contained by the cloth he experienced the terrible sensation of cutting the child out of a woman's belly. But out fell — not a child, or at any rate not a recent child — but bones. Bones. With them descended a greyish dust that unnerved him as it settled on his sleeve. And something carved, in the shape of an apple, that rattled as it fell out of the bundle, bounced and struck his foot.

The priests began to wail as if he had committed murder. One of them flung himself on the bones and picked them up with great gentleness, crooning to them. The Captain watched him for a moment. He had lost his bearings. He had not meant to destroy the bundle and didn't know why he had. There were worse offences than bundles here.

He went to one of the wall hangings, a painted cloth depicting one of their malformed deities, and ripped it down. He left it where it lay, on the floor, and went to another. God would be served. He would cleanse this place. He would burn it. The priests were now tearing their hair as they wailed. They had been penned against the wall and the one with the bones had been made to yield them up again. Olid had them, and he was throwing them down the stairway.

All around him, his men were taking the shrine apart. Pulling down statues, wrenching objects out of walls, stamping on canework and gouging wood with their daggers. There was such confusion that it would be dangerous to start a fire. In any case, he remembered as he took a pike from a soldier and swung it at the gold mask so that it clattered to the floor, what they were supposed to be doing was driving out the Devil and installing Christ. He picked up the mask and put it inside his shirt. Olmedo would do it. What were priests for, if not to exorcise and consecrate? There would be a figure of Our Lady shedding radiance where that monstrosity brooded.

So elated was he by this thought that he felt not at all surprised when Brother Olmedo appeared in front of him. He then noticed the friar's agitation.

'*What in the name of Heaven are you doing?*' Olmedo demanded.

The Captain's gaze travelled beyond him.

The emperor, carried in the arms of four attendants, was at the top of the stairway. His face was stiff and pale. A high-pitched hum of fury came from his throat.

'Who let *him* come here?'

'I did,' said Olmedo.

The next morning, as dawn broke, the Indians came to take the idols away.

The Captain, alerted by a sentry, went up to the palace roof by an inner staircase.

There were still stars in the fast-paling sky. The vast bulk of the pyramid was barely more than a silhouette, but even as he watched it took a faint flush of colour, a reddish tint, naturally, since everything to do with it concerned blood.

The Indians, featureless and shadowy, moved on the stairway in silence. They had brought . . . what had they brought? He strained his eyes. Something was thrown and uncoiled in the air. Ropes.

And other things. Armfuls of cloth, by the look of it. Large square things: mats? And some long poles, which caused him a moment's uneasiness.

Something was going on inside the shrine. He could hear banging, scraping and a persistent ringing of those infernal little bells they put on everything. There was a sudden, very heavy, thud, followed by a silence. It was too much to hope for that the monstrosity in the corner had fallen off its perch.

He was nervous and excited. When the emperor said that the *teotl* would be taken away, since it seemed nothing else would please his guests, the Captain had only half-believed him. Muckety was as skilled at prevarication as a Spaniard.

The east had lightened. Indigo bars of cloud floated in a yellowish sky. The sun, rising, looked hard like a boil.

His heart jumped as the drum in the sanctuary began to beat.

It had the deepest note he had ever heard from a drum. It was struck at festivals. But on those occasions there would be other instruments also playing. This time, the drum sounded alone. The beat – slow, unvarying – was that of a lament.

Out of the shrine came two men, moving slowly and carrying between them one end of a stretcher made from the poles and mats. They were walking backwards, towards the almost sheer drop at the edge of the platform.

On the stretcher lay a huge and muffled form. The Captain knew it for the Moloch of the bloodstained mouth whom he had seen two days before. He sensed the presence of the monster under the wrappings, felt the baleful stare of the piscine eyes and the vicious slant of the teeth. The thing was tightly wrapped, a gigantic version of the bundles that adorned the wall of its shrine. (What would happen to them? On the fire, if he had anything to do with it.) The stretcher, now carried in all by eight Indians, advanced to the edge of the stairway and stopped. Something complicated was being done with ropes. All the time the drum tolled, beating out what was happening, fingering some inner part of him that God couldn't reach.

The stretcher with its burden of damnation inched forward over the perilous edge of the stairway. Its end was supported, with a muscular effort it hurt him to imagine, by two Indians standing on what must be the fourth or fifth step below the top, those steps so narrow that he couldn't see how a man, even an Indian, could balance on them to support such a weight. As the stretcher was extended further over the (nearly vertical: look at the angle it made against the sky!) staircase, they were obliged to move to a lower and then a lower step, at the same time changing their grip and reaching higher, until their bodies made a straight line with arms extended fully upward, and he was reminded of something but couldn't think what it was. But what was extraordinary was that the men who were holding the stretcher and were presumably intending to carry it down that terrible stairway were still *facing backwards*. Facing the shrine. Their feet blind upon the steps.

After this there was no movement for a while. The men watching with the Captain stirred and shifted. Indians took a long time over things. Would they, perhaps, go on standing where they were for the rest of the morning?

No.

In the space of a few drumbeats (the drum had never ceased), everything changed.

It was the ropes. They had been attending to the ropes. The ends of which, he now saw, were held by at least a dozen priests.

These priests took up a half-crouching position, legs apart, on the platform and began to pay out their ropes as the Indians holding up the end of the stretcher lowered it very gently, until they were holding it parallel to, but a couple of feet above, the steps. It pointed downwards at a terrifying angle; the strain must be immense. The Captain moistened his lips. He felt an anxiety on the Indians' behalf, as if he were their father, while the other part of him, the part that had brought four hundred men this far, considered the desirability of the thing's plunging to the ground and shattering into pieces and found it much to his taste.

Could it survive the downward journey in any case? Bumping over the edge of step after step?

That wasn't what they were going to do.

From nowhere, Indians had appeared with bulging sacks or mattresses. Some were laid on the steps below the stretcher, and it was pulled over them. More stuffed sacks were placed on lower steps and the head of the stretcher was again let down over them, and so the thing descended, the two Indians going before it, bracing their bodies against a fall they would surely be power- less to stop, all that would happen would be that the Moloch would crush them . . . and *going backwards*, what madness, and yet still neither of them had missed his footing.

The drum sounded.

The idol descended.

The men had felt the tension, too, and were joking now that the image was safely on its way. The Captain relaxed. The drama was over. The Indians would bring out the other idols and trans- port them away in the same manner. They knew what they were doing. After all, they had got the objects up there in the first place.

He had already extracted Muckety's promise that the shrine would be cleaned. Scrubbed of all traces of blood, and lime- washed. Indians could work quickly when they wanted to, and the place would probably be ready for the installation of a Cross and Blessed Virgin by Thursday.

'You have told me many stories about your *teotl*,' remarks the emperor peaceably, for all the world as if the events of the previous days had not taken place, 'so now I shall tell you a story about ours. It concerns two *teotl*, who some say were enemies.'

The Captain resigns himself to some bloodthirsty farrago.

'The first *teotl* was a magician, a trickster, always changing himself into different shapes, always making trouble. We call him Smoke-of-the-Mirror. The second *teotl* was a holy man and a ruler. He ate no meat. He never drank *pulque*. He listened to music and poetry, and studied the stars. He was celibate. He was very ugly, but he did not know it. We call him Serpent-with- Feathers.'

The names are so outlandish. But the names — or perhaps it is something else — have provoked a flurry among the interpreters and they fall to bickering in the way that exasperates the Captain. He tells them sharply to stop it.

'One day Smoke-of-the-Mirror visited Serpent-with-Feathers and showed him his own face in a mirror. Serpent-with-Feathers had never seen his own face, and he was horrified. His skin was like a crab's shell, his lips were thick, his beard was long and ragged. Smoke-of-the-Mirror offered to use his magic arts to make Serpent-with-Feathers beautiful, and Serpent-with-Feathers begged him to do it.'

Perhaps the story is not so bad, after all. At least one can understand it.

'So Smoke-of-the-Mirror used his magic and his knowledge of transformations to make the face of Serpent-with-Feathers beautiful. When Serpent-with-Feathers looked in the mirror again, he was overjoyed, for his skin was soft, his lips were noble and curved, his eyelids did not sag any longer and his beard was shaved. Smoke-of-the-Mirror said, "We should drink a cup of *pulque* to celebrate your new appearance."'

The Spaniards smile.

'"I cannot do that, for I never drink *pulque*," said Serpent-with-Feathers, but Smoke-of-the-Mirror reproached him, saying, "When I have done so much for you, how can you refuse to drink with me?" And he said, "You are supposed to be wise, but how can you be wise when you have never tasted this simple thing that all your subjects know how to enjoy?" So Serpent-with-Feathers allowed himself to taste a drop of *pulque*. He found it very agreeable, and he drank a whole cupful of it. Smoke-of-the-Mirror persuaded him to take a second cup. Before long, Serpent-with-Feathers was drunk.

'Just then, a beautiful girl walked by. Smoke-of-the-Mirror had brought her there by his enchantments. Serpent-with-Feathers said to Smoke-of-the-Mirror, "Since you can do so many things, arrange for me to have pleasure with this girl." Smoke-of-the-Mirror said, "Nothing is easier," and so Serpent-with-Feathers got his desire. And in the morning he woke up and saw that the beautiful girl was his sister.'

A Spanish story-teller, the Captain considers, would not have done it better. The *tlatoani* has his listeners in the palm of his hand. They cannot wait to hear what happens next.

'Serpent-with-Feathers was grief-stricken. He threw away his robes and jewels, and abandoned his kingdom. He travelled over the mountains, taking only his faithful dwarves and hunchbacks, until he reached the sea. There he made a raft out of serpents, and sailed away on it in the direction of the rising sun. There are some who maintain that one day he will come back. But meanwhile we say that he is in the sky, and that you can see him there, shining brightly, just before the dawn.'

The Spaniards are quiet. They have been surprised to find themselves liking this story: it is poetic, it is dramatic, it has a moral. But something in it disturbs them. It is . . . *unexplained*.

Muckety is watching them. The Captain suddenly becomes aware of the sharpness of the emperor's gaze.

'Now, what do you think of this story?' asks the emperor.

'It is a good story, Your Majesty.'

'Have you ever heard a story like it before?'

'No, although we do have stories of trickery, and of quarrels between gods.'

'So. You do not have this story. Let us play *patolli*.'

The Captain is not quite ready to let the story go. 'Why did Smoke-of-the-Mirror do that?'

'He is a *teotl*. Do you ask your *teotl* why he does what he does?'

I wondered why Muctezuma had told us the story of the two gods. It perplexed me: it set up an echo in my mind that I couldn't trace to its source. Not for the first time, I wondered if the *tlatoani* was playing a very long and devious game with us.

If he was, it would make sense of what didn't make sense otherwise. After all, with a single word murmured in the ear of a single courtier, he could have raised his entire realm against us.

Why didn't he do it? He would have been the first to die, of course, but surely that wasn't what prevented him. The Meshica were warriors: they *sought* death. He had explained to us that, when they died in battle or on the stone, they went to join Hummingbird and for half a year accompanied the god's journey across the sky. After that, their souls became butterflies and danced in the sun for the rest of time.

I couldn't believe that the *tlatoani* feared death when his subjects revered it. He was a warrior himself, and also a priest. The Meshica said he was a *teotl*. I supposed that was why they wouldn't raise their eyes to his: they were afraid they might look into the eyes of the Lord of the Near.

I looked into his eyes on a few occasions – it was surprisingly difficult to do, it required an effort of will – but I never saw anything in them that explained anything at all to me. They were veiled. They told me I should not be looking at them. That was all. And I lowered my own.

The Captain looked Muctezuma in the eyes without any difficulty, as you might expect. It was, I thought, as if he had put a spell on the emperor. I think that this thought had occurred to him, too. But if it was a spell, he didn't know what spell. And if it was a spell, he was under it, too.

I went about my tasks in the palace of Axayacatl, where I was required to translate every day, wondering whether I was awake or dreaming. The city was as mysterious and beautiful to me as it had been when we entered it, and although so much had happened, I had a feeling that nothing had really happened at all. As if, in fact, *all* of us were under a spell.

One day, I thought, the *tlatoani* would act. He was waiting for something: a sign, an omen, the correct day of the correct month; perhaps he was making some military or political calculation which we had no inkling about. When the day came, he would murmur into the ear of his minister and the sky would fall upon our heads.

For some reason, this did not alarm me. It made me quite cheerful. I was altogether strangely content in this period, when time seemed to have stopped and every day brought new puzzles and fascinations and new glimpses – which of course might not be glimpses at all – into the mind of Muctezuma.

And I was feeling more hopeful about Taino. There had finally been an improvement in our relations.

Sandoval has sent wine from Villa Rica! It is greeted with joy. It happens that the casks arrive the very day the devilish images are taken out of the temple: a clear sign of God's approval, since it means that Mass can be said in the shrine.

The Indians scrub the blood off the floor and walls, and what can't be scrubbed off, since these practices have been carried on for so many years that the blood in places has become hard like paint, is covered with whitewash and a thick strewing of rushes.

Brother Olmedo exorcises the Devil from the place and brings in Christ and His Mother. Olmedo and Juan Díaz, the priest, conduct Mass. All the Captain's men attend, with the exception of four who are too ill to climb the temple steps and the Captain's interpreter, whom no one has ever seen take the Body of Christ and who is rumoured to steal out at night to attend the ceremonies of the Indians.

For several days after the Mass, there is an air of tranquil celebration in the Spanish quarters. It is as if they have reached the summit of their endeavour: because what more, now, could possibly be asked of them? In tune with the spirituality of the great event they have brought about, and deeply moved by the sight of Christian vestments and the Crucified Lord where pagan sacrifices formerly were, they abstain from uttering obscenities, more or less, and from blaspheming entirely, for two days. Gambling ceases. Gambling became a fever as soon as the gold was distributed. It was melted into flat, thin bars and the army lined up, each man to be presented with his share. Many of them went straight off and staked it in a card game. They said that that was all it was worth. There was a lot of discontent among the hundred-peso men, and talk about how the Captain had robbed them. The Captain is going to come out of this exceedingly rich. So they gambled, because gambling is a solace and also expresses contempt for what is staked. But after the Mass on the temple pyramid, there is no gambling. In respect for what has been done.

For two days. After that, the need is too great. Blaspheming resumes at about the same time, although the Captain (himself the worst offender in the army) has laid down severe penalties for it.

Underlying the resumption of gambling and blaspheming is a reluctant acknowledgement that perhaps what has been achieved is not a final victory over the Devil but simply the destruction of one of his citadels. The images have been removed: but where have they gone? They are being adored somewhere else. Everything necessary to the rituals has been carefully parcelled up by the priests and taken away. The sacrifices continue. Of course they do. There are at least a hundred temples in this city. And a hundred more girdling the lake.

After the rejoicing, a gloom descends. Really, they do not know what to do next. They sense that they have pushed their strength, or is it their luck, to its limits and still have no idea what the Indians, the ordinary Indians who avoid them in the streets, think about them. And there are so many of these Indians. That, still, is the problem, that numbing, beyond-calculation, imbalance of numbers. If the Indians should turn on them . . .

In short, they go back to doing what they were doing before.

Pedro de Alvarado watches the iron redden in the brazier. It is a branding iron, and he brought it along in his baggage thinking it might be useful.

The man stretched out prone on the wooden frame is Cacama, former prince of Texcoco. He is naked, and a day-old knife wound, untended, on his neck is starting to exude a creamy pus. Pedro de Alvarado, who has studied the prisoner's body carefully once it was lashed down and no longer able to resist him, has concluded that it has all the physical characteristics of a human being but in addition shows a slight prolongation of the base of the spine which is quite obviously the remnant of a tail.

It does not surprise him. He noticed the same thing with one of the Indian women he bedded. He can't at the moment remember which one, only the little bony projection where none should be, and his fascination with it.

Monkeys. They are some kind of cross between men and monkeys.

The iron is now slightly too hot. He lifts it out of the fire and balances the stem on the clay rim of the brazier. The brazier is a convenient height, though presumably designed for a different purpose from the one he is putting it to. The clay has a grotesque design modelled into its surface, a grinning fanged face in which spirals, like the whorl of a snail shell, stand for eyes. He has never seen a design of theirs that wasn't grotesque. Everything about them is an offence.

He presses the still smoking iron into the sole of Cacama's foot.

The Indian shrieks. Alvarado's nostrils flare at the smell of burnt flesh.

He takes away the iron. He waits for the Indian to recover his senses enough to understand. Then he says, 'Where is the gold?'

He has no interpreter with him, only a servant who will keep his mouth shut. He knew better than to ask for the loan of Hernán's prize pair. He reckoned he could do without an interpreter for this business. He has brought a gold plate under his shirt.

'Gold?' he says again, and thrusts the plate under the nose of the bound Indian.

Cacama turns his head aside. He says nothing.

Pedro de Alvarado returns the iron to the fire.

He knows there is more gold in Texcoco. Cacama surrendered five thousand pesos' worth when the tribute for Spain was demanded. *Five thousand pesos!* It's nothing. There must be ten times that amount secreted away in this rich lakeside city. Look at the luxurious furnishings of this house, apparently only one of Cacama's former palaces. Inlay and polished woods, painted screens, turquoise, jade and all manner of coverings and cushions, ornamented with that silly featherwork they dote on. Why, there's probably a thousand pesos' worth hidden in this very building, if only he knew where to look for it.

Frustrated, he withdraws the iron from the brazier and plunges it into the heel of the same foot as before, with only the briefest pause for cooling.

This time, when he asks for gold, there is, after some minutes, a hoarse whisper.

'What?' frowns Alvarado.

The whisper is repeated.

He bends down and unties the Indian. He smiles down at him, a tender smile which Cacama, lying face down, can't see. He helps him get off the frame, on to his one good foot, holding the burned one away from him and away from the floor with an expression of agony. Cacama hops to the wall and stands supporting himself on it. They look at each other.

'Show me,' smiles Alvarado.

He makes the naked Indian take his arm to lean on, and together they go out of the room and down a corridor, Cacama pointing the way.

Off the corridor leads another, narrower passage. Off that, after half a dozen paces, opens a small room. There is nothing in it except what Alvarado takes to be a shrine, a low platform on which stands one of their ghastly statues and a smoke-stained incense-burner.

'What have you brought me here for, you wretch?'

Cacama points at the wall to their left. It is panelled in a dark wood.

'Behind that?'

The Indian points again. Then he suddenly cries out, and tucks his burned foot under him with such a piteous expression that Alvarado has to laugh.

There is nothing to break the panelling with, and he has no intention of leaving the room until he's got what he came for, so he kicks it. It sounds hollow. Panelling usually does sound hollow. He kicks again.

This is doing his boots no good, but he has made a split in the wood. The panelling is done in narrow strips. Not too difficult to break. He moves back and thrusts at the wood with the sole of his boot, putting his weight behind it.

In the course of about ten minutes he has demolished an area of panelling some three feet square. There is nothing behind it except the stone wall. He peers into the gap at the sides, puts his hand and then his arm into it. Nothing.

Pedro de Alvarado manoeuvres his captive out of the room, down the corridors and back into the room they came from. He ties him again on the frame.

Taino was not his name, as it turned out. It was the name of his people. They were the Taino nation.

I apologized for making this mistake and asked what name I should call him by. He said it didn't matter; I could go on calling him Taino, since that was what I was used to, and he was used to hearing me say it. He said that it was probably good that I should call him by the name of his people because soon there would be none of his people left.

He had turned his anger, which he could not express openly, into bitterness, and covered the bitterness over with an appearance of docility. With me, since I did not beat him or threaten him or even force him to cook my supper, he did not feel the need to be docile, and he was merely bitter. This was the *winic* whom I had, so I thought, rescued from Juan Díaz, and who might at least show a bit of gratitude. He had never shown a scrap of it. The only time he had ever smiled was when I gave him the fish. I treated him with gentleness and he was surly. I talked to him and he was silent. I tried to make him understand that we were equals and he reacted with contempt.

He was like this throughout our journey to Tlascala, which was miserable enough in any case, and throughout the fighting and the negotiation with the four lords and the horror at Cholula and the descent to the lake and the first weeks in Muctezuma's city. Then, without any warning, as if something had been breached inside him, he began to talk to me. Except that it wasn't talking.

'You want know what happen in Cuba? In Cuba they kill us, that what happen. Chop off head, hang, open stomach, throw to dog. Burn. Yes, they like burn. And children, they take children from mother and throw on to stone, so head break. You want know more?'

He was screaming at me. He was possessed. His eyes blazed. He looked like a vengeful god.

I backed against the wall. I thought, he will kill me.

'Why we go to Cuba from Bohío? Because in Bohío they kill us. We think, in Cuba is safe. We go in canoes. But they come after. Kill us. Burn our king. They say him, "You become Christian, not burn. Hang instead." He say, "I prefer burn." So they burn.'

I thought, he isn't saying 'they', he is saying 'you'. The Spanish is the same.

'Why they kill us? We bring them gift. Food, other thing. What we have. They happy. But then they kill us. Why? They make us work in mine. Work, work, not eat. Die. They take world away.'

His rage so filled the tiny room we were in that I could scarcely breathe. My heart was pounding. His words fell on my body like blows. I expected him to leap for my throat.

Abruptly, he fell silent. He stood as motionless as a statue, then shuddered violently. A moment later, he was shaken by a tempest of weeping.

I let him weep for a time. Then, approaching him cautiously as you would a wounded animal, I laid my hand on his head. He didn't strike it away, so I kept it there, and after a while he became quiet.

All this while I hadn't said anything. What was there to say? I was so filled with despair at the plague that was my countrymen that I was ready to hang myself. I went on not saying anything as I hunted for and found some maize cakes, went to warm them on the brazier in the corridor, brought them back and shared them out between us.

We ate them in silence, too. But it was a different silence from the one that had previously existed between us. This was a silence that had been broken, and could be broken again.

And was. Many times. When next he stormed at me I was prepared for it, although by now a new anxiety other than my own safety had occurred to me. Suppose someone overheard one of these outbursts? We had our quarters in a little room that had once been a storeroom: it still had a bundle of reeds stacked in one corner when we moved into it. It was on a corridor that didn't go anywhere of importance and which was therefore usually empty, but a Spaniard did sometimes walk along it, and the flimsy curtain that covered the room's entrance was naturally no protection at all against eavesdroppers.

If Taino were overheard, he would be whipped. He might be killed. And I might not fare much better myself. Not that he would care about that.

I did not try to silence him: how could I, having waited so long for him to speak? I simply prayed that there would be no one walking down the corridor when his rage was in full spate. I blamed myself for exposing him to this danger, making him more vulnerable than he was already; he would have been safer with Juan Díaz, I thought. But it was done now.

He did not seem to hate me personally, except that I was a member of the race that was doing its best to wipe out his people. But once or twice he did turn on me, not for being a Spaniard but for having pretended not to *know*. I protested that I had *not* known, but he brushed this aside and he was right, although it was also true that while the dreadful events he listed remorselessly for me had been taking place in Cuba, I had been tilling the fields in Chanek.

At first it seemed that he did not believe me about Chanek, either. He did not believe that such a place existed. But then he started to ask me questions about it, and in reply I told him about the shipwreck, Gonzalo, the slaves, the *batab* . . . and, without my intending it, these replies turned into stories, stories about Chanek. He liked the stories. They calmed him. (They calmed me, as well, and after one of his rages I was in need of calming.)

I noticed how, gradually, he was coming to think of Chanek as both a real place and a place that represented freedom. Freedom was what I would have loved to give him, but in the circumstances I could not, because his people were not free and where could he go? But when he thought about Chanek he could at least imagine himself as free. He started to refer to the people in the stories as if he knew them, had recently spoken to them, almost as if they lived in another part of the palace of Axayacatl.

On an afternoon that has seemed like any other, there comes catastrophe.

'You must leave our realm,' says Muctezuma, when the Captain goes to see him. 'At once.'

The Captain is shocked. 'I don't understand.'

'Our *teotl* are angry. You must leave.'

He has never seen the emperor look more composed, more full of his own power. He sits upright on his meagre cushion in his meagre apartment that is surrounded by armed Spaniards as if he were still the undisputed ruler of all his lands.

The Captain forces a smile. 'I think Your Majesty is making a joke. You know we cannot leave. My king would be very displeased.'

'We do not care about the displeasure of your king, of whom we had never heard until you came here. We care about our *teotl*, our city and our people. You must leave.'

The emperor's face is calm but remote. His lips have thinned to a line. There is something new in his voice.

The Captain tries to guess what has happened to change his attitude, but his mind baulks at the entrance to the labyrinth.

'It is inconvenient for us to leave now,' he complains. 'I have sent men all over the country to bring me back a report of it, so that I can describe it to the King. I have sent men to found a new town.' This is true: only three days ago, Velásquez de León departed to found a colony in the south-east with a hundred and twenty men.

'You must go, whether it is convenient or not.'

'And if I refuse?'

'Then our people will kill you. We will not be able to control their anger.'

The card he can't trump. He tries, of necessity. 'It is *your* people who will be killed. You have heard what we can do. You do not want fighting here.'

'No, we do not want fighting. But if it comes, it comes. You must leave.'

'We have no ships.'

'You must build some.'

'That will take time.' (Can he spin it out for three months? Six?)

'We will give you wood. But you must go.'

Alvarado wants to stay where they are and fight it out. He wants to strike first, not wait to be attacked. They should, he says, start by killing Muckety and the other prisoners.

'They're hostages,' the Captain protests. He notices Marina, waiting for him, as he comes into the room, and dismisses her with a wave of his hand.

'Hostages don't make threats,' says Alvarado.

The question is how much prestige Muckety still commands. If it has lessened with his captivity, he is of little value as a hostage. However, the Captain believes that Muckety's authority is as great as ever. The *tlatoani* is thought to be a god; how could that change, simply because his freedom of movement had been limited?

'He is everything to us alive, and nothing dead,' says the Captain simply. It is the nearest he has ever got to rebuking Alvarado in public.

'Perhaps we should start building some ships, to keep him quiet,' suggests Diego de Ordaz.

'We should not build ships, because there are still some gentlemen among us who want to go back to Cuba,' says Alvarado.

Ordaz narrows his eyes at him. 'What were you doing in Texcoco, Pedro?'

'I was not in Texcoco.'

The Captain puts a stop to this, whatever it is. 'We can start building ships, and spin it out for as long as we can.'

'But what are we waiting *for?*'

This question is asked by Ávila, and it is an uncomfortable one. Are they waiting for reinforcements from Spain? Sent flying across the ocean by the news brought to Seville by the Captain's emissaries? It is beyond hope. Can he send for men to Hispaniola? He could, if he had a ship. Just one ship. It would set sail and Muckety would not know where it went.

The fact is, he hasn't known what he's waiting for since he abducted Muckety. Since before then. The whole business has been an inspired blundering in the dark. Now it is beginning to look as if it might not have been quite so inspired.

Something will turn up.

He smiles into their eyes. He feels his ability to win them flowing through his veins. It isn't just the gold they follow him for.

'Gentlemen,' he says, 'we have got this far, and no one would have believed that we could. Our luck is not going to desert us now. We'll play for time. And I promise you that we will not let go an inch of what we've gained.'

The Captain orders work to start at Villa Rica on three ships, a good Christian number. One can go to Hispaniola. One can go to Spain (why not?). One can go ... oh, what does it matter? It will never get finished anyway.

His instructions are to build all of them as slowly as possible, short of actually doing nothing. To finish even one would be dangerous. It would start the business about going home to Cuba all over again, and more seriously than before. Lest anyone even begin to imagine that the ships are real, he calls all his men together and explains to them that the ship-building is only a ruse to keep Muckety quiet. He has given orders, he says, that faulty planks should be built into the hulls, so that if the ships do set sail they will founder in the shallows.

It isn't true, but it is believed, because it is just the sort of thing he would think of.

Several weeks pass.

The city has changed its character. It used to be open, bustling. Now it feels closed. Spaniards who go into it venture there only in large, well-armed groups. They come back reporting silence, hostile glances and the way the Indians go indoors to avoid them.

The priests have made no attempt to take the Cross and the Blessed Virgin out of the temple. Indeed they have not been near the sanctuary. The Captain falls to wondering about the welfare of the holy images which he has placed there and which look down on the pagan dances that are still held in the temple precincts. Perhaps what he has done has offended God, rather than pleased Him. Nor has it made any headway with the Indians, who are still cutting out hearts in every other temple in the city.

The army of Christians averts its eyes from this spectacle, and holds on, waiting. For something. The Captain amuses himself with two of Muckety's nieces, given to him by the *tlatoani* in better times.

Then one afternoon a Droopy-ear who went down to Villa Rica with Sandoval rushes breathlessly into the palace. He says that Spanish ships have been sighted off the coast.

Toxcatl is coming, lord.

The temple stands in the lake. Its stairway has eight steps.

At evening, He-who-has-become-You crosses the lake. He mounts the
stairway.

On the first step he breaks his first flute, and throws it away.

On the second step he breaks his second flute, and throws it away.

On the third step he breaks his third flute, and throws it away.

On the fourth step he breaks his fourth flute, and throws it away.

On the fifth step he breaks his fifth flute, and throws it away.

On the sixth step he breaks his sixth flute, and throws it away.

On the seventh step he breaks his seventh flute, and throws it away.

On the eighth step is the Lord of the Near, lord.

4

It takes a week for a man to get to the coast and back again. The Captain has sent to find out what ships have come, but his scouts have not yet returned. He has heard nothing from any other source. He has never been so conscious that the city is an island, and that entrance to it is by a long and narrow neck of land that might be cut anywhere, suddenly, as a man's throat may be cut.

He can't ask Muckety what he knows, for surely he knows something. The whole, increasingly desperate game rests in part on the bluff that Spaniards are godlike, omniscient. The Meshica seem obligingly to have accepted this pretence, if their use of the same word to mean 'god' and 'Spaniard' is any guide. Being intelligent, they cannot, of course, truly believe this; yet there is a doubt in their minds, the Captain thinks, and Spanish safety may hang on keeping that doubt alive.

He watches the emperor keenly on his daily visits, alert for small signs, but Muctezuma, whose manner has cooled towards him, is inscrutable.

The envoys who visit Pánfilo de Narváez at his sprawling camp on the sand dunes have painted faces and nodding feather head-dresses. Each wears a jewel in nose or lip. Their clothes consist of the inevitable loincloth, of which the ends are embroidered, and a short cotton cloak that leaves the arms bare. They are just Indians, really, but they are not like the ones Narváez is accustomed to seeing in Cuba. They are finely dressed, in their savage fashion. They carry themselves with pride. And on their wrists is gold.

The Spaniard standing beside him says confidently, 'They're Meshica. You can always tell.'

Narváez conceals his distaste. The man is garrulous, slippery and vulgar. However, he has picked up enough of the language to interpret, and has been of use in other ways. He has sung Hernán's discreditable secrets (a fifth of the gold, indeed! and half his men in revolt about the distribution of the rest, and no wonder) with no need for persuasion.

The Indians are bowing and speaking. His interpreter tells him they have come from 'the emperor Muctezuma' and welcome him to their master's realm. Narváez introduces himself: he is the servant, he says, of the Governor of Cuba and the King of Spain.

Wicker baskets covered with white cloths are now brought forward, and the covers are lifted to show what lies beneath. Fruit, fish, poultry. Narváez is restless. The sun is blinding on this beach, and the mosquitoes plague him without mercy.

Then they uncover the gold.

He supposes there isn't so very much of it, because it is all worked into little figures and necklaces and beaten into thin patterned discs. Nevertheless, at the sight of it his heart leaps. He knows it is only a foretaste. There will be many more such baskets, their covers deferentially turned back for him to glimpse the wealth beneath.

He thanks them. A conversation begins.

'They're saying that their people have been very cruelly treated by Hernán,' says his interpreter with a complacent smile. 'He has stolen gold and feathers from the royal palaces, he has burned the governor of a province and all his family with great brutality, and he has imprisoned Muctezuma and four other princes against their will.'

'I have heard these things, and they are serious crimes,' replies Narváez gravely. He hadn't heard about the burning. Hernán has certainly been busy. However, he's lost his grip if he's stealing feathers.

'The emperor wants to know if you intend to punish him for these crimes.'

'Most certainly. I have come here to punish him. He is a rebel, and when I catch him I shall hang him.'

Narváez does not doubt his ability to accomplish his mission. He knows Hernán Cortés of old, and thinks little of him. A lawyer, not of the best family. Loose-tongued, and a ladies' man. A gambler, who has been lucky.

The Indians are looking solemn.

'Naturally, as soon as I reach . . .' (Damn it, what is the name of the place?) He slaps another mosquito, but the weal on his skin is already rising.

'Tenochtitlan,' supplies his interpreter.

'As soon as I get there, it will be my first task to free the emperor and the four princes.'

The Indians brighten. They are still waiting, though. What else could they want?

It comes to him.

'Once I have punished Hernán Cortés and restored your ruler to his rightful throne, I shall leave this country together with my men.'

He remembers that he is founding a town a few miles from here. The ground has been marked out already. He hopes the emperor hasn't heard about that.

The envoys depart, apparently satisfied. It is the following day before Narváez learns that the town Hernán illegally founded, to which he sent his officers demanding its surrender, has not surrendered. On the contrary. Its commander, a boy of fumbling speech called Sandoval, has sent his men as prisoners to Tenochtitlan.

✻ ✻ ✻

'I have just received news that will make you very happy,' says Muctezuma. An attendant brings forward a rolled cloth and opens it.

Ten, fourteen, *eighteen* ships are painted on a ground of blue. They look a bit like canoes and a bit like pyramids, but you can tell what they are. In another part of the picture are horses: these really look like horses, a Spanish painter would not have done better. There are a lot of horses, at least forty. The Captain's mouth is dry. Alvarado is leaning over his shoulder, swearing softly in his excitement.

'You see, your friends have come,' says the emperor. 'Now you can go home.'

Alvarado whoops for joy and pretends to beat a finger-drum. Tapia and Ávila dance. The Captain feels a stone in his chest.

'This is wonderful news. As you say, our friends have come. In many ships.'

'Yes, yes, many.' The emperor laughs gaily. 'It is very fortunate. Now you will not have to wait until your own are ready.'

'Very fortunate.' (Who is it? *Eighteen ships!*) 'I am surprised that I didn't receive a message . . .'

'No doubt your messenger is on his way.'

The Captain's smile is slipping: he puts it back. 'Perhaps I will go to the coast at once, to greet these friends.'

'Perhaps you should,' agrees Muckety.

The news, somehow (who has been listening at the doorway?), has got out, and in the distance he hears joyful shouts and the firing of a hackbut in celebration.

Damn them. We may need every pinch of powder.

Brother Olmedo seeks to avoid trouble, in whatever guise it presents itself. He sees no reason why, on his journey to the coast to carry out certain services for the Captain, he should not avail himself of a native porter, although his Order enjoins walking on his own feet. He walked enough on that frightful journey to Tlascala, and a sore on his right foot, which became infected, still bothers him.

As a race, the Indians are strong. The porters are very strong. Short and stocky, their legs knotted with muscle. He admires their endurance. It is a feat to carry another man on your shoulders over steep, uneven ground for mile after mile. Particularly a man of the girth of Brother Olmedo.

He has a fine view from his perch. A beautiful country. A virgin field for the evangelist, but he has a suspicion that the work will not be as easy as it looks. The Indians are intelligent and – rightly treated – tractable, even sensitive; yet there is something in them . . . Unregenerate? He has been labouring diligently with Muckety, who has as keen a mind as Olmedo has encountered, and the emperor has shown genuine interest in the truths of the Gospel. Yet his devotion to his pagan sacrifices is undimmed.

There is going to be fighting. Olmedo knows it. Not between *cristianos* and Indians, which is one thing and perhaps the only way of bringing Christ to them, but among Spaniards, which is nothing but bad.

The Captain has penned a letter, and here is Olmedo bumping his way down to San Juan to deliver it.

He has read it, naturally. It's a good letter.

> *Gentlemen,*
> *I do not know who you are or what you want, and pray you to communicate these things to me as soon as possible. I serve His Majesty and have reduced this country to docile obedience to him, and I trust that you have not come here to disturb that condition. The messenger who carries this is empowered to speak for me and to receive your reply.*
> *Your most obedient servant in Christ,*
> *Hernán Cortés*
> *Tenochtitlan, the 28ᵗʰ day of April, anno domini 1520*

Olmedo will take the Captain's side. He deplores the Captain's impetuousness and some of his other qualities, but he finds a breadth in Hernán that he enjoys. Against whom will he take the Captain's side? Against even the King? Pray God it doesn't go that far. If it does, his cloth will protect him. But against the Governor of Cuba, for certain.

Olmedo does not like Diego Velásquez. There was the matter of an estate in Cuba, willed to Olmedo's Order, which Diego Velásquez confiscated and gave to one of his many relations. Say what you will about the Captain (and much was said after the distribution of the gold), he would never do anything as high-handed — as *stupid* — as that.

The three men whom Narváez sent to Sandoval to demand the surrender of Villa Rica, and whom Sandoval with unconcealed glee sent as prisoners to the Captain, arrive in Tenochtitlan goggle-eyed and subdued. They have had many surprises on this journey up from the coast, not the least of which was the sight of a fat friar on his way down, but nothing has prepared them for the city on the lake.

The Captain rides out to meet them at the Turtle Gate. He was informed of their coming by a Tlascalan scout, but does not yet know who they are. They are covered in dust and look, on their perches, like startled parrots. He sits his horse comfortably, enjoying the coolness that rises from the lake.

'Gentlemen, you are welcome to Tenochtitlan. Whom do I have the honour of addressing?'

All that matters is the name of their commander. Obligingly, they tell him straight away. Pánfilo de Narváez.

Red hair. Overbearing. Excellent swordsman. Lazy.

'I had the pleasure of his acquaintance in Cuba,' smiles the Captain. 'I hope he is in good health.'

It is difficult for them, lurching in their high wicker seats, to maintain their dignity. He lets them feel the lack of it, as the little procession paces back into the city. He's taken six mounted officers with him. It looks good, and the horses need the exercise. From his saddle, he tops his visitors by a head. They are thunderstruck: the sight of the city has already done half his work for him.

He will hold a banquet. Discreetly, he will give them gold.

Pánfilo de Narváez's town consists of a huddle of huts by the seashore, but he has hopes that by Whitsun it will be as large as Villa Rica. He has not visited Villa Rica himself, but he gathers from the people he has sent there that it is a shabby place where the church doesn't even have a proper roof.

His church will have a fine roof. He has brought the best carpenters from Cuba. He also has silversmiths, candle-makers and even a glass-maker. The glass-maker should at least encounter no difficulty in finding sand.

To tell the truth, he has more men than he needs, but the Governor encouraged him to accept all who volunteered. Narváez does not fool himself that his army of more than a thousand enlisted out of affection for him or dislike of Hernán: he knew it was the smallpox, that they were desperate to get away from Cuba. And no doubt they hoped to turn a profit.

Narváez has been talking to the chief of Cempoala. A gross fellow, his eyes half-buried in little pillows of fat, out of which they gleam sharply. He laughs a lot.

'Oh, he is nothing at all,' the chief said, between peals of laughter, when asked about Hernán. 'He made a lot of trouble here. But he is nothing at all.'

'Are you friendly with him?' Narváez pressed.

'Oh, no, no, no,' said the interpreter, summarizing an agitated speech.

'When I march against him, can I count on your help?'

'Of course,' was the chief's reply.

Whatever Hernán did here, it has turned the natives against him. Narváez doesn't bother to find out what it was. A Spaniard's dealings with Indians are not important. What interests him very much, on the other hand, are Hernán's dealings with his own countrymen.

A handful of Sandoval's men have deserted to Narváez's camp. He won't rejoice too much over that, since approximately the same number of his men have deserted to Sandoval. But the deserters from Villa Rica are a rich source of information. What he has learnt about Hernán's intrigues will fill thirty pages in his report to Diego Velásquez and enliven many a dinner in Cuba.

It takes him a while to realize that these deserters from Sandoval are doing his cause no good. They have seen too much gold.

They have seen too much gold, they cannot forget it, and when they talk about it it grows in their imaginations. It becomes the only thing they can think of, and the more they talk about it the larger, in the minds of their hearers, waxes the man who has obtained it. Ornaments of gold clinking delightfully in baskets. Collars of gold hung about the necks of Hernán and his captains. A mountain of gold – that is what they say – piled up in Hernán's hut on this very shore, gift of the emperor who is now, no one seems able to deny it, Hernán's prisoner. At the dazzling centre of this hallucinated talk there shines the sun itself, that un-believable wheel of gold, as wide across as a man's outspread arms, they say with awe, and cross themselves as if they have seen a glory they shouldn't.

What is he supposed to say about all this? Try to belittle it? Say it was not so much, after all? How angry *that* would make them! But if he lets them chatter on like this, only one conclu-sion can in the end force itself into the mind of even his slowest-witted follower, and that is that if he has any sense he will attach himself to the leader who has obtained such fantastic wealth in so short a time, and has distributed it, however unevenly, among his men, in preference to one who has so far got hold of very little and not given away any. (He will, as soon as he has defrayed his expenses.)

And, of course, he can't silence them. In any case it's too late now. They have chattered all over the camp. And Olmedo has come.

Brother Olmedo is, in Narváez's opinion, a disgrace to his Order. It is not the business of the Church to support rebels.

Narváez scratches his bites. Then on a sudden rush of fear he raises his forearm and studies the weals on it. Two of them are infected, and the thin rivulet of yellow pus that had been trickling from each has now hardened. He picks off this yellow film. Painful they are, but they are mosquito bites and not the marks of smallpox. Aren't they?

He has no fever. And it's the Cubans, anyway, who are dying of it.

Under a hastily erected thatch in the south-eastern lowlands, Velásquez de León reads, for the fourth time, the two letters that have come to him.

One is from Hernán. It reminds him that Hernán has entrusted him with a hundred and twenty men and a sum in gold; further, that he, Velásquez, has sworn loyalty to Hernán and that Hernán has given him presents; and it asks him – most politely – to come with his hundred and twenty men to a rendezvous at Cholula, from where Hernán is planning to march against Pánfilo de Narváez.

The other letter is from Pánfilo de Narváez. It reminds him that he, Velásquez de León, is Narváez's brother-in-law and a cousin of the Governor of Cuba in whose name Narváez has come to these shores. It asks him – somewhat peremptorily – to make his way, with as many men as he can muster, to Narváez's camp where Narváez is preparing to march inland to capture the rebel Hernán Cortés.

Velásquez de León places both letters under a stone to keep them from blowing away and studies, abstractedly, the empty landscape. What is he to do? If this is about honour, he is pledged to both the men who claim his allegiance. If it is a matter of expediency, the matter is no simpler. Who has been the more generous to him? Hernán, and forgiven him, too. But there are the ties of kinship, and he might yet hope for something from his cousin. Who is the more likely to win the coming contest? Hernán is seriously outnumbered. But being outnumbered seems to bring out the genius in him.

Velásquez muses. Genius is a quality he lacks. He used to envy it in Hernán — that, at times, supernatural quickness, that ability to adapt to new circumstances. Occasionally he felt Hernán was laughing at him, for his slower understanding and his obstinate holding to a course. But it makes no sense to resent another man's quickness when it is not directed against you and when you might profit from it. So he reined in his envy, and his pride of birth, too, for a Velásquez of any degree is far higher in the scale of things than this threadbare son of a gentleman from Medellín.

He has reaped, to his own surprise, a rich harvest from it.

He gives the question another spin. Narváez knows nothing about the country. This thought presents itself neatly, with a little space around it. If Narváez knows nothing about the country, he knows nothing of importance. He has not fought the Indians of the country. He has not lived alongside them. He does not know how to weigh what they say, when to charm them and when to frighten them out of their wits. Hernán will be able to use the Indians against him even while Narváez is relying on their friendliness. And Narváez will be unable to fight on any inch of ground that Hernán does not know infinitely better.

But if he has *three times* as many men?

And if, in addition, Velásquez takes his hundred and twenty to join Narváez? Hernán will then be left with less than three hundred men, some of whom will be tied up in guarding Muckety. While Narváez will have at his disposal close on fourteen hundred.

And Hernán, fighting Spaniards this time, will not have the advantage steel, horse and cannon gave him over blades of flint.

It's a compelling wager.

The Captain makes a farewell visit. 'Your Majesty, I depart today for the coast. The Spaniards who have arrived here are, unfortunately, very bad men and not really Spaniards at all. They will cause trouble unless I deal with them. I shall not be away long.'

He is certain that nothing in this speech surprises the emperor.

'We are sorry you are going away,' says Muckety, whose manner has softened since the advent of Narváez. 'We enjoy our conversations.' He lowers his lucent dark eyes as he says it, and it occurs to the Captain that it might actually be the truth.

'The friends I am leaving behind will entertain you.'

'We are glad of it. But we do not understand who these Spaniards, who are not Spaniards, are. What do they want here?'

'They have heard of the riches of your kingdom, and of the friendship between Your Majesty and us, and they have come here to destroy everything.'

'How strange.'

'I shall leave Pedro de Alvarado in command here.'

'As you wish,' says the emperor. 'We shall hope for your success, since you say that these are bad men. But it is a good thing they have come, since, when you have defeated them, you will have their ships to go home in, will you not?'

The Captain leaves Alvarado with a garrison of a hundred, supported by Tlascalans. It is as many as he can afford, and if Velásquez de León fails him it will be more than he can afford.

Alvarado looks at him over a bitten knuckle. 'Good luck.'

'You shouldn't have any problems here,' says the Captain. 'They're waiting to see what happens between us and Narváez.'

'Yes. They're backing both sides.'

'How do you know that?'

'Because I would.'

'Be kind to Muckety. Cheer him up. Don't take your eyes off him.'

'They're preparing for another of their ghastly festivals.'

'I gave them permission. Just let them get on with it.'

They clasp hands. *He is the bravest and most enterprising of my commanders. He, if anyone . . .*

The Captain has made the garrison take an oath of loyalty to Alvarado. Of Alvarado's own loyalty he has no doubt.

He swings into the saddle.

The Captain takes his little force to Cholula and waits for Velásquez de León, who may not come. He waits also to hear how successful he has been in bribing Narváez's commanders. A lot of gold has gone to the coast in the pockets of the trio sent to him by Sandoval: some is theirs to keep, and some is to be spent on the Captain's behalf.

He is waiting for the gold, the fantastic tales and the uncertainty about the dangers of this unknown country to have their effect on Narváez's men. As, presumably, Narváez is waiting for contemplation of the penalties for rebellion and his own overwhelming superiority in numbers to have their effect on the Captain's men.

The Captain waits three days. The men he sent to snoop in the enemy camp return to say that Narváez has established himself in Cempoala.

Next morning he sniffs the air and his nose tells him it would be a mistake to wait any longer.

Ever since the Droopy-ear had brought the news about the Spanish ships, I had been in a state of dreadful suspense. When the Captain said he would take the Tongue and me with him to the coast, 'since we might have to deal with the chief of Cempoala all over again', I hastened back to my quarters to tell Taino.

He was talking to one of the *winic* servants, who slipped away when I appeared. 'Pack everything up,' I said. There wasn't much to pack. I still had the jaguar's head from Potonchan, wrapped in a sack, and the cotton armour the Captain had given me. And a couple of tin plates and a gourd for water. That was about all.

Taino cast a glance around. No doubt he was thinking I was mad.

'We're going home!' I rejoiced. Then, realizing this might have been a bad mistake, I put my head around the frayed curtain and looked up and down the passageway. Fortunately there was no one in sight.

I turned back to Taino, who was looking at me in bewilderment. Controlling my excitement, I said, 'We are going down to the coast. There's going to be fighting. It's our chance to get away.'

'Get away?'

We had never talked about this. Fearful of raising Taino's hopes, I had kept to myself my plans for slipping out of the camp and going over to Narváez, putting myself in his hands. I was certain that, even if Narváez did not defeat the Captain, the two of them would strike a deal and then Narváez would go back to Cuba. Or, at the very least, one of his ships would return, it *must* return, if only to take back the news of what had happened. And Taino and I would be on it, sailing to freedom.

I now explained this to him, breathlessly, watching for his eyes to light up at the prospect of escaping from the palace of Axayacatl. To my dismay, they did not.

'I not go back to Cuba,' he said.

'What?'

'I not go back there.'

'But . . . you will be with *me*.'

His face set. 'I not go back.'

I cast desperately about for some way out of this.

'But it won't be the same,' I tried to explain.

'Why?'

'I know that terrible things happened there . . .' I stopped, unsure what I was going to say next. That those things were over and finished with? He had told me they were not. Even if they were, would that wipe out the memory of them? How blind I had been not to foresee this. 'You will be with *me*,' I said again. I was not even managing to convince myself. 'I will protect you.'

'You cannot,' he said flatly. 'You not know anything about Cuba.'

It was true.

'Then we shall go somewhere else,' I said, with a certainty I didn't feel. After that, inspiration came to me. 'We shall go to Spain.'

And why shouldn't we? Sooner or later there would be a ship leaving for Seville, from this coast or from one of the islands (not Cuba). In Spain, Taino would be safe. No one there would make him labour on a plantation or send him to the mines. There was the problem of how I would pay for the passage, but perhaps, I thought, the Captain would give me some gold. I then remembered that I was planning to desert the Captain, but I decided to consider this difficulty later.

'Spain,' repeated Taino. This idea did at least seem to have aroused faint curiosity in him. 'But Spain far away.'

'Yes.'

'So how we go there?'

'I will find a way.' I thought of all that had befallen me so far and how I had survived it, and it began to seem quite possible that after I had been rescued from the shipwreck and lived in Chanek, and then been given the opportunity to rejoin my fellow Spaniards at Ix Chel, I should now be rescued once again, from the Captain and his ambitions, and end up in Spain where I had started. Indeed, the more I thought about it, the more likely it seemed that this would happen.

'What I do in Spain?' asked Taino. He did not look much happier about Spain than Cuba.

'What you do now,' I laughed. 'We will say you are my servant.'

'I am your servant,' he said.

I was shocked beyond speech.

But he was not thinking about what he'd said, but about Spain. He made the upward movement of his head that meant no. 'That not for Taino,' he said.

I saw at that moment, or thought I did, what he saw. A city like the one we were in, but even more incomprehensible. Its buildings taller, its sights and sounds more senseless, its smells more alien. Its inhabitants, without exception, the pale-skinned, brutish beings who had persecuted him. The fruits, the birds, the animals not like the ones of his homeland, nor yet like the ones here, but unimaginably strange. The gods unknown and hostile. The sky changed, perhaps the sun itself a different sun.

How could I propose to do this to him and tell myself it was for his sake?

With an effort I shook off a growing feeling of hopelessness. 'There will be somewhere we can go,' I said. I had no idea where it might be.

'We go to Chanek,' he said.

Tenderness and exasperation fought in me. I picked up the two tin plates. 'Are you coming with me or not?'

'I come with you,' he said, 'but not to Cuba.'

Alvarado was uneasy. He had been left a slender garrison with which to guard an emperor who was no longer docile and control a city in fiesta. The fiesta was not one he understood and he had reasons for thinking it was a cloak for rebellion.

He had been plainly told so, by a Tlascalan.

'They will fall on you from behind and above,' said the Tlascalan. 'They are making holes in the wall of the palace where you sleep. When they have killed and eaten you, they will put Hummingbird back in his shrine and throw your own teotl down the stairway.'

Alvarado personally inspected the outer walls of the palace and could see no sign of attempts to break through the stonework. However, it was obvious that something was afoot at the temple, because piles of rope had been moved to the bottom of the stairway, together with poles and other things.

'What are these for?' he asked an Indian who seemed to be in charge of them.

He was using as interpreter a Droopy-ear who had not gone home with the others, and had learned some Spanish.

The Indian standing beside the ropes said he didn't know.

Alvarado looked around him and hated everything he saw. Every part of it baffled him, or was a perversion of what it ought to be, or else was startlingly clear in its meaning and its meaning was death. The peaked canopies from which hung coloured paper streamers, red, black and blue, and he knew without needing to look again that the red was blood. The stewing of meat in one corner of the temple precinct, in enormous copper pans – he did not recognize this meat, he did not like the appearance of it, he thought it might be human. The solemn, skeletal circle of Indians that occupied the very centre of the area: men of middle age, their ravaged faces smeared with chalk, their feet blackened, squatting with lowered heads, intoning a chant that set his flesh creeping.

The Indians had erected a high screen of reeds in front of one wall of the courtyard, and nothing behind it could be seen. Immediately suspicious, he went to investigate.

There was a clutch of priests in attendance, but he shouldered his way through. At first he thought he was looking at a pile of corpses. Then he saw that it was a single object, pale and fleshy but with a hue to it that he greatly disliked, and that it was of human form but of gigantic size. If it stood upright on its gilt-sandalled feet, of which each toenail was a piece of shell, it would be higher than the doorways in the palace. It lay on its back on a wicker bed, scowling upward with its nightmare of a face. It was dressed in a grotesque mixture of feathers, plant fibres, precious stones and gold. Its vileness, its affront, was that ruddy hue that shone through the pasty flesh. Blood. Mother of God.

He seized his sword, but his companion laid a hand on his arm.

'You gave them permission to make it, Pedro.'

'Did I?' When had he? He could not have known what he was doing.

'It's only an image. Come away.'

He consented to be led.

His unease persisted. Several more Tlascalans came to him

with stories about the Meshica plot. One of them said that the Meshica were going to burn the *cristianos* in the temple plaza where the *cristianos* had burnt the governor and his sons. Alvarado had in fact noticed some piles of wood there. He had thought they were part of the preparations for the festival.

He didn't believe everything the Tlascalans told him. He thought they would say anything against the Meshica, and take anyone's side against the Meshica. But he had to listen to them because he had no other informants. In this city he was like a man blind and deaf. He understood nothing he heard and nothing he saw. He wished he had Hernán's gift for getting into the heads of these people.

Then something happened that he did understand. The Meshica stopped bringing them food.

You did not have to be a Daniel to interpret this.

He had to do two things straight away. One was organize a food supply. The other was find out exactly what was planned and when the attack would start. He selected a resourceful fellow to go to the market, buy what he could and pay for it with whatever the traders would accept. Then he turned his attention to the other matter and was at a loss, since he could only get hold of the information he needed by capturing a Meshica and that in itself would be an act of war.

Fate played into his hands.

He was walking through the temple precinct one evening on his regular gloomy vigil, with two companions and his interpreter, when he saw by the light of the braziers that the disgusting idol he had seen behind the screen had been set up in a corner, that flanking it were two smaller, equally hideous, images, and that sitting motionless in front of each of them was an Indian with a shaved head.

Alvarado made haste to the spot. His nerves were quivering. The three Indians – trussed like calves – looked dully at him. They were waiting to be sacrificed.

Alvarado glanced around. The precinct was deserted. He drew his dagger and his companions drew theirs. In a moment, the cords were cut and the three dazed Indians were being pushed towards the palace of Axayacatl.

There, with the aid of the Droopy-ear, Alvarado questioned them for many hours. They were asked what was going to happen at the festival, whether the Meshica planned to kill all the *cristianos*, when the attack would take place and what the signal would be.

They wouldn't talk. It occurred to him that perhaps they really didn't know anything, but he dismissed the possibility. They knew *something*. They had heard talk in the temple or the street. Of course they knew.

They were silent, stupefied.

He burned them with iron. It had never failed before, but he thought it was going to fail this time.

The first one died under it. Weaker than they'd thought. He hadn't said a word, only prayed to his gods.

The second began to shriek and gibber. So far, the fire had only burned him a little, but he had seen what happened to the first one, who was, truth to say, a bad sight by the end. There was clearly no sense to be got out of him after that point, and his shrieks would disturb the neighbourhood, so they stuck a knife in him and threw him into the canal.

Alvarado turned to the third. The youngest and perhaps the fittest. On closer inspection he looked the most intelligent, too. They should have questioned him first. Or perhaps the fate of the other two had cleared his head.

'Slowly,' said Alvarado. 'I want this one to last.'

He lasted well. They laid burning embers on his stomach and he called on his god, but he told them nothing. Until the end. Then, with the interpreter urging desperately in his ear – because all of them were exhausted and the air was getting difficult to breathe – 'Is it true that they will kill these *teotl* at the festival?' – the wretch as the fire bit deeper whispered with his dying breath, 'At Toxcatl the *teotl* will die.'

Alvarado looked at his companions in triumph.

* * *

Narváez had made his headquarters in the temple. On the lower level were sixty of his best men and a falconet; on the top platform, in what he took to be the shrine (there was for some reason a wooden Cross there, a Christian cross no less, that had been smeared – diabolically – with blood), he lay down to sleep among his personal guard.

The base of the temple was completely surrounded by his artillery. The main body of his force was encamped outside the town. He assumed Hernán to be somewhere in the foothills.

It was raining heavily. The rain beat on the thatched roof and some of it dripped through on to the stones, where it splashed with a monotonous, soothing rhythm.

He fell asleep.

Someone was shouting in his ear. Narváez struggled through the tatters of his dream. A torch dazzled him: beyond it loomed a wild-eyed figure with dripping hair.

'What is it?'

Something hurtled through the flimsy screen that covered the entrance to the shrine and smashed into the wall behind him.

Narváez sat up abruptly and felt for his boots. He pulled them on, rammed his helmet on his head and reached for the broadsword that lay under the mattress. Grasping it, he went outside.

It had stopped raining. The stars were bright. Hemmed in a corner of the temple precinct, his hackbutteers were shooting wildly from behind pillars and benches. Above the crackling of gunfire, the crossbows of his enemy hummed.

He swung his sword at a creeping shadow, which went down in a straight line like a tree falling. Then a tide of Hernán's men came surging up the steps, his guards rushed to meet them and the air shuddered with the collision of steel.

Narváez raised his massive sword and waded into the fight. He brought the blade down on the shoulder of a fellow who was coming at him but it glanced off a well-made steel corselet.

He lifted the weapon again and, holding it aloft, whirled to see who was behind him and kicked the sword out of the hand of a surprised trooper whose face he recognized from a gaming-house in Cuba. Narváez put his foot on the dropped sword, but it was almost the last thing he was able to do because of the press of men around him, which gave him no space to swing the broadsword but reduced him to trying to keep his feet like a bullock in a fast-flowing stream, holding the weapon impotently above his head.

He was being forced back into that cursed shrine by an irresistible wave of attackers, among whose faces he glimpsed the youthful features of Sandoval. He was being called to surrender, to which he shouted back angrily that he would surrender to no rebel. There came an answering roar from Hernán's men of 'Long live the King!', the insolence of which made his blood boil as he stumbled backwards through the curtain into almost total darkness.

'Give yourself up or we will set fire to the roof!' someone shouted.

Narváez sensed them grouping on the other side of the curtain, off guard for the moment because they had driven him and his men into the shrine and now they would concentrate on trying to fire the rain-soaked thatch, and a bloodlust seized him. Grasping his sword with both hands and holding it before him like a battering ram, he charged at the entrance, aiming straight through the curtain at the unsuspecting soldiers on the far side of it. But the sword in its passage ripped the curtain from its hanging and it fell over his head. The pikeman had a perfect target, and struck.

Narváez howled. He staggered back into the shrine, one hand pressed to his face, which was still covered by the curtain but was streaming blood, and worse.

The pain and the rage at his mutilation so blotted out all other things that he didn't know his boots were on fire until he smelt them.

* * *

There was blood on the ground, or was it mud? Narváez's horses slipped and plunged as their riders mounted. It looked, to an innocent eye, as if the plunging of the horses was responsible for what happened next – the riders all falling out of their saddles, as one man, all slipping to the wet ground in a heap of legs and armaments. Brother Olmedo, who did not have an innocent eye and had cut the girths with his own knife, watched long enough from the shadows to see the results of his handiwork, then hurried away to attend to his priestly functions. In a battle, there might be deaths. He had heard enough confessions in the past twenty-four hours to wish never to hear another one, and it was partly to give his mind a rest from other men's sins that he had cut the girths of the horses, but a man of God never knew where he might be needed.

A report of the capture of Narváez was brought to the Captain as he was directing the assault on a building where one of Narváez's commanders was fighting like a tiger. He left Velásquez de León in charge and went to see his adversary.

Narváez was nastily wounded. Blood was seeping down his face from a pulped eye socket which had been inadequately covered by a strip of cloth. He sat on a wooden bench with his body twisted in anger and his hands clutching the wood. Sandoval stood over him with a drawn sword and a grim smile.

'I hope you will spare my life,' the prisoner growled.

'I wish you no harm, my friend,' said the Captain, dropping easily on to a bench opposite and helping himself from a jar of olives that stood nearby. It was a long time since he had bitten into an olive. He would have olive trees planted on his estate here. A sheltered slope. They would do well.

'Did you try to negotiate with Muckety?' he enquired.

'*He* tried to negotiate with *me*.'

Olmedo had told him as much. He hadn't wanted to believe it. 'Did you say you would give him back his kingdom?'

'Of course.'

The Captain chuckled.

Narváez's men would join him now, increasing his force four-fold. Narváez's horse and cannon would be his. He would be able to start in earnest on founding colonies. More men would come from Cuba, because Diego Velásquez had shot his bolt and would not try again. The King would smile on him, in recognition of his services.

In these circumstances, the recent difficulties with Muckety seemed unimportant.

Pedro de Alvarado had known this would be the day, even before the dying prisoner told him. From what he had learned of the festival, it was obvious. This was the day when they would dance in the temple, this was the day on which the idol made with blood would be paraded through the streets and later eaten. Therefore this was the day on which Spaniards would be killed, unless he struck first.

He had taken four officers into his confidence, in addition to his brother, Jorge, and told them to hand-pick half a dozen men each. He did not want the whole garrison knowing what was planned.

He had not fixed on a time. He would know the moment. He had a flair for these things. That was why Hernán had left him in charge.

He bit his knuckle half the night. It was a heavy responsibility. He hoped he would nip trouble in the bud. The Meshica had never tasted steel. They would be shocked by what Spanish swords could do. He knew that, instead of averting a war, he might start one. But there was going to be a war if he did nothing.

It wasn't his way to do nothing, in any case. He was sick of the waiting game in Tenochtitlan: it had been eating him away. As dawn broke he went up to the roof. On the maze of canals that threaded the city, a pale light glittered. Mist rose from the lake, and with it some wildfowl, crying. Alvarado's spirits lifted. They were going to do something. By God and His Mother, they were.

He was again on the roof about two hours later when the drumming started in the temple precinct. He knew it was for the dance, but he could never hear an Indian drum without thinking of war. There were about sixty paint-and-feathered Meshica there, young men, decked in finery, drawn up in a phalanx. The dance, when it began, puzzled his eye and he looked away impatiently. He saw, at almost the same instant, two things: lurching through the streets, held up by its blood-streaked priests, the disgusting image he had seen two days earlier; and, at the edge of the precinct, a masked and feathered youth playing a flute, while before him people abased themselves in postures of adoration, and the stinking incense they could do nothing without rose in clouds.

Enough. Enough of this. He ran down the stone stairs with his hand on his sword.

The drumming was loud. The street was crowded and it seemed to him that the Indians returned his gaze boldly instead of avoiding it, as they normally did.

He divided the chosen men into four groups and told each to go to a different gate of the precinct. They were to mingle with the crowds until they saw his own group attack. Then they were to do the same.

He gave them a few minutes to get among the people. Then he drew his sword, shouted 'Santiago!' and rushed forward.

It was as it always was with him: the sword moving of its own volition, more spirit than steel. And he himself dreaming, at peace.

He heard the cries. They came from somewhere distant. He was aware the drumming had stopped. It was because he had sliced off the drummer's hands. They had flown through the air like clumsy birds.

All around he saw the screaming Indian faces. He hated them with a calm hatred, and his sword bit. Bite, for their womanish screams. Bite, for their narrow eyes. Bite, for their sodomizing. Bite, bite, bite for their tearing out of hearts and their sordid banquets of flesh and their reeking temples.

Oh, he was dispensing justice.

An Indian with one arm lopped off spun howling towards him, and he smiled and lopped off the other.

There was a woman . . . what was a woman doing here? — running in circles and flailing her arms like a crazed thing. He watched her for a few moments with curiosity, but as she continued doing the same thing he opened her belly with a sword-cut.

Still working calmly, he glanced to left and right to check on his men. The Indians were making such an agonized flurry in the precinct, like panic-stricken fowls, with their bloodsoaked feathers and dangling limbs, that he could hardly see his sturdy *cristianos*, but he knew they were there by the stir they were creating. He saw his brother Jorge behead an Indian with a particularly fine stroke. The Indian's blood was all over his face but he seemed not to notice it.

Alvarado stepped forward to slash at a running bundle of feathers and almost slipped. Sweet Saviour, the ground was mucky. Blood was the least of it. Brains and splinters of bone. (Their bones are just like ours.) Entrails by the yard, together with their contents. It was like a market.

Then he heard the conch blown. A wild, eerie noise: he had always hated it. It was being blown on the wall of the circular temple behind them. He had no doubt what it meant.

He shouted to his men to return at once to their quarters. Swords still in hand, they left unfinished what was still to do and ran from the precinct, jumping over the corpses and pushing aside Indians who blundered into their way.

Back inside the palace, Alvarado counted his men. All present, blood-covered and wild of eye. None injured, except for a few bruises. Some of the dancers had tried to fight back with wooden poles.

Alvarado drew breath. His heart was thundering but his head was quite cool. All the same it seemed to him that the ground shook. He ran up to the roof.

The street below him was entirely filled with a raging sea of Meshica warriors.

The news that Alvarado and his hundred men were fighting for their lives inside the palace of Axayacatl was brought to the Captain by a Tlascalan runner.

As it happened, the Captain had celebrated his victory over Narváez the previous night. He and his commanders had made good inroads on Narváez's stock of wine, the fumes of which had not yet dissipated from the Captain's head. He had spent the final hours of the night in a game of cards.

The result of this was that the words had to make their way to him across what seemed a great distance. Thinking he had misunderstood, he asked his interpreters to repeat what they had said, and then, still unwilling to believe his ears, told them to ask the Tlascalan to repeat the message.

Patiently, the Tlascalan said it again. It was at this point, before the translation came, that the Captain admitted the meaning of the words into his mind.

'No,' he said vehemently. 'It can't be.'

He assumed that it was Muckety's doing. But while Muckety's attempt to treat with Narváez had angered him (and hurt him, too), he found it understandable. This perfidy was of a different order.

'I cannot believe it of him,' he said, and went on saying for the rest of the morning, uncertain whether to order an immediate return to Tenochtitlan or not.

It was quite likely to be a trap. But what difference did that make? If it was a trap and Alvarado was the bait, he would have to walk into it.

He hated having to rely on the Tlascalans for information. The messenger had explained nothing. However, if Alvarado's men really were besieged, he could not hope for news from the one quarter he could trust.

He was in this racked state when a distraught delegation from Muckety arrived.

Lord of the Near, all-seeing one.
I am He-Who-Speaks.
Put words into my mouth, for it is empty.

5

The city allows them back into itself in silence.

In their descent from the mountain, the only sounds have been the clank of armour, the rumble of Narváez's gun carriages and the huff and whinny of horses. There was silence over the valley as they looked down on it, silence and uncanny stillness on the lake when they came to it, its opal surface unmarked by the passage of a single canoe.

The horses are nervous and shy at things that aren't there. An apprehension settles over the whole army, now about a thousand strong, as it embarks on the causeway. The Captain has ordered two of the falconets fired from the lakeside. It's his message to Alvarado, but there is no answering shot.

Four-fifths of the army is composed of the men Narváez brought. The Captain has won them over, with gold or the promise of it, sometimes just flattery. It is his genius that he knows what to say to a man. In this case it has not been difficult. Accompanying all the gifts, underlying all the promises, has been the promise of a share in a dazzling conquest which is already assured.

It is assured no longer.

And even the slowest-witted of them, as they begin their march along that narrow causeway, can see the trap they are walking into.

*　　*　　*

'What happened to the boats?'

'What boats?' Alvarado is haggard.

'The boats we built for the lake.'

'The Indians burned them.'

'They were our escape route.' The Captain is almost too angry to speak.

Alvarado lays his sword on the bench between them. 'Perhaps you would like this.'

'Pick it up.'

'I'm sorry, Hernán. I didn't know what else to do. It worked at Cholula.'

'*This is not Cholula.*'

Nothing can mend the disaster. The Meshica have only let him into the city in order to destroy him. No help will come because there is no quarter from which it *could* come. Narváez and Alvarado between them have undone him.

He lets two days elapse before visiting Muctezuma. The emperor looks wan. His eyes kindle as the Captain enters his prison.

'You have not visited us, Malinche. You have not come to play *patolli* with us.'

'You have not dealt honestly with me,' growls the Captain. 'You had dealings, behind my back, with my enemy.'

A faint surprise flits across the emperor's face. '*You* have not dealt honestly with *us*, Malinche. You have talked about friendship, but you have made us a prisoner and killed our people.'

'I have come to tell you that the market must be opened.'

'Is it closed?'

'Yes. My men have no food.' A well has had to be dug in a courtyard of the palace. The water is brackish and tastes of ordure.

Muctezuma does not reply. He is not merely listless but seems distracted.

'You must order your people to open it again.'

'Ten years ago,' says the emperor, rousing himself, 'the rains failed for two years in succession. Many people died of hunger. It is a sad death. The *teotl* send it.'

Alvarado steps forward violently. 'Listen, you dog . . .'

The Captain puts a hand on his arm. He is getting tired of putting a hand on Alvarado's arm.

'If we speak to the people, they will not listen,' Muctezuma says.

'Of course they will,' says the Captain with forced calm. It is the very thing he fears.

An attendant murmurs something in the emperor's ear. The emperor tilts his head, purses his lips and appears to give the matter, whatever it is, serious thought.

'It is possible,' he says at last, 'that the lord of Iztapalapa will be able to persuade them to open the market.'

'Who the Devil is the lord of Iztapalapa?' demands Alvarado.

Marina, the Captain's mistress and interpreter, answers, in Spanish. 'He is Kweetl-awac, the brother of lord Muctezuma, and he is in the next room.'

'You mean he's a prisoner?'

The Captain recalls them. A sorry sight they looked on his last visit. He has been in the habit of selecting two or three, from time to time, unchaining them and taking them in to talk to Muckety. An act of charity. He doubts if Alvarado bothered, in his absence.

'Do you know which one he is?'

She says she does. He sends her next door with Tapia and a key to the fetters.

They come back a few minutes later with an Indian whom the Captain does not recognize as the lord of Iztapalapa or anything else. Since they have been in there, in chains and what are fast becoming rags, stripped of their feathers and all the other things they wear, they have been indistinguishable to him.

The man prostrates himself before Muckety. There pass between them, on the one hand, fealty; on the other, tenderness. The Captain sees it and, despite himself, is moved.

They exchange words. Then Muckety speaks to the interpreters.

'If you release this man, he will try to get the market opened again,' the interpreters say.

What are the alternatives? The Indian is doing no good sitting there with a chain on his feet; and at the moment, *they* have to feed *him*.

The provisions the Captain brought into the city do not last beyond a few days. The market is not opened.

'Why not?' the Captain demands of Muctezuma. Muctezuma doesn't know.

Life inside the palace of Axayacatl, since at the moment there is no fighting, becomes bitterly focused on finding something to eat. Every day, a few *cristianos* venture out into the street to see what they can beg or buy. Sometimes they come back with a string of fowl bought from a farmer or some grain. It keeps hope alive. If the worst comes to the worst, there would be the rats.

The dogs come in for some eyeing, but there isn't much meat on them and in any case they are too valuable. They have fought well in all the battles and the Indians are afraid of them. No one even thinks about eating the horses. A horse is worth more than a man, and particularly – it is widely thought but only said under the breath – the sort of man who joined Narváez's army to escape the smallpox in Cuba.

It troubles the Captain, when he has time to think about it, that not all the men who came over to him from Narváez have reached the palace. Fifty or so whom he sent up – with horses – from the coast, before he received news of Alvarado's folly, have failed to arrive. He fears the worst. On the other hand, it cannot be denied that if they turned up now they would only make the food shortage more acute.

Every day, three times a day, a procession of attendants brings his meal to Muckety.

It is less of a banquet than it was in the first days of his imprisonment, when the number of dishes brought to him in his rooms was never less than fifty. Now it is more like twenty. Perhaps the emperor is trying to be tactful, or fears provoking his captors to violence. Or perhaps he is losing his appetite.

Nevertheless, the state with which he is served, the haughty demeanour of his attendants as they carry the dishes, each under its white cloth, past the noses of the *cristianos*, and the heavenly aroma of those dishes in the nostrils of the famished garrison, do not decrease.

The Captain, observing the effect of these daily processions on his men, the involuntary twitching of the muscles, a dangerous dilation of the eyes, makes sure that only his most reliable soldiers are on duty at the times of the emperor's meals.

One day, some men who have been out looking for food come back in a hurry. Blood is streaming from the heads of three of them and they have only one sorry fowl to show for it. They have been set on by Meshica.

The same day, the Spaniards guarding the entrance to the palace have to retreat inside under a shower of stones. Later, a soldier goes out to check on the artillery and gets an arrow in the throat. A falconet is dragged off that night, under cover of darkness, and is not seen again.

'They're going to attack,' says Alvarado. Hunger has made his face wolfish.

Brother Olmedo says Mass and hears confessions.

The assault, a well-coordinated attack by an overwhelming force of Meshica, comes the following morning.

The cannon are fired until the iron scorches the hand. They plough bloody channels in the enemy ranks, which close at once, as if they had been furrows ploughed in water.

The Captain has a spearhead in his right calf and a stone has paralysed his elbow. He drags himself up to the roof.

From a cluster of houses to the south, Meshica are loosing arrows, stones and javelins in a lethal hail at the palace of

Axayacatl. Spanish marksmen are doing their best to pick them off, but make no impression on their numbers. Still the hail falls, and still the Meshica hurl themselves against the walls of the palace, howling murder, wanting the hearts of Spaniards in a stone dish.

They have got inside the palace twice. Olid sliced the head off one and threw it back to his fellows. They don't care what their losses are.

The Captain limps back down the staircase to be told that the Meshica are trying to break through the wall of the palace where it backs on to the canal. He is thinking about how to defend the building from attack by water when a drift of smoke disturbs his nostrils. They are trying to set fire to it, as well.

It is essential to create a space around the palace for manoeuvre. The buildings from which the Meshica launch their missiles must be destroyed. In other words, there is a need for sappers, and a means of protecting them while they work. Using beams torn from the palace, a machine is constructed.

The monster that, after several days of sawing and hammering, is trundled out of the gateway on four gun carriages has been sired by a siege catapult on the Trojan horse. As soon as the Captain sees it upright in the reddish glare of the fires the Meshica keep burning all night, he knows it won't work.

Nevertheless, when day breaks, he has his men inside it. One at the top with a crossbow, eight on the deck, variously armed and looking out of the small windows, and fourteen on the ground, to fight and push. The machine will be propelled from the inside. Those who push it will have the protection of the wooden skirt that forms most of its lowest section, interrupted by two leather flaps that allow them to get in and out (and will also, unavoidably, allow Meshica to get in and out). They have been told to keep walking in a straight line until the men on the deck, who can see where the thing is going, tell them to stop.

The Meshica are greatly excited by the machine. They gather, shouting insults, on the temple steps and neighbouring rooftops as soon as it is day. A light shower of stones falls, the morning greeting.

The Captain orders the machine to proceed into battle as soon as the men are ready. He is fighting against the north wall of the palace when he sees its improbable outline lurch forward. He cuts his way through Meshica and reaches the place. An Indian has monkeyed his way to the top of the tower and clings there with one hand, while battering at the timbers with an axe. He falls, moments later, in a graceful headlong dive, preceded by his axe, the hand that had held it now grasping in protest at the crossbow shaft in his chest.

The Meshica throw themselves in waves at it and eddy round its skirts. They seem infuriated by it; they yell defiance. They launch themselves at it with flint swords whirling, and already they are managing to hack pieces of wood from the carapace although their blades splinter on it, the wood of the palace beams being so hard. Some throw their blunted swords away and wrench at the structure with their bare hands.

The Spaniards inside the tower blast away at them with hack-buts. Meanwhile, at the flanks of the machine, Spaniards fight hand to hand to defend the men inside. The machine gains ground inch by inch. They are half-way to the temple from which most of the stones are launched when the tower lurches to a sudden halt.

From inside comes an angry tumult. Meshica have got into it. The Captain duels his way through the bloodsoaked flap with a warrior whose head is encased in the mask of an eagle. In the gloom, in the confined space, steel glints and is dyed red.

The Captain puts his shoulder to the wooden frame.

It takes a great heaving to get the thing in motion again, and then it sways violently. But it stays upright and he has to cut his way outside, because although he is needed in there he is needed outside even more.

Stones fall like thunder on the wooden shell. Arrows skid or bounce off its sides, and hit another mark. A lad fighting at the Captain's side falls with an arrow through his cheek.

Press forward. Twenty feet to go before the stairway.

The tower sways.

Push forward.

It sways again, in the other direction.

Fifteen feet.

'*Get outside!*' roars the Captain. For the tower is toppling.

It falls slowly, so slowly that it looks as if it could be stopped, although nothing on earth could stop it now it has begun that stately descent. It is going to crash on the temple steps. The crossbowman on the top stage will certainly be killed. The others . . .

The Meshica, in their battle-delirium, seem not to notice that the tower is going to fall on top of them. They go on launching their stones and arrows.

Spaniards are scrambling out of the yawning space below the skirt and running from the contraption like rabbits. Two remain in the trap, their limbs caught.

It falls.

There is a huge shivering, like armour falling off a giant. A choking cloud of brown dust rises, cloaking the stairway from sight. The din of the crash dies away and is followed by a stupefied silence.

It is the Spaniards on the ground, in front of the stairway, who recover first. As soon as the first rift appears in the dust cloud, they rush the steps.

The Indians who weren't caught under the machine as it fell have fled. The Captain picks his way up through the wreckage, the wooden spars, splintered panels, torn bits of leather, and underneath them the crushed bodies of Meshica.

The priests have taken refuge in the shrine. They are pushed off the sides of the platform. The idols are thrown down the stairway. The fragments come to rest alongside the wreckage of the tower. Underneath both is a carpet of dead Indians.

The Captain surveys the scene and the cluster of Meshica commanders watching from a nearby rooftop. He sends for his interpreters.

'Ask them if they will accept a truce,' he says.

The answer the interpreters bring back is that the Meshica will wage war until there is not a Spaniard left alive.

The capture of the temple has achieved nothing, since they can't hold on to it. They can't pull it down, either.

They can't do anything, in fact, except defend themselves, knowing that each day some of them will die and each death is a subtraction from a figure that eventually will be zero.

And they have nothing to eat. The lord of Iztapalapa, whom the Captain was persuaded to release, not only has not opened the market but is *directing the fighting.* (This they have learned from captured Meshica.) In the circumstances, it is too much to hope that even the wiliest Spaniard could go out there and find, and come safe home with, *food.*

Rats are killed.

'Get Muckety up on the roof to talk to them,' says Alvarado.

'He says they won't listen to him.'

'He's a lying snake.'

The Captain doesn't hope for anything from it, but he sends Muctezuma up to the roof in the company of two men

There is a lull in the fighting at the moment. The Meshica are milling noisily in the open space around the palace, throwing a few stones, shouting the occasional taunt. In a few minutes, or perhaps a few hours, the confusion will resolve itself into another assault.

The emperor walks meekly between his guards. He at first said he could do nothing; but then he agreed to try. He looks to the Captain, watching him go up the stone staircase, like a man sleep-walking.

The Captain does not go up to the roof. It would make it too obvious that Muckety is his prisoner, and in any case he wants to be on the ground, where the trouble will start if it is going to.

Standing with the men who are guarding the gateway, the Captain can't, of course, see what is happening on the roof. He will have to rely on what the footsoldier Morales later tells him. And what Morales tells him is not clear.

Morales will say that he and the other soldier took Muckety to near the edge of the roof so that he could be seen by all the people below, and that they waited there for a short time for the Indians to realize that their ruler wanted to speak to them, and to become quiet. They never did become completely quiet (as, watching the crowd from the gateway, the Captain was aware: it was like watching the seething of water which hasn't quite come to the boil).

Morales will say that the Indians were restless and that when Muckety started to speak they all began murmuring and shouting, with the result that many of his words were lost. Since they had no interpreters, Morales didn't understand what the emperor was saying, but his voice was completely calm, Morales will say, and that surprised him, that at such a time Muckety's tone was so lacking in urgency.

No one saw the stone thrown. It came from out of the midst of that seething crowd. But hundreds of people saw, or will say they saw, the emperor reel backwards into the arms of his guards, blood spurting from the side of his head.

Later, the Captain goes on to the roof and looks for the stone. He finds it without difficulty. Against his expectation, it is not one of the smoothly rounded stones the Meshica use to such effect in their slings. It is a nasty little rock, a lump of that reddish-black, pitted stone that hides behind the decorated plaster of the buildings. There is a livid crust of blood on its broken surface, which transfers itself to his hand.

He sends his own surgeon to the *tlatoani*. Shortly afterwards, it is reported to him that Muckety has torn the bandages off.

✶   ✶   ✶

The fighting continues every day. It begins at dawn with a hail of stones and a blaring of conch shells and ends at dusk, the battle ebbing and dissolving into shreds like the light in the sky. At the end of each day, the corpses of Meshica lie piled in the streets down which the falconets have been fired, and against the palace walls where they have hurled themselves as if flesh could beat down stone, and on the roofs of houses and the platforms of temples where crossbows and hackbuts have picked them off as they slung their stones and loosed their arrows. These corpses are taken away the same evening: the Spaniards retire and allow the Meshica to put away their weapons and remove their dead without molesting them — for, as the Captain says, they have enough problems without a pile of corpses outside the door. There are fewer Christian dead, far fewer: they have lost, since Alvarado's fateful escapade, about forty men. But forty is still too many and no way offers itself of putting an end to the fighting.

The Captain goes to see his prisoner.

The emperor, in addition to his usual attendants, now reduced to four, has with him a priest who comes to see him every day. The visitor looks up at the Captain with open hatred as he enters with Sandoval close behind him.

Muckety has become frail. The stone that made such an ugly wound on his head seems also to have knocked the vital force out of him. There is another thing in its place. The new thing alarms the Captain. It is a kind of remoteness.

'I have come to ask about your wound,' he says.

'What is it to you?' asks Muckety.

'I care about your health.'

'You have a strange way of caring for our health. You have destroyed it,' says Muckety.

'Some of your people have rebelled, that is all,' protests the Captain.

'All of them have rebelled,' says Muckety.

'Will you speak to your people once more?'

The *tlatoani* points, with a thin and mocking smile, to the wound in his head. 'Do you not see what they think of us?'

The Captain rests one knee on the ground, so that he is at the imprisoned emperor's eye level.

'For the sake of the friendship there has been between us . . .' (wasn't there? some unaccountable mutual liking, not to be denied?) 'I beg you to try again to persuade your people to make peace.'

'If you want to save yourselves,' the emperor says, 'you must leave the city.'

'I will not leave,' the Captain says an hour later, when his commanders come to him.

That morning, Meshica broke through the south wall of the palace. They were speedily dealt with and the gap filled up with rubble and sacking. But it was a shock.

'Hernán, we must get out of here while we still can,' says Tapia.

The Captain surveys the half-circle of grim faces. Not cowards, any of them. 'I'd thought better of you.'

Alvarado (*Alvarado!*) says, 'There's no fodder for the horses. In a few days they'll be useless.'

Once, the Meshica brought bundles of fresh grass, neatly tied with creeper.

'I won't give up everything we've gained,' says the Captain.

Ávila gives him a steady gaze. 'You'll wait for them to kill us all?'

'If we l-l-leave,' says Sandoval, 'we can come back again.'

No one troubles to tell him he's mad.

From outside the walls comes the *boom* of the falconet. Ávila and Sandoval excuse themselves to return to the fighting.

Before long, all of them have gone back to the fighting. It is at the end of the day, when the brief sunset draws all the crimson of the streets up to itself, that a soldier runs to tell the Captain that Muctezuma is dead.

✶   ✶   ✶

302

The decision makes itself as he stands looking down at the corpse. The *tlatoani* lies on his side, his body apparently fallen, as if he had been walking and his foot gave way. His eyes are open wide and their pupils reflect the flickering light from the brazier.

Muctezuma is alone. His attendants have fled. The Captain, in the depth of his despair, nevertheless glimpses the pathos of this.

'We'll leave tonight,' he says to the two who accompany him.

'What about the gold?' says Ávila.

'Pack it in boxes.' The room smells of decay already.

'What about the other prisoners?' asks Velásquez de León.

Indeed.

He goes to see them. Something might occur to him, other than what is already in his mind. But nothing new occurs to him when he sees their subdued forms, manacled to the ship's chain that unites them, their sullen and sunk faces, and smells the stink of their captivity.

'We can't take them with us,' he says to Velásquez, and leaves it at that. There is no need for him to say more, and it's not politic. He is seeing far beyond this night.

He names a man to conduct the King's gold to safety. In a room of the palace, a mare is loaded with the wealth of Tenochtitlan.

They will leave at midnight. They will muffle the horses' hooves. The Meshica don't go out at night, don't — as far as is known — post sentries, certainly don't expect to fight by night.

The cannon will have to be abandoned. Too heavy, and the wheeled carriages make a din that can be heard on the other side of the lake.

The gold . . .

Suddenly there is too much of it. Suddenly, the weight of it is more important than anyone realized. What it weighs is almost more important than what it's worth.

But not quite. In the end, no one who has it leaves it behind. The Captain, finding a chest of it — in those convenient thin bars — unaccountably without an owner, not the King's, not *his*, just a chest of the stuff which presumably should have been distributed among the army but got overlooked, announces that anyone who wants some of it may help himself. The chest has been emptied when he walks past it a short time later.

The bridges have been raised on the causeways. He knows this from interrogating prisoners, but would have expected it anyway. His men will have to make a bridge, and carry it to lay across the gaps. More beams are pulled from the palace ceilings, and a hammering begins. The Meshica who hear it will think another machine is being built.

He has made his dispositions. The rearguard, which will be in the greatest danger, will be under the command of Alvarado and Velásquez de León. They will have most of the horses. Sandoval will lead the vanguard, in which will be the women. He, the Captain, will command the main body of the army, the un-tidiest and most unreliable part, containing the baggage and the men who came with Narváez.

Midnight.

The lords of the Meshica are knifed in their chains.

Two soldiers from Zamora, brothers, do it, swiftly, without speaking. The strange thing is that the prisoners, too, are silent. They accept their deaths as if they have always been preparing for them. The only sounds they make are involuntary, a gasp as the air leaves the lungs for the last time, a gurgle of blood or mucus. The thud of the body falling forward on that unyielding chain; the steady drip of blood. And the padding of the soldiers' feet on tiles that are decorated with a pattern of seashells.

There are fourteen prisoners, as it turns out. No one was quite sure. Now the bodies are released from their shackles, laid in a row and counted. All this has to be done by candlelight, but it is good enough.

What must be done next? Just 'kill them', Velásquez had ordered. Should they be left on the floor, like fish ready for salting? The brothers go to seek further instructions. Only one needs to go, but neither wants to be left alone in that room.

Velásquez is not to be found. Such is the confusion in the rooms and corridors of the palace — never has it seemed such a labyrinth — that the one thing that can be depended on is that you won't find the person you are looking for. Half the confusion, in fact, consists of men who are looking for someone who is looking for someone else.

The other half is a wrestling with things. With boxes, armour, a towering pile of saddles, sacks of something or other, armfuls of green feathers. The things are stronger than the people: they refuse to be vanquished.

The two executioners find the Captain. 'Oh, they're dead, are they?' says the Captain. 'Take them to the north gate and throw them outside.'

The brothers enlist help, and the fourteen are carried to the north gate, where in the course of the night they will be found by the Meshica.

It is starting to rain. A fine rain, at the moment not even a drizzle, more like tiny drops condensing out of saturated air and continuing to hang there, with not enough weight to fall.

In a room at the heart of the palace, a mare raises and lowers her hooves as box after box is strapped to the harness on her back. She is strong, but they are loading her as if she were a peasant's donkey.

The coming and going is continuous. Men bring heavy wicker baskets, set them down, go away again. They come back carrying more.

Another man is fastening each basket tightly with rope. Yet another is running his hands over the harness of straps on the mare's back, checking it. The straps run over a thick woollen blanket, woven in Andalucia, which protects the mare's back and flanks. Three of the baskets have already been tied to the harness of straps: the man checking the harness finds it secure, and lifts another basket to add to the load.

In the baskets is gold.

It is in the long, flat bars into which Muckety's goldsmiths have rendered it, and each bar is stamped with the King's stamp. It is the King's gold. It is the fifth of the treasure that Muckety gave to the Captain, weighed and calculated as precisely as possible in the circumstances (which are not ideal: a pair of scales could not be found and in the end had to be made by a blacksmith, grumbling that this was not his trade and he would not accept the blame for any inaccuracies). However, there are limits to the preciseness of this fifth which have nothing to do with scales. It does not, for instance, include a fifth of the gold that was taken without Muckety's permission from the House of Birds. It certainly does not include a fifth of the gold that Alvarado eventually extracted from the wretched Cacama. There are many fifths this fifth does not include, and one of them belongs to the man who is loading the mare. He, as he loads the mare, is thinking of many things, one of them being the possibility that he will die tonight, another being the share of gold that fell to the Captain: the Captain's fifth. By agreement, the Captain took a fifth of all gold that remained after the King's fifth had been taken. There isn't a man in the army who doesn't think that is too much. However, the Captain didn't stop there, as everyone knows. At least a score of stories are circulating the camp about gold the Captain stole, seized or was given by Muckety or some other prince that was never declared, never subjected to the King's fifth or shared with others — stories of people going to the Captain's quarters with a message and seeing the gold piled up there, in a corner of the floor, chains and trinkets and jewels, just waiting for another piece to be thrown on to it.

The man loading the mare catches his finger painfully in a tightening twist of rope.

He will carry his own gold, in those handy foot-long bars,

under his padded armour. It will buy him an estate in Spain, and a fine house. And a whole stable of horses as good as this one. The gold is heavy, of course, but then the cotton armour is light, and the two together will not be much heavier than a steel cuirass, such as the one he wore in a dozen battles in Italy.

His name is Bartolomé, and he will die tonight.

At midnight the retreat begins.

The men muster in their positions, except for those who are on their knees praying, or are still trying to decide the best way to carry their gold to safety, or, although it is difficult to believe this, are asleep. Officers go through the rooms of the huge and gloomy palace, now more melancholy than ever in its desertion, rounding up laggards. Some rooms are wrecked from the tearing-out of the ceiling beams. Candles gutter, possessions lie discarded since no one wants to be burdened tonight with anything that is not essential.

The dogs lope up and down the lines of assembled men. They are in a frenzy to be off, but are too well trained to bark. Their tongues loll and their eyes blaze. They wear small suits of armour, narrow sleeves of chain mail that encase the chest and belly. As the dogs run past each other, the small steel corselets clash and clink together, drawing muttered curses from the soldiers.

The horses lift their feet. One whinnies, others answer. It is time to be going and the Devil take anyone left behind, or the whole city will be awake and they will not even have started.

In the street outside the palace, Sandoval, at the head of what is not yet a column but is still a muddle, stands in his stirrups, draws his sword and raises it high. He circles it above his head, so that the steel reddens and flashes in the light of the temple braziers. Then he sheathes the sword, takes up his lance and puts spurs to his horse. The little squadron of cavalry that will lead the cristianos out of Tenochtitlan moves forward down the street that goes to the western causeway.

Astonishingly, it is done almost without a sound. Rags have

307

been tied to the horses' hooves. Every harness bell has been removed, and strips of cloth have been wrapped around the corners of the bits so they will not jingle. Equipment has been reduced to a minimum. No cannon. No powder, only what is in the flasks of the hackbutteers.

But there is the bridge

The bridge, made from the planks and beams of the palace, is heavy. It is a stubborn, unwieldy, vile-tempered beast, and it numbs the shoulders of the men who carry it. They long to put it down, but dread the moment when they will put it down, because it will be a moment of extreme peril. Before them will yawn a gap in the causeway, and how is this fractious monster to be manoeuvred across it with no one on the other side to help? Suppose it pitches headlong into the water? No one has thought of an answer to that. It has been left to God. If God wills, the bridge will work, and if it works it will save them.

They walk as fast as they can, with the bridge on their shoulders. Since, for obvious reasons, they are at the front, just behind Sandoval and the cavalry, and since in any case the army can't proceed without them, the speed at which they walk is the speed at which the whole encumbered procession moves. It is *not fast enough.*

Sandoval, at the head, steps his horse carefully, sways as little as possible in the saddle lest the leather creak, and scours the darkness with his eyes. It is not really darkness, when your eyes are used to it and have forgotten the glare of the braziers with which the Meshica have surrounded the palace. But it is raining harder now, the drops are splashing upward from the paving and are puddling in the hollows of the stone. The rain is a curtain through which things appear indistinctly, unreliably. What is that dark shape? A gateway? He doesn't remember a gateway there. Yet a gateway it is, or seems to be as they pass it, a gateway to another courtyard to another building in this indecipherable city, but nothing emerges from it, no devil or armed Meshica, to answer the jumping of his heart. His horse treads on.

The Captain, at the centre, has one eye on the rooftops and

one on his men. From horseback he looks down on the top of the bridge, glistening with wet as it sways twenty paces ahead of him. His view of it is interrupted by the rain and by a line of pikes. He prays to God that the bridge will hold and the powder will stay dry.

His heart is beating fast, but it is with excitement. His despair has lifted. Tonight he will either lose everything, or free himself to start again. Under his breath, he is humming a ballad from Extremadura.

Alvarado, captaining the rear, is also exhilarated to be on the move. However, he does not underestimate the horrible danger of each yard of this retreat. Pacing forward, at the too-slow pace of the column governed by the speed of the men who are carrying the bridge, he rides turned in the saddle and looking behind him. The buildings are dark. The red, mist-haloed braziers fade slowly from his view. The Meshica don't like the rain, and in any case don't fight at night, and it seems they have all shut themselves up in their houses. He commends himself to Saint Christopher, protector of those who make a perilous crossing.

None of them sees a woman leaving her house to fetch water for the morning's gruel, who stops as the army of shadows passes and puts her hand to her mouth.

A conch is blown from a temple wall.

Alvarado knows that conch. He heard it on the day of Toxcatl. In a flash he sees what is to come. Even before the night is rent by other sounds – shouts, and the throbbing of the great drum that has returned to its home in the temple of Hummingbird – he is whirling his horse, ordering his men to close ranks.

It starts within minutes. A volley of arrows. A footsoldier goes down with a shaft in his neck, and a horse has been struck in the flank.

Impossible to move faster. He can't, damn it, even *see* the enemy. The Meshica are somewhere behind that glimmering curtain of rain.

Another volley. Two more horses are hit. Now, in the rain-streaked darkness, he begins to see Meshica faces, and it seems to him that they are grinning.

Fire crackles from hackbuts. The painted faces, the plumed faces, the eagle-and-ocelot masked faces are suddenly all around him. The air is filled with their rage, their javelins and arrows and their murderous stone blades. Alvarado hears again the drum, their master, hears its unrelenting beat, and he takes his Florentine sword and begins the first slaying of that endless night.

The Captain hears the drum and the lilting tune dies on his lips.

He turns his horse. The column of men and horses is too long, the curtain of rain is too thick, for him to be able to see the rearguard. But soon afterwards the eerie whoosh of arrows comes to his ears and he knows the battle has started.

Twenty paces in front of him, the wet black back of the bridge bumps along on the aching shoulders of men who do not want to lay it down yet.

He is in time to see the Meshica gathered on a rooftop, and to shout a warning.

Sandoval has reached the causeway. His heart lifted as he saw its open path ahead of him and the lake an unbroken misty darkness on either side. He has escaped the city which he feared would be his tomb.

But now he hears the drum, and he knows that the city will not easily release him.

He turns in his saddle and looks behind. He sees his detachment of horsemen also turning their heads to the sound, and behind them the moving black platform of the bridge. Then a feathery line of pikes that wavers in the rain, and behind that nothing, only the sensation of a great and moving bulk, of metal and flesh in the wet night.

And the drum.

He turns again to the front and spurs his horse.

The Captain holds up his shield under a rain of stones. They clang a deafening message on his shield and the shields of the men around him. How many stones can be stored on a rooftop?

The horses hate it. The riders shelter them, shelter their heads, with the shields, though it means leaning far forward on the horse's neck, but it is the terrible noise of the stones raining down on the steel, just above their heads, that most frightens the animals. They back and whinny. Some of the horses that came with Narváez are threatening to bolt.

When the Meshica run out of stones they will loose arrows or javelins, or just throw themselves at him in a great howling wave.

He wonders how Alvarado is faring.

Sandoval has come to the first breach.

He stares into the blackness at his feet. Only his horse saved him from it. He was riding, as fast as he dared and too slowly, with his eyes raking the mist for Meshica, when his horse shied. Another step and they would both have been in the lake.

The vanguard bumps to a halt behind him. He turns in his saddle.

'Bring the bridge forward.'

For the bridge to be brought forward, the horsemen who are at the very front have to get behind it. This is a tricky manoeuvre because, although the bridge is no more than half the width of the causeway, there is room for only one horse between it and the causeway's sloping edge. The horsemen turn their mounts carefully in the narrow space, and are about to start on the cautious single-file along the strip of stone available to them when, shivering the darkness, out of the depths, it seems, of the black lake itself, comes an avalanche of arrows.

They strike his little troop like a mighty fist. Riders fall out of their saddles into the water and the loose horses blunder into the path of the men bringing the bridge. One of these men, too, has fallen, pierced in the chest, and the ones behind stumble over him so that there is nothing for it but to throw his body into the lake before it brings the whole army to a halt.

The lake is full of Meshica. They are in canoes. A warrior has leapt, apparently out of the air, in front of Sandoval and is slashing at his horse, which rears in panic. Sandoval spears the Indian with his lance and sends him back into the lake, but there are more, they are everywhere, swarming like wasps.

'Bring the bridge!' he shouts again.

The bridge, somehow, is got to the edge of the chasm and the men on whose aching shoulders it rests begin at last to lower it. Meshica standing in canoes hack at their legs. They cannot defend themselves, being occupied with the bridge; their comrades, trying to defend them, get in the way.

'Drop it on its end,' Sandoval directs.

They want to drop the back.

'The *front* end. Then *topple* it.'

It may fall short. (Who measured the gap? No one: it was guessed at.) It may fall back on the men raising it. It may, when it falls . . .

'*Now!*'

An arrow buries itself in his horse's leg.

The bridge, its broad back shining wet, is raised upright. It begins to be lowered, gradually — dangerously, because there is not enough purchase for it. But the shorter the distance it has to fall the better, because, when it falls —

'Let it go.'

It falls with a crash that terrifies the horses, but it falls true and does not shatter. And there it lies, and the chasm is bridged, and it is the most beautiful thing Sandoval has ever seen.

Already, on the far side, Meshica are leaping.

He spurs his lamed horse across to meet them.

✣   ✣   ✣

Alvarado is fighting for his life. He draws a bloody space around him with his sword and at once it is filled again. He stays horsed with the greatest difficulty, for there are always half a dozen Meshica at his stirrups or his bridle, snatching, pulling, trying to drag him off. His sword is coated in gore to the hilt and above it. His hand is so bloodied that the weapon threatens to slip in his grasp.

He switches it to his left hand and wipes his right hand on the horse's flank. While he is doing this he stabs an Indian in the throat.

The rearguard has moved barely a hundred yards since the fighting began.

When the Captain, battling for every foot gained, reaches the bridge, about twenty Spaniards have already fallen off it, pulled down by Meshica in canoes or struck by arrows. Their bodies bob palely. Some are still alive. Beseeching voices call up at him to rescue them.

There's nothing he can do, under this hail of missiles. Saving one man from the water will cost another four. He spurs over the bridge, which is treacherous with blood and muck.

His horse has to step up from the end of the bridge to the next section of the causeway. He notices this. With the weight of men and horses passing over it, the end of the bridge has sunk into the rubble that was exposed when the wooden section of the causeway was taken up. He wonders how difficult it will be to raise it again.

Velásquez de León is conscious, after two hours of incessant fighting, of the weight of gold inside his shirt. It is starting to be a nuisance. As he swings ceaselessly in the saddle, jabbing and slashing at Meshica faces, he can feel it, doing its best to slow his swing and impede his blow.

He fights on, ignoring the weight. The gold is what he came for, it is why he is here, killing Indians in the darkness. He urges his horse. They are on the first stretch of the causeway still, he is not sure where but they haven't reached the bridge yet. When they have crossed the bridge they have, somehow, to pick it up and bring it with them.

There is an Indian leaping at the horse's head. The horse rears and strikes out with her hooves, and the Indian falls back into the night he came from. Already another has taken his place.

The horse is wounded. Blood is pouring from a slash on her neck. He feels the wetness in his hand. He himself, he finds, has an arrow in his leg.

Alvarado is laying about him like a man possessed, just a few feet away.

Velásquez de León fights on.

The rain has cleared. Stars canopy the sky.

Sandoval sees this in a glance that also takes in the lake, a glinting shield of greys emerging from darkness, and on it, stretching as far as he can see, the dark shapes of a thousand canoes.

How far has he come? He has been fighting for an eternity and it is not yet dawn. From his saddle he gets glimpses of part of the causeway, a paleness, beyond the attacking Meshica. Of the shore he can see nothing.

He pushes his spurs into the horse's flanks. Forward. Lancing the leaping forms, thrusting them off the causeway. Stab and thrust. Over and over. His arm is weary. On an impulse, he frees his right foot from the stirrup and kicks out. He catches an Indian in the throat, but it is a mistake because another grabs the foot and pulls, and he is only saved by the sword of the man behind him.

Soon it will be dawn. Then he will be able to see the shore.

There is abruptly a clear space ahead of him. No Meshica. He is about to urge his horse forward when something stops him and he reins it instead.

He has come to the second breach in the causeway.

✴ ✴ ✴

The bridge can't be lifted. Whatever they do, straining, sweating, they can't pull it up. It has lodged itself firmly in the rubble at the edge of the gap.

'Leave it,' orders Alvarado. He has lost a dozen men already in the effort to raise it. The arrows are still coming as if the sky was made of them. 'Leave the cursed thing.' It is starting to fall apart in any case.

An idea strikes him.

'Get that beam free,' he shouts, and then has to shout it again because there's such a din of drumming and whistling from the Meshica that he can't be heard. So five of them set to wrenching and tugging, while he and Velásquez de León lay about them, defending the men who are trying to free the beam, and he prays that it will come free quickly or the few of them who are doing this will be cut off from the rest of the rearguard, and will not last long enough to say *Ave Maria*.

The bridge was supposed to be taken up after the first crossing and passed forward so that it could be used again. 'Where is the bridge?' shouts Sandoval into the chaos behind him. He guesses the answer.

The second breach will have to be swum.

The canoes swarm in the water. From them, and from the causeway on the other side of the gap, comes a hail of darts and arrows.

A dart embeds itself in Sandoval's shoulder. He plucks it out.

He shouts to those behind him that they must follow him into the water. Then, throwing down his lance, he jumps his horse into the lake.

In mid-leap he finds the horse slipping away from him, slipping sideways in a rolling movement that throws him from the saddle, and he pitches, flailing, into the water. The horse is wounded. He opens his hand and lets the reins go, and dives away from the stabbing javelin-points, away from the dying horse, seeking the stony backbone of the causeway, along which he will grope, and up which he must try to climb, in the face of the sharp-as-glass blades of the Meshica.

Behind him, Spaniards jump into the water and die.

The mare laden with the King of Spain's gold treads along the causeway, her great load swaying but well secured. The man who secured it is dead already from a blow with a club that broke his skull.

The mare is the special care of the rider who leads her by the bridle, Alonso de Escobar, whom the Captain appointed to guard the treasure when he went down to the coast. The appointment brought him more trouble than honour, and tonight he wishes it had been given to anyone else.

His task tonight is to get the mare and her burden to safety. His task is not to fight. But he has to fight, like every other man in this beleaguered column, he has to fight or die. And he has only two hands. One to defend himself, one to lead the mare. He guides his own mare by the pressure of his thighs. He needs another hand. He has no shield.

His cotton armour is stuck with arrows like a porcupine. One of them, shot with great force from a canoe close at hand, has gone right through the tough skin of the armour and into his chest. He feels this arrow with every step of his horse along the causeway. It is as if the stepping of the horse drives the arrow-head further into his flesh. It burns hot. It is a tiny piece of Hell embedded in his chest.

The larger Hell boils around him. The Meshica hurl themselves on the Spaniards without respite. They do not fear Spanish swords, although they die by them in hundreds: and why should they, if death is glorious to them, and if they know that they will in the end prevail by overwhelming weight of numbers?

'We shall not get out of here alive,' thinks Alonso de Escobar, as he cuts and chops a way through Indian flesh for the King's gold.

✳   ✳   ✳

It is dawn. The sky is white and the lake a gleam of silver. In the cold light, the Captain looks at the terrible scene that is the second breach in the causeway.

Forty, sixty, who knows how many Spaniards have died here – not, most of them, struck by Meshica arrows, but pulled down by the weight of steel armour or the gold they were carrying, and drowned. They have sunk into the mud of the lake and others have fallen on top of them, and others again on top of those, and in the charnel pit that the gap in the causeway has become the Captain sees the bodies of two horses wedged. His soldiers are spreadeagled, some on their backs, and the faces of those are starting to puff already with the water that half-covers them, and some have been buried standing, only their heads stare in horror at the corpses piled all around them; and those lying face down seem, with their outflung arms, still to be trying, pathetically, to swim.

On the other side of the gap, the Meshica throng and taunt him, blow their deafening whistles and loose darts. The canoes swarm on the water.

The Captain looks down at the ghastly breach and in that brief moment when his sword-arm hangs idle four Meshica hurl themselves at him from the lake and pull him from his horse.

He struggles desperately but they are determined. The sword has been knocked from his hand. They are dragging him towards the edge of the causeway. They will cut out his heart.

He wrenches an arm free and drives his elbow into his captor's throat, but the Indian scarcely loosens his grip and the nightmare movement towards the lake, the canoe, the sacrificial stone continues.

A sword flashes at his right and the Captain's face is drenched in blood. A to-and-fro swaying ensues – he can see nothing – and then he is being pulled to safety, back into the press of his own men, indebted for his life to a humble footsoldier from Aragon. And now he is a footsoldier himself, because the Indians have killed his horse. There it is, he sees as his vision clears, lying in the terrible gap with its fellows.

Still *the gap must be crossed.*

The Captain jumps down into the breach, on to the bodies of the dead and dying, and crosses to the other side by walking on them.

The army follows him.

Alonso de Escobar leans forward over his horse's neck to deliver the death-blow to an Indian costumed like an eagle, and feels himself falling. It is the fire in his chest that draws him down.

The eagle figure with its raised stone sword grows until it fills the world. He hears the thunder of a cataract falling in a vast cavern, and darkness has come on his eyes. He is weighed down, he cannot rise, he struggles but his limbs don't move. He tastes blood and pine.

The bridle of the mare carrying the King's gold slips from his hand.

The mare blunders forward a few more steps, missing the guiding hand and confused in the fray. Only the artilleryman making his way behind her, who came here with Narváez and will die in the next few minutes, sees her lose her footing and tumble with her burden into the waters of the lake.

The latest canoe-borne wave of Meshica, landing on the causeway from both sides, has succeeded in cutting off the rearguard from the main body of the army.

It is the thing every soldier in the rearguard has fought hero-ically to avoid. Now they will have to fight just as hard – harder – in order merely to stay alive for a few more moments. If in the course of those moments of superhuman effort they don't manage to fight their way back to their companions, back through those surging and now triumphant Meshica, there is no hope for them.

Velásquez de León is fighting in a trance. Indians appear, weapon in hand, before him and he cuts them down. Sometimes he kills two with one blow, thrusting or slicing with such force that the blade careers from one willing — it seems — sack of flesh to another. That is all they are to him now, sacks of flesh, impaling themselves on his sword, sometimes requiring to be jousted with beforehand but always succumbing, in the end, the difficulty being that there are so many of them. He has felled a thousand already, or so it seems to him, with the unwearying movement of his arm. Perhaps it is a little weary. But only a little. He is a strong man. He is known for his strength. When he was a boy in Valladolid, he picked up a yearling bull calf and carried it on his shoulders. The incident comes back to him now, and he fancies he hears the shouting of the crowd in the plaza, and that is what it must be because he can even feel the weight of the calf on his shoulders, trying to bear him down. He resists it, as he resists the unkind weight inside his shirt that wants to impede him, as he resists the hands that have come from some-where and are attempting to drag him from his horse.

He struggles. He is a strong man and brave, and he is a Velásquez. But something is wrong, his strength has ebbed just when he needs it most, and he is powerless to prevent what happens, the hands, the blow to the head, the fall into water. It is deep, the water. It is the water of the Duero, in which he swam as a boy. It was his friend, in those days; it allowed him to play. This time it will not let him go.

Alvarado sees Velásquez de León snatched from his horse but cannot save him. He has just lost his own horse, killed under him by a spear in the chest. He is fighting on foot, duelling with two Meshica who are circling him, waiting for the moment when he will tire or misjudge a stroke. They are both masked, and between the jaws of the masks their eyes glitter as they weave about him, trying to disable, waiting to pounce. They won't get what they want. No Indian is going to have his heart on a plate.

He catches the blow of a flint sword on his shield, uses the shield to push the weapon away from him and drives his sword into the warrior's exposed armpit. As the Indian crumples, he kicks backward into the knee of the other before the second flint sword can find its mark, whirls and lunges. The second Indian falls away from him into the turmoil of the battle, but at once others crowd into his place. They swarm like fish in the sea, and they are between him and where he needs to be. He sees, far ahead of him, a fluttering patch of orange, the Captain's banner, kept flying at God knows what cost.

Before him is an open stretch of water.

He has only just seen this and his head reels. What has happened? He has traversed two breaches in the causeway, the first by means of the bridge and the second over the bodies of Spaniards, and here is a third which the Meshica can only just have opened.

And so they have: on the other side of the gap, they are still hauling beams out of the way. One remains, perilously bridging the chasm.

He is breathing hard. He is wounded in the shoulder, leg and side. He has lost more than half his men. Some were killed fruitlessly trying to wrench a beam free from the first bridge. Now here is another beam, as if in answer to his prayer, except that it is too narrow. Surely it is too narrow.

Across the breach, the Meshica tug at it. In a moment they will have it free.

There is no time to lose, no time to balance risks or even to consider that he is supposed to be the last man on this side of the breach, not the first one over it.

His feet run along the beam so fast it is like flying.

Sandoval has reached the shore.

The fields lie quiet and unpeopled in the sunlight.

He gives thanks to God and sheathes his sword.

He sits his horse (he lost the first, but God sent him another) and counts the men and women he has brought to safety.

Then he leaves them in the care of his second-in-command and rides back to help the Captain.

✠   ✠   ✠

It is the middle of the afternoon.

It will be another six hours before the last Spaniard is off the causeway.

By then, for every three that set out from the palace of Axayacatl, two will be dead or in the hands of the Meshica.

V
Maize

I

The storm had blown us off course. It tossed us for three days and nights. When it had passed, the ship's master did not know where we were. He set a course to the north-west, saying it would bring us to the island called Jamaica. That night we struck a reef. The ship went down almost at once. It was surprising she had weathered the storm, Gonzalo said later. In the condition she was in, she should not have left port.

It was Gonzalo who pulled me out of the water. He hauled me into the ship's boat, into which he and a few passengers had flung themselves as the waves swept over the deck. In the end there were about a dozen of us in that boat, including two nuns, and a cask that we had managed to heave aboard, not knowing what was in it. There proved to be water in it. If there had been anything else, salt pork or cassava or wine, we would all have died.

There were two oars in the boat. We thought ourselves very lucky when we found them, but trouble started as soon as we had to decide in which direction to row. We couldn't agree. Several of us nearly came to blows over it, but the problem was solved by the oars themselves because one of them snapped as soon as it was pulled on. They were worm-eaten. After that, Gonzalo took charge of the other one, saying it might still serve as a mast, and he wedged it somehow so it was upright and tied his shirt to it, and we agreed to let the wind take us where it would. But there was no wind, or hardly a breath, and for day after day our sail hung limp as a ghost.

The cask had been broached and was far from full. We took turns to drink, watching each other closely. It became such torture to watch another person drink that in the end it was almost a relief when the cask was empty. We tipped it overboard, but it bobbed alongside us for a long time, an eerie bulk in the moonlight, like a second boat, until we cursed it as if it were the cause of our misfortunes. That was when people began to die. Of thirst, which we had made worse by gnawing the leather of our shoes and belts. Of the sun, which had no mercy on us. Of simple weariness, perhaps, of being in that boat.

We pushed them overboard. As my mind began to stray, I used to see them, at night, climb back into the boat to sit with us.

All this time, without our knowledge, a current was taking us. One day it cast us up on the shore of a country that had never been heard of.

Chanek was a little white-walled town that perched above the sea. When the *winic* who found us on the beach took us there, carrying us, for we could not walk, I did not believe that anything I saw was real. My eyes had deceived me for so long, showing me land where there was none, streams of water where there were none, that I assumed that this town, too, with its strange painted buildings set on platforms, its brown-skinned people decked with shells and feathers, was just as much a fantasy. But when they brought us before the chief of the town, I became frightened.

He was sitting cross-legged on a mat, playing with something. When we were brought in, he did not at once raise his head to look at us, but turned it to say something to an attendant. I saw his profile. The nose was large and hooked, but it was the high, sloping forehead that astonished me. It sloped backward as if it had been pressed back by a huge hand, and the skull rose almost to a point like the narrow end of an egg. From the top of the head to the tip of the nose was an unbroken line. It was a profile utterly savage, like that of a bird or animal of prey. Sweet Saviour, what place is this? I thought.

Then he turned his gaze on us, and it was not ferocious at all but aglitter with curiosity. He motioned for one of us to be brought up to him, and he felt the man's clothing, peered into his eyes and pulled his beard. It was Gonzalo, of course.

I don't remember the day the others were taken away. Gonzalo told me about it when I recovered. After we came ashore I was ill for a week — raving, he said, as if I had held madness off for as long as I could and now that we were safe it had overtaken me. He said that eight of us had come ashore, and the other six had been distributed among three of the neighbouring chiefs. He and I would stay in Chanek. I was sorry that we had all been separated; I thought it would have been a kindness to keep us together. But I told myself that, since the others had gone to neighbouring towns, it would not be long before we met again. I was quite wrong.

We were put to work in the fields. The fields lay between the town and the forest. They had been cleared from the forest, and they were doing their best to go back to it. We had to get the roots out so that the soil could be used for planting. The under-growth had been burnt off, and a crust of grey ash covered it. A new growth of vegetation was already springing up through the ash. Below, the ground was knotted with roots.

I was given an axe. I didn't know how to use it. My hand was used to steel, the weight of it, the sureness of the bite. This tool, which was too light, its beak of flint bound into the socket with creeper, would not cut a root. It only bruised it, and my palm grew raw with useless chopping. I had to be shown how to send the flint at the correct angle into the root's fibres, how to peck instead of chopping, how to use my arm and not just the axe.

Then, when the clearing was at last done and the rains began, how to sow. How to drive the long, bladed digging-stick into the soil with the strength of my shoulders. How to place, in each hole that was dug, three seeds of maize as white as the sun.

Gonzalo helped me, particularly at first, when the labour exhausted me. He was very strong, and was generous with his strength. But it was the other slaves who taught me. They taught me with patience and smiles. Their smiles were innocent, they were the smiles of children.

Gonzalo had adapted easily to the place we had come to although it could not, I thought, have been more alien.

I watched him with amazement. He crouched on his heels like a *winic* as if he'd always done it; he folded and wore his loin-cloth (the *winic* had taken our clothes away: they were rags) as if he had never worn anything else. He walked barefoot in the forest, where there were snakes, without fear, and barefoot on the burning sand of midday as if he didn't feel the heat. He ate the food we were given, a tasteless cake of maize and a bean stew fiery with peppers, with relish when I could barely swallow it. He did his work without complaint. When he lay down on his sleeping mat he fell asleep at once, while I lay staring up at the thatch, listening to the sounds of love the slaves made in the darkness (it shocked me that they did this, and did it without shame), and thinking of the life I had lost.

I reproached him once for his acceptance of all the things that had befallen us.

He said, 'There's no use in not accepting a thing if you can't change it.'

He was carving a piece of wood with a flint he had set into a handle. The *batab* had taken away his beloved knife.

'Are you happy here?' I challenged him.

He looked up at me calmly. 'I'm content, I suppose.'

'But you're a *Spaniard!*' I protested.

'Am I?'

'What else could you be? Do you think you're one of *them?*'

'No,' he said. 'I don't speak the language, do I?'

He was learning it, though. I had heard his stumbling attempts at conversation with the slaves.

'Once I lived in Palos,' he said. 'Then I lived on a ship. Now I live here.'

'You're still a Spaniard.'

'I'm Gonzalo,' he said. 'That's who I am.'

'What a stupid thing to say!'

He laid aside his carving and said, quite gently and seriously, 'We have to forget where we came from.'

'No!' I cried. 'We must remember! And if we remember, if every day we remember, a day will come when we are rescued.'

He said nothing more. But the next day I saw him do what the slaves always did at the start of a meal. Before eating, he took a morsel of his food and threw it into the fire as an offering to the hearth-god. When I spoke to him about it, he didn't even seem to know what he'd done.

We lived in a long hut with about thirty other field slaves, who were all youths or men. The hearth was at one end of it, and consisted just of three large stones between which the fire was made. A big pot of stew was brought every day from the *batab*'s kitchens and put there for us. We ate it sitting around the fire, or on the earthen platform outside, spooning it from clay bowls with our maize cakes.

The hearth and the clay bowls, the sleeping mats and a pile of tools at the far end, were all there was in the hut. There were no windows and no doors, just an opening at either end. The *winic* did not seem to know about doors, or perhaps didn't see a need for them. The hut, like all the buildings in which the slaves or the common people lived, was built of wooden stakes planted upright in the ground and bound together with creepers. A thick jumble of thatch covered it, made of many different kinds of leaves and twigs all woven together. There was a hole in the thatch just above the hearth, where the smoke was supposed to go out, but often the smoke didn't, but hung around making our eyes smart. The rain, on the other hand, always came *in* through the hole in the thatch. The rain was wiser than the smoke, the *winic* said, laughing, shaking the rain out of their sleeping mats if they had left them too near the hearth.

The rain came heavily in the summer months, and was the reason why all the houses were built on platforms. During a downpour, water would rush in torrents through the streets. The streets were mostly mud, but a few in the centre of the town, where the temple and the *batab*'s palace were, were paved with limestone. The temple and all the official buildings were made of stone and stood on stone platforms, approached by wide, shallow steps. They were plastered and brightly painted, these odd, blocky buildings with their squat pillars and carved roof lintels, and in the clear, sparkling light of the ocean they shone like sea-washed coral.

I used to say my prayers, at first. After we had eaten our stew of beans, I would kneel down on my sleeping mat, fold my hands and close my eyes.

The slaves were very interested by this habit of mine. When I had done it several times, they began imitating me. They, too, would kneel down, fold their hands and close their eyes. Knowing they were doing it didn't help me, as I knelt there, to pray.

Nothing would have helped me in any case. It was as if I'd used up all the prayers that were in me on the night of the shipwreck. My mind was empty, as empty as the cask we had thrown back into the sea. Because it was empty, it filled itself up with nonsense. Something irritating that Gonzalo had said. Something particularly baffling that one of the slaves had done. A picture of the field we were working in, with its snaking roots and its white-brown soil. Or another picture, that often drifted into my dreams, of a blinding sea and the bleached curve of a hull.

I was distressed by my inability to pray. I wondered what it meant. Perhaps, I thought, it meant that I was damned, although

I did not see why I should be damned simply because, through no fault of mine, I had been shipwrecked on an ungodly shore. After all, *I* had not thrown *my* food into the hearth as a sacrificial offering. However, if it was not my fault that I couldn't pray, it must be God's fault, and that was a sinful thought so I tried not to think it.

As a boy, I had been devout. I had wanted to be a priest. I had served at the altar. I had fastened my eyes on the crucifix and believed that He was talking to me and I to Him. When I had closed my eyes, in those days, to pray, He would appear before me, white against my eyelids, His arms stretched out on the Tree. He would stay there for as long as I was talking to Him.

In this new place, He was reluctant to appear. By a great effort of will, I sometimes conjured Him. He did not stay long. After a very short time in which I fumblingly tried to frame a prayer to Him, He would fade, and I would find myself looking, strangely, at the bare wood of the Tree.

It was all the more necessary to pray, I felt, because of the spiritual darkness of the place we had come to.

It was not that the *winic* had no gods: they had hundreds of them. In every street there was a wayside shrine or two. It was always spotted with blood. A little clay censer stood in front of it, burning pieces of pine resin. The smoke was rich and heady, and I supposed kept away flies, for there never were any, in spite of the blood. It was the blood that upset me, and that I couldn't connect with the gentleness of the people. It was human blood. It was their blood. This was the way they worshipped their gods.

They would cut their ears. The lobes, if these were not already too scarred; if there was no room on the lobe, they would try devotedly to draw a drop of blood from somewhere on the fleshy rim of the ear. They used, for this purpose, a specially shaped flint, a piece of oyster shell or a spine which they got from a certain fish. The instrument they did it with was treated with

331

great respect, as if it were a person, and kept in its own pouch. When they had drawn a drop of blood, they would flick it on to the image of the god, and perhaps light a bead of incense as well. In time, I found that cutting the ears was only one of the things they did; that sometimes, if greater devotion needed to be paid, they would mutilate their tongues, and that the nobility would offer their blood smeared on to the bark paper they made, for this paper was precious, and they would burn the blood-stained paper so that the offering would be carried to the god.

All of this seemed to me to be horrible, and it was the first thing I noticed because there was an image just outside the hut to which the slaves paid their devotions every day. However, it also touched me, because clearly they loved their gods very much. I pitied their state of ignorance; they did not know that the only blood that had needed to be shed was that of our Redeemer. I wondered if I should try to tell them, but hastily put away the idea. I couldn't say my own prayers: who was I to teach them? In any case, I didn't speak the language.

Some of their gods were of human form, but others were grotesque and I supposed they were demons. They had faces that were half-human and half-cat, or half-human and half-lizard; they had pointed fangs or long arms like monkeys. The god whose image stood outside the hut, however, resembled a young *winic* with a serene face. He had the high, sloping forehead the people admired and curving lips. He was seated on a kind of throne, and behind his head rose, like the plumes of a headdress or the rays of the sun, the spear-like leaves of the maize plant.

Gonzalo was not respectful about my attempts to pray.

'How long are you going to keep it up?' he asked me one evening.

I pretended not to know what he meant. 'Keep what up?'

'Saying your prayers.'

'And why shouldn't I say my prayers?'

'Because there's nobody listening. God isn't going to help us.'

I was not greatly surprised to hear him say that. 'He will help us if we have faith,' I said.

'He didn't help all those poor souls the night the ship went down, did he?'

I had had the same thought myself, and not been able to answer it. At least a hundred people must have lost their lives that night, in the inky water. I could not answer Gonzalo now.

'God has never heard of this place,' Gonzalo said.

Because we must remember, I would not become like the *winic*. I would not learn the language. I would not sit on my heels. I would not use the maize cake to scoop up food, but made myself a spoon out of tree bark. Because we must remember, I kept count of the days.

I had started it in the boat. Each day, I cut a notch in the wooden side with Gonzalo's dagger. As our condition worsened, I sometimes forgot to do it or did not know if I had already carved the notch for that day, or even if it was the day I thought it was. In the end, Gonzalo wouldn't lend me the knife in case I dropped it overboard. After that, I stopped trying to count the days.

In Chanek, as soon as my strength began to come back, I started again. I worked out what was likely to be the date we came ashore, and counted forward from that. It was a guess, but it was something. It made a foundation for the world. But then we were taken to work in the fields, and for the first days I found the work so overwhelming that I simply forgot about keeping a calendar. It was quite a long time before I remembered, and by that time I had forgotten the date I had decided it was when we came ashore.

One day I began the count again. For some reason I fixed on the fifth of April as the date for that day, and I looked for a means of keeping my calendar. In the fields there were a lot of little white pebbles. They were a nuisance when you were preparing the ground: they were forever forcing themselves to the surface of the patch you had cleared. However, they were a handy size. I collected a pile of them and put them beside my sleeping mat. Then I took out five and put them at a little distance from the others. Tomorrow I would take another pebble from the pile and add it to the five. I would do this every day. Later, I would find a means of recording the months.

The slaves noticed the pebbles straight away, but did not touch them. Probably they thought the pebbles had something to do with my kneeling on the mat with my eyes closed. Gonzalo asked me what they were.

'My calendar,' I said, with pride.

'Oh? How does it work?'

I told him.

'So what day is it today?'

I told him the date.

I was disappointed in his response: he merely looked perplexed. But afterwards he said with a smile that he was glad I had found a way of doing it.

Gonzalo and I didn't talk much. It was partly because the work didn't give us much chance to, and when we weren't working we were usually too tired to do anything but sleep. But it was also because, in spite of all we'd been through together in that open boat (which we never spoke of), and in spite of the fact that we were both Spaniards, we had very little in common. Often I thought that Fate had played a rather cruel trick in giving him to me as my only companion. He seemed to be closer to the *winic* than he was to me. Seeing him squatting on his heels made me feel betrayed. He said it was comfortable. I said it wasn't Christian. He laughed.

He didn't think about things, as I did. If I wanted to talk about Spain, he was unwilling to. He said it was over, that part of our lives. We would never leave the country we had come to, and the sooner we accepted the fact the better, he said. This filled me with despair.

We argued often. That is, I argued with him. His simplicity maddened me. His ability to make himself at home in the slaves' hut struck me as an insult. I picked quarrels with him because I couldn't bear the situation we were in and I felt that he should not be able to bear it either. The arguments were usually about nothing – what name the *winic* gave to a certain fruit, whether the animal that had come into the hut one day and looked like a pig *was* a pig, what had been the name of our ship that went down – and they were unsatisfying because Gonzalo would not argue back. He would put up, patiently, with my outbursts until I pushed him too far, and then he would either walk away or tell me I was being stupid. It was impossible to provoke him. It seemed to me very unfair.

The days went by. I marked their passage with pebbles, occasionally missing a day but always making it up the next day. I would say to myself, 'Today is the twelfth of May,' or whatever the pebbles told me it was. Saying this was like throwing out a very long, slender rope to the place I had come from. The rope meant that the place I had come from was real and therefore that I would one day go back to it. It meant that Chanek, the fields and the slave hut were not all there was. It meant that I was a Spaniard, for the calendar I kept was the Christian one of saints and fasts and memorials, even though these things were becoming immeasurably distant to me, and like husks from which the fruit has gone.

One day I came back from the fields very tired and lay down on my mat to rest. Beside the mat was a pile of pebbles. I glanced at it and fell asleep.

Gonzalo woke me: he was holding out my bowl of food. I thanked him.

He pointed at the pebbles. 'What day is it?'

For a moment I didn't know what he meant. I had forgotten that the pebbles were supposed to tell me the date. I had not moved a pebble from one pile to the other that day, or – I suddenly thought — the day before. Or had I? It was difficult to remember. I supposed I had done it the day before that. It was something I did every day: I always did it. Except that I could not remember when I had last done it.

Gonzalo looked at my face, and went away.

I felt as if I had fallen into a pit. I lay on my mat and stared blindly up at the rafters. I do not know what day it is, I thought, and I shall never know again. For it was clear to me that there was no point in starting the reckoning for what would be the fourth time. By now, my calendar was beyond rescue. It could not have any connection with the calendar kept in Christian lands.

I gave in to my hopelessness and wept. The slaves gathered round me in concern and waited silently until I had stopped weeping; then they left me. While I was weeping, the thought came into my head that I had known all along that this would happen.

I washed my face with a handful of water from the pitcher and ate my bean stew. When I had finished eating, I gathered up all the pebbles. I took them outside into the fields. By now there were only the stars and moon to see by. I walked into the fields a little distance and began throwing the pebbles away, one by one and then two by two, like sowing seeds, throwing them back to the soil they had come from. In the end I finished and stood there looking out over the shadowy field and it seemed to me that I could see them, under the starlight, in the pattern they had formed when I threw them back, like stars themselves, and perhaps, I thought, that was what the stars were, pebbles thrown by God. A moment later, I couldn't see them at all.

I entered on a state which must, I thought, be like that of animals. The sun rose, the sun set; these were the events that marked the passage of time. I lived each day as it came, and saw how the maize grew and the beans began to twine around its stalks. I began to feel the earth's rhythm of growth and decay, and how it gave shape to time. This slow rhythm, which was the circling

336

of the seasons, would have to be enough for me, for it was all there was. It sufficed the *winic*.

I was finding the labour less exhausting now. My body had learnt ways of preserving itself. Every stroke of the axe, every plunge of the digging-stick, had to be done at a measured pace, otherwise you would have no strength for the end of the day. Breathing itself had to be done with care. In the middle of the day the air was so hot that, if you took a gulp of it, it burnt your lungs.

I learnt from the slaves. I did what they did. I squatted in the shade when the sun was at its fiercest, and drank from the gourd. In it was *k'eyen*, water that tasted of maize, from a little bit of fermented maize dough that had been mixed into it. It had made me feel queasy at first, but after a time I found that it gave me strength. I had begun to enjoy the taste of maize. It did have a taste. It was a mild taste, but it filled the mouth. There was a depth to it. It was slightly milky. I found myself wanting it, when the day was over.

When harvest came I worked along the maize rows, picking the ripe cobs and throwing them into the basket which was held by a strap across my forehead. This way of carrying a load, which at first had horrified me (it turned a man into a beast of burden; and mightn't my neck snap?), now seemed the obvious way to carry a burden, although nothing reduced the weight of it. Feeling the sinews of my neck I found them as tough as forest creepers.

As I worked my way along the maize rows one day I wondered what the Spaniards I had known before the shipwreck would think if they could see me labouring in the fields like a *winic*. Then my gaze fell on my sunburned, calloused feet and the looped end of my loincloth, and I knew that if a Spaniard saw me he would not know I was not a *winic*.

One day a terrible thing happened.

Gonzalo was called away from the hut when we returned from the fields. He was away for quite a long time. I got his food and put it by the hearth to keep warm. I began to worry when it was completely dark and he still had not come back. But then I heard his step, and he sauntered in and made his way by the dim glow from the fire to his sleeping mat.

I brought him his food. 'Thanks,' he said. He started to eat it.

'Where were you?' I'd hoped he would tell me without being asked.

'They're building a road.'

'What?' He had spoken with his mouth full, and a road didn't seem a very likely thing for him to be talking about.

'They're building a road. North of the town. It goes into the forest.'

'Yes?'

He munched. It was the usual soup of beans and peppers, with a bit of squash.

'It's going to be a good road,' he said. 'They've put in the foundations and the drainage.'

'Gonzalo, for heaven's sake! I'm not interested in a road!'

'Well, you asked me where I'd been.'

'They took you to see it?'

'That's what I'm telling you.'

'Why?'

'They want me to work on it.' I couldn't see his grin, but I heard it in his voice. 'They obviously don't think much of me as a farmer.'

The news was not welcome. I was so used to working alongside him that the thought of working without him, of not feeling his solid presence near me as I hoed my maize row or rested in the shade to drink, was dismaying. However, I would see him in the evenings.

'It means,' he said, 'that I'll have to move to another hut.'

My belly went cold. For a moment I couldn't get my breath. I must have made some small noise, because he said, 'Are you all right?'

'Yes.'

A little time went by. The ashes of the fire settled down.

'When?' I said.

'Tomorrow.'

The following day he left the hut, taking his flint knife, a deer antler he was carving and his sleeping mat. He gave me a funny half-salute as he went, and looked as if he wanted to say something, but all he said was, 'New berth, then.'

'I will come and see you,' I said.

'Good.' He ducked through the low entrance and walked away.

2

When Gonzalo left, I watched him walking up the dirt road that led to the town, not looking back. I thought, he did not say *he* would come and see *me*. And I knew he wouldn't.

I became very angry. How could he care so little about being taken from me? How could he walk away with such a jaunty step? He thought he could do perfectly well without me: let him find out. Let him pine for the companionship of the hut and the maize field. Let him hate his wretched road.

I knew that all this was nonsense and that he would manage perfectly well without me. The question was how I would manage without him.

When my anger, which was a sad flurry pretending to be a storm, had died down in spite of my attempts to keep it alive, I could not hold off my grief. It was as if he had died. He *had* died – to me. I knew that when I went to see him again, trudging through the town to where he would be living, in a different hut among different slaves, he would already be different himself. I knew this because Gonzalo adapted himself instantly to wherever he was. Without me, he would quickly become just like the *winic*, because there was nothing to stop him. He had almost achieved it already.

I mourned him, but I mourned my own state as well. There wasn't another human being in the world to whom I could talk.

I wondered if it was possible to die of loneliness and, if so, how long it took. To hasten the process I stopped eating, but started again after I fainted in the maize fields and the overseer forced some water mixed with a bitter herb down my throat. The *winic* were kind to me, but they were not going to allow me to die because Gonzalo had gone. Or to stop working, either.

I found a thought in my head when I awoke one morning. It was a simple thought and it had probably been there for some time, but I had ignored it. It was, 'I have to learn the language.'

I still knew only a few words of it. Obstinate, and afraid of becoming like the *winic*, I had always left it to Gonzalo to do what talking was necessary and explain to me what he thought the slaves were saying. I suddenly saw this behaviour in a new light: not just obstinate, but stupid. And now, a luxury I could not afford.

I began learning the language that day. I asked the slaves, humbly, to teach me. I would point to something, and they would tell me what it was called. Hut. Earth. Foot. Stone. Maize. Simple words. The names of things.

After a while, I went to see Gonzalo in his new quarters. It was as I had known it would be: there was a shyness between us, and we hardly knew what to say to each other.

I asked him how it was in the new hut, whether the labourers were as friendly as the slaves in the field hut, and whether the work was very hard. He replied in his usual way, with not many words and none of them telling you much about how he felt. The hut was all right, the *winic* were friendly enough, the work was not too bad and the road was going to be a good one.

He took me to see the road. We had entirely run out of things to say by that time. It was certainly a good road. It was wide enough for four to walk abreast and as straight as an arrow. They had dug the ditch for it as far as the edge of the forest and put in a bed of small stones, well packed down. A short stretch, just outside the northern entrance to the town, was paved already with white slabs.

'It's a fine road,' I said, to please him. 'What is it for?' It seemed to me that if it only went as far as the forest it would not be very useful.

'Some festival,' he said.

'All this for a festival?' There were frequent festivals: I did not bother to go to them. I would take advantage of the day of rest, and sleep or sit on the beach. Sometimes I wrote messages no one would ever read in the sand.

'Well, they make a big thing of them, don't they?' he said. Then, to my surprise and pleasure, he added that there was going to be a festival in three days' time and suggested that we go to it together. I accepted, of course.

Normally Chanek was a quiet, drowsy town. On the day of the festival the streets were in a ferment. The cries of fruit-sellers rose above a general hubbub of greetings, laughter, the shouts of children and drumming from the temple. Pushing my way, with Gonzalo, through the crowds, I passed men selling caged birds and monkeys on perches, women carrying great circular baskets of yellow fruit, a boy with a stick over his shoulder from which hung dried and salted fish, another boy exhibiting live fish in a wooden pail of water – and then, as we entered the market, I saw a whole world for sale. Vendors sat behind heaps of maize cobs, beans, straw, coloured ribbons, clay pots for cooking, fire-wood, seaweed, flint tools, face-paint in glazed dishes, ropes woven from creeper, grinding-stones, feathers, weavings and fowls with their necks wrung, sold singly or by the string. Every few paces I wanted to stop and stare, for some of these things I had never seen before and some I could not even guess the use of, but Gonzalo would not let me linger. He wanted to get to the temple, where the dancing would be.

The dancers were taking their places in the square in front of the temple when we arrived. They wore deerskin sandals and their bodies were painted black: Gonzalo said this meant that they were warriors. Below their knees, like leg-guards, were tied string upon string of brown nutshells that rattled as they moved.

Great care was being taken to make sure that every dancer was in the right spot. The drummers pattered the drums with their fingertips, lifted them to their ears and seemed to talk to them. I studied the paintings that glowed in blue, green and yellow on the long stuccoed wall that flanked the stairway: seashells, fish, a god with bulbous eyes, another that had the horns of a deer, a creature that resembled the small dogs the *winic* bred for meat, and a branching plant-like form in whose top perched a bird with long tail-feathers. To the right of these, presumably extending behind the temple and standing between it and the cliff, I glimpsed a collection of slender upright stones like fingers.

When I looked again, the dance had started − or, rather, some subtle change had taken place between not-dancing and dancing, and the whole group of dancers, forming a perfect square of eight men by eight, was moving with a quiet and stately motion like the swaying of maize in a breeze.

It was a patient, beautiful dance and, before long, I could not take my eyes from it. It was both simple and not simple, for, however long I watched, I could not work out the sequence of the steps. Just as I thought I had it, I would find I had been fooled; and then, when I least expected it, they would turn. The whole group would turn together, a square locked in a wheel, to face another of the four directions. Each direction was danced to in turn. Over and over. From time to time, incense was lit in bowls in the space separating the dancers from the crowd, and the resinous smoke drifted heavily on the air.

When we left I was light-headed from copal and hunger. Gonzalo found us something to eat. They were little pies of steamed maize, fresh from the pot, filled with sweet fruit. They were delicious. We were supposed to pay for them with the small black beans the *winic* used for money, but we had none and were excused because the woman selling the pies knew who we were. Then Gonzalo found us something to drink.

At the time I knew nothing about *balche*, the intoxicating drink of the *winic*, and accepted a cup gratefully. I gulped it because I was thirsty, and accepted another, but found I had to sit down when I was only half-way through it as my legs had become weak. Gonzalo laughed and finished my cupful.

'It's a good job they only have one of these every twenty days,' he remarked.

I had no idea what he was talking about. I said goodbye to him, staggered back to the hut and fell asleep. It was quite a while before I gave his last remark any thought.

Very quickly, as I began to learn the language, I discovered that the simple words were not simple. No sooner had I learnt what I imagined to be the meaning of a word than a second meaning came along, like a jealous twin, to join it. And there was hardly ever any connection that I could see between the second meaning and the first. *Can*, for instance, meant both 'sky' and 'serpent'. It wasn't just the names of things that were twinned; the words that described them were, as well. An adjective, after all, was only the name of how a thing *appeared*. So that 'blue smoke', for instance, could also mean 'shining water', and again, it could also mean 'shining smoke' or 'blue water'. How could you possibly be sure what was meant? And why on earth did the *winic* not simply make up more words, if they didn't have enough?

As I grew more ambitious in what I attempted to say, I discovered other frustrations. What kind of tongue was this in which there seemed to be no verbs? Words that expressed something being *done* were reduced to little syllables that attached themselves to words that were more important, the naming words. You couldn't say, in this language, 'I caught a fish today.' You would have to say something about the now-caughtness of the fish. Past and future weren't important either. Everything happened, in so far as it did happen, in the present. But, really, what the language seemed to say was that nothing happened. Things *were*: or rather, *they had always been*.

Nor did mastering the sounds of the language come easily to a Spaniard. It was full of rise and fall, of indrawn breaths and little clicks made at the back of the throat. Often I would think I had got a word right but the *winic* would correct me, laughing, making me say it again and again, because not only must the pronunciation be right but the tone of voice must be right as well. I despaired every day of learning to speak this language. I persevered because I had no choice. I told myself I must not keep trying to say in it things that could not be said, and that if it forced me to say something I did not want to say, that was the price of speaking it – and *I* would know what I meant.

I gave it a name, this language, for the *winic* did not have one for it: they called it simply 'our-speaking'. I named it *Ahau*, which means 'lord', because I could not make it do my will.

The second time I went to see Gonzalo was much the same as the first time. For something to say, I mentioned that I was learning the language and I told him some of the thoughts I had had about it. He seemed puzzled. He could talk quite freely in it by now, or so it seemed to me (at any rate, the *winic* under-stood him), but the idea that a language was something you could *think* about had not occurred to him. You spoke a language or you didn't. If you wanted to learn it, you did.

'I suppose so,' he said, when I remarked on the way every word in Ahau meant two different things. His brow creased. 'But you can usually work out which it is.'

I concluded, as I walked home (for the field slaves' hut was home now), that I wanted something from him that he couldn't give. Well, he had given me enough, and now that I no longer saw him every day and breathed the same air as he did, I knew what I owed him. I was sorry that I couldn't say so. I was certain he would not let me get the words out, and I wasn't sure that I could frame them in any case. Thinking what I would say, I even fell silent in my mind.

Perhaps I could do something for him, or give him a present, to say thank you. I liked this idea, but it was hard to think of anything. There was nothing he needed. There was nothing I had. I supposed I could make him something . . .

The idea came to me of plaiting a reed pouch he could keep his flint knife in, and perhaps other small possessions. I thought with embarrassment of how he might laugh, although in fact it was not such a bad notion.

I found that the seasons ruled more than just the agricultural cycle. They ruled an activity that was extremely important to the *winic*: war. The season for war started as soon as the rains were over.

The first time there was a war, I knew nothing about it until it happened. The town was suddenly full of young men swaggering, and one day it was impossible to cross the public garden near the *batab*'s palace because they were practising their slingshots there. I did not give it any thought. Two days later they marched off to fight. But before they marched off, they paraded.

The whole town went to see them muster.

When we arrived, they were just filing into the plaza. Their bodies, naked except for the loincloth, were painted black, with a pattern of red and white triangles on the chest. Their arms were tattooed, and their heads shaved to leave only a long braid of hair at the back, which was stuck with feathers. Each carried a round leather shield high on the shoulder and his weapons: a spear, bow or the wooden, flint-bladed sword called *macana*. The black paint on their skins glistened like oil and had a pungent smell, for it was made from a fungus that grew in the forest. This smell mingled powerfully with the scent of copal that was burning in the braziers.

Above them rode their banners. Eagle, snake, coyote, squirrel. The banners were elaborate: they were fringed and studded with coloured stones and sewn with hundreds of tiny, bright feathers. The warriors made a fine sight, drawn up under their floating banners, stamping their feet in rhythm so that their plumes waved and jostled. But what most held my eye were the drums.

346

The drummers stood apart on the temple steps, and their drums were of many kinds. Some hung at the drummer's waist and were tapped with the fingers. Others came up to a man's chest and were beaten with both hands. There was a drum that was like a finely carved log of wood, that was struck with the antler of a deer. There were drums that were the shells of sea-turtles and were beaten with sticks. There were four drums that were simply clay pots which, struck across the opening with the flat of a hand, gave out a sound between a boom and a sigh. Lastly there was the drum I could not see, that lived in the temple, that was the lord of them all and paced out their music with a single, deep throb that seemed to come from the ground beneath my feet.

While the drums were still speaking, the captains came into the square. They carried their huge war-masks in their hands. When they had taken their places, each in the middle of his company, all the drums ceased, and in the hush that followed each captain lowered his mask on to his head, becoming eagle, snake, coyote, squirrel.

Down the temple stairway then stepped a man wearing round his shoulders the tawny, spotted skin of the animal the *winic* most revered. His body was so lithe and spare, and his eyes, in a face that fasting had reduced nearly to bone, burned so fiercely, that I was uncertain for a moment whether it was a man or a beast I was seeing. He walked through the assembled companies, where mask now answered to mask and beaked head to fanged one, and there, in the very centre of the host, he set on his shoulders a huge and gaping mask through whose jaws his face showed as if being born, and all the drums leapt.

Five days later the war was over.

The warriors came back into town with music and triumphant shouts. Those at the head were leaping and dancing. At the back, roped together in a line, walked their prisoners. About a dozen men, walking with bent head. They would become slaves, I supposed.

That night and for two days following, the warriors, captains and town elders feasted and drank. Through the evenings, warriors stunned with *balche* caroused in the plaza and staggered through the streets. On the third day, all of this stopped abruptly and one of the prisoners was sacrificed in the temple.

I did not know what was happening. I had gone with the field slaves to what I thought was a festival like all the other festivals. I saw the prisoner, dressed apparently in paper and holding a *macana* made of paper, climb the temple stairway with a guard holding either arm. Behind them, walking alone, came a warrior in full war costume. The prisoner did not seem reluctant: he climbed steadily between his captors. There were smoking bowls of incense on each step, and clouds of smoke billowed from the censers at the top of the stairway, where there stood a smooth, curiously shaped boulder.

At the top of the stairway the priests, with the prisoner between them, halted. I saw the man's paper robes stiffly outlined against the blue sky. Then four priests came forward, with a fifth behind them. The four seized him and flung him down on the stone. The fifth held a flint knife. He raised it and brought it down in a savage, unerring swoop on the prisoner's breast. He pulled out, and held up, the heart.

After this had happened, I was so shaken and frightened by what I'd seen that I could hardly bring myself to speak to the other slaves. Everything around me now presented itself in a new light. Behind every ritual I now saw a human sacrifice. The gentle smiles of the slaves concealed the souls of murderers. Even worse than murderers: I had been told, by the slave standing next to me in the crowd, that the victim's flesh was going to be eaten by the family of the warrior who had captured him.

I was sickened. I drew away from the slaves, into myself, until they asked me in concern if I was ill. I said brusquely that I was not. What I meant was that my soul was sick and they had poisoned it.

If Gonzalo had still been in the hut, I would naturally have talked to him about it, but I did not have the strength of will to make my way through the town, passing the temple, to where he would be. I should have turned to God. I should have prayed. I had never been more in need of prayer. But I could not pray. I had given up trying to pray months earlier.

It had become usual for me to forget, as I knelt, what I was supposed to be doing, and my mind would go off and amuse itself. When I recollected why I was on my knees, in that un-natural position, I would hastily cast around for the appropriate words. They would not come. Even the prayer all Christians are taught as children, the prayer Lordjesuschrist gave us, slipped away from me. How could I forget it? It was part of me, it had grown with me. But it had gone.

I would abandon the search for the Our Father, then, and try to make up a prayer of my own. It should not have been hard to find things to say. If nothing else, 'Please deliver us from this place' would have done. But often I did not get even that far. It eventually dawned on me that the reason I could not pray was that I did not believe there was anybody listening.

Of course I couldn't admit it. I went on trying to pray. Telling myself I *was* praying, although the words were without meaning and my head was empty, and Lordjesuschrist was no longer on his Tree. He had faded like a bleached cloth on which you can't see the pattern any more. I could still see the Tree, if I concentrated, standing tall and bare against the sky. But not Him who had hung there. Not once.

In the end, I stopped doing it. It was not something I could one day just abandon, as I had thrown away the pebbles. I could only stop doing it by not noticing I had stopped doing it. One night when I hadn't tried to pray for quite a long time it occurred to me to kneel down and I knew I was not going to, that I didn't want to, because there was no point in it. I admitted then what I had fought against knowing: that God was not there, that he did not know this country existed, that Gonzalo had been right.

✳   ✳   ✳

349

I did not go to visit Gonzalo for quite a while. Gradually, when there were no more terrible events at the temple, my spirits recovered from the shock they had received. Life went on as normal. The slaves took on again, in my mind, the nature they had always had – mild, helpful, mysterious. The work was the same as ever. The crime I had witnessed had left seemingly no mark on either the town or its people. I put it to the back of my mind, since there was nothing else to be done with it.

I gathered some reeds at the edge of the pool and wove a purse for Gonzalo. When it was finished, however, I still did not hurry to take it to him. I wasn't sure that he would like it. As long as I hadn't given it to him, I could imagine his pleasure at receiving it. In any case, at the end of a day's work in the fields I could always tell myself I was too tired to go visiting.

I don't know how long had gone by when I eventually picked up the purse I had made and walked to his hut. He wasn't there. They told me where he was, but I didn't understand the directions, so a slave came with me. He left me outside a hut in another district.

Gonzalo was resting on his elbow, on a mat, smoking tobacco. The front of his head was shaved and his hair at the back was long and braided. He had dyed it to make it look blacker, and wound a thread of crimson into it. In the holes in his earlobes were two discs of painted clay. Blue spirals like the whorls of sea snails were drawn on his cheekbones, and a leather bracelet sewn with small blue feathers circled his left wrist. The other wrist, and the arm above it, were covered in a web of fresh scars.

I simply gazed at him.

'Come in,' he said. 'You don't have to stand half-in and half-out.'

I took a few steps towards him. The tobacco smoke hung thickly. I was bewildered. I said in the end, 'Gonzalo, you've become an Indian.'

'Have I?' He ran his hand over his shaved scalp. He smiled. 'What do you think *you* are?'

'Do you cut your ears and sprinkle the blood on the altar? Do you have an idol that you deck in bits of paper?'

'No,' he said.

My eyes moved down his body. His skin was burnt as brown as a *winic*'s, and down the centre of his chest from the collarbone to the belly was painted a column of red and black triangles. His loincloth was as white as a sail.

He said, 'I'm a warrior.'

'What?'

He pointed to the nasty mess of scabs on his arm. 'That's the badge of my company.'

I was filled with anguish. 'How proud you must be,' I said bitterly. 'Once you were a Spanish seaman, but this of course is much better.'

'It's better than chopping roots and heaving stone.' As always, I could not provoke him to anger. 'They know how to fight, and no mistake,' he said. 'But there are a few things I can show them. I've done a bit of soldiering.'

'I'm sure you have.' Then the horror of what I had recently seen rushed at me, and I burst out, 'Gonzalo, they *sacrifice their prisoners!*'

'Is it worse than killing them on the battlefield?' he asked.

'Yes.'

'Why?'

I did not know why.

'It's more difficult to take a man alive,' he said. 'It's more dangerous. There's glory in it.'

'And is there glory in what happens after the sacrifice? The body is *eaten!*'

'Only a bit of it,' he said mildly. 'They don't think of it as food. It's a religious thing. They eat a bit of the flesh with maize. They say it's to acknowledge that they will die, too.'

'And you accept all this? You think it doesn't matter?' He said nothing. 'Gonzalo, it is *horrible!*'

He met my eyes but his were unreadable. He would not let

me into his mind. We stayed like that for what felt a long time, he reclining on his elbow on the earth floor, I leaning at the hut's entrance, not speaking.

'What's that you've brought?' he suddenly asked. He had noticed the purse that I had in my hand.

There was nothing for it but to give it to him, although in the light of the conversation we had just had it seemed a ludicrous gift. 'I made it for you,' I said. It sounded like a reproach. 'I thought you could keep your knife in it, perhaps.' I wished I had got rid of the thing on the way.

He turned it over in his hands. 'I like it,' he said, to my great surprise. 'Thank you.' He scratched his ribcage idly and drew on his tobacco pipe. His muscles moved like cats under the body paint.

I did not know what I felt. I was terribly confused. Part of me was humbly grateful to him for liking the purse, and part was furious with him for what he had done. It was a few moments before I realized there was a third element to my confusion: a feeling I was wholly unprepared for and couldn't at once identify. A painful longing swept me, and I could only stare at him. Then, as I understood what it was, this feeling, and that it was utterly forbidden to a Christian, I had to make some excuse to get away from him, so I said that I was very tired, and went back to my hut.

Little by little, as I learnt the language, I was learning how the *winic* reckoned time. For they did, of course, and Gonzalo had known it before I did, with his casual remark about how they held a festival every twenty days. Twenty days was the length of their month, and the festival was the celebration of that month. The *winic* thought of months as people, and the words for 'month' and 'human' were almost the same. Both words had in them the sound that meant 'twenty'.

Since twenty days were a month, it took eighteen months to make a year. Five days were left over, and these days were said to be unlucky. No one did anything, if they could avoid it, on these five days. Certainly you would never embark on a journey. Then the New Year would be brought in with great rejoicing by one of the year-bearers, whose image was set up at the appropriate gate of the town, and there would be a festival that went on for days.

They thought that years were a burden carried by the gods. There were four gods who were year-bearers, and these four were connected with other fours: the four directions (which the *winic* held to be sacred), the four holy colours (which were the four colours in which maize grew) and the four who held up the sky. Pondering these fours one day, I saw that I could set alongside them the fourfold way in which the *winic* named things: blue smoke, shining water, shining smoke, blue water.

I did not understand why they called the years by the word that meant 'stone' until one day, at another festival, I went to look at the grove of upright stone slabs that stood behind the temple. Each had engraved on it a sinuous design, similar to a picture but not quite a picture, and all different. There were many of them, there must have been fifty or sixty. Some were much newer than others. I studied them, puzzled, for some time, before it dawned on me what they were. They were year-markers. The *winic* erected one of them at every New Year. A year *was* a stone.

They used the same word for 'day' and 'sun'. I liked this very much, and I was pleased to come across a pair of meanings that at once made sense to me. Each day also had its own name. But here things became very complicated, and I could get no further until someone explained to me that there were *two* calendars, two independent ways of reckoning time, and that one was used by the ordinary people and the other by the priests for divination. In the people's calendar, a day was known by its numerical position in whatever the month was (just as the Christian calendar reckons). In the other, it was known by its own name (there were twenty day-names, such as 'monkey', 'flint' and 'wind') paired with a number from one to thirteen. Each day that came, therefore, had a twin designation, which itself had two parts, the name and the number, so that here was yet another four.

However, there was more to it than this. In the priests' calendar, the 'year' was 260 days. In the people's calendar, it was 365 days. They ran alongside each other, their four-part combination of names and numbers different each day, until finally a day came in which the combination had already occurred. The count, in other words, had run to its full length and was back at its starting point. This happened every fifty-two years. It was a moment of great danger, the *winic* believed, for there was no way of knowing whether the gods would allow time to begin again.

Something else also followed from the circling of time. The days would follow in the same intricate order as they had before. But days were not just 'one sun'. Each day was a divine being with its own character, at which its name hinted. It brought its own fate and was shadowed by its own omens. This meant that events would repeat themselves. Past and future could not be told apart.

Learning and practising the phrases the slaves taught me, I built on them. I built them up as you build a picture out of bits of coloured stone. I, too, was building a picture. It was a picture of the world. Because it took shape so gradually, I was hardly aware of how it was starting to eclipse the picture that had been there before.

One day I had to take a basket of the fruit we had been picking to the *batab*'s house for a banquet. I walked through the gardens behind the palace, seeing for the first time the tended shrubs, the fishponds and birdcages. Fish was being grilled on open fires in a courtyard; behind the yard stood a wide thatched building from which came gusts of steam, the clatter of pots and women's laughter.

I went through one of the tapering doorways and for a moment my eyes, accustomed to the afternoon sun, were blinded. The kitchen was a huge, dim space lit by flaring fires, over which clay vessels bubbled, smoked and steamed. Intent *winic* faces reflected the glow of the fires, and turned to survey me as I stood uncertainly there.

'What do you want?' one of the women asked me. They were all women.

I said I had brought fruit for the banquet. A plump, toothless woman dressing a fowl said never mind the banquet, what had I brought for *them*? and thrust her hand into the cavity of the bird and held it up in a gesture so frank that I didn't know what to do, and there was much laughter.

I was rescued by a girl who, carrying a plate of quails' eggs, beckoned me to follow her. I did, down the length of the kitchen to where large crocks of water seethed on platforms of brick above a charcoal-fired stove. A mound of uncooked maize glistened ready by the pots. A short distance away stood three baskets heaped with melon and other fruit. I set down my own basket next to them.

Then I noticed what the two women at the stove were doing. Each had taken a handful of maize and was breathing on it, hard.

'What are you doing?' I asked, curious.

They said they were going to cook it. The *winic* always answered patiently, even when the question appeared to them stupid.

'But why are you breathing on it?'

They laughed. 'Because it needs heart.'

I thought this over. Perhaps I had mistaken a word.

'The maize needs heart?'

'Of course.'

'Why?'

They could not believe my slowness. 'Because it is going into the fire!'

Maize cannot be afraid, I thought as I walked outside. This is a childish idea. But I thought it without much conviction. I was not sure of thoughts like this any longer. Living every day among the *winic*, living *as* a *winic*, I was seeing things I had never seen as a Spaniard, feeling things I had never felt. I knew the *winic* thought of maize as a living being that had a soul, and I did not find that foolish. But if maize lived and had a soul, why should it not dread the fire? And if it did, was it a childish notion that human breath should give it courage? Or was it touching, even beautiful?

At the New Year that belonged to the colour red and the direction north, the year's image was carried into the town along the road Gonzalo had helped to build. It was the height of the war season. Warriors danced to the tall drums. They danced in the square below the temple from dawn until the sun went down. The drums could be heard far out into the fields. In the mud streets beyond the walls, little boys with turkey feathers stuck in their hair stamped and leapt to the beat.

In front of the temple, with their heads tilted back, the dancers trod the step that looked simple but wasn't. Each direction was danced to in turn. I looked for Gonzalo among the dancers, but couldn't find him.

The priests moved about the town, thin as shadows, with their censers and strips of paper. Many people were going to the temple to give thanks. A gong sounded in the shrine every few minutes, to show that a sacrifice of quail had been made. At the bottom of the stairway, children were giving away coloured ribbons to the people who had sacrificed. Men tied theirs on their wrist, women to their blouses. Quail for offering were being sold in the streets, two cacao beans for five.

I wandered through the crowds, enjoying the bustle and the colour. A man with a jar of *balche* gave me a cupful to drink. As always, it made my head fuzzy, and after a while I went back to the hut.

A bit later, the other slaves began coming back. They brought *balche* with them. The drinking began early that day. I drank only a little.

I was sitting outside on the platform with some of the slaves in the late afternoon when an official arrived and said that ten of us were needed to carry jars of *balche* to the warrior house, where there was a feast and supplies had run short.

I was chosen as one of the ten because I was still sober. We set off. The slave in charge of us also appeared to be sober, but in fact he was very drunk and fell down as soon as we got into the streets. We propped him against a wall and went on.

We had to go to a warehouse where the *balche* was stored. After several mistakes we found it, but now the sun had set, the town was lit by pine torches and everything looked different and confusing. We couldn't agree about where the warrior house was. None of us had ever been there. Two of the slaves said it was useless, sat down on the ground and refused to go any further. They opened their jar of *balche* and began to drink it.

We left them where they were, too, and tried to find the warrior house. The streets were narrow and twisting and, away from the centre, dark. We bumped into one another. A jar of *balche* was dropped and broke. *Balche* spilt everywhere, splashing our legs, and a slave cut his foot on the broken pot.

We found the place by accident. We were trying to get back to the centre of town in order to start again, when we found ourselves outside it. We knew it by its four thick pillars and by the torchlight and the strong smell of drink that came from inside. We carried our *balche* up the two shallow steps, past the pillars and into the warriors' hall.

It seemed they had found another source of drink. Either that, or they had gone beyond needing it.

The torches lit glistening mounds of melon rinds and sticky pools of *balche*. Half-eaten pastries, broken clay cups and charred plugs of tobacco mingled on the floor. Warriors lay slumped and snoring, or sat looking puzzled at the ruin of their clothes, or were coupled in the form of love that was now familiar to me from the slaves' hut.

I set down my jar of *balche*. It was not needed, but I had done my job. Then I saw Gonzalo. Over in the shadows of a corner where the brazier threw a warm, unsteady glow. He had cast his clothes aside. I saw how he tended the youth whose body was turned to him. I saw how in the act of love he arched himself like a porpoise in its leap.

I could not bear it, but I watched.

When I went back to the warrior house it was about the third hour of the night. The moon rode overhead, nearly full. The streets were empty. Some dogs whimpered from a yard.

I went into the hall, where the pine torches still flickered, not knowing what I might find. My heart was drumming and I was feverish with desire and fear.

Gonzalo was asleep in the corner where I had last seen him, one arm flung out as if to caress his lover. But the boy had gone.

I walked over the strewn floor, past the slumbering forms. I stood beside him. I let my loincloth fall to the ground.

He stirred, then opened his eyes. His eyes went very wide. He took in everything, my look, my nakedness.

Slowly he shook his head. 'Not you,' he said.

I felt as if he had struck me. 'Why not?' I whispered.

'You are a Spaniard,' he said. 'It would not be right.'

I picked up my strip of cloth and slunk away.

3

A morning came when I cut my ear with the edge of a shell and sprinkled the blood on to the image of the maize god. Then I lit a bead of copal and watched the blue smoke curl up.

The maize god was the spirit of the young plant. I had grown to love the noble serenity of his face, but that was not why I sacrificed to him. A simple and mysterious thing had become clear to me. I lived on maize. I ate it twice a day and drank, in the fields, a drink in which maize was mixed with water. It was not only that I ate and drank it: it came closer than that. Maize became my flesh. I *was* maize.

That was how the *winic* regarded themselves. They were maize. They loved the maize plant with passion and reverence. That — not so that he would bless the harvest — was why the maize god stood outside the hut.

There was more. One day they would die, and their bodies would go back into the earth. Their bodies would feed the earth, and the earth would in return produce more maize. They would be reborn as maize. The maize would again become *winic*. The cycle was perfect and eternal. But what touched the heart was that the maize could not seed itself. Every grain had to be planted by a human hand. This plant, without which the *winic* could not live, could not live without them.

Their reverence was reflected in the many names they had for maize. There was a word for the sprouting maize plant, another for the plant when it was full-grown, and another for the plant when it began to die. There was a word for the grain when it was white and another word for when it was golden, and yet another for the grain stored as seed. There were more words still for the young cob, the mature cob, the cob with and without its silken tassel. And all of these were the names of gods.

After I had laboured for a few years in the fields, the *batab* took me into his household service. Instead of clearing and planting the ground, I had to weed the *batab*'s gardens, sweep the paths, feed the fish and birds and clean the birdcages. It was lighter work and my tasks were different every day, and I preferred it.

However, I did not want to move to a new hut. My feet knew every hollow and bit of flint in the earth floor of the hut I had lived in, and the way the wind stirred the thatch just before rain came, and I had grown very attached to the field slaves. I asked if I couldn't go on living in the field slaves' hut and work in the gardens, but I was told this was not possible. I said goodbye sadly and went to live in a long hut behind the *batab*'s house, across a courtyard from the kitchens.

It was quite unlike my previous home. It was always noisy, always busy, because the courtyard was used for all manner of things. The women ground maize there, on slabs of heavy dark stone with rollers of the same stuff; children played; washing was put in the sun. We ate our meals there, sitting on our heels around the clay stove. The slaves gambled there, using a wooden board and dried beans. They were forbidden to gamble and did it all the time. They would gamble for anything – beads, a woven bracelet, a feather.

The hut was larger than the field slaves' hut, and divided roughly into sections with a few strips of coarse cloth hung from the rafters. At first, until I grew used to it, the presence of so many other people in that wooden compound pressed on my thoughts at night. It was as if I could feel their dreams. I could certainly hear their sounds of intimacy. I lay awake in my desolation. But that, too, passed.

I could not find the courage to visit Gonzalo for a long time after I had gone to the warrior house. So long that, by the time I did, the war season had started and he had already fought, and distinguished himself, in a battle.

In the end I had to see him. It was ridiculous not to. It was not even as if I was angry with him. I understood the reason for his 'not you', and I told myself I should have expected it. I could not forgive myself for my stupidity. I could not forgive myself for inviting that humiliation. But as for forgiving him . . . surely I had done that, long ago.

I went to the hut where he lived. I prayed that he would not refer to the night when I came to him and took off my clothes. I prayed that he would not even look at me in a way that suggested he remembered it. What on earth we would talk about, I didn't know.

We talked about fighting. It seemed that the way *winic* fought battles was altogether different from the way Spaniards fought battles. The difference was not just in the weapons and the tactics, and in the main object of the battle – to capture, not to kill – but also (and this in fact was the greatest difference of all) in what the battle was thought to *be*.

'It's a divination,' said Gonzalo.

'A what?'

'A divination. You know what that is?'

'Of course I do. I just don't understand what it has to do with battles.'

'The battle *divines* the will of the gods.'

'Whoever the gods favour, wins?'

'That's right. It's a sort of game, really. A sacred game.'

I had no difficulty in fitting this into the way the *winic* thought.

'It means that there are rules,' said Gonzalo. 'You can't just attack someone. There has to be a proper declaration of war. Then you have to present the enemy with shields.'

'In case they haven't got any?'

Gonzalo's look reproached my levity. 'It's a ritual. But it means something. The two sides have to be evenly matched. Otherwise . . .'

'Otherwise it doesn't reveal the will of the gods.'

'Exactly.'

'It doesn't sound,' I said, remembering something he had told me, 'as if anything *you* could show them about war would be welcome.'

Gonzalo grinned, the impudent grin that once had so exasperated me. 'I don't know about that,' he said. 'We'll have to see.'

I was greatly relieved that the conversation had been an easy one and had kept away from dangerous areas. I was preparing to leave when he said casually, 'By the way, I'm getting married.'

I went to the wedding. By that time Gonzalo had risen to be a captain of five, and had an amber disc in his lower lip. I asked him if it was painful. He said of course it was.

I didn't stay long at the celebrations. His friends were bent on getting drunk as quickly as possible

The marriage had been arranged by the matchmaker, I was surprised to hear. The bride's parents had been correctly approached, a bride-price paid. I do not know why I expected Gonzalo to have behaved like a ruffian rather than following custom: perhaps I wanted him to.

The girl was not at all pretty, I thought.

Gonzalo said to me, 'I always wanted to get married. I like family life.'

'In that case I wonder that you weren't married before,' I said.

'I was,' he said. 'I've got a wife in Palos. But that's not much use here, is it?'

I was summoned to the *batab*'s presence one day. It was after I had begun to work in his gardens. I was afraid I had done something wrong, but he received me without any appearance of anger. There was a frail-looking and much older man, a priest in white robes, sitting with him on the mat. I had seen this priest before, being carried through the town, but did not know who he was.

'You speak our language now,' the *batab* said to me. 'I have some questions to ask you. This is my friend the Chilan, who is the priest of the oracle and wishes to hear your answers.'

'As the *batab* wishes,' I said. I had been told that I should say this.

'From where did you come?'

I was about to say, 'From Spain.' I knew that Spain was, originally, where I had come from. I knew it because I had always known it. But Spain was a place I could no longer believe in except as a story, and when I examined the story, all it turned out to consist of was that I had been born there and had one day left it. Accompanying this were a few colourful shreds of memory that did not fit together. It occurred to me that there was another answer. The ship that was taking me to a destination I never reached, on an errand that had long since vanished from my mind, had set out from a place much nearer to Chanek. And this, surely, was a better reply to the *batab*'s question. Or it would be if I could remember the name of the place.

They saw me struggling to answer, and waited. In the end the *batab* said, 'Then in which direction does it lie, this land?'

I would gladly have told him if I could. How many times, in my first year in Chanek, had I stood on the cliff outside the town, gazing at the ocean, wondering where in its immensity was the place I had come from? (And, after that, where was the place I had come *to*?)

I had to say something. I pointed, at an angle, towards the wall of the *batab*'s house that faced the sea. I was pointing roughly north-east, to where, surely, Spain was.

'That is the right hand of the sun,' murmured the Chilan. He had an old, dried-out voice that made me think of the seed-head of a poppy.

'He is not sure.' The *batab* threw some knobs of copal into the censer.

'On the day One Deer,' pursued the Chilan.

'The day One Deer, the day Six Wind. What does it matter?'

'The day always matters.' The smoke coiled up from the censer and the Chilan followed it with his eyes.

'And how far away is this land?' the *batab* asked me.

'*Batab*, I am sorry but I cannot tell.'

'Then how many days were you at sea?'

Did he mean the voyage from Spain or the one on which I was shipwrecked? It seemed to me that it didn't matter, since I couldn't answer either. '*Batab*, our canoe had no paddles and drifted. I do not know for how long.'

'They were near death,' said the Chilan.

The *batab* shrugged. 'They did not mean to come here.'

'He has not said that.'

'Ask him.'

'Did you know of our country before you came here?'

'No, lord.' I said this with relief, because I was certain of it.

The macaw climbed noisily in its cage and let out a squawk.

'Who is your god?' asked the Chilan, in the same quiet, dry voice. The *batab* gave him a sharp look.

I stared at the ground. The question was not straightforward.

'When you came here,' prompted the *batab*, who was getting bored, 'you spoke to your god every night.'

I knew then what to say. '*Batab*, his name is Lordjesuschrist.'

'His name is not Kukulcan?' asked the Chilan.

'No, lord.'

The *batab* said to me, 'Tell us something about this god.'

Brightly lit pictures came into my mind: a sick man on a plank, being lowered through a roof; a savage crowd demanding blood; a woman holding a jar. They were not the important thing. I did not want to speak about the important thing, because it shamed and still saddened me, but after I had gazed at the floor a little longer I did because it demanded to be said.

'He went away,' I confessed.

They both leant towards me.

'To where?'

I said I did not know.

'And will he return?'

Again, I had to say I did not know.

'We should question the other one,' suggested the Chilan.

'It will be fruitless. This one is more intelligent.'

'But he knows nothing.'

'He knows nothing,' said the *batab*, 'because there is nothing to be known.'

Ignoring the Chilan's protest, he dismissed me.

Now that I worked in the *batab*'s gardens, I walked through the town almost every day. Almost every day I passed the temple with its gods and creatures painted on the walls in the clear colours of sea and sky. You can see a thing many times before you truly see it and, when you do, what has made you see it? There was nothing different about the morning when, several months after my interview with the *batab*, the strange half-plant half-tree, with a bird perched atop it, reached out from the wall of the temple as I went by and stopped me.

It was elaborate, this plant, it had many curlicues and plumes that confused the eye, but on this particular morning my gaze ignored all these decorations, seeing them suddenly for what they were, mere ornament, and went straight to the place where the fan of branches leafed at the top. There, inside the stem or trunk, at the thing's heart, the cross sprang cleanly out. Two simple lines, the vertical slightly longer than the other. It was the Christian cross.

I trembled. Tears came to my eyes. Here, where I thought Lordjesuschrist had never been, was the cross on which He had hung. Here was the Tree on which He had always shown himself to me, until I came to Chanek and He vanished from it. His cross was here on a *winic* temple, and what it was telling me could not be misunderstood. He had not abandoned me. This was the form in which He wanted to be worshipped in this country.

I saw it, after that, in many places, either the tree or the cross, or sometimes both together. I learned that the tree was the Yaxché, and the cross was its sign. And I realized — indeed, the way it was depicted on the temple wall was telling me this — that the sacred tree was also the maize plant.

One day I was ordered to go to a place half a day's journey away and bring back a basket of freshwater fish for a banquet at the *batab*'s house.

I set off at dawn. The path was sometimes a path, sometimes a few snapped twigs. The sun opened brilliant halls into the forest. I walked with sure feet and open eyes. I picked out at a glance the mushrooms that could be eaten from the mushrooms that must not, the tree that bore a fruit the same colour as its leaves, so that only with the sharpest eye could they be found, the creeper that stored enough water for my journey, the creeper that was not a creeper but a snake.

Before midday, I came to the lagoon. A reed hut had been built on the shore. Canoes were drawn up on the sandy beach. The fishermen were out in the lagoon, standing in water up to their thighs, the fringes of their loincloths tucked in to keep them dry. They were raising and dropping long poles in the water. They worked in pairs, holding the poles between them, each gazing into the distance over the other's shoulder.

The water foamed with the churning of the poles, and a greenish scum, in which pieces of leaf appeared, was forming. The poles made a thudding sound, and after each thud came a sucking noise as the pole was pulled out of the mud and leaves. They were pounding into the water a drug to make the fish sleep.

I squatted on the shoreline, watching. The figures of the fishermen wavered in the heat. Behind the thudding of the poles I heard the chirp and hum of insects and the baying croak of the marsh frogs. My eyes began to close from the heat and the hours of walking, and I opened them to see the lagoon a plate of silver and the men wading to the shore.

We rested in the hut, talking, and the fishermen smoked tobacco which they had dried themselves and which hung in sweet-smelling flags from the rafters. While we talked, they told me something that would lengthen my journey home.

We went out again when it was a little cooler, each one with a wide reed basket. We waded into the shallows. The fish floated just under the surface, as if pushed up by an unseen hand, a still harvest. Their gills opened and closed pinkly. We picked this cold-fleshed fruit out of the water and laid it in our baskets, where it shuddered and began to die.

I lined my own carrying-basket with fresh leaves, packed into it the fish I was to take and set it on my back. I said goodbye to the fishermen and set off through the forest again. They could not spare a man to show me the way, and I was afraid of missing the path. But when I came to the fork they had told me of, the way was quite clear.

I arrived in the town soon afterwards and stopped at a long hut outside which a group of youths sat gaming. I asked them where I could find the women with pale skins.

They laughed and said I should wash the smell of fish off myself before I approached women. They directed me to a large house with red gateposts in the centre of the town.

I found it without difficulty. I went through the courtyard, where a huge steward with rolls of flesh like ropes asked me what I wanted.

He turned his head, when I told him, and at the same moment I saw them. They crouched just on the other side of the open doorway, with the grinding-stones between them, grinding corn with the patient movement I had seen countless times. They raised their faded eyes to me without interest.

I said in Spanish, 'God be with you.' I had prepared this greeting in the forest.

They did not stop grinding at once. The words had to sink

down a long way, and then be tested against the knowledge that they were impossible.

The hands faltered on the stone.

'Who are you?' said one.

'He is Gonzalo,' said the other.

'He is a ghost,' said the first, and made the sign of the Tree.

'No, he is Gonzalo.'

'Gonzalo is dead.'

'Gonzalo is alive,' I said, 'but I am not he.'

I told them that Gonzalo and I were both living in Chanek, the town we had first been taken to. They listened, but with a sort of dullness, as if they thought I was lying. Then they spoke to each other, in a rapid Spanish that made me realize how heavy, like something waterlogged, mine had become.

'There were others,' said one of them to me.

'No, they have killed them all,' said the one who had said I was a ghost.

The steward came past and said to me, 'Are you still here? Haven't you got your own work to do?'

I apologized and said I would not be much longer. He went away, grumbling. The women started grinding the maize again. As they pressed the shaped stone into the yellow grain, they remarked that I could speak the language of the country.

'Don't you?' I asked in some surprise.

They shook their heads.

'I hate it,' said one. 'It sounds to me like monkey-chatter.'

This offended me, and it must have shown in my face.

The other smiled, rather unpleasantly. 'You are at home here,' she said.

I did not know what to reply to this, understanding that it was not kindly meant, so I said, 'What is your life like? How do they treat you?'

The one who had said she hated the language set her mouth bitterly and said, 'We grind the corn all day. That is all we do.'

'Yes,' said the other. 'And that is all we will ever do.'

'All we have to look forward to is death,' said the first. They both made the sign of the Tree.

A moment later they both looked at me with the same thought.

'You are a *priest!*' they cried. And although I protested that I was not, they threw themselves at my blackened feet, babbling prayers.

I pushed them from me in horror, picked up my basket and fled. As I hurried through the courtyard I heard one say to the other, 'It was a ghost, you see,' and the reply, 'But it was not Gonzalo.'

I found, in time, a lover. He came shyly to my mat one night. He said he had waited, because he knew my soul was with my friend, but now he thought perhaps it had been long enough. His name was Kuna. I did not send him away.

The seasons passed and I was content. The world of the *winic* came close, I breathed its breath. It was my world now.

I spread my hand, seamed with toil, on the seamed bark of the Yaxché. I gazed at my brown feet and saw that they were part of the earth. In the forest a *kukul*-bird flew up from its branch straight at the sun, cascading emeralds into my eyes.

When the maize was harvested we all went to the fields to help. I worked alongside my old companions, laughing and joking with them, showing them I had not forgotten how to pick a crop. I tossed the ripe cobs into the basket at my back. The cobs pressed themselves into my hand, full, magnificent. The stalks of the maize bent towards me. Their heads rippled, their floating banners were silken, their fruit was proudly borne. And they sang: the field of maize was singing.

Then the maize parted, and I followed the path. At the heart of the maize where the light was brightest, where the song was loudest, I saw Him again, His features as they were on the clay image the slaves adored, His head crowned with radiant spears.

The seasons passed. The season for sowing, the season for harvesting, the season for war.

369

There came a disturbed time in which rumours bred like flies. Some of them were about a new invasion from the north. Invasions always came from the north, which was the region of bad luck and where the land of the dead lay. The invasions of the past, of which no one remembered anything except that they had once happened, were a part of the story of the *winic*.

The rumours were believed, not because there was anything convincing about them – in fact the stories were fantastic, they were clearly inventions – but because the past and the future were the same to the *winic*. They were not-the-present. It was certain that there would be more invasions, or, more accurately, dreams of invasions, since the past was a dream and so, in a different way, was the present.

The slaves looked at me and joked when they talked about all this. My stupidity amused them greatly. They asked what kind of country I came from, where people did not count the years in a great circle, or know that there had been other worlds before this and would be after.

Because of the rumours, there was talk that the ancestors would be consulted.

The priests, it seemed, were divided about whether this should be done. Some sided with the oracle priest, the Chilan, and some with the *batab*, who was scornful of the ancient prophecies.

This disagreement, people said, was bad, and Chanek was not the only place where it had happened. The times were changing. Once the *winic* had possessed magical powers, they had known how to see things far off and divine the past and future, and the gods and ancestors had spoken to them every day. And at that time gods and ancestors had spoken clearly, not as now, when everything said was a riddle and like something seen through smoke; and the speaking had been freely given, not as now, when it must be painfully sought and bought with blood.

Shortly before the New Year of Yellow, it was announced that the rite would be performed. All the people of the town, whatever their rank, must attend.

When I went to the plaza it was already crowded. People were standing on the flat roofs of the buildings. The noise of talk, the shouting of vendors, the beating of a drum in the distance, the screeching of parrots in a cage near by, all combined in a deafening hubbub.

The noise stopped quite abruptly. Into the hush came a silvery percussion of shells and, immediately after it, the shrilling of flutes. Then into the plaza from the direction of the temple threaded a procession headed by four temple slaves carrying a sumptuously draped litter, and on the litter, his back resting against a carved wooden pillow, sat the Chilan, clothed from head to foot in white.

Behind him came a line of priests carrying incense. And behind the priests, walking with his courtiers and wearing an expression of solemnity which might have hidden a profound boredom with the proceedings, came the *batab*.

The procession wound its way around the plaza and the litter halted in front of a tall carved stone. The Chilan stepped down on to a mat which had been placed for him. He stood there quietly and alone for a few moments, a frail figure in the very centre of the plaza. Down the stone steps of the temple now came a fantastically decked figure in yellow and scarlet, plumes nodding at his shoulder, a mask of snakeskin on his head and bracelets of shell and bone on his wrists. He held a glazed bowl in his right hand, and in his left long strips of paper that floated upward behind him over the steps.

This priest came to stand behind the Chilan, who took something out of the bowl and held it up. It looked like a blade of some kind, perhaps shell; at any rate, the people recognized it and greeted it with acclamations. The Chilan turned it and it caught the sun with a hard glint. He lowered it slowly, until his arm was almost straight down at his side but the wrist was crooked a little, so that the object in his fingers was held pointing upward.

With his other hand, in a swift and sudden movement, he tugged at the loop of his embroidered loincloth and it fell to the stones, where the snake-headed priest bent and picked it up.

The old man now stood in his cloak and sandals on the plaza, his nakedness exposed to public gaze. I glanced for reassurance at the faces of those around me, but they did not answer my look; they were all entranced, it seemed, by what was taking place in the centre of the plaza, except for some who were gazing not at the spot where the Chilan stood but at a place in the sky above him, where there was nothing to be seen but a few wisps of cloud.

I was looking, myself, at this spot in the sky when there came a sound from the assembled people which was between a cry and a groan. The Chilan had done something, and for a moment I did not understand what it was, but gazed in horror at the blood which darkened his thighs.

He had driven the thin blade of shell through his penis.

He held the dripping blade up to the people. They shouted.

Above, in the sanctuary, a drum began to beat. Incense drifted heavily on the air.

Again the Chilan plunged the blade into the wound he had made. His intention seemed to be to make it wider. In his pain his eyes had rolled upward so that the whites showed under the iris, but still he stood firmly and did not sway as his blood fountained anew and pooled shining on the ground.

The drum beat again, more insistently, summoning. They had lit burners of incense all around now, so that the blue smoke wreathed in the air and the smell overpowered the senses. The air itself was getting heavier; the sky was clouding as if the wisps of vapour I had seen were drawing others to them. There would be rain, out of season.

Remorselessly the Chilan drew blood and yet more blood from his flesh. I was bathed in a sweat that was partly horror, and could scarcely breathe for the suffocating incense. Nor could I move. I was wedged tight in the crowd, who seemed hardly to

372

be breathing either, and whose gaze was now entirely fixed on the spot in the sky where there was nothing to be seen but a cloud rapidly becoming denser.

The rhythm of the drum grew faster and became complicated. A series of quick running taps now preceded the dominating boom, and then between the main beats that were summoning something, or someone, came a slithering half-beat that was gone as soon as you'd heard it, like a snake into grass.

Something moved on the air that I could not quite see. It was huge and elemental. The sky was changing.

The costumed priest took the crimson blade from the Chilan and handed him one of the strips of bark paper which he was holding. The Chilan held the paper up for the people to see, and then, as my knees began to shake and the sky grew every moment more terrifying, he inserted the paper into the piteous hole he had made in his flesh and pulled it completely through.

Again he held the paper up, drenched and dreadful, for the crowd. Who were sighing, weeping, praying and seemed to see everything that was taking place on the plaza without removing their gaze from the sky above it.

The priest took the bloodied strip from the Chilan and dropped it into the burning censer nearest him. It flared and smoked, and the smoke spiralled dense and black straight into the heart of the coiling thundercloud.

The drum tugged and smote me, and the reeking smoke took away my wits. As my knees gave way I saw it at last, the thing at which the *winic* had long been gazing. I saw the serpent of the sky, in its vast misty coils, its infinite jaws agape and its neck bent down in tenderness to its people.

The rains came again, and the maize was planted in the cleared ground. While the shoots were young, bean seeds were sown a hand's span from their roots so that the beans, as they climbed, should have support. At the edge of the field the beehives were set out, and the beekeepers brought offerings of honey and danced their dance at the festival of bees.

At the festival of fish, the fishermen danced, and the nets were brought to the temple to be blessed. At the festival of the carvers and painters, the tools were daubed with blue, and the children's hands were touched so they would be able to practise the crafts of their parents. At the festival of the new images, the images were anointed, and the carvers, who had lived apart from their wives while the images were being made, returned to them. At the festival of children the infants were baptized, and at the festival of hunters, animals that had been caught in the forest were offered at the temple.

At the festival of warriors, victories over enemies were celebrated and the warriors danced.

The years melted together. At one of the New Year ceremonies, a bearer stumbled when carrying the image to its house and it fell to the ground.

But it was not that year, but the next one, that a trader came down the coast with a bag of beads and a message curled in his hair.

VI
Iron

I

The lower slopes of the mountain are covered in a crust of black stones and boulders, or not quite black but, rather, the colour of charcoal. As if the stone itself had been burnt, were the result of burning. It is dull and pitted; quite light, too, in the hand. Francisco de Montano puts a small piece in his pocket.

The slope at first is not particularly steep, but the myriad loose stones that coat it move under your foot, so that with every step forward you also slip back a little. After you have climbed in this way for half the morning, only to find the angle of the slope increasing harshly, while at the same time the air can no longer nourish your lungs, which snatch at it and never get enough, the ascent begins to seem serious and you feel a deeper respect for those half-dozen of your comrades who a year ago returned with wild stories and scorched clothing, driven back from a summit which as yet Montano and his four companions are nowhere near.

It is getting very cold. Montano feels the cold on his face while his back and chest run with sweat. He feels it on the backs of his hands, too, a chill wind blowing from the higher slopes. They are messengers, those winds. They tell him what lies beyond the steeply rising field of stone that fills his view – snow, that's what, and ice, scarcely to be believed at this latitude but he has seen the white peak from the pass below and it was proved by Ordaz the year before with his icicles, icicles a yard long and as thick as your thigh, and stained a bitter yellow, at which the Captain stared.

It is because of that yellow that the five of them are here, slogging upward into the crystal sky.

They come to the snow before he expects it. A patch of startling white in a hollow of a crag. After that, a larger drift, patterned by a bird's track, and then another flung on the shoulder of an overhang, and a short way beyond this the drifts have merged to form an unbroken blanket of snow that winks in the sunlight. The boots of his companions sink and crunch. This comfortable crunching, their effortful breaths and the occasional creak of the basket one of them carries are the only sounds in the pure morning. The mountain greeted Ordaz with thunder and a rain of ash. For Montano and his friends it waits in silence.

At the end of another hour, they come to a place where the mountain rises up almost sheer above them. To the right, the ground yawns into a crevasse. Ordaz spoke of this and said that a route would lie to their left, over a narrower cleft which was spanned by a natural bridge. Towards this they pick their way.

The bridge is hump-shaped, the snow presumably blanketing a boulder which rolled long ago into the crevasse and stuck there. A false step on the rounded surface would send a man plummeting to the crags below. Montano, conscious how the rope coiled around his waist hampers him, inches his way to the further side and then calls for the basket, which has bumped all this way on the broad shoulders of Herrera, to be thrown across to him. Hauling it out of the snow, he straps it on his own back.

The bridge is the start of more difficult terrain. Above the next field of snow they must cross a ribbed sheet of ice, stained in patches with a blackness that makes him think of ink but that must in fact be soot. And now they have to climb in earnest, seeking handholds in the frozen rock, thankful for the warm sun on their necks because it does something to lessen the cold in their groping fingers.

Still the mountain is silent. But then, lifting his gaze above the expanse of rock on which he clings like a fly, Montano sees a drift of white in the sapphire sky like foam on the sea, and a hiss of vented steam comes to his ears. The vapour above him thickens. The rock seems to shiver, and then suddenly, with a terrifying *boom!* a black cloud shoots upwards and covers all he can see of the sky.

He and his little party go on climbing. They climb through the soft warm rain of ash that settles on their beards and faces and pause on the last ridge, from which, amid the drifting shreds of vapour, the summit can be seen. A strange summit. The top of the mountain has been scooped off as you scoop off the top of an egg.

A quarter of an hour's steady trudging takes them there. The mist, or cooled steam, wraps itself briefly round them as they slow their steps towards that sinister edge, but it clears just as they are starting to fear that they will walk too far. A breeze whisks it away, and there is nothing between them and the winking evil of the pit.

Red. A baleful red, burning far down in a nest of darkness. Not quite darkness: a fitful light flickers on rock walls, illuminating for a moment great crags and spurs of rock and caverns gouged in the walls of the crater as if one vast emptiness were not enough. Not that it is really empty, only empty to the sight, being filled with suffocating fumes and exhalations and a heat that makes your eyes smart. And Montano can hear the hissing now, like a million snakes getting ready to strike, and he can see the vapour rising from the huge rim of this ungodly hole like devil's breath, and going up to mark its message on the sky.

I am to be lowered over the edge into this?

Wordlessly, he loosens the straps of the basket and takes it off.

The way in which this is to be done has been agreed between them before they set off. But then, naturally, they hadn't known what they were preparing for. Would there be a projection of rock to which the rope could be secured? If there wasn't, they would have to take his weight, and the basket's weight together with whatever else was in it, with their own bodies, and how would those bodies fare on the edge of the fire? For all they knew, the ground would be too hot to kneel on, perhaps even too hot to *stand* on; perhaps there wasn't even any ground but something else, treacherous and consuming. But since there was no point in such speculations, they would assume that the normal laws of nature applied up there on the top of the mountain and they would tie the rope around their waists and secure the basket to the end.

Then Montano would get into the basket.

It turns out that there is no projecting rock. The ground is seamed and tortured and into its cracks a coarse black grit has settled. This grit, which is sticky, also lies everywhere in mounds, some of which are capped by snow like tiny mountains. But, for all that, the rim of the great hole is as smooth as an Indian's cheek. There are no boulders, no outcrops. They themselves will have to be the rock.

They begin to tie the rope around them, starting with Herrera, who is the stoutest. Montano watches him, at first with the unminding attention with which you watch any man who is tying a knot, but suddenly with the awareness that his life will depend on the tying of it. After that, it seems improper to watch how the other knots are tied, so he occupies himself by walking a little distance. He does not look over the edge. He looks out at God's earth with love: a far-off valley, green, darkly furred with trees, and a village from which rise wisps of whitish smoke and – does he imagine it? – a woman's voice.

His companions stand roped in a line like an ungainly string of beads, and here is the basket at the rope's end, glaringly empty, perched on the rim of the crater.

Montano walks to the edge and lets his gaze fall.

It is still there.

He picks up the basket and drops it over the edge, catching

the rope so that the rim of the basket is just below the level of his feet. A choking vapour gusts into his face but he keeps his grip on the rope, crouching there on his heels on the edge of the abyss until one of them comes and takes it from him. The others move back, taking up the slack in the rope, getting ready to brace themselves.

His eyes are streaming. He wipes them on his sleeve. He crosses himself and steps into the basket.

They begin to lower him. At first all he can see is the wall of the pit in front of his face, curtained in shadows and fleetingly lit by the pulses of the fire. But as he goes lower, and the blessed blue of the sky withdraws from him, the surface of the rock emerges from its darkness and he begins to see what no human eyes have ever seen.

The rock is mostly as black as soot, and pitted like a sponge. Here and there, a patch of lurid red or greenish-yellow blooms on it like a huge lichen, and he supposes that these are minerals that have been spewed up from the depths. Tiny needle-points of crimson glint at him from the blackness, catching the flare of the burning below. Shards of rubies, he thinks, and tries to scrape some off with his fingernails, but the rock is as hard as iron for all its strange look of softness and he breaks his fingernails instead. The basket, which swayed outward with his reaching for the wall, on its return strikes the rock and brings a warning shout from above.

Montano squints upward. The black rim of the crater cruelly cuts off the sky. A head leans over the edge, its contours disguised by a helmet.

He goes back to his wall. But now his eyes have lost their wisdom in the dark, and he must wait for them to recover it.

Carefully, trying not to make the basket sway, he reaches forward and feels the rock with the palm of his hand. A steady warmth comes off it at a distance of an inch or so. It is only when he lays his palm flat on it that he realizes it is covered in moisture, a sticky sweat that has condensed out of the steam-laden air. He brings his hand to his nostrils and sniffs. A foul and cloying smell, somehow sweetish, but acrid, too, a smell that hits the back of the throat and burns there.

Sulphur.

As his sight returns, he begins to see it all around him. There it is, and there, and again there, mushrooming on the dark walls in rippling stains. As he touches it with his fingers it crumbles away from the rock; it can be picked off between a determined thumb and forefinger. He will be able to cut it away easily with his knife.

Hernán has given him a sack, previously containing cassava bread, which has imparted a musty smell to the hessian. He is standing on it, that's the trouble. The realization of what he has to do next, stand on one leg, thereby tipping the basket off balance, reach down and pull up the sack, transferring his weight as he does so from one leg to the other, thus tipping the basket in the opposite direction, and all this while steadying himself with only one hand because the other hand is needed for the sack – the thought of this brings him out in a violent sweat and he convulsively clings to the sides of the basket for a few moments before shame gets the better of him. Gingerly he lifts his right foot. The basket tilts to the side where his weight rests. To compensate, he leans on his right arm. The basket lurches and sways outward over the pit, then careers back towards the rock face and strikes it hard, with a terrible sound of splintering wickerwork. From above comes an anguished shout.

Montano stands still in the basket and waits for his heart to stop knocking at his eardrums and for the sweat that bathes his forehead to trickle down the sides of his nose to his beard. After a short space, he takes his knife from his belt and lays the point under the edge of the nearest pale incrustation that glimmers at him from the rock. He pushes the blade gently forward.

It is as he hoped. The stain begins to peel from the rock like a skin. By careful working – he needs both hands for it, which leaves no hand to steady himself – he has the crust entire and free in his palm at the end of five minutes. Feeling triumphant, he drops it into the basket at his feet.

He removes a second circle, then a third. He drops them into the basket. They land on his boots. He will worry about that later. He looks for more sulphur.

There is a fourth deposit to his right, a lumpy coagulate that arouses a hunter's lust in him, but he can't reach it. The basket can only be moved up or down. He will have to go down. He calls out that he wants to be lowered.

After a moment or two, the basket begins to rise.

'No! No!' shouts Montano. '*Down!*'

The movement stops. An incomprehensible question floats down to his ears.

'*Lower me!*'

The basket lurches. He clutches the sides. An unsteady descent begins.

After about six feet they stop him. Montano gets out his knife.

The sulphur glistens all around him. He digs at it and brings it away in lumps. He drops the lumps into the basket and the cargo begins its steady rise towards his thighs. The basket, at erratic intervals, continues its descent into the heart of the volcano.

The campaign will be arduous, or so the Captain has to assume. The preparations must be exact. He lacks everything: money, soldiers, equipment, horses, food. The Tlascalans will feed them for three weeks, after which they will have to fend for themselves.

He is occupied for much of each day with such things as crossbow bolts, gunpowder (ingenuity has suggested a source for this), horseshoes, ropes, anchors, sails and timber. Not to mention the state of his army, part of which — a predictable part — is mutinous.

He issues an order that all gold must be handed in. Alvarado's eyebrows rise.

'No money, no war,' points out the Captain.

'It all went into the lake.'

'Nonsense. How much do *you* have?'

Alvarado smiles warily.

'There's enough gold out there, stitched into saddles and armour and stuffed into boots, to buy another fifty horses,' says the Captain. He isn't sure of this, but he is gambling again. It can't be that the Spaniards who died on the causeway were the only ones carrying those thin bars of gold.

'Where are you going to get horses from?'

'Hispaniola.'

A comfortableness exists between them, the old understanding, now that there's a new campaign to plan. For a time, it has been absent. After the killings in the temple that provoked the Meshica rising, the Captain was slow to forgive his second-in-command. As a matter of fact the Captain has still not forgiven him, but Alvarado doesn't know that.

'There's talk about Cuba,' remarks Alvarado.

'There is always talk about Cuba.' The only time the word was not mentioned was when they were holding Muckety, and the empire, in the palm of their hands.

'This time it's different.'

'How? The argument is always the same.'

'This time, we have lost six hundred men.'

'I know what we lost,' says the Captain. 'It's nothing.'

Alvarado looks levelly and long at him, as well he might. Then he says, 'They won't want to give it up, their gold.'

'Tell them I'll hang them if they don't.'

'And *will* you?'

The Captain's reply is stony. This is not to be a piece of road-side theatre about stealing chickens. 'Yes, I will.'

Once they were off the causeway, most of them wanted to go straight back to the coast. It was natural. And they made it clear to him, when he gathered them together on the shore that devastated midsummer morning and spoke to them about what must be done next. Half of them were too weak to stand, but they hadn't lost their voices. He had to explain to them that if they tried to get to the coast they would never reach it, the Indians would kill them all in the mountains, that their only hope was Tlascala, where (he did not say this, he did not have to) they must pray they would find a welcome, when there was every reason to expect the opposite.

In Tlascala they were welcomed. He is still astonished by this. The Tlascalans have uttered not a word of reproach to him for the loss of two thousand of their people, for the failure of the dream of glory. If they understand the completeness of the disaster that has befallen him they avert their eyes from it, as they pretended not to see, on his arrival, the beaten, ragged, exhausted army he dragged behind him like an unravelled bandage. When, at his first interview with the four lords, he declared, 'I have received no more than a setback. I intend to return and conquer Tenochtitlan,' there was no smile of incredulity, no laughter, only a long, long pause as the import of this statement settled into every corner of the room.

Then: 'That cannot be done,' said Shiko Tenka calmly.

'You are mistaken,' the Captain told him.

There was a glazed bowl on the cloth. It made a bid for his attention, but he could not attend to it because he was watching Shiko Tenka. Shiko Tenka put out his hand and moved the bowl towards him. He made a graceful gesture in the space around it.

'Tenochtitlan is surrounded by water,' he said. 'On the water are the canoes of the Meshica. As you approach, they will take up the bridges, as they did before. What will you do?'

The bowl contained salt.

The Captain pulled a breath deep into his lungs to steady himself. Then he, too, put out his hand and touched the bowl. He drew it towards him, claiming what it represented.

He looked round at them, the four lords, Shiko Tenka, a clutch of councillors. 'This is what I shall do,' he said, and he told them.

✻   ✻   ✻

385

Perhaps they made up their minds at once and are only pretending caution. He has had an audience with the four lords every day since his return. Talking, explaining, bargaining. Never begging. For in his position of absolute weakness, absolute dependence, the one thing he must never do is appear to be asking favours. It is an equal enterprise. Tlascala will supply materials, manpower, food, a secure base and a number of warriors yet to be agreed on; Spaniards will supply what only they can supply, their armaments, strategy and skills of war. The old lords haggle. They demand this and that as part of the bargain. Some of their demands betray a touching faith about what the future will be like. Thus, they ask to have their own fortress inside the conquered city. (Yes, he says, after delaying as if to give it thought; yes, that is possible.) The fact is that they can ask him for anything, anything at all, and he will have to grant it. The difficulty is to prevent them from realizing this.

Shiko Tenka is not usually present at these meetings. His absence has been explained by the oldest and most sympathetic of the four lords, Maxicatzin, with the words, 'His attendance is not necessary and he has many things to see to.' The Captain speculates as to what may lie behind these words. Shiko Tenka has never been friendly to the Spanish alliance and has recently been at the centre of a furious dispute within the ruling council, news of which has come to him from several quarters. It turns out that, while the Captain and his men were slogging around the northern edge of the lake, skirmishing daily with Indians, the Meshica were sending ambassadors to Tlascala to propose an alliance of their own. That was what the salt was doing in the bowl. Together, the ambassadors said, they and the Tlascalans could drive the Spaniards out of the country.

The four lords, thank God, refused the offer: they could not bring themselves to make an alliance with people they hated. But Shiko Tenka argued passionately in favour of the Meshica alliance. He said that these invaders from who-knew-where were a far more serious threat to Tlascala than the Meshica could ever be.

He said they would end up destroying the Meshica and Tlascala and the whole land if they were not wiped out. He accused the four lords of being unfit to govern his country. His aged father threw him bodily out of the council chamber.

At least one inference may be drawn from this disquieting event. It is that the Meshica have got themselves a new ruler who knows what he's about. He is, lamentably, a man the Captain once had under lock and key: Kweetl-awac, Muckety's brother, whom Muckety suggested be set free to reopen the market. A sly fox, Muckety. It may also be inferred that Shiko Tenka is a man of strong and consistent opinions. But the Captain always knew this.

It is not all scheming, haggling and making lists. God will be served. The lords of Tlascala are receiving instruction from Olmedo, and will be baptized in ten days' time. Periodically the Captain raises his head from his many practical tasks to contemplate this prospect – the baptism, freely sought, of the rulers of a native kingdom, to be followed presumably by mass conversion of the country – and is awed by it. He sees before him the whole vast land, from ocean to mountain crag, subdued beneath the sign of Christ, and his heart swells with the magnitude of the task to which he has set his hand.

He rides out one morning with Alvarado, Sandoval and a Tlascalan guide to look at trees. A lovely morning, with mist hanging in a white scarf above the tops of the forest. Such a stillness. Then a flock of birds rises in a cacophony of fright at the horses, and caws into the distance. He thinks of Spain, the rooks that inhabited the trees around the castle of Medellín.

The trees here are not so very different, with a few exceptions he can't identify. There are fir and pine on the slopes. Tall, yes, but is the timber strong enough? There's oak, he can see it, though not much. He wanted to bring Martín López, who would know about the timber, but the man is too sick to ride. He won't die, God won't let him die, and if God lets him the Captain won't.

It occurs to the Captain now that, after all, the timber does not need to be of the stoutest, because how long does it have to last? A year, at most.

The thought that, within so short a time, everything will be accomplished or he will be dead sets his pulse running like a hare.

The sun draws the mist up to itself and in their groves they stand waiting, his ships.

If anything was going to go wrong, Brother Olmedo thought it would be the font. The Captain had ordered it to be made. By native craftsmen, using a hard reddish stone. Olmedo visited the workshop with him and picked up some dust under his fingernails. Rubbed into the palm, it made streaks the colour of blood. That wasn't the problem. The problem was the weight. This font was going to weigh more than a brace of falconets, and the cannon had already crushed more Tlascalan arms and legs than anyone wanted to talk about. Brother Olmedo knew what would happen, he saw it every night as he closed his eyes for sleep. One of the bearers would stumble, the load would slip, there would be blood and mangled flesh, and the first baptismal font in what Hernán was optimistically calling New Spain would be inaugurated with an Indian sacrifice.

This did not happen. With humble gratitude, Brother Olmedo saw the font carefully, precisely lowered on its ropes to the plinth on which it would rest. To the accompaniment, it's true, of a great deal of jabbering, gesticulating and excitement, but that was normal. Tlascalans couldn't move anything without making a noise, as if it helped muscular effort. Now there sat the font, and he strolled over to inspect it.

Massive, you could say. The outside surface left unfinished, showing the chisel marks. This not for reasons of time, although indeed there wouldn't have been time to finish that surface and it was a miracle the thing was ready at all; no, the Captain had ordered it that way, saying that the roughness, the naturalness, of the unfinished stone would represent the still savage nature of the country, soon to be tamed by the spirit of Christ, as represented by the smooth hollow within.

Such a pretty turn of speech the Captain had.

Brother Olmedo ran his fingers over the pleasing concavity in which the holy water would rest. They came up stained with a reddish dust that looked like blood.

The baptism, performed in the open air several days later, was designed to be a grand affair. All the noble families of Tlascala had been invited, and sat on benches talking avidly. The Spaniards were also present in great numbers. The Captain had indicated that not to attend would incur his displeasure, announcing, 'This is the most important thing we have done since we arrived in the country,' to the considerable irritation of quite a few scarred veterans.

Well, he was right, Olmedo thought as he raised the crucifix and began the Communion service that would be followed by the baptisms. Hernán was standing as godfather to Maxicatzin, Pedro de Alvarado to the father of Shiko Tenka, Sandoval and Tapia to the two others. The Latin would not be translated, and Olmedo, belatedly thinking of this, decided that he should deviate slightly from the normal order of service for the benefit of the hundreds of watching Indians who, more than anyone, needed to understand what was taking place.

Accordingly, at an appropriate point he put a question directly in Spanish to the baptismal candidates themselves. It was the question at the heart of everything, and they had been well prepared for it.

'Do you agree to give up the religion of your fathers?'

When this was translated to them, the four lords looked puzzled. They asked Marina to repeat what she'd said. Olmedo's heart sank in foreboding. Beside him, the priest Juan Díaz, who disliked all dealings with Indians and therefore, thought Olmedo, had no business here, scowled in disapproval.

The lords conferred, and then gave their answer. Marina translated it to Gerónimo, who turned to Olmedo.

'No.'

Olmedo shook his head vigorously. 'The question was, "Do you agree to give up the religion of your fathers?"'

The process was gone through again. Olmedo knew what the answer would be before the lords spoke.

'No.'

The congregation of Spaniards, whose attention had been wandering, became aware that something was amiss and fell to staring and whispering. Even the Tlascalans knew that something was up.

'Just carry on,' said the Captain in an undertone.

Olmedo wouldn't. He took Christ more seriously than that.

'I have been instructing your lordships for the past three weeks,' said Olmedo, 'and I have explained why you must give up your religion, and you have agreed to do it. Why are you now refusing?'

The interpreters squabbled over the translation. Then the lords needed to discuss their reply, at some length. It was getting very hot. A fly settled on Olmedo's neck.

Finally the interpreters spoke. 'We thought it was politeness. Here, we say to a guest, "This is your house," but no one imagines it is true.'

No one stirred. It was as if a shroud had fallen over the assembly. The Captain, one hand on his belt, the other holding his doffed hat, seemed paralysed. Then he blinked like a man rousing himself from a daydream.

'We shall not delay this baptism on account of a foolish misunderstanding,' he said. And, when Olmedo was about to protest, 'Proceed, Brother Olmedo, or I will do it myself.'

I had not expected to see Tlascala again. First, I expected the Meshica to kill us all on the causeway, and if the Captain hadn't placed me in the middle of a company of ferocious Basque lancers I don't suppose I would have lasted an hour in that battle. Then I thought the warrior bands that harried us every step of the way around the lake would finish us off, and at least once, on the second day of our march, they nearly did. As, at last, we began our climb into the mountains, I was convinced that as soon as we crossed the border into Tlascala we would be dead men for certain. The boundary was marked by two large boulders about six paces apart. In my mind, a Tlascalan army waited behind each of them.

The mountainside was deserted. We were at least a league into Tlascalan territory before its defenders rushed out to meet us. They were children from the nearby village, and they brought us flowers and maize cakes.

I should have been relieved and grateful to be in a place of safety. I wasn't. I'd never felt at ease in Tlascala after we made peace with them. I knew we were making them promises we wouldn't fulfil. I'd felt easier in Cactus-on-the-Stone, where at least the game we were playing was obvious to everyone from Muctezuma down to the street vendors. Tlascala had made my skin itch, and it still did.

But it was in Tlascala that my happiness came to me.

I came back to my quarters one evening and I couldn't find Taino.

Almost from the moment we arrived, I had been ceaselessly busy. The Captain wanted me to interpret at his first, crucial meeting with the four lords; and the first meeting was followed by another the following day, and then another. Often there were two meetings in a single day. When he wasn't talking to the four lords he was talking to Shiko Tenka or the Tlascalan commanders, and then he might be giving instructions to a Droopy-ear messenger who had to be sent to the coast. And then back to the four lords again. Very often, as soon as I thought my duties were over for the day, I would find that one of the Captain's officers required my services. Or Brother Olmedo.

At the end of one such day, very tired, short-tempered and hungry, I returned to the house that Taino and I shared, to find no Taino, no supper, not even a couple of maize cakes, and the hearth cold.

I looked at the room, its emptiness. It seemed to mock me.

I felt my anger rising like water into a well. It was a pleasurable feeling, heady. I strode off to find him.

I knew where to look. He liked to spend time with the other *winic* from Cuba. Two of them had been killed on the causeway, which had brought the others even closer together. Normally I had no objection to his being with them: it was perfectly natural, and since I didn't force the duties of a servant on him, he didn't have much else to do. I found myself thinking, as I walked quickly through the lanes of the caneworkers' district where the Tlascalans had billeted us, that it wouldn't do him any harm to have rather more to do.

He came out of a house with a foolish grin on his face, fastening the cord of his pantaloons.

Something seized me. I did what I had seen other Spaniards doing but never thought to do myself: I grabbed him by the ear and yanked him forward so that he almost fell on his face.

'You wretch!' I bellowed at him. 'What do you think you're doing? Where is my supper?'

He righted himself and gazed at me in pure astonishment. Still holding his ear, I dragged him back to the place where we were living. A little crowd had gathered and watched with approval.

Back in our quarters, I turned on him. 'There is no fire in the hearth and nothing to eat. And you are enjoying yourself.'

I had released him from my grip. He stood up straight and gave himself a little shake, like a dog shaking off rain.

'If fire is cold, then light it,' he said.

I had a tremendous desire to hit him.

'You light it,' I said.

'You say I am not servant.'

'Whether you're my servant or not, you need to eat as much as I do.'

'I just eat with friend.'

'Well, I didn't. I have been working hard all day. You have been doing nothing. You could at least light the fire and warm some maize cakes.'

'Why?' he said. 'You say I am not servant, now you make me servant. Why my people serve your people?'

I looked into his eyes and saw steel there. I saw that he knew exactly what he was doing, knew he could not count on my forgiving this, knew I was so angry that I *might* kill him, and that he did not care. I understood also that he was provoking me, not in spite of the fact that I had been kind to him, but precisely because my kindness was unbearable.

I think in that moment I saw him for the first time. Shorn of all my thoughts about him, and unconquered. Standing there in his slave pantaloons, with his ear reddened where my thumb and fingers had pinched it, he looked both ridiculous and noble. I ached for him.

I turned away abruptly, to hide what must show in my face. And I said, in a curt tone, 'No, you aren't my servant. You aren't anything. You do nothing for me in return for my protection. You only exhaust my patience. I don't care what happens to you. So go.'

'Muluc,' he said quietly.

It was my Chanek name. He had never used it before. I went on glaring at the wall.

'Muluc.'

I looked at him. The steel had gone. In its place was a softness. There could not be a softness; I was deceiving myself.

I took a step towards him. He waited. His hands rose slightly from his sides. Ready to . . .

Strangle me?

They were a warrior's hands; they could have. But they were on my waist, my back, my shoulders, weaving and crushing. My mouth sought his mouth like a bird its nest. I drowned in it. My body drowned in his. There was nothing else, only him. Only him.

* * *

In sackfuls and barrels, strapped on to horses or carried on the strong backs of Indian porters, things necessary to the enterprise begin to arrive from Villa Rica. Several Tlascalan granaries are emptied to store them. Rigging, falconets, masts. Blacksmithing tools, sets of harness, spare wheels for gun carriages, woollen blankets, cooking pans. A quantity of long copper-headed lances the Captain has had made. Boxes of hackbut shot, or at any rate of something. By the dozen, cannonballs, escaping from their pyramids and rolling everywhere. They appear in the Spanish living quarters and the men play bowls with them, until the Captain puts a stop to it. He has sent Ávila to Hispaniola to buy horses. Narváez's ships are going to be useful.

Then the four lords make one more request as their part of the bargain.

'Malinche, we want you to attack Tepeaca.'

'Where?'

A map is constructed on the floor. This pine-cone is Cholula, this beautiful feather is Tlascala, this sprinkling of dust is the mountain range. Here, not far from the pine-cone, is the pebble that represents Tepeaca.

The Captain isn't pleased. He isn't ready to fight, and the mention of Cholula reminds him that he did what he did there partly at Tlascalan urging. Now here they are again, urging him on to battle with another city with which they have an ancient feud. He hasn't come to New Spain to fight Indians' battles for them. Rather the reverse.

'It is only two days' journey away,' the lords say, to encourage him. 'The Tepeacans have done us many injuries.'

He half-listens as the interpreters drone about the bad behaviour of the Tepeacans. He enquires about their relationship to the Meshica. He is told that they were conquered by the Meshica a generation ago and now pay tribute to Tenochtitlan. The same is true of many towns in the region.

Then, seemingly as an afterthought, 'We think,' says Maxicatzin, 'that this was why they killed seven of your people when they came from the coast.'

His lost troopers! One of the groups of Narváez's men whom he sent up to Tenochtitlan, with Droopy-ear guides, before he knew of the fighting that had broken out in the city, and who never reached it. He had been less able to spare the horses than the men. Most of Narváez's men, to tell the truth, are more trouble than they're worth. But the horses . . .

'The Tepeacans did this?'

Yes, says the old lord, they did it to please the Meshica, of whom they are afraid.

A helpful anger floods him. He pictures the seven unsuspecting Christians, probably leading their horses because the terrain would be strewn with loose rocks, fallen upon as they enter some narrow defile. Did he warn them to be careful? Of course he didn't, he wanted them to think the country was completely pacified and under his hand.

Maxicatzin says more. That the Spaniards were taken to the temples to be sacrificed, that their skins were afterwards removed and the priests danced in them. Every Spanish face in this room has gone like marble, and now it is clear that the Captain has no choice, and it is as well to do the thing in any case because Tepeaca occupies a strategic position on the plateau. He can use the opportunity in another way, too: it offers itself smoothly. Exemplary punishment. The message will not be lost on the Meshica.

In the general rejoicing as the pact is sworn, no one wants to make anything of the fact that Shiko Tenka will not be commanding the two thousand warriors sent by Tlascala, indeed will not concern himself with the Tepeacan campaign at all.

In a rough stone hut on a Tlascalan hillside, Martín López, whose wound has almost healed and who has spent the day supervising the felling and trimming of trees, draws plans of ships by candlelight.

There are to be thirteen of them. He will say nothing about this number, having had enough to say about other matters. The Captain expects more than can be done, either by a man or a boat. Cannon, a strengthened prow, deckroom for a score of soldiers, and the qualities, at the same time as these requirements, of speed and agility. Well, the ships will be what they can be. What they have to be is flat-bottomed, like the canoes they will be chasing, because the lake is too shallow for a keel. That fact in itself will govern how manoeuvrable they are. He can't work miracles.

In fact what is being asked of him is not much short of a miracle. Thirteen ships, to be built in four months and then carried eighty miles overland to Lake Texcoco. Carried over the mountain. On the shoulders of Tlascalans. It can only be done by making them in sections and transporting them that way, or perhaps – he has not decided on this crucial point – even in individual planks, numbered. When the pieces are put together, they have, of course, to float.

Twelve months ago he knew nothing about the activity that now occupies his every waking moment and intrudes on his dreams. He learnt how to build a boat by building one. He built four, in the end, so that the Captain, under cover of wildfowling, could explore the lake. (It turned out to be not one lake but several, separated in some places by strips of marsh, in others by dikes built by the Meshica in order to control the water level. That the Indians burned these first-fruits of his labour still pains him.)

He has learnt everything he knows the same way. He learns quickly. With materials, tools, measurements and plans he has a sympathy. He understands them and they obey him. This happens even when he has apparently no knowledge of a craft. It will happen now, with this seemingly impossible problem: how to design something in bits and pieces that in all human history has been made as a seamless whole, and then how to get it eighty miles to where it will be assembled without losing any of the pieces, meanwhile taking care that the respective pieces of the different boats do not get mixed up, because these boats are not all the same – the Captain wants some, for instance, single-masted and others double-masted, while his own boat will be bigger than the rest – and, finally, how to be sure that the vessels *will* float, because one thing is certain, that if thirteen ships turn up in sections on the shore of Lake Texcoco and, having been assembled, then sink to the bottom of the lake, that will be the end of the siege of Tenochtitlan and probably of everyone embarked on it.

Martín López draws with fine, firm strokes on paper that was salvaged from one of the scuttled ships at Villa Rica and that he dried out himself, carefully, sheet by sheet in his palm thatch. It has a bumpy surface, like a landscape of gently rolling hills, such as one doesn't see in this country which is all valleys and precipices, but it is good paper and will do well enough. He is drawing a section of a hull. It is the hull of a single-masted ship. Privately he thinks they should all be single-masted: it would simplify his task and the resulting fleet would be a more flexible instrument, not less so, as the Captain imagines. The single-masted boats will be modest, simple, fit for their purpose. He is at the moment departing from his instructions and designing one that will be lighter and therefore faster than the rest. One day there will be a need for it. His hand moves with love over the paper.

The Tepeacans are given a chance. The Captain's messengers demand surrender and an explanation for the death of seven *cristianos*. Unless both are forthcoming, the consequence will be war. Neither is forthcoming: the Tepeacan reply is insolent. The Requirement, setting out the reasons why they must submit to Spain (that their land was given by the Pope to the monarchs of Castile), and the consequences of refusing, is read to them. They do not respond.

It isn't much of a contest, a battle fought in maize fields where

397

horses can charge and manoeuvre and cannon can plough furrows in unsuspecting flesh. The Tepeacans lie heaped in bloody rows, and those the Spaniards don't kill the Tlascalans haul off.

It is all over in an hour. At once, the vultures start to gather. It's August, high summer, and best to leave the vultures to get on with it, because the Captain has plans for the survivors and they won't be building funeral pyres.

He orders them to be rounded up and separated: men at one end of the town, women and children at the other. He says they need not be rounded up with any particular gentleness, and as a result two are spitted on Alvarado's lance as they try to run into the temple precinct. Several more are thrown from a rooftop.

When all the inhabitants of Tepeaca who are still living are penned in two terrified herds between the swords of Spaniards, the Captain orders fires to be lit and the branding irons that were brought in the baggage from Tlascala to be found. The Tepeacans are now slaves, they have brought this punishment on themselves by rebelling (they shared in the oath of fealty given by the Meshica rulers to the Spanish crown: he does nothing without justification in law), and as slaves they will be branded on the face.

Some resist. They are killed on the spot.

After all this is over, and the corpses of the Tepeacans who did not survive the branding have been thrown outside the town to join the ones who did not survive the battle, hackbut shots are heard from a house in the temple complex where it turns out that four wretched Indians, two men and two women, have been hiding. The dogs have found them.

They cower in a corner, their eyes wild with terror, as the snarling dogs strain against the hands of Spaniards.

Some thoughts present themselves too strongly to be denied. The Captain wants to strike fear into Indian hearts: he *needs* to.

He orders the shrieking Indians to be given to the dogs.

✻   ✻   ✻

For three weeks, blood flows in the towns and fields that surround Tepeaca. The Captain gives licence to his men to commit whatever deeds they harbour in their hearts; he encourages them to remember their friends who died on the causeway. As a result, Indians who are not even offering resistance, who are trying to submit, are run through with a sword or have their stomachs ripped open with a pike or their arms or legs cut off, or are torn by dogs or thrown from rooftops or precipices, or are burned or trampled under the hooves of horses or crushed by stones or hanged from trees, or are drowned in rivers or suffocated in swamps.

When the men have been disposed of in these ways, the women and children are branded with the slave-mark and the Captain sells them to his rank and file for ten pesos apiece. Most soldiers can afford that, even if they really have given him the gold they've brought from the city; and if they haven't, well, here is a good way of extracting some of it from them. The money will go into the army's funds, he says. Most people don't believe him. The slaves are useful, though. They can be sent out to look for food, of which there is a shortage.

The Tlascalans, who have been killing Tepeacans enthusiastically, are eating them. At least, that's what is said in the Christian camp. That's how *they* solve *their* food shortage.

The Captain suspects that this is more slander than truth, because it will work to his discredit if it gets back to Spain and the men who are saying it are the men who are always against whatever he does. But he doesn't care to enquire into the matter. There is nothing he can do about the Tlascalans.

At the start of September, by which time a region roughly half the size of Cuba has been laid waste and driven out of its wits with fear, the Captain calls a halt. Enough has been done. The people he has killed, tortured and enslaved are not Meshica, he knows that: they are subjects of the Meshica, or their allies, or their vassals – the precise relationship doesn't interest him. The point is that any other subjects, allies or vassals of the

Meshica within twenty leagues of what has been done will think seriously about their allegiance to the Meshica from now on. They are doing so already. He has taken oaths of fealty from a dozen local potentates who probably have no idea what they are swearing to, but what does that matter? It's a tool, nothing more: it will strengthen his arm if they are troublesome later, and it is a triumph to report to the King.

He begins a long letter to his sovereign. He dips his quill in the inkpot that has been brought to him as the sun sets on the stilling camp. The letter will take many days to write. The writing of it is as important as anything else he has to do, perhaps even more important, because without the King's favour everything he is doing will come to nothing. An attempt to undo it has already been made, and nearly succeeded. He will paint the intervention of Narváez in the blackest possible colours in his account. He will say it was entirely responsible for the disaster in Tenochtitlan – which is true, except that he cannot afford to admit that it was a disaster. Important letters are never simple. However, his quill scratches rapidly over the paper. Words come easily to him, they always have. It makes him enemies. Lots of things make him enemies.

He intends to found a town here, and use it as a base for operations. When he is quite sure there is no remaining threat to him on the plateau, he will take his army back to Tlascala to put the finishing touches to a campaign that will make this one look like a game of *patolli*.

Tlascala is in mourning when the Captain returns to it in early December. He learns with dismay that the oldest of the four lords, Maxicatzin, has died.

Maxicatzin has been the Captain's staunchest ally. In any disagreement in the ruling council that concerned the Spaniards, he took the Captain's side. His successor has not yet been chosen. The Captain will insist, now that Tlascala is a fief of Spain, that he is consulted.

Knowing the mutual respect that existed between the old lord and the Captain, the Tlascalans have kept Maxicatzin's body for him, violating the rule that the dead must be burned straight away. It would have been better, the Captain feels, approaching the room in which Maxicatzin lies waiting for him, if they had followed custom. The elder has been dead for two days. It was very sudden, people are saying: the thing that killed him, which has never been seen before, came upon him in the morning and he was dead by nightfall. They say that, by the time he died, his body had already begun to rot.

They have preserved him as best they could, in scented wrappings and with the use of honey, but his body is melting. Two polished pebbles of jade lie over his eyes, but the flesh around the eye-sockets is dissolving and a thick river of liquid makes its way from the rim of each pebble to the black pool below.

The Captain holds a cloth to his nose and leaves the room as soon as he decently may. Something is nudging his mind. He puts it aside until later; he has everything in the world to see to. During the evening, in the interval snatched to take a frugal meal, it comes back to him. More precisely, several things come back, some seen many years previously and some just recently overheard. That's it. Smallpox. Maxicatzin died of smallpox.

2

The Captain leaves Tlascala again on the third day after Christmas. It is almost fourteen months since he entered Tenochtitlan for the first time. From the ridge he looks down again on the glittering city. His eye returns, over and over, to the western causeway, from this vantage point the furthest and least impressive of the three. It angers him that it should look so unconcerned, so bright in the sunlight, as if nothing had happened on it.

Coming down the mountain on the far side of the pass, he is ambushed. It is only one small company of Indians, presumably from one of the valley towns, and they are driven off without any losses. However, the same thing happens the next day and two horses are injured. The Captain carries on down into the valley and at the end of the third day camps at an abandoned village not far from Texcoco.

Texcoco is where he wants to make his headquarters, and he does not know what difficulties he might have to surmount. It is the second city of the Meshica empire, its rulers linked by blood to those of Tenochtitlan. On his first arrival in the valley, its lord was Cacama, who ended with a Spanish knife in his ribs. After Cacama's rebellion, Muckety bestowed the throne on a youthful brother of Cacama's who swore allegiance to Spain. The Captain does not know who rules it now.

In the middle of the night, a visitor comes to the Spanish camp. The Captain knows him at once. He welcomes the Indian, who has brought only one attendant, into his own lodging, asks Marina and Gerónimo to come to him, and has the brazier lit. He waits while the young aristocrat, as haughty as any of them but with something else in his make-up (is it petulance? or is petulance the result of it?) that has always prevented him from getting what he wanted, settles himself on a mat. This is Ixtlil, Cacama's brother who, on his father's death (as Muckety explained), wanted the throne of Texcoco but was not given it, betrayed his brother for it but still did not get it, and presumably wants it still. He brought Cacama with his hands bound to the Captain one misty night in the palace of Axayacatl. Who else would it be, paying a call on Spaniards after dark?

'I can help you,' says Ixtlil eventually, when pleasantries have been exchanged.

'Your help will be welcome,' the Captain replies. 'What do you have in mind?'

'I can help you conquer Tenochtitlan. I can bring ten companies, and I shall fight at their head.'

Ten companies amount to about two thousand men, the Captain guesses. It will be a useful addition.

'They will be valuable. How soon can you do this?'

'Straight away.'

In the original settlement with Cacama, Ixtlil was given the northern part of the province of Texcoco. The larger but less fertile part. The division was made by Muckety. Ixtlil never accepted it, and has been fighting, on and off, ever since. All of this was told to the Captain by Muckety, who was often talkative over a game of *patolli*. No wonder Ixtlil can supply his warriors at once: they are probably permanently under arms.

The Captain studies his guest covertly, while offering him refreshment. (How far has Ixtlil come? The Captain has never heard of Indians travelling by night.) The young man is tense, elegant and shifty.

403

'You will need to provide food for your own troops,' the Captain warns him.

'Naturally.' Ixtlil waves away a dish of something that the Captain's page, rubbing sleep from his eyes, has offered.

They arrive at last at the delicate point that, in Ixtlil's eyes, is presumably the goal of the interview.

'What are you asking in return?' prompts the Captain.

He believes the answer to be so obvious – what else but Texcoco? – that the reply he gets is startling. He has to lower his gaze and stare fiercely at the ground lest Ixtlil see his surprise and, worse, amusement.

'I want nothing,' announces the chieftain with pride. 'I only want to help you. I shall help you conquer Tenochtitlan, and when it is conquered I shall rule it for you.'

Texcoco, when the Captain reached it, was deserted. The granaries and storehouses were empty, too. The Texcocans had fled across the lake; some of them were still paddling over it, taking their food and belongings with them.

This was a blow. He had been hoping that something might be done with the Texcocans, that they could be won over with the mixture of promises, threats, arguments and flattery that he deployed as skilfully as a cavalry charge and often to better effect. Words were always his preferred weapon. When he had planned to use them and couldn't, when he saw his intended audience fleeing over the water in canoes, he became bitter. He was exasperated by the loss of the food stores, too; he had been planning to seize them, they were part of his calculations. Disappointment and also policy – everything he did was being watched, and any leniency would be interpreted as weakness – combined to make him vengeful. Those Texcocans who hadn't managed to escape were rounded up. They were killed if they resisted. The remainder would be enslaved.

The Tlascalans had nothing to do, so burned down two palaces. It was a beautiful city, smaller but more charming than its great cousin across the lake. The eye was everywhere greeted by tree-shaded gardens and green orchards, ornamental ponds stocked with fish, transparent streams. Several large aviaries housed flocks of brilliantly plumaged birds. The Captain took time from his many cares to stroll through the streets with Sandoval. At least, now that he didn't have to be pleasant to the Texcocans he was free to choose where he would make his quarters. Perhaps he would live in the palace that had a large circular room overlooking its own private lake. The kings of Texcoco (one of them was a distinguished poet, Muckety had told him) had certainly looked after themselves.

Two visitors came in the afternoon. They were local rulers. They said they had been responsible for the ambushes on the mountain. They had been trying to please the Meshica, it seemed. They had now decided it was not the Meshica they should be pleasing.

The Captain put on a show of severity, but this was exactly the sort of thing he had hoped for. He took oaths of loyalty from the two chiefs. A couple of days later, having established himself at Texcoco, he led a raid around the southern corner of the lake on the town of Iztapalapa.

It's a bright morning, and little spots of gold dance on the water.

The town is right on the lakeside, at the end of one fork of the southern causeway. It was here that the Spaniards passed their last, wide-awake night before entering Tenochtitlan for the first time. It is still, today, what it was then: very pretty, with many of its houses built on posts above the water and having brightly painted canoes moored under them. There are little platforms, like balconies, around the houses, and the townsfolk have come out on to them and stand staring at the Spaniards.

The Indians are drawn up on a low rise, ready for battle. The breeze from the lake ruffles their standards. They look colourful and doomed. The Captain has eighteen horse, a large company of crossbowmen and hackbutteers, about a thousand Tlascalans and a company of Indians commanded by Ixtlil, an earnest of his pledge.

The defenders have chosen to fight on ground that is perfect for horses, and their ranks break under the ferocious charge the Captain leads against them. The charge is followed up by volleys from the hackbuts and crossbows and then, when a large, mangled gap has opened in the defenders' ranks, the Tlascalans pour ravenously into it. Long lines of prisoners are taken off the battlefield, their hands bound, their eyes fixed on the ground, their legs and arms streaming blood.

It is quickly over. The Iztapalapans who haven't been killed or captured flee to the town. From there, soon, smoke starts to rise. The Tlascalans are burning the houses. They burn easily, being built in clusters through which the breeze carries the flames. From a distance it looks as though the water itself were burning.

The townspeople crowd into canoes and escape across the lake. Some don't manage to get away. The Tlascalans commence a massacre. The houses are methodically looted of anything that might be of value, and every last handful of maize is seized from the granary.

The Captain allows this. Later, he will explain that he can't keep the Tlascalans on a leash all the time. He will add that he brought them to Iztapalapa so that they could take what they wanted from it, because their provisions had been used up and he couldn't feed them in Texcoco. About the dark innuendoes that the Tlascalans are eating their prisoners he will say nothing. Nor will he comment on reports that Ixtlil took a prisoner in single combat and sacrificed him by fire.

By the time the day is well advanced, about a quarter of the town has been burnt to ashes and the water of the lake is red. The bodies of dead Iztapalapans bob about in it: warriors, women, even babies. So do the things that have been thrown out of the houses when the Tlascalans were looking for loot. Birdcages, mats, benches, bowls, curtains. They bob about among the corpses and the upturned canoes.

The Captain calls a halt and sends the Tlascalans back to the shore to make their camp. He gives his men permission to sleep in the houses on the water if they want to, but says that he himself will sleep on land.

It has just got dark when the lake begins to rise.

The first thing anyone notices is a strange, deep gurgling that comes apparently from underground. This noise grows louder, and now it is accompanied by a rushing sound like a wind in a forest. Then little waves start to break over the ankles of Spaniards who had thought themselves on dry land, and in moments the water is half-way to their knees.

Spaniards come splashing out of houses, cursing and stumbling into each other. They can't see what's happening, because the only light is from the stars and from the still-burning houses in one part of the town. In the confusion they lose their weapons and anything else they are carrying. It all goes into the water, to join all the other things that are already in the water and that nobody wants to think about, and the water is rising all the time.

They shout to each other as they try to keep their footing and lose it and resign themselves to swimming. Some can't swim, and cling grimly to whatever there is to cling to. They shout for help and to ask what the Devil is happening. A few have already realized what's happening. They have swallowed a mouthful or two of water and it's salty. It's many other things as well; it has a taste of scum and a taste of blood, both of which are enough to make you retch, but it is definitely salty. The water in this part of the lake is normally fresh. The Meshica have breached a dike.

The water has already risen to engulf the lower parts of the houses built on poles. As it rises, it puts out the remaining fires that are still flickering on the lake, and a deeper darkness descends. At the same time, the incoming water must have breached some obstacle that has been holding it back, because a half-dozen *cristianos* who had lain down to sleep in a house comfortably provided with mats and weavings find themselves all at once in a swirling torrent that is carrying them out into the open lake.

The current flings them against the last of the looted houses. They grab the roof-posts and cling to them, and continue to cling with all their strength while the objects the torrent is carrying along with it hit them painfully in the back and sides. It is a long time before they know from the slowing movement of water at their backs that the current has stopped, which means that the levels of the two parts of the lake have become the same. It is very cold by now, and their teeth chatter. They gaze around over the cluttered, dubious water for where the shore might be.

Far away is a line of small fires. They are probably Tlascalan cooking fires. They might, however, be Meshica fires.

The six men pray that they are Tlascalan fires and strike out, hampered by their padded armour, which has become saturated, in that direction.

I said to Taino once, when we were in Texcoco, 'Did Juan Díaz ever try to make a Christian out of you?'

'Yes,' he said. 'He whip me.'

I said, 'Did you think I was going to whip you?'

'Of course.'

I was taken aback. I had thought my good intentions were as clear to him as they were to me. I had a sudden thought.

'Did you ever think of running away?'

'From Juan Díaz?'

'No. From me.'

'Yes.'

'Taino, you don't mean that!'

'Of course. You not whip me, but that not mean you not going to.'

I gazed at him in consternation. He began to laugh at the look on my face. It was a free, merry laugh, and in that camp an open challenge. I put my hand over his mouth. 'Shush,' I said. One day he would go too far; *we* would go too far. His lips were dry and full against my palm. My heart thudded again.

The sweetness of our nights followed me through the days. I carried out my duties scarcely knowing whether I was interpreting to Tlascalans, Iztapalapans, Chalcans, Huexotzingans, Cholulans or Droopy-ears, waiting for the evening when I would go back to him. I knew I had no right to my happiness. The war was about to begin: it had begun already. The prelude had been a massacre, the thing itself was not likely to be any better. There was nothing I could do, so I refused to think about it. I wrapped myself up in my lover. His voice, the sheen of his skin, the grave smile in his eyes that greeted me.

So absorbed in my private world was I that when I encountered Salvador and his friends strolling through the streets of Texcoco I was as startled as if I'd met a trio of ghosts.

'What are you doing here?' I said.

'Looking around,' said Salvador. They had a singing bird in a cage. I supposed they'd taken it from one of the palaces.

'You got off the causeway, then,' said Salvador.

'Yes,' I said.

'Nasty business. We was there, too.'

They had stayed on the coast on our first journey to Cactus-on-the-Stone.

'We came up here after Narváez,' Salvador explained.

'Did all right,' confided Vasco. 'There was a box of gold bars in that palace, and people just told to help themselves.'

A likely story, I thought. I wasn't surprised they had survived the causeway. I thought they would probably survive anything.

'You be careful, now,' said Salvador as we parted, and something in the way he said it made me think that he knew what relations existed between me and Taino. As if to confirm this, he gave me a look I didn't know what to do with. I worried about this briefly, but then gave it no more thought. I never did know what to do with Salvador. He confused me utterly. Every time I looked at him, I saw Gonzalo.

At Texcoco a ditch has been dug. It stretches for a hundred paces. It is about waist-deep and there is a trickle of brown water at the bottom of it. Mounds of excavated earth and heaps of the timber that will be needed to shore up the sides lie along its route. A rope strung on posts hammered into the yielding ground accompanies it for its full length and vanishes into the distance, where the lake is a glimmer of blue.

For the city of Texcoco is not quite on the lake. It is separated from it by a strip of marshy land roughly a mile and a half in extent. When the ships that are being built in Tlascala are brought here, in sections, on the shoulders of Tlascalans, they will be assembled at Texcoco because it is too dangerous to assemble them on the lake shore, where they will be vulnerable to Meshica attacks. But, assembled, they will not be portable. Therefore a canal must be dug. This unpromising ditch is the start of it.

The Captain, returned in sober mood from his adventure at Iztapalapa, goes to inspect it. His eye follows the rope until it loses itself against the gleam of blue, and he fancies he can see, resting on that distant gleam, the white and crimson tops of the temples in Tenochtitlan.

'It will take a month,' he says, thinking aloud. He will have five hundred Tlascalans working on it, under Spanish supervision. They are sturdy workers.

But it will take longer. It will be late March when the last Tlascalan lifts the last shovelful of earth, the wooden barriers holding back the lake are pulled away and the water gushes into the channel that has been made for it.

The channel now is ten feet deep. At a certain depth the soil becomes ungenerous, and then it ceases to be soil, and the bottom of the trench has had to be pecked and gouged out of a multitude of stones that have wedged themselves into a mass that is almost as hard as rock. And it is wide, this channel, twice as wide as a normal man can leap; it is wider, even, some people are saying, than the breach in the causeway Alvarado jumped when he left his men behind on the Night of Sorrows.

The Captain rides the length of his canal on the evening after it is flooded. You would not know, out there on the flat, loamy, abundant fields, what was going on in Texcoco just behind them. Here there is no sound of hammering or steel being sharpened, there is no smoke of a blacksmith's fire. There is no patter of a Tlascalan drum. There is quiet and birdsong. Insects rustle near the feet of his resting horse. In the channel a fish jumps out of the water, looking surprised to see where it is.

There are no Meshica, either. The land appears empty, or under some spell. But then he does see an Indian – in a canoe, out on the lake, fishing with a net. The Indian sees him, and stands motionless in the stern of his boat with the net on his arm, ready to cast it.

The Captain, on an impulse, raises his hand in greeting. After a pause, the Indian raises his.

He does not cast the net, though. He replaces it on the floor of the canoe, picks up the paddle and, with a stroke, turns the canoe towards a further part of the shore.

'Why Gonzalo not come with you?' Taino asked me after I had told him about Gonzalo becoming a warrior.

'He liked it in Chanek.'

Taino nodded with approval. The explanation satisfied him completely.

I felt ashamed.

'The truth is,' I said, 'I didn't ask him.'

'What?'

'I didn't tell him about the trader bringing the message. I didn't tell him the Spaniards had come.'

'But you go look for him. You tell me.'

'Yes. And then I turned back.'

He studied me. Lies always puzzled him. 'Why?'

The *batab* had lent Gonzalo to the *batab* of Putun. The *batabs* were always borrowing warriors from one another for their wars. Once I had permission to leave, I set off for Putun. It was two days' journey away.

On the first day, my journey went well. On the afternoon of the second day, a sudden weariness overtook me and I stopped in the shade of a fruit grove to rest. A woman offered me water. I drank it and put the gourd on the ground, and my gaze fell on my brown, splayed *winic* feet. I saw them with a shock. I thought, whose feet are these? They are not the feet of a Spaniard. What do I think I am doing? I can never become a Spaniard again.

A panic gripped me. I tried to tell myself that the man who had sent the beads knew very well that Gonzalo and I had lived among the *winic* for a long time, and *he* believed we could become Spaniards again.

It is like gold at the bottom of a stream, I told myself. It sinks right down among the stones and gravel, it is impossible to see, but it is there, and if you want to, you can find it. I can find the Spaniard in me.

I thought, for Gonzalo it will be more difficult.

The next thought was as clear as day and it hit me like a stone. It was, *I* can never become a Spaniard again if *he* is with me.

Why hadn't I thought of this? My heart began pounding like a hammer. Gonzalo knew something about me that in Chanek hadn't mattered, but that in the place we were going to would matter a great deal. I might have forgotten most things about Spain, but I hadn't forgotten that men in that country who practised the form of love the slaves practised in the slave hut were killed for it.

Of course, I knew the same thing about him. It should mean that we were both sworn to silence, that we could trust each other. Yet, *could* I trust him? I felt I couldn't. By a look, a smile, a joke, he might betray my secret, and it wouldn't stop him that

412

he was also betraying his own. Gonzalo was Gonzalo, and he said what came into his head.

Even if he never said anything, I would always know that somewhere in the corner of his mind was the memory of the night I had gone to him in the warrior house. And when I thought about *that*, I realized that none of this was what made it truly impossible that he should come with me: what made it truly impossible was that I wanted him still and I could not conceal it.

'Muluc.'

'Yes.'

'Why you turn back?'

It was the hardest thing I had ever done. If I was not going to tell him about the message, I could not see him again. He would want to know why I had come to Putun. I could not lie, not at our last meeting. It meant I could not say goodbye to him.

I remembered the lofty reasons I had manufactured for myself as I left that fruit grove and began to walk back in the direction I had come. That Gonzalo by now was so completely a *winic* that he could never go back to our people and would not want to. That, in Putun, I would merely present him with a choice he couldn't make. That, as a Christian, he had a duty to return to a Christian life if he could, but, since he would be unable to, it was better for me to save him from having to make the choice, and take the blame of it on my own shoulders. I had almost believed all this fabrication by the time I got back to the coast.

'Muluc. You not answering my question.'

'Because I loved him,' I said.

In the time the canal is being dug, many things happen. They all tend in the same direction, however, and, for the Captain, they are all part of the same necessary and exceedingly complicated task.

One by one, he is winning over the rulers of the towns around the lake. They come unannounced, generally, and with few attendants, and although they walk with dignity to the Captain's lodging they have the look of men who are glancing over their shoulders.

All of them are taking a deadly gamble. If they ally themselves with the Spaniards and the Meshica win the war, they are all dead men and their people will be brutally punished. However, if Spain wins the war and they have fought on the Meshica side, they believe the Spaniards will kill them all. The Captain encourages this belief: he has already encouraged it by his behaviour at Tepeaca.

They come before him, having heard what he did at Tepeaca, in fear but also, it may be, with the beginnings of excitement. It is the excitement with which people realize that a burden they have always thought there was no remedy for might in fact pass away, perhaps quite soon. For there is no doubt, as the Captain maintains, that the Meshica have more enemies than friends. They have never been interested in making friends. They have Hummingbird.

The Captain is very pleasant to these Indians who come to see him. He exerts himself to charm them; he gives them small presents. He shows them, as far as is prudent, the preparations he is making for the war. He whets their appetites by talking about the treasures the Meshica keep in their storehouses — the green feathers, the jade, the turquoise. He speaks of the generosity of his sovereign, who will become their protector.

They go away content — or so it seems. They promise to send warriors.

It isn't always so easy. It has happened that several cities wanted independently to make peace with him, but then tried to withdraw the pledges they'd made when they found they were in an alliance that included cities they'd had a quarrel with for years. The Captain has to try to patch things up between these quarrelling nobles. In view of the obscurity, generally, of their disputes, he is more successful than might be expected.

But sometimes it takes a battle. He has realized he must never say no to a fight. When chiefs of towns come to him and say, 'Since we made peace with you, the men of such-and-such a place have been attacking us,' he will send a small force of Spaniards and Tlascalans to help them. For weeks, there isn't a day when some of his men aren't fighting somewhere.

It is at this point that he learns who was responsible for the murder of the largest group of Narváez's soldiers whom he sent up to Tenochtitlan. They were ambushed near a town in the hills. He is told its name. On the same day, he receives word that the ships are ready.

The Captain deems Sandoval the best man to escort the precious ships to Texcoco. He orders him to make a detour on his route to Tlascala and visit retribution on the town that killed forty-five Spaniards.

The town is in the mountainous terrain that divides Tlascala and Meshican territory. Sandoval, stepping his horse with care along a stony ridge that winds between precipices, has no need to coax his imagination about that ambush.

He sees the town, perched on an outcrop, and spurs towards it. Fourteen sets of hooves clatter behind him, accompanied by a soothing clank of steel. There follows the tramp of a column of Spanish footsoldiers, and behind them come the allies, light-footed, straining like dogs who haven't had enough, looking forward to another sacking. People of Zoltepec, leave your homes, for Sandoval is coming.

Many of them have fled, in fact. At first he doesn't bother with that. He goes straight to the main temple, as experience has taught him to do.

The walls are a carnival of dead horses. Their taut flayed skins are stretched flat like huge starfish as if they have been pressed down under a great weight. Their heads have been removed, so that at first sight it is only the still-magnificent arching tails, and the eloquent feet, that identify them. The tails hang downward, looking oddly like plumes, and then he sees that indeed coloured feathers have been bound in among the hairs of each one, neatly with a scarlet thread. The tails hang down and the mutilated neck is at the top, so that the horses appear to be swimming to Heaven.

Something glimmers at him from a recess. A horse's head, entire – they have somehow preserved it – has been fixed on a stone pedestal. The eyelids are sewn shut, the great soft mouth bound up with a white ribbon. And in the ribbon, too, feathers have been tucked, tiny green ones with an iridescence that is visible in this gloom. The pedestal is sticky with a black, pitchy substance that he knows is pine resin, but it is mingled with reddish streaks and spots of blood.

'Here are the saddles,' says a soldier behind him.

They are piled up in an alcove behind a curtain. Sandoval picks one up and takes it to the light. It's a good saddle, more ornate than he has a taste for but well made. A strip some ten inches long has been hacked clean off it with a flint blade.

Forty-five men. What has happened to them? So far, there are the remains only of the horses.

He makes a thorough search of the temple, its precincts and the principal houses. Nothing. Not a belt-buckle, not a coin, not a scrap of velvet or a powder-horn or a quill-sharpener or a locket with the likeness of San Cristóbal. There is not a trace that forty-five Christians have come this way and died.

'They must have been sent to Tenochtitlan,' he mutters. He is bitter that Spaniards can vanish as though they had never been, as though God wasn't watching.

Finally, riding out of the town, watched at a distance by a huddle of frightened townsfolk, they find what they are looking for. Or some of it.

In a straggle of tiny houses on the outskirts, a heap of steel armour, rusting, and a chest of jumbled, bloodstained clothes.

In the last house, which is no more than a hovel and will transform itself in Sandoval's memory as a kennel fit only for a dog, a Spaniard has written on the wall his name, that he is a prisoner and that he despairs.

Sandoval weeps. He weeps for his countrymen and their horrifying end, and for the darkness of their last days. He weeps for the faithful horses.

Then he turns his mount. He rides straight at the crowd of Indians on the plaza. They flee, but they cannot escape him.

The strangest and most unwieldy procession that has ever been seen is making its way across the foothills of the Tlascalan frontier.

At its head rides Martín López. At its rear walk hundreds of Tlascalan porters carrying baskets of food, piles of clothing, ceremonial headdresses, weapons, firewood, incense and many other things. Between these extremities, forming the vastly extended, slow-moving body of the snake, walks every able-bodied man the republic of Tlascala can spare from agricultural, priestly or military duties, laden with timber. Not in rough lengths, this timber, but cut to size, shaped and planed. Planks and ribs, struts and braces, bulkheads and masts. They are carrying, between them, thirteen ships. Ships for the siege of Tenochtitlan.

The ships have already been built. They have been launched. Martín López, who leaves nothing to chance, has tested each one on the waters of the Zahuapan river. No point in taking it eighty miles to the lake if it's going to sink when it gets there. Having tested them, he took them apart again.

Each piece of timber, each section, bears a letter and a number. These denote which ship it belongs to and whether it is part of the hull, decking, or some other component. The letters and numbers are done in a rust-red paint of which the Tlascalans were able to supply a great quantity. They like this colour and decorate their temples with it. It has the advantage of being visible both on the plain wood and on pitch. The pitch has been used to coat the bottoms of the boats. These bottom sections are being carried complete, on long poles resting on the aching shoulders of many Tlascalans, since once they were sealed with pitch they could not be taken apart again and if they had not been sealed with pitch they would not have been watertight.

The pitch was made on the slopes of the mountain from the resin of pine trees. The Tlascalans were astonished. They did not know about pitch. One of them, as a method of finding out, dipped his finger in it when it was being brought to the boil. After this, the other Tlascalans refused to have anything to do with the substance, and López had to caulk the thirteen boat-bottoms himself.

They are very heavy, these boat-bottoms. If the ribs on which they are built were fully planked, the sections would be impossible to carry. They are difficult enough as it is, their elephantine bulk perched on those hundreds of patient shoulders and threatening with every unevenness in the ground to topple over, in spite of the steadying hands of the carriers: left hand if the burden rests on the right shoulder, right hand if it rests on the left. From behind, the procession itself resembles a ship, the upward-slanted arms its ribs, the rhythmically moving legs its oars.

There are oars, too, real ones. In the sort of circumstance these ships are designed for, it's no good waiting for a wind.

So the planking of the hulls rises to just above the water-level, where the ribs curve in gracefully like the horns of an antelope, and above this point the ribs continue their rise as bare as the bones they are named after and end abruptly, and rather forlornly, reaching into the sky.

López prays they won't fall, those boat-bottoms. If a rib snaps or a plank is staved in, there is no spare timber with which to replace it. How could there be, when every piece of timber is slightly different (and that is why they are numbered)? Wood for any repairs will have to be found at Texcoco, and there will be enough to do at Texcoco without running about measuring trees.

He prays, too, that he has forgotten nothing. A tiller, a foremast, a poop, anchor, nails. He prays that the triangular system of communication that has come into being between himself, the Captain and the commander at Villa Rica has worked properly. If it hasn't, he will get to Texcoco and find that numerous essential pieces of equipment that should have gone to Texcoco have gone to Tlascala instead, arriving just after he set off.

The poop decks, of which there are five, are also being carried complete. Each one is slung on a pair of poles, with four Tlascalans to a pole. They swing too much for his liking. On a steep slope they will be difficult to control. If absolutely necessary, they can still be taken apart. But the more that is taken apart, the greater the number of loose nails that must be carried and the greater the likelihood that something will be forgotten. Or dropped down a ravine.

It has been all right so far. And everything is in the hands of God, after all.

It is a comforting thought that God has the ultimate responsibility for what happens to these brigantines, whether they sink, whether they stay afloat, whether they destroy fleets of Indian canoes. Martín López cannot, however, quite divest himself of the heretical idea that the ultimate responsibility is his: that the outcome of this war – and, needless to say, all their lives – depends on the exactness of his calculations and on the stoutness of the tens of thousands of pieces of timber snaking laboriously ahead of him up the mountain path.

At the top of that path, Sandoval reins his horse. Below him sways a gigantic wooden armadillo, a twenty-thousand-footed, million-jointed monster, whose tread shakes the mountain. All

419

around it, in an exuberance of feathers, drum and dance the
warriors of Tlascala who are escorting the lumbering beast on
its way.

Sandoval's mouth drops open in astonishment.

3

There were a dozen or so of them; the Captain doesn't want to run the count in his head. Roughly a dozen, starting back with popping eyes as he came through the door. There and then he could have pronounced death on all of them and carried out the sentence himself, by strangling – steel was too good and his fingers were hungry. But first things first.

The paper was on the bench. The conspirators had drawn back from it as they recoiled from his entrance. A little white rectangle with a list written on it, written in an elegant hand. The eye sees everything, the brain is slower.

He and Villafaña grabbed for it at the same moment. Villafaña got it. He needed to: he knew what was on it. The Captain's hand, thwarted, flew to Villafaña's throat. Another hand – Alvarado's – fastened on Villafaña's wrist.

Alvarado took the paper out of Villafaña's hand and gave it to the Captain. The Captain put it in his pocket. Simple.

By now the conspirators had begun to recover from their shock and it had occurred to them, for some reason, that all might not be lost. They began to bluster. Starting with Villafaña, who did not know that as soon as he opened his mouth he sealed his fate.

'I demand to know by what right you burst into my quarters.'

'Information has been laid,' said the Captain.

He didn't speak as the miserable place was ransacked – yielding

421

nothing, as he knew it would; what else would they need to do after they had committed themselves to the stupidity of making that list? – and as the more astute of them challenged him on the legality of laying hands on a Spanish gentleman without a writ. (He should have laughed, but he didn't feel like it.) He kept his silence, aware of how it was disquieting them, and kept his gaze roving over the shadowed corners of the room with its ghastly niches for gods, as if the men before him weren't worth his sight, until the fruitless ransacking was finished and he could turn his back on the scene.

What to do was tricky. If his informant had been telling the truth, this was not only the most serious plot that had been hatched against him but by far the nastiest. Once the details were made public, he knew he could count on a swell of indignation in his favour.

But if it were made public, that never-quite-healing wound from which the army suffered would break open again in full and hideous view. Minds healthily focused on fighting the enemy would swivel inwards, to the contemplation of thoughts that could not possibly do any good. Worse: to reveal the details of a conspiracy, and particularly such a conspiracy as this, was to put into every mind the idea that *such things were possible.*

'How were you going to kill me?' he asked Villafaña a few hours later. He had studied the list by then.

'They were going to stab you at dinner,' replied the young man. His thin beard wobbled just a little, as did his voice. It had turned out he was the son of some impoverished branch of the extensive Velásquez clan.

'*They?* Weren't you one of them? By your own admission, they met in your quarters.'

There wasn't much that needed to be said to the wretch. Villafaña was questioned twice and on the second occasion, considerably paler now that he knew the others had been questioned, he confessed. Yes, he had been the ringleader. Yes, the plan was to murder the Captain and all his chief officers as they sat down to dinner. Yes, they would do it — his voice had the grace to become inaudible — having absorbed the Captain's attention in a letter which they would pretend had come from his father, Martín Cortés, on the ship just arrived from Spain.

'Whose idea was that?' asked the Captain silkily.

For men so stupid, they had done a lot of thinking. They had thought about who would lead the army and who would be chief magistrate of Villa Rica, who would be the King's treasurer, who the expedition's treasurer, who would replace Olid as quarter-master and who would explain to the Tlascalans that it was time to go home. Because, of course, the campaign to defeat the Meshica would be called off at once. What was the point? These gentlemen had endured enough privations and maize cakes: they were going back to Cuba.

The trial was held in secret in the Captain's lodgings. Antonio de Villafaña was found guilty of conspiracy to murder the Captain-General of New Spain and ten others, conduct detrimental to the good order of the army and treason against His Majesty the King.

His body hangs from the roof of the house in which he lodged and in which the conspirators met. All the others have been pardoned. Only they, the Captain and the men who accompanied him to Villafaña's house know who they are. Still fewer know the names of the men who were on the list but were not at the meeting.

It is better this way. The men who planned to kill the Captain are free, but they are his prisoners. They are forever in his debt. He will never forget the twenty-six names on that list, and they know it, although as soon as he had read it he burnt it in the flame of the nearest candle.

With drums, shell trumpets, shouts and whistling, twenty thousand Tlascalan warriors parade into Texcoco under the command of Shiko Tenka. Yes, Shiko Tenka! He has abandoned whatever lofty business kept him in Tlascala during the Tepeacan campaign, and he is here for the war. Behind the Tlascalans parade the other native levies, the warriors from the towns that have volunteered obedience to Spain.

The Captain is pleased. The allies have shown up when he asked for them, in the numbers he asked for, and they make a stirring, if confused, spectacle. What's more, they are spoiling for a fight. The Meshica have made themselves thoroughly unpopular. The region was a fruit ripe for the picking. (But it has taken him to pick it.)

He has ordered a precise count to be made of his own forces, how many horsemen, how many footsoldiers, crossbowmen, hackbutteers and artillerymen. What with the ranks constantly swelling on the one hand from new arrivals, usually sent up from the coast without being told that it's him they've come to join (the Governor of Cuba, unaware of the defeat of Narváez, has helpfully continued to send reinforcements), and dwindling on the other as a result of death from wounds, hunger, sickness or hanging for treason, or through the sending away of men on some essential mission to the King, to Hispaniola or some other place – the Captain finds himself writing many letters – what with these and other considerations, not to mention the major consideration of those hundreds of men of Narváez's who enlisted with him and then died on the causeway – as a result of all these complications, the Captain doesn't know how many men he has under his command, although he hazards a guess it's roughly the same number as he brought to the country in the first place.

When the count is made, he turns out to be right.

The Captain likes this numerical symmetry. There is something hard in it, something Roman. With fewer than five hundred Christians, he will capture Tenochtitlan.

The point of the count, the immediate point of it, is that he has to divide his force. This is a siege. The enemy must be prevented from getting out, and from receiving food and water, while the Spaniards and their Indian allies fight their way in. The causeways have to be blocked. In fact they can't be, not all of

424

them, a fact that keeps him awake at night drawing maps in his head, because there are too many, they ramify and supplement themselves with sub-causeways running alongside something else, like the aqueduct (for which he has plans), or dikes dividing the lake into sections for some occult purpose — or perhaps not so occult, as he realized the night the Meshica breached a dike and he nearly lost a hundred men at Iztapalapa. Nevertheless, the three major causeways running into the city from the west and south can be blocked. At their shoreward ends, he will station his troops. Most of his troops: some will go on the launches.

The launches are his masterstroke. Command of the lake. Never again that terrible double ambush from the water, with Hell behind and dancing in front of you, your progress along the stone bridge the progress of a piece of meat in the jaws of a tiger. However, the launches will need to be crewed: you can't ask a man to row *and* fight.

It turns out there aren't many men you can ask to row. They consider it an insult. The Captain orders that anyone with any sea-going experience at all, including fishing from a boat, be put to an oar. When there still aren't enough rowers, he extends the order to anyone who was born in a port. There is nearly another mutiny.

He will command the launches himself, directing them to where they're needed. He will divide the bulk of his force between Alvarado, Sandoval and Cristóbal de Olid, who distinguished himself in the fighting in Tenochtitlan. Tapia protests: he expected Olid's command. The Captain gives him a soothing reply.

None of this is any use without God. Standing orders have been issued of which the first is a prohibition of blasphemy. Further down the list comes a prohibition against gambling for a horse. The order that the Indian allies are to be respected and their booty is not to be taken from them is somewhere in the middle.

'Why we here?' asked Taino.

His head rested on my arm. We were both looking into the

darkness, which had a reddish hue from the Tlascalan fires that burnt late into the night. Shadows thrown by these fires moved on the back wall of the house we slept in, a humble place that had once belonged to a potter: there was a kiln standing in the yard and, next to it, a clutch of fresh pots. The kiln had still been warm when we moved in.

'What do you mean?' I said.

'I mean why we here. I not want being here. You not want being here. Why we here?'

'It's a perfectly good house.'

'I not talking about the house.'

I sighed. I knew what he was talking about. He had started mentioning it after we left Tlascala. Although my plan to defect to Narváez had come to nothing (within an hour, there had been nothing to defect to), Taino had not forgotten the idea that we might get away.

'Muluc.' I loved it when he called me that. He turned his head towards me. The arch of his neck and the curve of my arm fitted each other perfectly. His eyes glowed. 'We go now.'

'*Now?* It's the middle of the night!'

'Good time.'

'It isn't a good time. There are sentries. What possible reason could we give for walking through the town when everyone is asleep?'

'Tomorrow, then.'

'Perhaps. No.'

'Why?'

'Go to sleep.'

'Muluc.' He ran a finger down my chest, between the ribs, to my belly. He laid his hand flat on my skin, which roused at his touch. 'We must go soon.'

'To where?' I said.

'Anywhere.'

'Anywhere won't do.' It was why I did nothing. We had a refuge here. We were together and no one bothered us. Out there, anything might happen.

'I have bad feeling,' said Taino.

Of course he did. I put my hand over his hand, where it lay on my belly, squeezing his fingers between my fingers. Then I withdrew my arm carefully from under his head and propped myself on my elbow. I kissed his forehead, his eyelids. I ran my lips along the princely ridge of his nose. I kissed his mouth. I drank his breath.

'I will chase it away,' I said.

The water comes from a spring that rises on a high crag over-looking the lake. Behind the crag are pleasure gardens for the recreation of the monarch. The Meshica have a new monarch now, not Kweetl-awac, who has died of a plague, but a nephew of Muctezuma's. It seems the new *tlatoani* doesn't care for recreation: the gardens are overgrown. Alvarado's eye notes brambles, ivy, thin pinnacles of grass interrupting the paved stairway.

He hears the plashing of the water before he sees its silver thread, half-concealed by a brown fold of rock. It falls into a deep, natural basin from which feed the pipes the Meshica have constructed. Two pipes, not one, so that the second can be used if the first needs repair. They have thought of everything. They haven't thought of Alvarado.

He trots his horse along the flat, pebble-scattered ground. It's a fine May morning and a splendid day to start a war.

An arrow hums past his ear; the next one sticks in his saddle. Then comes a cloud of them. He spurs his horse, whirls his sword. Out of their hiding-places in the maize the Meshica erupt, and the exhilaration of battle takes him.

Meanwhile the real work goes ahead. For, all he and his troop and the three hundred Tlascalans are doing is protecting a dozen men who have waded out into the lake with hammers and pick-axes and now stand up to their knees in the water.

They are there to break the pipes.

The clay is a handsome red that has the sun in it. Under a sky as blue as this, it has the hue of a Spanish apricot. Splashed with the water of the lake, it darkens, it becomes brown, and in the brown there seems to lurk the rusty colour of long-ago-spilt blood. As it dries, the darkness retreats from the edges, fading inward like a mist being sucked to itself by the sun, until in the centre of the stain is just a dark point, like a wicked star, which suddenly has vanished.

A boy sitting with a hammer in his hand has just noticed this.

The pipes are stoutly made, the clay is as thick as the length of your thumb, and it resists the hammer. It protests, too, at this unprovoked assault. At the first blow, dealt by the boy, a red-haired lad who was a blacksmith's apprentice before he left Cuba, the clay sings out a deep, golden note of outrage that — who knows? — may travel all the way along the pipe and be heard with foreboding in Tenochtitlan.

The boy holds his hammer still in wonder, and listens to the sound.

A man seizes the hammer from him and drives it home with a powerful sideways swing as if cutting hay. The domed surface of the clay cracks in a fine, jagged line, like the coastline of a new country, and where the hammer bit there is a shallow crater you could crack an egg into.

The hammer swings again, pitilessly hitting the same spot. The clay shatters and a jet of water spurts full into the face of the man wielding the hammer, who curses and, wiping his face, looks for the boy so he can give the hammer back to him, but the boy, who just now was sitting astride the pipe, is no longer there. His body floats in the shallows of the lake, pierced by an arrow.

The three divisions of the army, each supported by a contingent of native allies, take up their positions where the stone bridges thrust out into the lake. Each is at once vigorously attacked by Meshica.

The ships are assembled. Martín López forgets to eat and barely sleeps. His calculations have not failed. Nothing — surely it is impossible, this — has been overlooked, lost or sent to the wrong place. The Tlascalans have not dropped anything, or at least anything of importance, the requisite number of anchors and sails have been sent from Villa Rica, and even the falconets, of which one is to be fixed in the prow of each of the larger boats, have turned up.

One by one the ships are launched on the channel the Tlascalans have dug, for the finishing touches to be put to them before they are rowed out to the lake. The Captain watches, holding his breath, as each is carefully lowered, the Indians letting out the ropes hand over hand, down the wooden ramp. Each is freighted with his hopes. One by one, their bows lift as they reach the water, lifting his heart with them.

Absorbed in thoughts of rigging, oars, sails and gunpowder, he is suddenly aware, as he passes by the Tlascalan camp one evening, of an unnatural quietness. The Indians, normally so friendly, avoid his eyes. Some, on seeing him, even get up and walk away, vanishing into the maze of curtained booths they have put up for themselves.

Alarmed, the Captain sends a message asking Shiko Tenka to come to him as soon as he returns to his quarters.

Shiko Tenka does not come. Eventually, the Tlascalan second-in-command presents himself, stiff-faced. He says that Shiko Tenka has left the camp.

'Where has he gone?' demands the Captain.

'He has gone home to Tlascala.'

'Why?'

'He did not tell me, Malinche. He did not say that he was leaving.'

'Then how do you know where he has gone?'

'Everyone knows it.'

'Do you mean he has gone back to stir up rebellion?'

There is no reply. The Indian's expression cannot be read, but the Captain believes there is fear in it.

'Whatever the reason, he is a deserter,' says the Captain.

429

The essential thing is to get him back at once. Get him back, and then there will be something that can be offered, something that can be threatened. The Captain directs that three Tlascalan officers be sent after Shiko Tenka in all haste. Men whom he respects, to whom he will listen.

Why should he listen? This, later, is what Alvarado will want to know. The Captain will offer him wine off the boat from Spain, and not reply.

'We cannot just walk out of the camp and trust to Providence,' I said. I was weary: I'd been interpreting between the Captain and the Tlascalans all day. Didn't Taino understand that I had work to do?

He was obstinate. 'We go before too late,' he said.

'It won't be too late.'

I flung myself down on what straw there was, miserable thin stuff that let the cold of the floor through, and closed my eyes.

He sat on his heels beside me. 'Muluc. Don't sleep.'

'What do you want to do?' I said.

'I tell you all the time. I want leave here. Go far away.'

'It's too difficult now.' Any time would have been better, I thought.

'It must be now.'

He said this calmly and with authority, like a man much older. I moved my finger and touched the young, taut, beautiful skin of his wrist.

'All right,' I said.

What had I agreed to? My eyes flew wide open at once with anxiety. How could it possibly be managed? Now, when the siege had started? With, all around, the Captain's spies? *Where could we go?*

'Good. We leave tomorrow,' said Taino. 'I pack up everything.'

'You'll pack up nothing. We'll take nothing.' I was not going to steal out of the Spanish camp carrying two tin plates and a jaguar's head. 'We won't go tomorrow, either,' I said.

'Why?'

'Because Shiko Tenka has disappeared, he's gone back to Tlascala, and I have to stay here because I may be able to do something.'

'You may be able do something,' he repeated.

'Yes.'

'Do what, Muluc?'

'Do something to help. If they find him there will be trouble.' If they didn't find him there would be even greater trouble, I thought.

'What you talking about?' demanded Taino. His eyes burned with anger. 'You have never been able help.'

It was true, but he had no business to remind me of it. I raised myself on my elbows to remonstrate with him and saw that it was tears burning in his eyes, not anger.

'You cannot leave that Captain,' said Taino. 'You cannot. That why you don't. It nothing to do with helping.'

'How dare you say that?' I said.

'Dare? Because I am slave, you mean? Slave you rescue from priest?'

This was terrible. The last thing I had said, the last thing he had said, vibrated in the air.

'I'm sorry,' I said. 'It is my fault. Forgive me.'

He turned and knelt on the floor, bending his head down so it rested on my chest. I felt his tears soaking through my shirt. I put my hand in his hair, his long fine hair as black as mirror-stone.

'We will leave,' I said. 'In the next few days. We must wait for a good moment, when the Captain is busy with something that doesn't involve me.'

He raised his head and I dried his tears with my fingers.

'But the question still is,' I said, 'where will we go?'

'To Chanek,' he said.

'We can't go to Chanek. It's a dream.'

He shook his head vigorously. 'No. We can do it. I know.'

'We can't.'

'*Why?*' His eyes, the set of his face, insisted that I think about this, that I properly consider it. I had never done so.

I took a deep breath. 'It's too far.'

'It not further than Spain. I know it not further. You said once we go to Spain.'

'That's a different thing.'

'How?'

And I saw that it was only different because I wanted it to be different. And that the reason I would not consider going back to Chanek was that I was afraid of something so obscure I couldn't even say what kind of thing it was, and also that it only existed in my head. Chanek would be what it had always been.

'I don't know where Chanek is,' I said. But even as I said this, I did know. It was east. It was directly in the line of the sun as it rose. I guessed it was about forty days' journey away.

We would need to take food.

Could we walk all the way? The shape of the coastline was argued about. Some people said there was a strait that had been overlooked.

Well, if we had to cross the sea there would be a canoe.

This time I would not have glass beads. I would have Taino.

I laughed. It was a laugh of exultation. 'All right,' I said. 'We will go to Chanek.'

Taino flung himself at me. I held him; we laughed and held each other. In my arms, he shivered suddenly.

'You've caught a chill,' I said.

It's Alvarado who makes the mistake first.

Alvarado is commanding the troops stationed at the end of the western causeway. This is the causeway over which the Spaniards fled from Tenochtitlan, and in the mind of every man who was there on that night it is the road of death. It fills them with hatred. Hatred of its bloodstained masonry (the blood is still there, its brown glitter visible in the cracks between the paving), hatred of the city from which they were driven in humiliation, hatred of the Meshica, who are the cause of all this misfortune and have had the insolence to build a beautiful city in the middle of a lake while being eaters of human flesh.

From these feelings springs, naturally, a ferocious will to win the causeway back and turn it into the avenue of a triumph.

However, before they can attack, they must defend themselves. The Meshica have assaulted Alvarado's camp since the moment it was set up. Every day, Indians flood down the causeway and leap from canoes. Every day, Alvarado's men must beat them off and strive to advance. They have to *capture* this causeway.

Then, having captured it, they have to hold on to it. That's the problem.

For every yard of the causeway is both road and island. Sections of it can easily be taken up, trapping whoever's on the wrong side, as those who survived the retreat know all too well. Their solution then, and it worked for as long as anything could be expected to work on that terrible night, was a portable bridge. However, all they needed to do, that night, was get out. The requirements now are quite different. They need to be able to move back and forth along the causeway at will. A portable bridge is no good, and in any case they would need ten of them. When the Meshica pull up the bridges, as they assuredly will, the only answer is to fill in the breaches with whatever material is at hand.

'Never,' the Captain has instructed his commanders, 'leave a gap unfilled behind you.'

For it is perilously easy to leave a gap unfilled. In many places, the lake is so shallow you can wade across it. The temptation to plunge into the water in pursuit of a fleeing enemy is over-whelming.

Fortunately, the material for filling the breaches is at hand. It means pulling down the houses and shrines that stand at intervals along the causeways, but that needs to be done in any case because the Meshica use these buildings to conceal bodies of troops and they launch arrows and sling-stones from the roofs.

433

Accordingly, houses are pulled down and breaches are filled with rubble. It's less glorious work than fighting but quite as dangerous, in fact it's very much like rowing a launch, and there are just as few people who want to do it, but it is – grudgingly – done.

One Sunday morning, Alvarado's force is set on by three separate companies of Meshica. One comes from his landward side, threatening to cut him off, while a fleet of canoes looses off arrows from the lake and a band of warriors bursts out from behind a wall that the Meshica have built overnight. The Meshica fight fiercely and they have got hold of – probably from this very causeway! – Spanish swords and pikes. Each canoe is a springboard from which may vault at any moment six Meshica warriors. And *where are the launches?* Hernán's got them, and is amusing himself by chasing canoes on another part of the lake.

Alvarado presses onward. After a time the Meshica fall back and he pushes on to the wall, a rough thing about breast-high, which of course they will defend. But the defence is half-hearted, the Meshica have clearly been shaken by his counter-attack. He presses home his advantage – and suddenly they've gone. Vaulting the wall, he finds he is looking at a gap of water about eight feet wide.

Do they really think he can't follow them across this? Without hesitation he plunges into the water. It takes no time at all to get across and pull himself up the other side, and he and thirty others are in full cry after a scattered band of Meshica apparently fleeing like startled poultry when those same Meshica abruptly whirl about, weapon in hand, and attack them.

At the same time, more Meshica pour out of a building thirty yards away and more leap on to the causeway from the lake. Cursing, Alvarado has to give ground, has to move back much more quickly than he wants towards that open stretch of water he crossed so lightly. This time, crossing it will not be so easy.

Then he sees that he will not cross it at all. It is thronged with canoes.

There is only one thing to do. He leaps into the lake from the side of the causeway; he leaps into the water prepared to fight and wade his way to safety and he finds his feet sinking, the lake is suddenly bottomless, he is floundering in horror, gasping for air, while hands grab at him.

His foot, thank God, finds something to stand on, and he swings his sword. At the edge of his vision he sees a canoe paddle away carrying a pinioned Spaniard, struggling like a fly in a web.

The lake reddens as Alvarado and his companions begin a desperate struggle to regain their camp.

Six of Alvarado's men are captured that day. None of the rest escapes a wound.

The Captain is angry. He sends Alvarado a letter of reprimand — *by launch.*

Alvarado rides to see him.

'I told you to fill in the breaches.'

'Wait until it happens to you, Hernán.'

'I shall take care that it doesn't.'

'They had dug pits *in the floor of the lake.*'

'You shouldn't have been in the lake.'

'Where were those damned launches? If I'd had a couple of launches it wouldn't have happened.'

Alvarado storms back to his causeway. The following day, four launches are rowed across the lake for his use.

The Tlascalan officers who were sent in pursuit of Shiko Tenka return without him.

'What did you say to him?' demands the Captain.

'Everything you told us to say, Malinche.'

The Tlascalans are embarrassed by their failure and lower their eyes. Or perhaps this is not what embarrasses them.

'What reasons did he give for not coming with you?'

Their faces close up. He knows he could put them to the rack and they would not reveal what Shiko Tenka said to them.

He wonders how many sympathizers Shiko Tenka has in the army, and how far the revolt has spread in Tlascala.

He thanks the Tlascalans and dismisses them. He sends for the new lord of Texcoco, another brother of Cacama (there is apparently an unending supply of them) who is under his influence and whom he has had proclaimed ruler. Shortly afterwards, five Texcocans and five Spaniards are despatched from the camp. Their instructions are to find Shiko Tenka, bring him back to Texcoco and hang him.

'Spare his life.'

They walk a little way.

'You're an odd fish, Pedro.'

Alvarado shrugs. He hates executions.

'He's a rebel,' the Captain points out.

'You have spared men who planned to kill you.'

'And now they eat out of my hand.' It's true, they do.

'They can still do you harm.'

'They're driven by malice, or cowardice, or some such thing. They aren't difficult to deal with. Shiko Tenka is not of that sort.'

'He's driven by love of his country.'

This is so simply put, and so unexpected, that the Captain pauses before replying to it. 'He has ambitions.'

'To rule Tlascala? Why shouldn't he? He's afraid of what we will do to his people. And he's right.'

The Captain flicks a pebble into the lake with his toe. 'That is why you would like me to spare his life? Or has your concubine put you up to this?'

He has just remembered, with satisfaction, that Alvarado was given one of Shiko Tenka's younger sisters. It was one item in the lengthy transactions that went on in Tlascala over the winter.

Alvarado frowns. 'I'm sorry you think I would ask for the life of an Indian simply because I bedded his sister.'

'Why, then?' He sees, and it consoles him, that his senior

436

commander is not sure why he wants this Indian spared. 'You surely can't be asking me to spare him *because* he is a rebel?'

Alvarado struggles with an idea, then gives up. 'I'm asking you to spare him as a favour to me.'

Alvarado presumes, thinks the Captain. Particularly in view of recent events.

'I will give it thought,' he promises, and they clasp arms and the Captain goes back to his camp.

He will not give it thought. Shiko Tenka could unseat every one of his plans, and it's a measure of Alvarado's lack of judgement that he fails to see it. There's a second reason. The Captain understands what Alvarado was trying to say and couldn't find the words for. Shiko Tenka is not really a rebel, not if one is to be absolutely honest. He never swore fealty to Spain and never accepted baptism: he merely said he would obey the decision of the lords of Tlascala. He is an unconquered chieftain. As such, he cannot legally be abducted and hanged for trying to resist a foreign army that has placed his people under subjection.

No one must be allowed to think along these lines, which is one very good reason for getting Shiko Tenka out of the way as soon as possible. Not only because it imperils the Captain's position in this particular case — and he is always looking ten years ahead of him as well as over his shoulder — but because that kind of thinking is the insidious, burrowing tip of a siege engine that will undermine the legal foundations of the whole enterprise. For if Shiko Tenka is not a rebel, but in law a free man, what about the inhabitants of the towns around the lake whom the Captain allowed his men to kill 'because they were rebels, having given allegiance to His Majesty', when they did not know they had given allegiance and would not have understood what it meant if they did know it? The Indians don't understand what is said to them even when it is in their own language. When the Requirement is read to them in advance of a battle, they take not the slightest notice, as who could expect them to, since frankly it is the most monstrous nonsense that has ever been devised.

And as for the voluntary submission of Muckety and his kinglets to the Spanish yoke, of what value was it when it was not voluntary, since he, the Captain, had just unchained them and they were going to be chained up again an hour later, except for Muckety himself, who had had his spirit broken?

Day after day, Alvarado's men fight off an attack on their camp, advance along the causeway and secure some wall or other obstacle the Meshica have built. Each step is won against furious opposition. When they have gained, laboriously, this wretched obstacle, they pull it down and throw the stones into any nearby breach the Meshica have made in the causeway.

By the time they have done all this, most of the day has gone and the Meshica are ready for the next ritual, a pitched battle forced on the Spaniards as they return to their camp on the shore.

Next morning, rubbing the sleep (if they have been lucky enough to get any: the Meshica keep up a fearsome racket all the night) from their reddened eyes, Alvarado's men grasp their weapons, do battle with the Meshica (who *have* slept: this is a fresh cohort), advance by painful degrees along the causeway and find that the obstacle they demolished yesterday has been built again and the breach they filled in is gaping as wide and deep as ever.

The remedy, it goes without saying, is to occupy the terrain that has been won so that it doesn't have to be won back, over and over again. But Alvarado doesn't have enough men – enough Spaniards – to guard the camp *and* occupy the newly-won terrain and the stretch of causeway in between. He hesitates to use the Tlascalans. He regards them as undisciplined – often they rush to fight the Meshica on the causeway just as the Spaniards are withdrawing to their camp, and have caused quite a few casualties by getting underfoot. He doesn't trust them at night, either; the dark seems to make them nervous.

He considers moving his camp to a stone apron into which the causeway broadens, about a bowshot from the shore. To do this raises, once again, the spectre of being cut off from land. However, if the Tlascalans can be got to protect just the first stretch of the causeway, stiffened by the horsemen, who still won't risk their horses except on the shore (when this is over he will have a few things to say to certain gentlemen), then his line of retreat may be secure enough.

Assuming there is no attack from the landward side by the towns that have not submitted to Spain. That is the real danger they all stand in. Cut off again on the stone bridges, with the Meshica in front of them and the Meshica's friends behind, and the ships no help against so many.

The ships have turned out, shockingly, to be vulnerable to a Meshica ruse.

Two launches on patrol one evening, pursuing some canoes that appeared to be taking food to the city, struck an underwater obstruction and were held fast. More canoes poured out of hiding in the reed-beds and after a fierce battle the launches were captured. Investigation showed that wooden stakes had been planted in the bed of the lake. They had been set in at an angle and sharpened to a point. It was quite obvious that the launches had been lured on to them.

In an abandoned orchard near Texcoco, Shiko Tenka is brought to be hanged.

He has not spoken since the moment of his capture, when he uttered a lacerating sentence to the five Texcocans present that they will never forget. The five Spaniards, who did not understand what he said, hustled him away at swordpoint. The journey through the mountains has been hard and dangerous; now, at the end of it, they are all tired and full of resentment. They resent their task, hunting a man down and hanging him when there is fighting to be done. They resent the prisoner, for his calm, his indifference, his contempt.

His silence has spread out to engulf them. They cannot find anything to say to each other. Even necessary things are not said, but communicated by a raised eyebrow, a pointing finger, a jerk of the head.

It is early morning, the right time for a hanging, but nothing is going as it should. The horse stumbled, not once but twice, as they went into the orchard, and the branch over which the rope was first thrown, which had appeared to be perfectly sound, snapped and fell from the trunk as soon as the sergeant put his weight on it.

Another tree is selected. The only possible branch is rather too high; the rope they have brought turns out not to be a long one and, thrown over the branch, its end dangles just above the reach of the tallest of them.

The sergeant mounts his horse and retrieves the end of the rope. He ties the end in a noose. The noose, naturally, hangs still higher than the untied end had done. With his eye the sergeant measures the height from the ground of the branches of all the trees in the orchard. There are only two other trees that have branches capable of taking a man's weight, and the branches of both of them are either too low or inaccessible.

The hanging cannot be postponed. His orders are very clear. In any case, he is sick of the business and he does not trust the Texcocans, who have become sullen since the arrest was made.

'We'll have to hang the villain from horseback,' he says, dismounting. These are the first words that have been spoken in nearly twelve hours.

The prisoner, who during the night has been shackled, is freed from his ankle-fetters. A faint breath of what might be relief or surprise escapes him. He is still wearing the full regalia of the Commander-in-Chief of the Tlascalan armies and the eagle-claw pectoral of the nobility. His Spanish captors did not trouble to strip him of these things and the Texcocans did not dare. Stained by the mud and dust of travel and the greenish dirt of the poultry house where they made him pass the night, this ceremonial finery — the brilliantly dyed cloak, the inlaid featherwork shield, the floating heron's crest, the armlets of

440

carved bone and shell — has acquired a sombreness that lends it added dignity.

Shiko Tenka's gaze passes over the untended orchard with its rioting grasses and frayed thatch, but seems not to see it. Then he lifts his wrists as if he has suddenly become aware of them, and looks at the iron chain that links them. His gaze moves to the Texcocans, lingers for a disdainful moment and returns to the hills, at which he has been gazing almost without interruption since he was allowed to crawl out of the poultry house.

Two Texcocans are holding the end of the rope. The other three loiter near by, having nothing to do. Two Spaniards, one on each side, are guarding Shiko Tenka with drawn swords, a purely symbolic precaution since he is unarmed as well as being fettered. The other three are trying to catch the horse, which, being left to its own devices since it has always been a tractable horse, has wandered out of the orchard and is unexpectedly reluctant to return to its duty.

The sergeant swears as the animal lunges past his outstretched hand and his foot slips in a patch of mud. It rained heavily the previous afternoon, and the ground here holds the water. He has fallen on his knees, it is humiliating, and on the faces of the watching Texcocans is the ghost of a smile. He rights himself, and walks stiffly to where someone is holding the horse by the bridle.

There is not much left to do, but it seems to take a long time. It takes a long time to get the horse to where the rope is flung over the branch (the horse backs and steps sideways and turns its head aside; what is the matter with it?), and to get Shiko Tenka to where the horse — at last — is standing; it seems to take even longer, it seems to take an eternity, to get Shiko Tenka on top of the horse. He has not, of course, ever been on horseback, he has no idea how to mount, but that, thinks the sergeant in fury, is no excuse. Three men are needed to hoist Shiko Tenka on to the horse's back, and he is not even resisting, although he is not helping, either. It's the horse that is resisting, all at once, as it belatedly realizes what is happening to it and tries to make another bolt out of the orchard. The two Spaniards who are not engaged in getting Shiko Tenka on to the horse are occupied in restraining the horse, with the help, when they see that help is needed, of the three Texcocans who are not holding the rope; at which the two Texcocans who *are* holding the rope seem about to let go of it so that they can help as well, and have to be recalled to their task by a roar from the sergeant.

Finally it is all in place. Almost. Shiko Tenka is on the horse and the horse is, for the moment, under control, but the noose dangles a foot from Shiko Tenka's head and it is plainly beyond reason to ask him to put his head into it.

The sergeant, who has not hanged anyone before and whose clothes, moreover, are covered in mud, beckons a Texcocan to come to him and climbs on the man's back. Balancing precariously, grimly aware that the repertoire of things that can go wrong with this enterprise has not yet been exhausted, he succeeds, in spite of Shiko Tenka's vigorous attempts to evade the noose, in placing it around the prisoner's neck.

He jumps down from his perch and gives the horse a thwack on the rump to make it step forward. The horse, to nobody's surprise, does not move.

It's a Texcocan who solves the problem. Standing dangerously close to the animal's left ear, he gives, without warning, the terrifying yell with which Indians like to launch their attacks. The horse, accustomed to such sounds on the battlefield, is not expecting them in a peaceful orchard. It leaps forward as if catapulted.

There is a chance, since everything else has been such a muddle, that the Texcocans holding the end of the rope will let go of it. But they do not, and the body of Shiko Tenka drops straight down, the first thing that has gone right all morning, and hangs, turning slowly in the air, the head fallen sideways, the proud heron's crest drooping emptily, the expression in the eyes — as if everything were not already lost — implacable.

* * *

The Captain has established his own camp at a point where two branches of the southern causeway meet. With his back protected by Sandoval and Olid, he ranges along the stone bridge. He beats off attacks from the Meshica, he captures fortified places, he pulls down houses and throws the stone into the gaps the Meshica have made, only to find, next morning, that everything is back where it was.

He has himself rowed over to Alvarado's camp one evening; he wants to see how Alvarado is getting on.

Alvarado is getting on famously. His causeway is shorter than the Captain's by about half a mile, which naturally helps, and he has established a camp on the causeway itself, but even taking this into account the Captain is impressed by how far he has got. Alvarado's men have actually penetrated into the city. Not far, it's true, but they have gone *the whole length of the causeway* and fought Meshica in the suburbs.

And got back again. That's the thing.

Have they managed to hold on to what they've won? Of course not. If it were that simple . . .

Audacity, thinks the Captain. It has always served best. Enough of this advancing and retreating, filling up breaches and finding them cleared the next morning . . . what is needed is a base *in the city*. He orders a combined assault of all the armies, aimed at capturing the marketplace of Tlatelolco.

It starts in good order. From all three camps, Spaniards advance, banners flying in a stiff breeze that is coming off the lake. The launches keep pace with the standard-bearers, for the launches have now been distributed among the three divisions of the army. Behind the Spanish soldiers march the massed ranks of Tlascalans and the other Indian allies, the Texcocans, the Cholulans, the men of Huexotzingo and the numerous towns in the lake region that have submitted to Spain. Some towns have sent canoes to fight alongside the launches. A vast, colourful, three-armed beast parades and sways along the causeways to the beat of many different drums.

It does not get far before it is checked by the front-line cohorts of the Meshica.

'What happened?' Sandoval is later to ask his grey-faced commander-in-chief.

Rallying his men, leading charge after charge (for they had levelled enough buildings for horses to be used now), the Captain was exhilarated and God was in his right arm as he came to the gap. It wasn't much of a gap, you could leap across it, and on the other side the Meshica were grouping. At the Captain's back pressed impatient horsemen, a hundred and twenty eager foot-soldiers and two thousand Tlascalans wild for glory: he couldn't have stopped if he'd wanted to.

He jumped his horse across the gap. In a joyful rush the cavalry spurred after him, and the lances bit Meshica flesh, and the dogs were with them, too, running and leaping in their jackets of steel.

It was then, with the sun high on his advance, that the Meshica sprang their trap.

It was like the breaking of a great wave which you had not seen gathering. One moment, he and his men were fighting in the way all of them were used to. The next, they were engulfed in an earthquake.

The Captain's horse slid and slipped on gore, and he jumped from the saddle rather than be caught under her. She went down and he saw the spear in her side. He fought where he stood, though barely able to swing his sword in the confusion, and all around him was disaster: blood poured from head wounds, faces were smashed into a pulp, arrows found fatal gaps in armour. He shouted an order to fall back, to keep together, but it was hard enough to keep your feet, so narrow and overcrowded was the causeway, and already he had seen a white mare that was a fine trooper fall into the water like a sack.

Soon afterwards, he judged from the commotion behind him that he had got back to the small breach, which presumably had been filled in since he had ordered all breaches to be filled.

Probably it had not been done well and was tricky to negotiate, and that explained the commotion.

But the breach had not been filled. In the narrow gulf, deepened by the digging of invisible pits, Spaniards were drowning, were being clubbed to death from canoes, were being snatched out of the water as prisoners. Two launches, one on each side of the breach, were, to judge by the frantic efforts of their oarsmen, stuck fast on stakes. The lake was a heaving mass of war-canoes. On the far side of the channel, those Tlascalans who had managed to escape the onslaught were running away as fast as their legs could carry them.

A burning pain in the Captain's thigh made itself felt at the same instant as the crush of bodies plunged him into the breach. He spat out water that was half blood, gained purchase on a footing of God knows what, and smashed his buckler into a Meshica face. His sword-arm was entangled somehow: he wrenched it free, found he was still holding his sword and swung it at a grinning devil stooping at him from a canoe. Before the stroke could find its mark his feet went from under him and he flailed back into the mud.

He was not going to be allowed to drown. Meshica, shouting in their excitement, were hauling him out of the muck. He struggled desperately. He was already half into the canoe when help came. Saving arms clasped his waist, pulling him out of the clutch of his captors, and another arm made such havoc among them with a blade that they fell back stricken into their boat. The arms that held him delivered him to a strong hand that hauled him on to solid ground. He looked for the men who had saved him but in the confusion could not make out who they were.

A soldier holding a horse was at his side. A second miracle. He needed help to get into the saddle because his left thigh, from which blood was pouring, would not bear his weight, but once there his body fell into the balance it had always had. From horseback, he surveyed the carnage on the causeway. It was like a painting of the Last Judgement, even to the colour of the lake, a Biblical crimson, with, swarming on it, the black canoes of the Meshica.

The retreat to the camp was as bloody as any battle he had ever been in. His men could only hold up their shields and stab blindly as they fought to control the pace at which they were pushed backwards. They slipped on gore, they stumbled over the bodies of dead comrades, they fell under each other's feet and were trampled by their own horses. Still the drums pounded, the conches blared and the bone whistles keened.

At last the safety of the few stone buildings that stood at the junction of the causeway was reached. The camp was still there, praise God, but no sooner had the Captain reached it than he realized that today it was not safety.

Normally, the Meshica retired when the Spaniards returned to camp. There was an unspoken agreement that it was all over until tomorrow. Today the Meshica had changed the rules.

'They want to finish us off,' said the Captain. His wound burned malevolently. He handed command over to Tapia and went to his hut, where he wound a strip of cloth around his thigh and then lay open-eyed on his mattress listening to the fighting.

The noise of battle suddenly stopped. Everything had stopped. The world was holding its breath after some dreadful event.

He pulled himself off the mattress, grasped his sword and limped outside.

The men made way for him. They were grouped around a pool of awfulness on the ground, something clumped, hair, eyes . . .

'*Tona-tiuh!*' The Meshica burst into a savage chant. It was their name for Alvarado. '*Sando-valtzin!*' They leapt with exultation.

He forced himself to look coldly and saw that although, flung on to the stones, were the blood-matted heads of four Spanish soldiers, none was the head of either Sandoval or Alvarado.

Rage flooded him and drove out defeat. He launched himself

446

at the nearest dancing Meshica and brought his sword down on the Indian's skull. The battle flamed again.

The head of Sandoval, in its proper place on his shoulders, is now outlined against the wall of the hut by a flickering candle flame. It is bruised and blood-encrusted: a stone has chipped his cheekbone.

'They said one of the heads they threw down was yours,' the Captain tells him.

'They threw one in front of P-Pedro and said it was *yours*.'

Sandoval has ridden to Alvarado's camp for news of the fighting on the western causeway, and only just managed to get through because of bands of Meshica roving on the border of the lake. By the time he arrived at the Captain's camp, several hours later, everybody had a fairly clear idea of the events of this disastrous day.

From the Captain's company, sixty-six men have been taken prisoner. That is in addition to a number killed. Eight horses have been lost.

Having put the Captain's men to flight and captured so many, the Meshica then turned their fury on Alvarado's company and drove them back to their camp, destroying their launches. They threw the severed heads of six Spaniards into Alvarado's camp, saying one of them was the Captain's and one Sandoval's.

But that is not the worst of it.

'While I was with P-Pedro,' says Sandoval, 'the Meshica sacrificed some of our p-people.'

The Captain won't look at him. 'How many?'

'T-Ten.'

'How do you know?'

'You can see the t-temple. We counted them.'

How horrible. His fault. 'May God have mercy on their souls,' he murmurs.

He will have masses said, if he ever gets back to Spain. At the moment it seems unlikely. He can feel a lowness of spirits such as he hasn't felt for years advancing in his soul.

447

'What happened, Hernán?' asks Sandoval again.

'I am a sinful man,' says the Captain, 'and this is my punishment.' Nothing else can account for the disaster of this day, because it is inconceivable that God does not want His soldiers to triumph.

'They say you forgot to fill a b-breach.'

The Captain is silent.

Next morning, the Tlascalans have gone. Vanished. There is not a feather or a curl of incense.

The other Indians have gone, too. The ones who came to offer their allegiance when they saw how the Spaniards had freed towns from tribute to the Meshica, or who submitted out of fear.

Not quite all: a handful remain. No more than a hundred, out of more than twenty thousand. A few are with the Captain, a few with Sandoval. They are the ones who have so profoundly thrown in their lot with the Spaniards that they have nowhere else to go.

The Captain understands this, with the part of him that sits aloof. The rest of him, which oscillates between a despair as deep as he has ever known and a wild optimism that the war can still be won in the face of any difficulties, prefers to ascribe the loyalty of these few Indians to a personal devotion to himself.

The departure of the Tlascalans has sunk the entire army into gloom. There are many Spaniards who did not like their Tlascalan allies, who objected to their chattering and drumming and the smell of copal drifting over the camp, and who looked askance into Tlascalan cooking pots and wondered if there was Meshica flesh bubbling there. But it was mightily reassuring to know there were a thousand fighters at your back, ready to hold bridges and guard the rear, ready to scout, to create an ambush or to make havoc in the countryside if that was what you wanted.

Without the Tlascalans (they have never esteemed the other allies much), the little force of Spaniards feels itself suddenly to be no more than that, a little force, and like a man on a cliff-face who is half-way up and half-way down and cannot move in any direction, clinging to a tiny foothold, hearing the sea beneath. Worse, without the Tlascalans to share the burden of this war, it comes face to face with itself, it sees itself, steely, heartless, impudent, led by a man obsessed, and it has to acknowledge what it is doing here, an unprovoked war of conquest, the lunacy of this venture. The illegitimacy.

4

Every day the Meshica attack, and are repulsed. There are no more forays into the city. The wounds of some Christians heal. The wounds of others don't, and they die.

When they die, they are thrown into the lake, covered in whatever will serve as a shroud. Their hands are crossed over their breasts, and Olmedo or Father Díaz says a prayer. It is the best that can be done. It's much too dangerous to take the bodies to the shore and bury them. The shore might be anybody's.

The besiegers are themselves besieged, but nobody cares to say so.

There has been a problem with the severed heads.

Once it had been established whose bodies they had been severed from, Olmedo asked what the Captain expected him to do. The Captain replied ill-humouredly that *he* was the priest. Olmedo said that God permitted the resurrection of a body which had been disunited from itself in exceptional circumstances, and would undoubtedly permit it in the case of these four heads, but he did not feel it was proper to compound the offence by throwing the heads, in knotted sacks, into the lake. Moreover, they would keep reappearing, as things thrown into the lake did, because the lake was so shallow and was constantly being churned up by battles, the digging of pits, the filling in of breaches and the fixing of stakes on which to impale launches. Being small, they would instantly be recognizable as heads and not corpses, which would lead to a renewed lowering of spirits in the camp.

'God and His martyrs!' exploded the Captain. 'We are fighting a *war!*'

Olmedo's look reproached him.

'What do *you* want to do with these heads, Olmedo?'

'I will say a Mass, and I want you to have them buried at the end of the causeway.'

'It's too dangerous.'

'God will ensure that it's done safely.'

It went against the Captain's judgement. But he had to do something about the heads, they were in a house of their own at the edge of the camp which nobody went near, although some soldiers had drawn crosses with chalk-stone on the wall. Olmedo refused to say Mass until the Captain agreed to the burial, and in a very short time everyone in the camp knew that was why the heads were still there.

'Am I Captain-General of this army or not?' demanded the Captain, but Olmedo had judged the mood of the men better than he had, and he sensed it. There was also the fact, undeniable although unstated, that those four heads would still be on their shoulders if the Captain had not neglected to fill in a breach.

The burial was carried out by night, aided by a slip of moon. Two men with spades dug a trench in the soil of the lake's shore, while twelve stood with their swords drawn facing out into the silent countryside. Olmedo pronounced the committal and a prayer for the souls of all Christians who had died in this land. The party returned safely to camp.

The Captain now concedes that Olmedo had a point. It has also occurred to him that the lake is in a pretty terrible state, what with one thing and another, and is starting to smell bad. No doubt the less that is thrown into it, the better.

His officers try to cheer him up in the bleak evenings when wounds are dressed and the fires of the Meshica glow red on the causeway. He listens bitterly. Anyone who is an optimist in these circumstances does not understand the circumstances. Soon, the Indians in the region beyond the valley will rise, and then it will all be over.

His despair endures for a week. It is brought to an end by a reproach quietly uttered by an old Indian, a relative of the new lord of Texcoco (and thus also of Ixtlil, who has vanished).

'You should not be sad, Malinche.'

'Why should I not be sad?' The Captain stops in his pacing of the tiny stretch of causeway (five strides in either direction) that is out of bowshot of Meshica archers. 'Fortune's wheel has turned and I am again at the bottom of it.'

His interpreter on this occasion is his mistress, who, he is savagely aware, will make nothing of the bit about Fortune's wheel and will not bother with it. Her Spanish is good enough now for Gerónimo not to be needed, except for the look of the thing. This is as well, because Gerónimo has got into the habit of absenting himself. Something will have to be said to him; in this war, everyone has a grief.

'But you have won the victory.' The Indian's eyes are bright.

The Captain swallows his anger. He tells himself that he is not being mocked. 'Why do you say that, uncle?'

'They have no water. They are drinking salty water from a pool they have dug.'

The Captain seats himself on a falconet. The sun has been just long enough on it to warm the iron after the chill of the night, and it is comforting to his buttocks.

'How do you know this?'

The Indian's seamed face crinkles with laughter and he has a bantering exchange with the woman. She translates. He has said, 'An old man who has nothing to do but watch the birds can tell a lot from the way they fly.'

'Where is the pool they have dug?'

'In Tlatelolco, where the market used to be.'

The phrase 'where the market used to be' floats at the surface of the Captain's mind, gently releasing its meaning. He stares out at the lake, at the strangely-lit water and the things that populate it. There is no market now. Of course there is no market. It was the living heart of that great city, and he has throttled its arteries. The causeways are blocked. The canoes are chased by his launches. There is no food. There is no water.

He feels light-headed. There is an unnatural stillness, as if everything is waiting for something. It is waiting for him.

'Are they hungry?' he demands.

'Yes, they are hungry.'

'How much food do they have in store?'

'None. There are many warriors in the city, because they have come from all the allied towns to defend Tenochtitlan. And the granaries were nearly empty already, because you had eaten the maize.'

The Captain calculates. It is June now, two months to harvest.

'They don't *look* as if they're hungry,' he objects. 'They don't *fight* as if they're hungry.'

'They are Meshica.'

'But they will weaken?'

'They will weaken and they will die.' This is said as calmly as if the old man had already seen it pass before his eyes.

'Thank you,' says the Captain. He gets to his feet.

Taino died two days after he fell ill.

At first I thought it was the fever that afflicted a lot of men in the camp and that the Captain himself was particularly prone to. It was weakening but not usually fatal. The Captain had his own recipe for dealing with it, a vile black potion made up by his physician. I thought of asking him what was in it, but I quickly realized that what ailed Taino was not a fever. Or not that fever.

It burned hotter and deeper and gave him a thirst that nothing could quench. It twisted him in pain. It took away every ounce of his strength, so that he could do nothing but lie on the straw

453

that I had to renew constantly because he had lost control of his body and the waste began to pour out of him like a foul river. It ravaged him like a fire sweeping through a thatch. The black and purple marks of the end were already blooming on his cheekbones on the second morning.

The pustules appeared on the first day. They were hard and crimson, but ripened almost immediately into yellow boils. They appeared on his chest in the morning, had risen to his face by noon and by evening covered every part of his body. That was when the first dark patch appeared on the skin. On his stomach.

The pustules told me what this was. Other *winic* in the camp had died of it. I knew then beyond a doubt that he would die, although I went on praying that he would not, praying to anyone who might listen, praying to his own gods as well as mine. I offered myself in exchange. I offered anything. No one was listening.

He died early in the morning, before dawn. I had kept a candle burning so that he could still see me, if there was sight in his eyes, and so that I could see him. I heard him stop breathing. I fell to my knees at his side. I cried his name. I implored the gods to bring him back, to unmake this moment. The air was still, it was heavy with corruption. I blundered out into the night, where the stars were shining. I could not understand how they could shine. I went back to him. He was still dead.

I prayed that I might die, too. I knew that this prayer would not be answered, either.

Eight days after they went away, the Tlascalans and the other allies come back. They offer no explanation for either their absence or their return. The Captain summons their commanders and tells them they deserve to be hanged, but so great is his relief that he cannot put much thunder into it.

And who can tell what has really taken place in these eight days? It is as if some tipping-point has been passed, so that the balance from now on will inexorably favour him; but what it was, that point, at what moment it was reached, the Captain will never know. What is certain is that both his men and Alvarado's have filled breaches in the causeways *that have remained filled*. This was such an astonishing occurrence the first time it was reported to him that he mounted his horse and went to look. It was true: there was the low, ragged hill of rocks and timber still rising like the back of a turtle between one section of the causeway and the next.

What does it mean? That the Meshica *are* weakening. Alvarado says it is his impression, too, that the Meshica are in difficulties, and that the very high losses the Spaniards are inflicting on them are at last starting to tell.

'But I haven't noticed they're sending fewer men to attack the camp,' says the Captain. 'Have you?'

'No.' The reply is thoughtful.

'What?'

'There are corpses in the streets.'

Alvarado has returned to his sorties into the city.

'Warriors?'

'No. Women, old people.'

'Can they be dying of starvation already?'

'They're dying of something.'

The Captain sends a message to the new *tlatoani*, Kwah-temoc, calling on him to surrender. It is not the first such message he has sent. Like the previous ones, it is ignored.

With the Tlascalans to guard their backs and fill breaches in the causeway, the Spaniards embark on more raids into the suburbs. The Meshica make them fight every step of the way.

It seems to the Captain that his causeway has got a little shorter. What has happened is that there are fewer open channels to fight around and worry about: the rubble now often stays where it's thrown, becomes compacted by the feet of many men and horses (they are using the horses every day now, stabling them in the camp), and in the end could not be removed by the Meshica if they tried, so solidly is it wedged into the gap. He is constructing a road into Tenochtitlan that can't be unbuilt, can't be turned into a trap, can't be made the site of an ambush from every wayside temple and every cluster of little houses built out charmingly on the water. There are no wayside temples, now, or houses built out on the water. They have been levelled, they are filling up the gaps in the causeway.

The process is remorseless: it has to be. Only by iron can this city be won. The iron enters the Captain's soul and he does not resist it, because it is the price. He sees, pitilessly, how the pretty buildings and their raised gardens topple, the children run screaming, the birds take flight into the sky and do not return, the lake changes colour and nameless things glide and ferment below its surface.

On this road he canters in pursuit of retreating Meshica. He knows they have only fallen back to regroup, and it is no surprise when they try to ambush him a few hundred paces ahead. Though well used to the shock of their assault, he is still not inured to it: the shell trumpets still chill his blood, the reek of incense and feathers and the paint they put on their bodies still nauseates him when he is in the press of them (and now there is the added anxiety: *what are they eating?*). He jabs viciously with his lance and hears with pleasure the crackling of gunfire and the clash of steel on flint. Meshica are still rushing forward with reckless courage and trying to take captives (they haven't learnt: they should be trying to kill); they are still utterly contemptuous of the harm his men are doing them — and then suddenly they've gone. Some signal was given, and they've vanished like deer.

It happens again and again and there are always more Meshica to fill the gaps in the ranks. But something is new. In the pauses between the attacks, there are no Meshica at all. The Captain finds himself riding through empty streets. Can they really be empty? Is there yet another ambush preparing? But no, he knows they are empty, they *feel* empty. There is a feeling here like a lowering cloud, like the circling wait of a vulture. His horse's hooves clatter in an eerie quiet. When the Meshica erupt again out of some place where they have concealed themselves, he is almost glad to see them.

On one of these raids, Alvarado's men come across the pool the old man had spoken about. Alvarado tastes the water: it's bad but drinkable.

A woman, very thin, her body covered in hideous sores, is lying dead in the doorway of a house. He has the corpse brought and thrown into the pool. They will drink from it no longer.

The Captain orders every building that is captured in the city to be pulled down. Sometimes a fierce battle develops as this is being done: the Meshica throw themselves in anguish against the Spaniards who are pulling the stones away and prising loose the beams, or setting burning brands in the thatch of temples. Occasionally a building has to be abandoned before the job can be finished, but it will be finished the next day, or the day after. Then the stone and timber will be thrown into the nearest canal, for the canals must be blocked up as the gaps in the causeway were, so that the horses can manoeuvre and so that there is no longer a danger of being ambushed by canoe. Then, on the levelled ground where the building stood, together with the former canal in which the building, reduced to rubble, now lies, the army can advance in security, deploying its horse and cannon as they ought to be deployed, having created at last, by superhuman effort, a battlefield fit for Spaniards to fight on.

The Captain again calls on Kwah-temoc to surrender. Kwah-temoc does not reply.

This is how things stand when the event every Spaniard has dreaded happens. The towns friendly to the Meshica that are far in the Spaniards' rear, and have never been subdued, have risen. Their warriors are heading for Tenochtitlan and are sacking, on the way, the towns that submitted to Spain.

The Captain receives desperate messages. The siege has reached a point at which any slackening of his grip will spell disaster, but he has to do something or the Indians who come from the threatened towns will go home again, and this time will not come back. In any case, the threat to his rear can't be ignored.

He sends Tapia, with a hundred Spaniards and a large force of Tlascalans, to deal with the problem. As soon as Tapia has left, the Meshica attack ferociously. All three camps are battered by wave after wave of warriors. The attacks start at dawn and continue until the evening. The Meshica are beaten off and come back, are beaten off and come back.

With the battles unabated on the second day, the Captain sends messages by launch to Sandoval and Alvarado, saying that this is the Meshica's last great effort: they need only hold it off a little longer and the city is theirs. He does not believe it, himself. He believes Kwah-temoc will not give up as long as there is strength in his little finger.

On the third day he begins to be seriously alarmed. The Meshica are still fighting furiously, and they have immobilized him. What's the use of all those battles fought up and down the causeway, all those channels filled and houses demolished, his stranglehold on the enemy's food and water supplies, when he is apparently back where he started? With his force diminished by a fifth, and not a single soldier who isn't wounded?

The attacks continue on the fourth day and then, without apparent reason, stop.

Two weeks pass. Then: 'It's time to make another push for Tlatelolco,' pronounces the Captain.

The faces around the candle flame are serious, with good reason, considering what happened the last time they made a push for Tlatelolco. But now the situation is different. How different can be judged by the fact that there are seven faces around the candle flame.

A month ago, to have got so many of his senior commanders in the same room at the same time would have been impossible. On that occasion, the Captain consulted them by launch. He wrote to them asking what they thought, and they wrote back. Without exception, they said it was a bad idea.

Now, 'You're right,' says Alvarado. He is picking his teeth and regarding the candle flame keenly. He has never had enough of any fight. And he has a particular reason to go to Tlatelolco.

'What about the p-powder?' asks Sandoval.

'There's enough powder,' says Alvarado.

'*You* may have enough.'

'Powder is coming from Villa Rica,' the Captain assures them.

It is being escorted by horsemen and Tlascalans. It ought to be safe. The Meshica seem never to have grasped the significance of gunpowder. If they had captured a keg or two and rolled it into the lake, they might have stopped the war.

'Do you intend to make a base there?' This is Tapia.

'Yes. We can hold Tlatelolco *and* the causeways now.'

'Suppose there's another rebellion in the countryside?'

'Who is going to rebel?' Tapia and Sandoval between them – for in the end the trouble was not confined to one region – have reduced all the countryside up to fifty miles away. 'Do you want to do this, gentlemen?'

They do.

Alvarado watched it every night. He would stand outside the flimsy wooden shelter that was his lodging (they had put these shacks up against the rain, but the rain came through) and watch as attentively as if it were a play put on for him. It happened always after the end of the day's battle, when he and all his men were back in the camp, at leisure (in a manner of speaking) to be entertained with a spectacle. It happened, also, as the sun went down, flooding the topmost steps of the pyramid in light, and striking brilliance from the golden mask above the entrance to the shrine. From his camp on the causeway, he had a perfect view of those steps, the broad platform they led to and the little, wicked, thatched house in which the Meshica kept their god. And in front of that little house, the stone slab.

459

There, every evening, in the short interval between the first perceptible cooling of the day and the disappearance of the sun behind the mountains, six Christians were sacrificed.

At this distance it was very hard to pick out features, and as they mounted the steps, the six of them looked as if they were all the same man, a man going to be executed. Walking stiffly yet disjointedly, like dolls, or as if they had been racked (but the Meshica did not have such an instrument). Heads bowed forward. Hands clasped in front of them — tied, he presumed. On their heads, a grotesque high crown of paper and feathers. And as they came more fully into view on the stairway, hauled upward by their captors, drummed upward by that merciless beat, he could see how the Meshica had tried to take away their dignity by robing them in paper, too, because their shrouds stuck out stiffly from them like stubby white wings.

The first one reached the platform. The drum was pounding now. The priests came out from the shrine. Alvarado's stomach contracted with hatred. There came a blast on the shell trumpets.

The prisoner, having reached the platform, was made to perform a series of leaping movements around a pole that the priests brought out from the shrine. It was horrible to see. The poor wretch was kept moving by pointed sticks which they jabbed at him and, as he leapt, the flutes piped up their intolerable whistling.

Then it would stop, quite abruptly. The leaping, the flutes. The priests laid down their sticks. They moved towards the prisoner, who stood between them like a bullock waiting for the knife. They laid hands on him.

It was then that he raised his head. He raised his head for his death, and Alvarado knew him. He was Guzmán, who had brought a horse for the Captain as he struggled out of the water on the day of the unfilled breach, and then been captured himself. He was young Cordero, taken many weeks ago in an ambush near Iztapalapa. He was Musa, who had boasted he could eat anything and downed a plateful of insects for a wager when they were living in the palace of Axayacatl. He was Alvárez, who cheated at cards. He was Banderas, who came from Alvarado's home town and had been forced to marry a girl he didn't want to marry, and had abandoned her. He was Lupe, who claimed to see the future in dreams, but had not seen this.

All of these raised their heads for the death that awaited them, and Alvarado bore witness that they went with their heads high to the slab at the top of the stairway.

He continued to watch. He stayed at his post while the hearts were lifted skyward and then placed in the stone dish, the shell trumpets meanwhile clamouring. He remained standing, stone himself, while the six plundered bodies were thrown down the long stairway, and although he knew his ears at that distance could not truly hear the thump of flesh and bone on the ugly steps, it seemed to him that he heard it nonetheless.

This happened ten nights in succession.

It has rained heavily the previous afternoon, a torrent of rain whipped by the wind, rain penetrating through the cracks in the walls of flimsy shelters and dripping through the patchwork roofs. Everything is still wet: the horse blankets, the harness, the sleeping-mats of the men who were on watch, the sleeping-mats of the men who weren't. It's difficult to get a fire going to toast the maize cakes, and they're unappetizing cold. Normally, there is a lot of grumbling in these circumstances.

Today there is only good humour. The sun is up and it will dry everything. The Meshica have not appeared yet. This is the second day they have not come to attack the camp in the hour after dawn. The causeway stretches ahead, empty, levelled, safe for Spaniards.

Alvarado rides out with a jingle of spurs, squinting and laughing into the sun. He knows exactly what he is going to do today.

Two hours later, he has got no further than the edge of Tlatelolco, where he is fighting hand to hand with a forest of Meshica. They were waiting for him: did they know this would be the day he came? The great square that used to be the market is now crowded with booths of a different kind, dispensing varieties of death. The vendors, the licensees of this fair wear headdresses of animal-skin and parrots' feathers, are beaked like eagles or tufted like owls; their faces glare from between the jaws of tigers and ocelots, snakes and wolves. They howl and jabber and screech their wares, they blow into shells and drum their fingers on logs carved to resemble alligators, they whirl great rattles above their heads that make a sound like trees falling. They offer death by the slicing of flesh, the death of the flint-bladed sword, and death by the spilling of brains, the death of the club. They offer the slow death of the copper-headed arrow in the intestine. They offer the swifter death by arrow in the heart or eye. They offer the dramatic death by the javelin that transfixes the throat and always leaves the recipient with a look of astonishment on his face. They offer the nameless death that destroys the face. They offer death by decapitation, by the severing of a limb, by disembowelling (the flint blades are cruel, but the black glass is crueller), by trampling (for in the crush of this battle, if you lose your footing you will not get up again). They offer, finally, the death they most prize, which today is the one least wanted by its purchasers, the delayed death, the death on the stone, the meeting with Hummingbird.

Alvarado kills them.

The sun is high now, and the colours dance. Ahead of him, far ahead but dominating his vision, rises the great pyramid of the temple. This, too, seems to dance as he fights his way towards it. So slowly. It is his fantasy that, for each step of the stairway he wishes to climb, he must kill a hundred Meshica.

There are many temples here, in fact, but the great pyramid towers over all of them, pyramid of Babel, temple of Moloch. He has been inside it, he has seen its webbed darkness and its eyes. He came here with Hernán when they had been only a few days in the city. Until that day it had all been like a wonderful dream. Then . . . *that horror.*

He slays three more Meshica for destroying his dream.

In the space between the smaller temples and the great one, which is the space where the market used to be, the Meshica have built a maze. Using trestles and banners, screens covered with rushes, fences woven from branches . . . none of it makes sense to his eye, until his mind perceives what it is and instructs his sight. It is a trap. You can't tell whether what confronts you is a solid obstacle or not, anything you put your foot on might give way beneath you, and the horsemen are at a loss because the horses, which don't flinch at cannon, shy at these strange ambiguous surfaces.

It doesn't deter him. He fights on, untiring, as the sun dances in his head and thirst sears his throat. There will be a time to slake it. Then at a certain moment an avenue opens – this sometimes happens in a battle, it is like the sudden clearing of mist – and this avenue points directly at the foot of the stairway of the great temple. Alvarado knows a sign when he sees one.

What follows next is what must happen. Alvarado is at the base of the stairway, handing the reins of his horse to his lieutenant. He is running up the stone steps, so recently befouled with the blood of his comrades, but he will cleanse them. Up and up. His men surge behind him, skirmishing with Meshica: he sees this in the corner of his eye but he is concentrating on the steps, on keeping his footing and his momentum. The platform comes into view, and with it the priests.

A flock of hideous crows they have always seemed to him, with their black clothes and blackened faces and stink of the slaughterhouse. But passive, he always thought, the mere servants of their demon, and too thin to have much strength. He is surprised to see them weaponed.

They fling themselves at him in fury. They have flint swords, staves, and one of them is holding a rock, which Alvarado twists his body on an instinct to find poised above his head. He sidesteps and runs the rock-bearer through, and the rock crushes the foot of another of them.

He breaks away and rushes into the shrine. Fire winks from a brazier that, like everything else here, is perverse in its shape, apparently standing on its head. The floor is slippery, the place is suffocating with evil. He snatches something from the wall, one of their feather tapestries, and flings it into the coals. The smoke is foul but the thing, after charring for a while, takes flame. He strides about the tiny room, pulling objects from niches and throwing them down or tossing them into the brazier, where the feathers now are burning like a sunset.

Others have joined him, which is right. Spaniards have died here, Spaniards should be here to witness. A soldier dips a rolled-up cloth into the flames and uses it to fire the thatch. Alvarado grunts approval. The fire will do the rest. It will deal with the vileness that lurks in the shadow at the back of the room. There will be no return of this devil to its temple.

The flames lick, then run like wind in a cornfield, and the roof is engulfed in a glory of flame.

Outside on the platform, standing by the altar stone (it is empty and washed clean: he feels obscurely cheated), Alvarado picks a burning twig from his shoulder. He finds he is resting his foot on the body of a priest. He lifts his foot and kicks the priest off the platform.

One day these stones will make a church.

The Captain has now sent ten messages to Kwah-temoc through captured Meshica. To most of them he has not even received an answer. So contemptuous is this prince.

'Consider,' the Captain said in his latest message, 'what your people are suffering. They have no food. They have no water.' (As he finds the wells they have dug, he poisons them.) 'I urge you to make peace, before there are none of you left.'

This time he receives a reply.

'Every one of us,' says Kwah-temoc, 'would die rather than live a slave. Cease bothering me with your messages.'

You would not think, from the pride in these words, that the man who uttered them was in possession of only one-fourth of his former city and that his warriors retreated to an isolated cluster of houses in the lake after each day's fighting.

But it is so. In the heart of the city where the palaces, temples and administrative buildings stood, the Meshica no longer control the streets. The Spaniards control them. They move warily, studying each movement among the heaps of rubble (usually a rat or a pecking vulture), scanning such roofs as remain, and always, as they ride past darkened doorways, alert for an ambush or a silent arrow. But these are Christian streets. There has been no ambush, since the three divisions of the army united at Tlatelolco. There have been only a few arrows out of doorways. One was fired yesterday. It caught a Basque footsoldier. His companions rushed the doorway and killed the archer. Then they fetched their commander, who fetched the Captain.

The arrow had been fired by a woman. She was wearing full martial costume (her husband's?), even to the wooden shield slung at her back. The Captain put her age at about twenty.

It was after this that he sent his message to Kwah-temoc. It was sincere. He has had enough of the killing. It is beginning to lie heavy on him. The very air is heavy. The rain freshens it for an hour, but then the heaviness comes back, the lowering-ness, the growing stench.

There are still battles every day. Each morning, the Meshica present themselves for war under their captains, with their signs and banners bravely held and their drums beating. It is the sixty-seventh day of the siege. Signs of hunger are evident in those he captures, but they deny that they are starving. He sent Kwah-temoc two baskets of food with his most recent demand for surrender. Kwah-temoc accepted the food, but sent in return two embroidered cloaks, thus turning charity into a ritual exchange of gifts.

The battles are still fierce. Very fierce. Kwah-temoc is defending like a lion the last quarter left to him. Every building the Captain needs to demolish, every canal he needs to fill up to make the terrain safe for horses, costs Spanish blood and leaves the ground strewn with Meshica dead. He allows the corpses to be taken away, and sees the smoke of the funeral pyres billow up from the shore.

But there are not enough funeral pyres, because the smell of death is everywhere in the city. It hangs in the houses, it comes out of the stones. It is the stifling heaviness in the air. It bursts upwards in the evil-looking bubbles on the lake.

Perhaps there are not enough still alive to dispose of the dead.

This thought comes to him every morning with an accompanying hope that perhaps today it will be over, but by noon he will be enmeshed in another bloody battle with a seemingly inexhaustible number of them, and at nightfall they will pursue him to his camp as if they never needed rest.

'I must finish this,' murmurs the Captain. He does not know how to, with an adversary who does not follow the rules.

The Captain lays an ambush. As the Spaniards return to camp, hotly pursued, as always, by the Meshica, his cavalry, supported by Tlascalans, burst out of hiding and kill about forty of the enemy. After this, the Meshica stop pursuing the Spaniards to their camp in the evenings.

Nothing else changes. There are battles to capture a bridge over a narrow, foul-smelling canal, battles to capture a house in which there is nothing but a broken pot and the corpse of a baby, battles to capture a pile of stones.

Reasoning that, with every day that passes, the situation of the Meshica worsens without his having to do anything, the Captain then does not send his men out to fight for several days. He hopes that hunger will do his work for him.

Kwah-temoc has read his mind. On the second day of this pause in hostilities, two unarmed Meshica, as thin and bony as they all are now, amble past the Spanish camp and sit down on a nearby pile of rocks. They have a woven bag with them. They indulge in a little ritual taunting of the Spaniards. By now most of the Captain's men have picked up a bit of Meshica and they are familiar with the names the Meshica call them. They respond in kind.

What the two skeletons sitting on the pile of stones do next requires no translation. They open the woven bag, take out of it two chicken legs and a handful of maize cakes and proceed to eat, in a leisurely way, without any appearance of hunger.

The Captain is called, and watches them in silence. He is awed. The two Indians talk to each other in a gentle, conversational way as they eat, and every now and then exchange a titbit.

After a long time, they prepare to go. He notices that they pick up the crumbs and put them in the bag. The Captain calls for his interpreters.

'I'm glad to see that you have plenty of food,' he says to the two Indians.

'Yes, we have plenty of food,' the Indians reply.

'Tomorrow I shall come and see where you're keeping it,' the Captain says. 'We could do with some meat here.'

'Come whenever you wish, Malinche.'

They walk away in the direction of the shore.

In the afternoon, the Captain sends another demand for surrender to Kwah-temoc. This will be the last. If, this time, Kwah-temoc does not surrender, he will send the launches against the refuge in the lake.

He receives a conciliatory reply. Kwah-temoc will meet him the following morning. They will speak across a water-channel that has no bridge. The Captain must bring only two officers, and Kwah-temoc will do the same. The Captain must not bring any weapons-that-kill-from-a-distance, and he, Kwah-temoc, will bring no arrows, darts or stones.

The Captain accepts these conditions.

He rides to the water-channel the next morning with Sandoval, Alvarado and the interpreters. They wait.

They wait until the middle of the day, when the sun is fierce. The buzzards circle. The flies drum. Dark clouds, bearing the afternoon's rain, start to gather.

The Captain turns his horse.

The landscape – the city – what is it? it is a desolation – appears empty of people. But then he sees them again, those figures that at first he confused with an image recalled from a nightmare, spectral, without colour, waiting motionless on the few remaining rooftops, waiting for the end.

The honour of leading the last assault will be Sandoval's. The Captain will watch from the platform of the great temple.

A thick mist cloaks the surface of the lake this morning, thinning as it rises, so that in its shifting gaps the roofs of Kwah-temoc's last fortress can be glimpsed. The houses are simple wooden huts built on stilts in the water. Under each one is a landing stage and a ladder that leads up to the house. They used to be the homes of fishermen and the people who tended the floating gardens on the lake. They are fragile, but from their upper platforms an archer has a perfect shot.

Sandoval orders a start to be made while fraying banners of mist still drift above the water. He hopes the mist will delay the moment at which his approach is seen. He has with him all the launches that have survived the fighting – seven. There is little breeze, the lake is barely rippling, so the oarsmen have to pull hard because, now that the thing is afoot, no time must be lost.

They draw closer to the wooden shacks. A shower of arrows falls like a curtain and hisses into the water.

'Row!' orders Sandoval sharply.

The timbers creak. Another shower of arrows falls. Not in the water this time: they strike the deck, one lodges in a sail and one has found its mark in an oarsman's neck. Sandoval can clearly see the archers on their flimsy platforms; they are lifting their bows for a further volley. But now he sees, too, something he is not intended to see.

Riding below the clustered shacks is a small fleet of canoes. One is larger than the others and has a seat in it, and over the seat is an awning hung with green feathers. In this seat, a figure sits. Into all the canoes, objects are being hastily loaded.

'Row!' shouts Sandoval again, for the first canoes are starting to move away and a desperate anxiety seizes him that the prey will slip from his grasp. A third curtain of arrows falls, thudding into the deck, and now he is so close to the shacks that he must divide his fleet to go around them, and hope to overtake Kwah-temoc on the further side.

Precious time is lost in signalling his orders to the ships that must peel off and go the other way. When he comes round the curve of the shacks, he sees the canoes fleeing for the far shore like minnows before a pike. His oarsmen strain, and still there is no breath of wind to help and the Indians are paddling as if possessed, the canoes leaping over the water. If his quarry reaches the shore, all is lost. Kwah-temoc will hide among his people, and no Spaniard will be able to tell him from any other Indian.

One of the launches under his command is lighter and swifter than the rest. He fires a shot to attract the attention of its captain and shouts to him to go after the canoe with the feathered awning. He watches with pounding heart as the launch breaks away from its fellows and starts to close on the royal canoe. But still it has not got enough speed. The canoe is darting away like a bird. It has nearly reached the shore.

What then happens will be regarded ever afterwards by Sandoval as a miracle owing to the Mother of God whose hair he wears in a locket next to his heart. A wind starts up. The launch, its sails filling, rushes down upon the canoe in which Kwah-temoc sits upright and motionless. Then, infuriatingly, a dense mist is blown across Sandoval's boat, blinding him. He has only his ears to tell him what is happening: shouts, a gunshot.

He curses impotently as the mist mocks his vision and the oarsmen rest their oars. Water slaps against the hull. From somewhere ahead of him drift Spanish voices and the knocking of wood on wood.

Then the mist parts. Caught in a pool of light are a launch and a canoe. An Indian garbed like a warrior, and wearing a broad collar of green stones, is setting his foot on the ladder that leads up to the Spanish boat.

* * *

The Captain descends the temple steps. He will wait for his prisoner on the jetty.

It is the thirteenth of August, 1521.

Already his exhilaration is starting to fade.

VII
This Beautiful House My Lord Has Built

Jade Wind came to me today and said that I must grind maize. I said I would not. I said if she wanted maize to be ground she must find someone else to do it or do it herself.

There is no lack of women to grind maize. In this house there are the kitchen-slaves, and if there aren't enough of them she will find a girl out there where the streets used to be who will grind maize all night in return for a meal.

Jade Wind wants to humiliate me, that is all. She will not succeed.

She is just the daughter of the sister of the lord of Texcoco, who died like a thief with a chain on his feet. I don't know who she thinks she is.

My lord has made me many promises and he will not forget them. He keeps me with him still, although there are other women now. I was the first, and they know it. The child is the proof.

That is why they are jealous. They know they cannot take away the three years I have been with him and what I did in that time. It makes them angry that they can't, and so they talk about me in my presence as if I were not there. I laugh at them.

It is quiet here, in this place near the lake shore where Lord-Who-Is-Severe had one of his palaces. I am used to it now, although at first I didn't like it. I had grown so accustomed to the noise. All the time we were on the stone bridges, the noise never stopped.

The Meshica didn't want us to sleep, so they screeched and whistled and beat their drums all night. Then there was the noise of fighting all day. I only realized what a din there had been when it stopped. I was glad, of course, when it stopped because who wants to be deafened and not to hear the birds? Not that, when it stopped, there were any birds. However, when the fighting ended there was a great deal for me to do. My lord was constantly talking to the Meshica: they came every day with their petitions, and if they didn't he had questions to ask them, such as what had they done with the gold that went into the lake. But after a while there wasn't so much for me to do, and one day there was nothing.

That was when I would have been glad to hear the noise again.

Sometimes, in the night, when I'm almost asleep, I think I hear it. I start up out of my bed. My head is full of the whistling and screeching and I think the Meshica are going to launch another attack. I am about to shout a warning. But the noise stops. My head is as empty as a wind-shell. And after that it is hard to go to sleep, because I am looking for something to fill it up again.

Another proof that I am first is the name by which the Meshica call my lord. Malinche. It is my name, the name he gave me on the sand dunes. By calling him by this name, the Meshica mean that he is my lord and I am his woman, and we cannot be separated.

And this is the truth. No one else could have done what I did, and I do not mean simply the speaking in two tongues. I mean the other services I performed as well, services which saved all our lives, which I was able to do because of my quickness and because I never trust anybody. These qualities have been bred in me by the life I have led.

When I began to speak for him I had no idea what he wanted to do or how dangerous it would become. It only became clear to me gradually. Even the business in Cempoala with the tribute collectors I thought was some kind of game beyond my understanding, although by that time I was beginning to think that he was never peaceful in his mind unless he was taking a risk.

I did not think he would carry out his promise to visit Lord-Who-Is-Severe.

I did not think that any of this that has happened since would happen.

Nor did he. He thought the Meshica would surrender. I saw tears in his eyes once.

There were no tears in my eyes. I don't cry. I have learned that it serves no purpose.

Lord-Who-Is-Severe was a very bad ruler and it is good that he died when he did. His own people killed him. I saw the stone that was thrown. There are whisperers who say that my lord ordered his murder, but they are lying. They will say anything.

In any case, even if he had ordered it, he would have been right.

The *tlatoani* was not as tall as I had thought he would be. His skin was pale and his face was haughty. His eyes were very sharp, very intelligent. Sometimes there was something moving and turning in the depths of them, which was his *teotl*.

When I met him for the first time my knees wanted to knock together. My body wanted to throw itself into the dust. I dared not raise my eyes to him. It was as if there was a weight, a lid, over my eyes that would not let me lift them up.

This was so for the whole time that my lord was speaking. Then Muluc was speaking. There was a pause, and I had to speak.

But the words I had to speak were not mine, of course not. They were my lord's words, which had to be put into the language Lord-Who-Is-Severe understood. It was not suitable that my lord's words should be spoken to the ground, instead of to the face of the one to whom they were addressed.

That was what gave me the strength to raise my eyes. I thought, it is not I who am doing this, who am looking Lord-Who-Is-Severe in the face, it is my lord who is doing it. And, strengthened by this and making my lord's will into my will, I raised my eyes. I looked Lord-Who-Is-Severe in the face. I spoke words to his face.

475

His face was like ashes. I think that in that moment he knew everything that would happen.

And it is so. I have said this to no one, because they would laugh at me. Silly woman, they would say: how important does she think she is? But it is true. Lord-Who-Is-Severe is dead, his lands are destroyed, everything is finished, because a woman, a low-class woman from the coast, a slave, raised her eyes and looked him in the face.

Jade Wind again came to me and said that I must grind maize. Her look was angry.

I pretended not to be bothered by it, but said that she was wasting her time with these foolish games.

I turned away to do something for the baby, and when I glanced at her a moment later, when she wasn't expecting to be looked at, I saw her gazing with hatred at his cradle.

Swiftly I moved between her and the baby, to block the harm. I sent her out of the room with some dismissive phrase or other. She is a witch. I pray I was in time.

I pretended not to be awed by Cactus-on-the-Stone but at first I felt like a mouse, crossing the floors of those great palaces.

I got used to it. Nothing was so hard again, after I'd looked Lord-Who-Is-Severe in the face.

On the other hand, I had to keep doing that. I had to do it every day, because my lord spoke to him every day. Every day it was a bit easier, but every day I felt What he was staring into me from his eyes. There were moments when I became faint from it. I thought, how can I do what I am doing? How can his *teotl* not kill me? Yet I was not harmed. It was a mystery. I thought the power of my lord's *teotl* must be protecting me. Certainly it protected my lord, who could not have lived otherwise. So I think it must also have protected me, although it has not done anything for me since.

Lord-Who-Is-Severe never got the measure of my lord. He tried everything he could think of. He sent magicians to find out who he was; he set tests and traps to make him reveal himself. All foolishness. None of it touched my lord; he did not even notice it. But he did know that he must conceal his mind from Lord-Who-Is-Severe, and I understood that straight away. I always seemed to know what he wanted. I knew that I must be especially careful in translating his words, because his power resided in them just as much as in what he did.

Therefore one had to be terribly careful with the words. And that was why Muluc so infuriated me, with his casual way of leaving out things my lord had said if he couldn't think how to translate them, or for some other reason. I know he did this because he admitted it, and in any case when I had started to learn my lord's language I could hear him do it. That was partly why I set myself to learn the language of my lord. Then when Muluc had left something out, I would put it back in again if I thought I understood it.

It was strange that Muluc accused me of doing the same thing. He claimed that I didn't translate everything that Lord-Who-Is-Severe had said. Well, it was true that I shortened a few speeches, but I never left out anything important and in any case it was not the same thing. Nothing that Lord-Who-Is-Severe or any of the Meshica said was going to make any difference, because their power was not in their words.

That would have been beyond Muluc's grasp entirely.

The house is large. It is built of stone and plastered, and it has many rooms. There is a staircase, made of wood, which joins the two levels. The roof is of baked clay, formed in pieces that sit above each other so that the rain doesn't come through. There is a fine courtyard, in which a well has been dug. My lord has planted a tree.

The house is as big as the *batab*'s house in Potonchan. It is bigger. But in Potonchan I was a slave, and everywhere I went I kept my eyes down. I did not speak, except to answer when I was spoken to. I wore the slave's garb and I ground maize.

Here I walk with my eyes raised and I say that this and that must be done. I wear jewels in my ears, which my lord has given me. I have bracelets on my wrist, so many that I cannot wear them all and I must keep some in a box, wrapped in cotton.

I eat hare and turkey.

Every day, men come to the house to see my lord, and often they enquire about me. Sometimes I am called from my room to meet them. They remember the great services I rendered.

I never go out without being recognized and respectfully greeted.

It is true that these days I go out very little. The air is still bad, particularly near the lake. And people are still dying of the spotted-sickness. But in any case there is no point in going out because there is nowhere to go.

I'm told there is a market, of sorts, in Tlatelolco. It is nothing like the market there used to be, of course. But I'm told you can buy a few things there – fruit, a rabbit, seeds for planting. Caged birds.

It is too far from here, and the roads are dangerous. Where there *are* roads. Mostly there is mud.

The canals are filled with stones and rubbish. In many places they have overflowed and made another lake, a shallow, evil-looking one. There are a lot of flies.

It is better to stay in the house. This beautiful house my lord has built, from which you can see the mountains.

I could not go to the market anyway. They are all Meshica people there. They would throw stones at me.

Sometimes I have a dream in which I see my mother again.

In the dream, I am with my lord and we are going on a journey. We have many soldiers and Tlascalteca marching behind us. My lord and I are both mounted on animals.

In my dream, the landscape changes. It becomes full of lagoons, like the place in which I grew up, and I know that we are coming to my village. I have a feeling of dread. I am sure that I will be cast out again, that I will be told I am bad and there is nothing to be done with me.

We stop outside a house. It is the house I grew up in. There is a crowd all round us, village people, saying things that are not friendly, and I wonder why the soldiers and the Tlascalteca don't protect us, but they have disappeared. Then I notice that my lord has disappeared, too. I am alone in the middle of this crowd, sitting on my animal.

I hear someone say, 'Here she is,' and I think they are talking about me. But then the crowd parts to make a path and along the path is walking my mother, and I understand that it was her they meant. She looks quite young, not much older than I am, and she is pretty.

She comes to where I am. She says to me, 'Why have you asked for this meeting? I am the ruler of this village, and I have many things to see to.'

I say, 'I have come in order to forgive you.'

She says, 'No, that is not it. You have come to ask my forgiveness. But what you have done cannot be forgiven.'

Then I am not sitting on my animal any longer, but standing on my feet beside a hearth, and she is grinding the chillies to make the smoke that will make me cry.

That is the end of the dream. Half of the dream is lying because if I saw my mother again I would not want to forgive her. But the other half is telling the truth. She would still not forgive me. For what I had done.

In fact I had not even done it. That was what she told me, the night she gave me to the merchants. It was what I was going to do. They had consulted an astrologer when I was born. He claimed to see in the stars that I would bring on my people and all my village some ruin he could not describe. My mother believed him. For that I was cast out.

It is a foolish dream, but I wish I did not have it.

The baby is doing well. I have kept him away from the sickness. He is two months old now.

There was a baptism ceremony for him. The fat priest did it.

The thin priest, who watches me all the time as if he thinks a bat is going to fly out of my mouth, rang a bell and held a burning wax. Words were said. For once, I did not have to do any translating. The words were in another language from the one I have learnt. I did not understand anything.

Afterwards they told me the baby's soul was now safe.

His name will be Mar-tin. I cannot pronounce it.

VIII
Hummingbird

Yesterday I went to the market, and as I was bargaining for a large earthenware storage jar there was suddenly Pérez the notary at my elbow, capering like a monkey and saying had I heard the news.

No, I hadn't, I said, because I keep myself to myself these days, and I didn't want to hear it either, but I thought it better not to say that.

Well, he said, with a grin so wide that spittle ran down from the corner of his mouth, Well then, I should, and he would do me the great favour of revealing it, because it had something to do with me.

I felt alarmed. So much so that I stopped haggling over the jar and paid what the seller was asking. I told him where to deliver it and that left me looking at Pérez, who was still looking at me with his little bulging eyes.

'There is going to be an Inquiry,' he said, 'into the Captain's conduct. What do you think about that?'

I said I didn't think anything. Which wasn't quite true.

'Everyone who might have evidence to give will be called,' he said. He was almost dancing with excitement.

I said, 'What does this have to do with me?'

'You were with him!' cried Pérez – he practically screeched it, and all the market people squatting in a line along the edge of the rubble turned their heads at the same moment. 'You saw *everything!*' Then he stopped abruptly and peered at me in a sort of puzzlement, because there was nothing on my face that he felt entitled to see.

'I was often with him, it's true,' I said, and I made it sound kindly and not as if I was defending myself. For, after all, it was possible he didn't know exactly what part I'd played. Pérez is one of the recently arrived ones; they strut about as if they took the city single-handed, and they understand nothing.

Almost without exception, they hate the Captain.

That is something that perplexes me, because what is it to them what he did, whom he cheated of gold? But there are more rumours here than carp in a pond, and a lot of them are about murder. A knifing on a country road, a dose of poison. In the centre of the rumours there is always the Captain.

'They will call you as a witness,' said Pérez.

'There are many people whose evidence is more important than mine,' I said, with as much dignity as I could.

He sniggered a little, then said, 'Well, if they call you, you won't have a choice. So you'd better get your story ready.'

I told him I had no story and did not know what he meant, but it didn't prevent him from shouting after me, as I left him, 'Aren't you going to thank me?'

I walked back quickly to the house they have given me, near the end of the southern causeway. It is a long way from the centre, and unfashionable, and for both those reasons it suits me.

The causeway still arcs over the water like the neck of a bird. But the lake is sick; unnatural currents disturb it and it is clouded by nameless things. After the fighting stopped the fish grew monstrous. Then soon afterwards there were no fish at all as if, having glutted themselves on men and women, they had gone on to eat each other.

Now there are creatures in the lake again, but they are not fish. They are eels and scuttling things. Sometimes, as I watch, a bubble as big as my hand rises to the surface and dies with a sigh like a soul escaping, while a green dust floats out from it and settles on the water, and doesn't go away.

An Inquiry into the Captain's conduct. They will waste their time. He has an answer for everything, and he has only to point to the city that is rising around us to give them the answer that stops all questions. That, of course, is what he has always counted on.

Nevertheless, there are things I could say.

I could say, for instance, that no one saw Muctezuma die.

The *tlatoani* was reluctant to go on to the roof to talk to his people. The Captain later claimed that he had wanted to go, that Muckety was a coward who always preferred peace to war and that was why he had allowed us to make him a prisoner in the first place. It wasn't true. Muctezuma was not a coward. His god had laid an intolerable burden on his back and he carried it nobly until it was taken away from him. But it is true that he didn't want war with us. He had his own reasons for that and the Captain was never privy to them.

He didn't want to go on the roof because he knew it was pointless. The war had started, in spite of all his efforts, all his acceptance of humiliation. In the fact that it had started, he read the decision of the Lord of the Near and his own sentence. What happened next would not be his responsibility.

But then, with the Captain's hand – unthinkable, once – on his shoulder, the Captain's voice, yet again, persuading, suggesting, explaining (his words translated, as ever, by the Tongue and me) . . . he went. He stepped out on to that roof with, you may be sure, a guard of Spaniards at his back but that they were some distance behind him is even surer, because no one wanted to be in the way of what might come out of that heaving, furious crowd of Meshica. As it happened, a stone.

Curiously well aimed, you might say. Considering that it was thrown steeply upward, at a man standing on a high roof who at that angle wouldn't have been at all an easy target. From the midst of a crowd so dense the thrower could hardly have had room to put back his arm for the throw. Added to which, no one who was on the roof or down on the ground guarding the entrance saw it thrown. All anyone saw was the stone itself, like a comet out of nowhere, hurtling up above the roof-edge straight at the head of Muctezumohatzin, which would have been better protected by a Spanish helmet than by its crown of *kukul* plumes.

It hit him on the side of the head, above the right ear.

His attendants carried him back down the narrow stairs to his room, his cell. Where for the next three days a procession of Spaniards, who could not be spared from the defence, who some-times were badly wounded themselves and could scarcely drag themselves the length of those long, increasingly foul-smelling corridors, came to look at him.

He lay on a bed that was made up from woven hangings taken from the walls of the palace. I don't know who did this: it wasn't something the Captain would have thought of, and his own people had deserted him. Carrying him from the roof was the last service they performed for him: after that they vanished. They must have found a way out of the palace that we didn't know about, because no one saw them leave. The fighting had started again, it had started as soon as the news spread that the *tlatoani* had been struck by a stone, and it was desperate – the Meshica filled with loathing and on fire to finish us off, and us fighting like cornered rats.

Nevertheless that line of Spaniards came to see him as he lay dying. It wasn't curiosity. Or not mostly. It wasn't sorrow or respect, either, things had gone beyond that, yet I know that some of them felt both those things. He had, after all, been open-handed with his gifts, and not all of them were ungrateful or thought generosity didn't count in an Indian. No, it was some-thing else. I thought they came because they needed to believe. He had been so important to them for so long, he had been the goal of their quest, the pivot of their schemes, he had been the treasure-giver and the unfathomable . . . he had been the obstacle they had to get around, the river they had to cross, he had been the one they'd had to trick and betray and they found to their surprise that he was also the one whose forgiveness they needed – I had even heard them confessing their sins to him, knowing he couldn't understand a word – yes, if he was dying they needed to see that, they needed to be certain, to be sure he wouldn't rise again, and to be sure in another sense, too, because they had never quite known what he was.

But *was* he dying? I thought he wasn't, although he wanted to die. The Captain sent his own surgeon to him. Muctezuma tore the bandage off as soon as the surgeon was out of the room. He did so each time the surgeon visited him. This was sworn to by the soldier guarding him, who went on to say that he had tried to make the emperor put the bandage back on again – not that anybody believed him on that point and not that we were talking about an emperor any longer. What is strange is that no soldier was on duty when Muctezuma died. This was strictly against orders and you might also say against possibility. The *tlatoani* had not been left unguarded for the blink of an eyelid since we took him into captivity.

Flea found him. The boy had spent a lot of time with Muckety before things turned against us. Flea came running with a face like candle-wax shouting that the *tlatoani* was dead, and a gross fellow told him to stay where he was and, without waiting to find out if it was true, rushed off to tell the Captain. I went with a couple of others to Muctezuma's rooms.

He lay on his back with his head turned to one side, so the wound stared at us, it was the first thing we saw. But the blood was caked and hard on it, it was bleeding no longer. And what next I saw was a shadow like a bruise on his neck.

The Captain came then, and he must have seen it, too, but he said nothing. He merely said it was a pity Muckety had died without becoming a Christian, for which we had to thank Olmedo. Neither then nor afterwards, so far as I know, did he ask any questions. Within a few hours we all had something else to think about, because he'd given the order to leave and we were embarked on that accursed causeway.

So I mourned Muctezuma later, when there was time.

I've wondered, of course, if the Captain ordered him to be killed. Once it was clear that he couldn't command his people any longer, he was no use to us. He was just another prisoner to be guarded.

I don't believe he gave any such order. However, I think he did something that had the same effect. I think he said, after Muckety tore off the bandages, that he didn't care what became of him. With those words, he allowed the soldier who was guarding him to leave his post, and he allowed any Spaniard who had a grudge against the *tlatoani* (and there were some, men who had seen other men receive presents and had received none themselves), or had seen the glint of gold when his cloak was loosened, to enter that room.

I hope the soldier who put his hand to Muckety's neck died on the causeway, because I don't want to pass him in the street.

But perhaps all of this misses the point. I know what Muckety himself thought. He thought Hummingbird threw that stone.

At first, the Captain didn't want to rebuild the city. I think it truly distressed him that we could only capture Cactus-on-the-Stone by pulling down each building as we came to it and throwing the rubble into the canals. It had been so beautiful, he said to me. It had. I can see it still, and there will never be anything like it again as long as the world lasts. But the horses, how could they manoeuvre in narrow streets that were cut everywhere by waterways? How could we fight under a permanent hail of missiles from the rooftops? And there were *so many* of the enemy. Right until the last days, when we saw that half the warriors mocking us at Tlatelolco were women, that all of them were starved skeletons, that they had concealed their hosts of dead lest we see how many they had lost although they could not conceal the stench, right until the moment when the last remnant of them lowered their shields and we looked around and saw the desert we had made, we went on thinking there were scores of thousands of them because for three months we had been fighting an enemy who seemed as countless as the sands of the seashore.

No, he did not want to rebuild it. It had cost him too much to destroy it. Better to let it lie. And it was in a most tricky location: set on wooden piles in the middle of a lake. Think of the danger that the whole thing would sink, think of the cost of transporting materials. And it had been the capital of a great and heathen empire. Better to leave its ruins as witness to his conquering sword. But then one day he changed his mind. And suddenly there was planning and clearing and laying of foundations everywhere you looked, because if the city was going to be rebuilt it was clearly going to be a very fine city indeed and no one wanted to be left out of it.

So it is quite a place now. Broad streets, attractive squares. Palaces.

Yes, palaces. What can you expect? Men who came here with nothing and became rich by armed robbery are going to *spend* their wealth. The Captain has a mansion in Coyoacan, a palace in Cuernavaca with sixteen turrets (I have counted them and am able to refute the slander that there are twenty-four), and a residence here in town so that he can keep an eye on things. He lost most of the contents of the town house when he was away in Honduras: it was ransacked, and they hanged the poor devil he'd left in charge of it.

He is refurnishing it now. What a pity a man can only be in one place at a time.

The building is done, naturally, by the Meshica. They are very skilful. They excel at all manner of crafts, and have great patience as well as a love of beauty. They are excellent copyists, and they can put up churches on the Spanish model and fill them with carvings of angels and Marys and Christian martyrs, to Spanish requirements, with only the slightest hint of anything Indian, a trace too much colour in a face, the cheekbones a shade too

489

prominent, the figure too earthy. You would never know they bury their gods under the altars and in the walls behind the saints. You would never know by what name they secretly call the Virgin Mary, or the other things they do.

The things they do aren't talked about. Not now, when it doesn't serve our purposes. Rather the reverse. What was the point of conquering them if they're still doing it? So we pretend they're not.

Many *winic* have been killed in the building work. It's rumoured that some of them were deliberately sacrificed. That isn't so. They never sacrifice without a ritual. They may have killed themselves, however. Why shouldn't they? Their lives are wretched, and they believe that suicides go to the paradise under the earth.

The Meshica themselves say that the stones are punishing them. For the city is being remade with the stones of the torn-down temples. The fabric of Hummingbird's house becomes the house of *Díos*. They say the stones cry out, that they fling themselves from their places, that beams will not rest where they are laid but fly up into the air.

Indeed, some of the deaths have been exceedingly strange. But you cannot expect Indians to give a reasonable account of anything. They are probably just still dying of the smallpox.

The new men, I suppose, hate the Captain because he has accomplished what they never could. With the old soldiers, the ones who went through it all, it's more straightforward. He has not given them enough Indians.

Indians, unfortunately, turn out to be all the country has to offer. The gold has gone, no one really knows where, and although there's more in the mines there have to be Indians to mine it. True, there is land, the country is vast, we have found the western limit of it and I saw that fabled ocean with my own eyes. Vast, and fertile. I saw the tribute rolls in Muctezuma's treasury. I saw the hundreds of dishes that were brought to him for every meal. I saw the thousands of plants, classified by their medicinal use, in his gardens, his collections of every animal and bird in his realms, I saw the teeming abundance that was brought to Cactus-on-the-Stone and sold in the great market. All of us saw these things. There were men among us who had come from hunger-stricken villages, from impoverished farms and from families who could not keep a horse although they kept their titles. They were filled with awe and envy and a brutal anger, because they knew what they were going to do and that it was a terrible thing. No one who saw it ever got over that first sight of the city, moored like a jewelled ship on its lake. No one ever forgot that vision of magnificent wealth. And the vision did not lie.

But the wealth comes from the land, and what is land without Indians to work it? No Spaniard will put his hand to a spade. One must have Indians. And where are Indians to be got? You can't just go out and take them. You have to apply for Indians to the governor, or whoever is acting as governor, and the number of Indians the governor can give you is laid down by the King.

Who, naturally, knows nothing of what is going on. Orders arrive and are, as the saying goes here, 'obeyed but not complied with'. It takes a long time for the boat to reach Villa Rica from Seville, for it to get back to Spain with the reply protesting that the orders are impracticable, for it to return with the new instructions. Which will be obeyed but not complied with. However, and hence springs the resentment, in the early days after the victory no one had any control over the Captain, and there was nothing to stop him from rewarding his followers lavishly with grants of lands and Indians. Did he? No. He was niggardly. He is only generous with his bribes. No one was happy with the distribution, and the men who'd come with Narváez and whom he'd enticed over to his side with dazzling promises were the least happy of all, because they got least. *His* men, the ones who'd been with him from the start, said it was fair that Narváez's men should get less because they had done less fighting, but Narváez's men said the Captain had tricked them, that if they'd known what was ahead of them (the flight, the deaths on the causeway and in the lake, hunger and sickness and three months' incessant fighting to capture the city, and at the end of it this miserly distribution and the gold vanished into thin air), they would never have agreed to follow him at all. Added to which (they were beginning to say again), he was, wasn't he, a common rebel?

So that you have here a recipe for great disturbance, and great disturbance was what broke out all over the country when the Captain went off to Honduras to teach a lesson to Cristóbal de Olid, who had defied him and set up his own fiefdom. A fool's errand in more ways than one: he was lucky to get back again, and by the time he reached Honduras they had hanged Olid in any case. The trouble started as soon as he rode out of the city. His own men, those he hadn't taken with him, and Narváez's men were at each other's throats in a trice. I spent as much time as I could at El Azul, the small estate he has given me in the hills towards Cuernavaca. But every now and then I would have to go into town, and then as often as not I would find myself in a mob of Spaniards trying to kill each other. The *winic* were terrified. They didn't know whose orders to obey. A lot of them ran away at that time, deserting their villages or their crafts. If they'd had a leader they might have revolted, but the Captain had taken Kwah-temoc to Honduras with him, and there was no one else they would all follow.

He was away for twenty months. Nearly everyone believed he was dead. Killed by a spear in the depths of the jungle. The man he had left as his deputy, a Johnny-come-lately called Salazar, was riding high. Anyone who said the Captain was alive was threatened with having his own life cut short. The old soldiers who were still loyal, in spite of the fact that he'd taken the gold and not given them enough Indians, holed up in the Franciscan monastery. And then news came, a letter in his own hand, that the Captain was alive and on his way home.

Salazar didn't last beyond the next day; by the end of it they had put him in a cage.

But things move quickly here. Today the street is full of gossip about the judge who will preside over the Inquiry and the letters he has brought from the King. Salazar is out of prison already.

I used to go and talk to Muctezuma when he was in the palace of Axayacatl. It hadn't been hard to learn enough Meshica: I had little else to occupy me.

'Lord Muctezuma,' I asked once, 'who is Serpent-with-Feathers?'

'He is a great *teotl*,' said the *tlatoani*. 'They say he had his kingdom in the land our ancestors came from. He taught us all the crafts we practise, and everything we understand about the heavens. He is the lord of the winds.'

'Is he the *teotl* of Cholula?'

'Cholula is his earthly throne.' His eyes dwelt on me. I wanted to say that I was sorry about what had happened at Cholula, but so much had happened to feel sorry about, starting with the fact that he was there sitting in front of me a prisoner in his own palace, that I could not say it; for some reason it seemed worse to say it than to say nothing at all. So I stared down at the floor and waited for the moment to pass.

The next question I asked was, 'Who is Smoke-of-the-Mirror?'

'He is the ruler of this world, and all its appearances and transformations. He is a magician and trickster. We call him the Lord of the Near, and we say he is closer to us than our own thoughts. He is the *teotl* of our people.'

I was confused by this because I knew the *teotl* of the Meshica was Hummingbird.

'They are the same,' he said, seeing my perplexity. 'It is as if the Lord of the Near turns himself, and in his turning we see the sun.'

He waited for me to show that I understood, and when I did not, he said, 'At night, the sun sinks below the earth and travels through the lands of darkness. So by day he is bright and we

493

call him hummingbird, and by night he is dark and we call him jaguar. But it is the same *teotl*.'

At El Azul I find I am happy.

I went there a week ago. Although they were not expecting me, everything was in order and my bedroom was swept clean with the mat laid out. I walked through the house, sniffing the smells of stone, wood, earth and the scent of growing things that drifted in from the fields. There was something else; I recognized it at once, faint though it was. Pine resin. They had been burning incense here.

For a moment I was angry, because it was against the law and did they think I was a fool? I followed the smell to where it was strongest and found a little clay brazier, blackened from burning and so sticky about the rim with resin that I could not afterwards get it off my fingers for days, standing in a stone niche in a corner of the kitchen. Presumably the spot was sacred. We did not know anything about the land we built our houses on. Whatever we built them on went on existing underneath what we built. We did not see it. The *winic* had never ceased to see it.

I called my steward, a Meshica who has been baptized with the name Diego. I knew he was there, waiting just out of reach of my eyes for me to do whatever I would do. He came. I pointed out the brazier. He looked astonished, as if he had never seen it before. I asked him how it came to be there. He said he did not know. I said that the laws of the Christians forbade the burning of copal because it was an offering to the heathen gods, who were devils, and he reacted as if he had never heard of such a law but would make quite sure that it was observed in future.

By this time I was feeling better than I had for a long while, so I told him to bring me a few maize cakes and some beans stewed with chilli, and said that I would go with him round the fields in the morning. I ate the food with a ravenous appetite

494

and drank water which had come from the stream. Then I lay down on my straw mat and slept soundly until daybreak.

'Lord Muctezuma,' I asked, 'why did you tell us that story about Serpent-with-Feathers and Smoke-of-the-Mirror?'

'Because Malinche wished us to believe that he was Serpent-with-Feathers come back to claim his kingdom.'

This answer bewildered me. Yet Muctezuma seemed to think that I must already know it, because his tone betrayed a slight impatience.

'He spoke of a ruler and teacher who long ago abandoned Anahuac and who, our people say, will one day return. He also talked about *this*' — and here the *tlatoani* made on the ground the sign of the Yaxché. 'This sign belongs to Serpent-with-Feathers. So, wanting to test him, we told him the story of how Serpent-with-Feathers was driven out of his kingdom, which is a very ancient story and which he would certainly have known if he had any connection with that *teotl*. It was clear that he had never heard it before, and did not understand it. But we did not believe his claim in any case, because of what he had done at Cholula.'

I was staring at the spot where he had drawn the cross. 'He burned the temple of Serpent-with-Feathers,' I said after a moment or two.

'Quite so.'

'Lord Muctezuma, is that sign truly the sign of Serpent-with-Feathers?'

'We have said so,' he replied, rather sharply. Then, softening his tone, 'Sometimes the priests show it by five dots instead of two lines, and then its meaning is clearer: the four directions and their centre.'

'In the place where I lived before, they say it is the Tree that joins the worlds.'

'It is the same thought, is it not?'

I said, 'This *teotl* is known there as Kukulcan. Which in their language is Bird-Serpent.'

'It may be so.' The emperor returned to his own thoughts. Eventually he said, 'Another proof that Malinche was lying is that Serpent-with-Feathers ate no meat, which is a way of saying that he refuses sacrifices of human blood. And in Cholula you had spilt a great deal of it.'

Honduras is not the only region that has been occupying the attention of Spaniards. There has been fighting on the coast near Ix Chel.

Don Francisco, whom seven years ago the Captain sent to Spain with a letter to the King and a lot of gold, has come back again. The King was pleased with the gold although he did not go so far as to say that he was pleased with the Captain, and he has granted Don Francisco the right to conquer the region that includes Chanek.

It seems the *winic* of those parts are not happy to be conquered. They have presumably heard of what happened to the Meshica and are determined that it shall not happen to them. There have been fierce battles. In some of them, it's said, the *winic* have been led by a warrior with blue eyes and a surprising grasp of Spanish military tactics.

I think about Gonzalo with great affection. I hope he wins his battles. I would not like to have deprived him of the opportunity of waging them, but I am now certain that he would not have come with me in any case.

'Lord Muctezuma,' I asked him not long before we fled from the city, 'what were the costumes you sent to Malinche?'

The *tlatoani* was more and more withdrawn. Sometimes I felt that talking was, to him, an unwelcome distraction from his thoughts.

'They were a gift,' he said at last.

'Were they the regalia of *teotl*?'

'Yes.'

'Of which *teotl*?'

'Of Serpent-with-Feathers and Smoke-of-the-Mirror.'

'Why did you send them, lord?'

He said nothing for a while. He gazed ahead of him, into the emptiness of the room, at the shadows cast by the brazier, the worn leather harness on the soldier's back. Then he said, 'What is it to you, who are both like us and like them, but will not die like us or see your world ended like us?'

I had never heard him speak bitterly before. I lowered my head. I said that if my questions were troublesome I would stop asking them. I said I only wished to understand what had happened.

'You only wish to understand?' repeated Muctezuma, and I saw that I could not have said anything that distressed him more. 'But who can understand it? We are He-Who-Speaks, and *we* do not understand it.'

'I am sorry, lord.'

'You did not mean to offend.' There was a long pause, and in it there could be heard the sounds of fighting around the palace wall. Finally he said, 'We sent those precious things, which Malinche disdained, because we did not know what you were, whether you were men or *teotl*, or who had sent you, or how your coming was to be regarded.'

'Why then were there only two costumes?'

'We sent only the costumes of Serpent-with-Feathers and Smoke-of-the-Mirror because those two *teotl* contain all that can be thought. Smoke-of-the-Mirror is the lord of this world, the ruler of things-as-they-are, and that is the meaning of his name, because everything here is merely appearance and illusion; and Serpent-with-Feathers is that which blows through the world and around and above it, and is not contained by it or by time; and that is the reason for their conflict and also why they require each other.'

'Do you mean, lord,' I said, 'that when you knew, after what Malinche did in Cholula, that he was not Serpent-with-Feathers, you then thought that he might be Smoke-of-the-Mirror?'

'Of course. Malinche is a warrior, as is Hummingbird. Furthermore there was a helmet in the keeping of one of his soldiers that was exactly like the helmet we see on Hummingbird's head. This likeness must have a meaning. Often he seems to favour the same colours, too.'

'When did you realize that he wasn't that *teotl*, either?'

'He defiled the Great Temple, which is the home of the Lord of the Near.'

I said, 'If you had believed, lord, that Malinche was either of those *teotl*, what could you have done?'

'If we had known what was required, we could have performed it, if there had been anything that could be done. But the *teotl* were silent.' For a few moments Muctezuma fell silent himself and I saw his anguish. 'If he had been Serpent-with-Feathers, it would have been simple, although it would also have been terrible. It would have meant that he was coming back to overthrow the *teotl* he found here. If he had been Smoke-of-the-Mirror, our own *teotl*, it would have been necessary to know what he wanted, why he was angry. We had given much thought to this and we surmised an answer.'

'May I ask what it was?'

'We wondered if the Meshica had left the true path by building this great city, subduing all other nations and holding such magnificent spectacles. Our forefathers walked barefoot in the desert. They lived on maize and chilli. At the beginning of our history, Hummingbird brought us here after a long migration. Was it his wish, we wondered, to begin another journey?'

He withdrew into his thoughts for a while, while I waited, astonished, for him to continue.

'Something could have been done. Penances, a giving away of riches. But it was not demanded.' Muctezuma's eyes rested on the copal-burner in front of him, but did not seem to see it. 'We knew when your people first appeared on the coast, with their clothes of metal and magical weapons and extraordinary animals, that this was a thing never heard of before. But there

498

can be nothing that has never been heard of before. An event is always to be found in the annals or the books of prophecy, because that is the nature of time. It was our task, as *tlatoani*, to answer this riddle. We were not able to answer it. We understood at last that the fact that it could not be answered was itself the answer. It meant that this was the end of days, it was the end of the world. There was no purpose in resisting this ending. Perhaps it was even forbidden to us, as *tlatoani*, to resist it.'

I could find nothing to say, and for a space Muctezuma and I sat listening to the fighting and the hiss of copal in the brazier. Then he said, as if musing, 'The Lord of the Near lacks a sacrifice.'

I did not understand, of course.

'When Tona-tiuh' (he meant Blue Eyes) 'attacked the dancers of Hummingbird on the day of Toxcatl, the youth who for a year had been the Lord-of-the-Near-made-flesh was killed.'

I remembered the young *winic*, of a touching beauty, who had played his flute in the streets.

'His life would have ended that day in any case, but with due ritual. Toxcatl is the day of the sacrifice. If the sacrifice is not offered . . . But it is always offered.'

I was groping my way towards his thought, I had half-reached it, when a servant from the royal palace who had managed to get through the fighting entered the room and I took my leave. That was the last time I talked alone with Muctezuma. Three days later, the stone was thrown at him as he stood on the roof. It was then that the thought completed itself in my head. There were two incarnations of the Lord of the Near in the city at any time. One was the youth who died and was born again at Toxcatl. The other was the *tlatoani*.

Last week I walked with Diego over my land. The land, that is to say, that is registered in my name in a document in the town hall at Cactus-on-the-Stone.

I know that Diego does not regard the land as mine or anyone's.

When we walk over it together, we are not seeing the same land. But while I know what he sees, he does not know what I see. He thinks I see what every Spaniard sees, a dead thing parcelled up, a net of ownership. Whereas what I see is something even stranger, a double thing that presents itself to me with first one face and then the other, like a sword hung twisting from a branch whose two surfaces in turn reflect the sunlight. I see, with half my mind, a pattern of maize plots and the money they will provide, and I am already tallying this up and setting it against my outgoings in Cactus-on-the-Stone and wondering whether I can afford to order some new furniture from Seville, because the house is scantily provided with chairs to sit on and I have noticed my – few – visitors casting scornful looks about them; and I see, with the other half, pulsing behind these maize rows which are really bags of coin or furniture from Seville, the true and ever-lasting earth out of which the maize springs and into which all, maize, furniture, Meshica and we descend and are reborn, as children of the earth and forms of maize, for ever.

The beauty of this second vision gives me such peace that I am silent and only wish to contemplate it, and the agitation resulting from the first puts me in such a terrible state that in the end I can do nothing but banish it from my mind and hope that the money from the maize crop will somehow produce itself without my thinking about it, because after all I have to live on something and this is the means the law provides. By the time I have finished walking around my estate and looking at it, I have reached an agreement with myself, but it takes all day to do it and none of it can be said to Diego, who believes he is in the service of a Spanish gentleman, albeit one of unusual habits.

It being January, there was no maize planted: it would not be planted until after the first rains. The dried maize stalks stood gaunt on the brown earth, rustling quietly in the breeze as if talking to each other. They stood like sentinels, I thought, or like the ghosts of warriors, a phalanx of dead warriors whose spirit still guarded the land. On the ground lay a few threads of silk from the cobs. I tried to remember the name for this in Chanek, but I could not get at it; it was like groping for something in a sack, all I could find were things I didn't want. The brown dead leaves of the maize, papery, brittle, dust-dry, would, if left to stand, last through the winter to the next planting. This never fails to move me. It means that the maize will never be absent of its own volition, that it will not leave the surface of the earth. It keeps man company. Man, for his part, sees to its renewal. For maize cannot seed itself. It must be planted by a human hand.

I walked with Diego through the ghosts of the maize and we talked about where maize would be sown in the coming year, and where the beans would be sown, and where the melons. Then we stopped at a spring which runs out from a rock above the valley. Someone worships there. I smelt copal, and saw the black stain on the rock face. We slaked our thirst and walked slowly back to the house as the day cooled.